Tara Pammi can't remember a moment when she wasn't lost in a book—especially a romance, which was much more exciting than a mathematics textbook at school. Years later, Tara's wild imagination and love for the written word revealed what she really wanted to do. Now she pairs alpha males who think they know everything with strong women who knock that theory *and* them off their feet!

Julia James lives in England and adores the peaceful verdant countryside and the wild shores of Cornwall. She also loves the Mediterranean—so rich in myth and history, with its sunbaked landscapes and olive groves, ancient ruins and azure seas. 'The perfect setting for romance!' she says. 'Rivalled only by the lush tropical heat of the Caribbean—palms swaying by a silver sand beach lapped by turquoise water... What more could lovers want?'

T0337321

Also by Tara Pammi

Fiancée for the Cameras

The Powerful Skalas Twins miniseries

Saying 'I Do' to the Wrong Greek
Twins to Tame Him

Also by Julia James

Destitute Until the Italian's Diamond
The Cost of Cinderella's Confession
Reclaimed by His Billion-Dollar Ring
Contracted as the Italian's Bride
The Heir She Kept from the Billionaire
Greek's Temporary Cinderella

Discover more at millsandboon.co.uk.

RINGS & RETRIBUTION

TARA PAMMI

JULIA JAMES

MILLS & BOON

All rights reserved including the right of reproduction in whole or
in part in any form. This edition is published by arrangement with
Harlequin Enterprises ULC.

This is a work of fiction. Names, characters, places, locations
and incidents are purely fictional and bear no relationship
to any real life individuals, living or dead, or to any actual places,
business establishments, locations, events or incidents.
Any resemblance is entirely coincidental.

This book is sold subject to the condition that it shall not, by way of
trade or otherwise, be lent, resold, hired out or otherwise circulated
without the prior consent of the publisher in any form of binding
or cover other than that in which it is published and without a
similar condition including this condition being imposed on
the subsequent purchaser.

® and TM are trademarks owned and used by the trademark owner
and/or its licensee. Trademarks marked with ® are registered with the
United Kingdom Patent Office and/or the Office for Harmonisation in
the Internal Market and in other countries.

First published in Great Britain 2024
by Mills & Boon, an imprint of HarperCollins*Publishers* Ltd,
1 London Bridge Street, London, SE1 9GF

www.harpercollins.co.uk

HarperCollins*Publishers*, Macken House, 39/40 Mayor Street Upper,
Dublin 1, D01 C9W8, Ireland

Rings & Retribution © 2024 Harlequin Enterprises ULC

Contractually Wed © 2024 Tara Pammi

Vows of Revenge © 2024 Julia James

ISBN: 978-0-263-32031-2

11/24

This book contains FSC™ certified paper
and other controlled sources to ensure responsible forest management.

For more information visit www.harpercollins.co.uk/green.

Printed and Bound in the UK using 100% Renewable Electricity
at CPI Group (UK) Ltd, Croydon, CR0 4YY

CONTRACTUALLY WED

TARA PAMMI

MILLS & BOON

CHAPTER ONE

SNEAKING INTO THE Manhattan penthouse of the intensely private and vengeful Greek billionaire Apollo Galanis, a man she'd already annoyed a few times, at nine in the night, wasn't how Jia Shetty foresaw her twenty-sixth birthday evening going.

But given that no one had even remembered the date, much less celebrated it—not unusual either—it was the most excitement she'd seen on one. Though it was a panic-ridden *OMG what's he going to do to me when he finds me here?* kind of excitement rather than a belly-filled-with-butterflies kind.

Honestly, Jia had no idea how that kind of excitement tasted. Except maybe that one time when her rough sketches for the new wing of a billionaire's private library had been accepted. But only a flicker even then, because her family's well-being had depended on getting that contract. When her designs had been lauded innovative and environmentally intelligent, there had only been relief.

Because it hadn't been her name on the design, or her being praised for designing an architectural marvel. Tonight, her degree in architecture—only allowed by her father because Jia had shown talent for it and his own had long-ago deserted him—had come in handy as she planned to infiltrate Apollo Galanis's penthouse in a luxury hotel he himself had designed.

Whatever else the man soon to be her brother-in-law was, he was a brilliant architect, an innovator who believed in achieving more with less, a billionaire who was determined to leave the world better than he had found it.

Except for her family, that is.

Having studied the blueprints and worked as a cleaning lady for the past month at the hotel, Jia had finally figured out how to get into his penthouse. Learning the man's agenda for a given week wasn't that much of a stretch. From the moment he arrived in Manhattan, he demanded the presence of her older sister, Rina, his fiancée, like a master calling his prized poodle to attention.

Just thinking of her sister made panic tighten Jia's chest. Rina's tears last night as she'd sobbed with her head in Jia's lap that Apollo Galanis was a ruthless monster who expected her to sit, stand and perform at his command, had been playing in Jia's head in a loop.

How was her gentle, tenderhearted sister supposed to survive the strain of being Apollo Galanis's society wife if she couldn't even bear the stress of being his fiancée? How was Jia supposed to protect the only person in her life who had ever shown her kindness, if not by throwing herself as bait at the monster?

Relief hit her in waves as the key card she'd stolen from Galanis's designated maid worked on the digital menu and the elevator carried her away to the penthouse.

She added another item to her increasing to-do list: make sure the maid didn't get into trouble for her actions.

The elevator opened with a swish and Jia stepped out, her eyes widening as she took in the architectural marvel of the penthouse.

Sweeping stairs made of wood and industrial metal straddled a palace-sized lounge with the ceiling stretching up to two levels. The ceiling and the walls were all glass, with load-bearing pillars breaking it up. Even those added to the modern industrial look of the space, fitting seamlessly into the concrete jungle around it. With the glittering lights of Manhattan and the sky itself open to the eye, it was as if one was standing in the midst of one of the most diverse cities in the world. As if one was both witness and a part of its constant reinvention of itself.

Other than a couple of turn-of-the-century art pieces in metal and wood again, the other adornment was lots of greenery. A giant fiddle-leaf fig and two monstera were the only plants Jia recognized among sturdier and more exotic greenery that warmed all the metal and wood, turning it into a much more intimate setting than the soulless chrome it could have been.

How could a man so eager and ruthless in his punishment of her family be the same one who had designed and given shape to this urban space full of such heart?

Jia knew she was violating his sacred space. He hadn't invited even her sister here. Maybe if Rina saw this, she would understand him a little better? But her older sister didn't have the same affinity that Jia had for old buildings and clean design lines. Neither was she as…worldly-wise as Jia was. Pampered and privileged and never having to doubt her parents' love for her. It was the first time life and their father were demanding something of Rina and she was simply crumpling against them.

In her case, life had forced Jia to learn to be tough, to understand that she had to provide value in any relationship.

Now Jia made a beeline to the kitchen, her stomach gnawing on itself. Munching on an apple, she looked through the state-of-the-art refrigerator that was big enough to hide in. Grabbing cheese and grapes and a wrapped bowl of what looked like pilaf with nuts, Jia spent the next few minutes trying to find the microwave hidden among the dark gray cabinets.

Finally, her pilaf was steaming, the grapes were cold and juicy, and the cheese perfectly crumbly as she reached the lounger that faced the Manhattan skyline.

Eating a meal with no one crying, losing their temper or conspiring in panic near her had become a luxury in the last few months. It also should have felt unnerving to sit in a space that belonged to the man who was turning their lives upside down.

Instead, Jia cherished the sweet tartness of the grapes and the buttery richness of the nutty pilaf. The cheese, she washed it down with a glass of chilled white wine and felt herself disappearing into the snug hold of the soft leather. Soon, she was snoring, her worries about selling herself to the devil all but forgotten.

Apollo Galanis walked into his Manhattan penthouse after a long, exhausting business trip to the Philippines and was in a sour mood since the property development deal there hadn't budged in two months.

His group of junior architects had made barely any changes to the designs he had already rejected. That they had the gall to invite him down there for another meeting pissed him off.

He'd wanted to fire the whole lot of them. Except these were the crème de la crème from the finest architecture programs across the world and if they didn't deliver, who would?

Neither could he fire them for something he himself was unable to deliver. He was blocked, or burned-out, or a bitter combination of both and he was beginning to see the reason.

It was this engagement he had talked himself into with the Shetty heiress. After more than a decade and a half of planning and strategizing and calculating ten moves ahead, he finally had Jay Shetty in his clutches.

The very man who had destroyed Apollo's father by stealing his designs and selling them as his own. His deepest trust betrayed, Papa had returned to Greece heartbroken and bankrupt, and had never recovered. Apollo was firmly planted on the board of directors of Jay Shetty's design company, with no way to gain controlling stock.

The older man, a conniving strategist, had shamelessly offered up his eldest daughter as a prize before Apollo could take even more drastic steps, like sending the man to prison. Jay's daughter would transfer her stock to Apollo after three years of marriage. It was clear that Jay was desperate to avoid other consequences Apollo could rain down on him. Was hoping to change Apollo's mind in three years.

The idea of reveling in Jay's desperation that Apollo might be sidetracked from revenge—a goal he'd pursued for nearly two decades—was immensely appealing. Giving the man a taste of the misery he'd brought on Apollo's family for years, by being present in his life as his son-in-law, by being the sword that was forever dangling over his head…sounded deliciously fitting.

Even though the last thing Apollo wanted was a wife.

One of the most beautiful women he'd ever seen, Rina Shetty was also demure, had acted as her father's society hostess for years, and was the kind of woman who would mold herself into whatever Apollo needed her to be.

Apollo had played into Jay's negotiation because Rina wasn't a bad choice for a wife for a man like him. A man who didn't believe in love and all that nonsense, a man who liked order and control in his every day, a man who would eventually need sons to carry on the legacy he was building. And really, who better than the grandchildren of the very man who had destroyed his family, to continue on the Galanis dynasty itself. There was a certain poetic justice in that.

Soon, Jay Shetty's company would be nothing but a speck absorbed into Galanis Corp, forgotten even by its own disgruntled, unhappy employees who were more than eager to prove their mettle and loyalty to the bigger, meaner predator that was circling their CEO.

And then maybe this hunger in him would appease, Apollo thought, with little faith in his own maybes.

Maybe then, after nearly two decades, he could take a moment to celebrate everything he had achieved.

He took off his jacket, undid the buttons on his shirt, poured himself a glass of red wine and walked to his favorite lounger—the only piece of furniture he had restored and brought here from his home in Athens—to enjoy one of his two favorite views in the entire world.

Only to find it already occupied by a woman in a maid's uniform.

An empty white wine bottle sat on the floor next to the lounger, along with a tray full of empty bowls and forks, all neatly stacked.

He had never invited even his mother or sisters to visit this particular project of his, and to find a member of staff not only breaking her professional code but invading his privacy, was untenable. He understood exhaustion and hard work but still…he paid exorbitantly well for his privacy.

Her white cap was on the floor, and the woman's gold-threaded dark brown hair fell in thick, lustrous waves, framing her familiarly angular face. He moved closer and turned on the Tiffany lamp, and let out a curse. Recognition came instantly and following it, *fury*.

Of course this was no maid transgressing his private space. This was a woman he had barely tolerated and he had known that the dislike was completely mutual.

In fact, in all of his thirty-nine years of life, Apollo had never met a woman, or even another person, who rubbed him the wrong way just by existing. Her mere presence had been like rubbing salt into a sunburn.

As if to provoke his ire even further, the sleeping

woman let out a loud snore followed by an awful belch. Apollo had had enough. Before he could think better of the juvenile impulse, he was upending the glass of red in his hand over her head. At least it wasn't cold, he told himself.

She came awake, sputtering and squealing, unfolding like a mangy dog, and then mumbled something incoherent.

He grinned, wondering when he'd had so much fun in recent memory. Not even as a poor undergrad student at Harvard, or later when he'd made his first million, or even when he'd won environmental awards for his designs.

Finally, she stopped mumbling, rubbed her eyes and smeared the wine all over her face. Belatedly, Apollo realized he had just ruined his favorite lounger and the pristine carpet. *Christos*, not even a minute near her and she'd reduced him to a playground bully.

A grin appeared on her face even as she threaded her fingers through dark, wispy bangs that almost covered her eyes. "Just realized you ruined your own chair, did you?" she said, looking up at him, and running the tip of her tongue against that wide gap between her front teeth.

It was the first thing he had noticed about her—the imperfection of her crooked smile next to the pearly, near-perfect smile of her sister.

The differences between this woman's tall, boyish figure, with her thick glasses and thicker, untamed hair and her gap-toothed smile and her purple lipstick and her entire forearm covered in colorful tattoos and her skinny jeans and combat boots, against Rina's full, curvy figure, her polish and perfectly pitched tone when she spoke, her cream-colored jumpsuit, her hair neatly cut into blunt shoulder-length style, and a barely-there pink lip gloss on her lips, and the way she carried herself had nearly…had discombobulated him. Bringing into sharp contrast what he definitely didn't want in his life.

At the first meeting with Jay Shetty, his useless bag of a son, Rina and this…wild creature who sat next to her sister and asked impertinent questions, even as her father sent her dirty, shushing looks, Apollo had been unable to look away from her.

It was like watching a car crash, he had thought then. But two more meetings with her—where she was supposed to keep her sister company and where she had asked him too many intrusive, invading questions about what their married life was going to look like—Apollo had amended his first impression of her, begrudging it every inch of the way.

She was like a wild sunset, all splashy colors and a warm blaze.

And now when she grinned at him, not even a little effaced by the fact that he had caught her inside his private sanctuary, Apollo admitted what about her provoked him so much.

There was a rough, untamable kind of beauty to her, as if she had been born to be unleashed in the world to create a maximum kind of chaos. And he loathed chaos anywhere near him with a visceral reaction.

Still, even as he acknowledged that she equally attracted and repulsed him, he began to wonder why Jay had never offered her up as the proverbial lamb being led to slaughter. Why it had been his eldest he'd pushed toward Apollo.

"You have two minutes to explain why you're here, Ms. Shetty. Or it will be the jail for you. Not a big surprise that you will blend in very well with your..." he ran a hand over her form "...colorful persona."

Standing up, paying no heed to the fact that he was standing close and threatening her with prison, she grabbed a napkin from the tray and started dabbing at her uniform. Which only arrested his attention. The damned dress was short on her, barely covering her upper thighs. When she wrung the hem to get out an extra two drops of wine, it revealed the tops of her lacy tights hugging her lean, muscled thighs.

His gaze went up, noting the tight tuck of her waist and the two buttons that had come undone at her chest, revealing small breasts and gleaming golden-brown skin. The tail end of another tattoo snuck up under the collar of the dress, playing peekaboo with him.

Apollo looked away too late. Lust coursed through him like a sudden bolt of adrenaline shot into his very veins. He let out a shocked curse, something he never did in company, for it revealed too much of his state of mind. No, not this woman. *Christos*.

Lusting after his fiancée's sister...smacked too much of that wildness he disliked about this woman. Of being out of control.

Standing too close, she ran her tongue over her teeth. "You have to tell me which vintage that is," she said, making a rude, smacking noise. "As a rule, I don't drink reds since they give me horrible headaches. For that one, I might risk it. In fact, maybe you can just gift it to me, seeing that we're going to become close soon."

He gritted his teeth and prayed for a calm that felt out of reach. "Jail, Ms. Shetty."

"Fine," she said, her breath hitting him on a shuddering exhale.

Apollo knew he should step back, give his lungs air that was free of that lush red rose scent threaded with a twang of sweet sweat. But he didn't. He liked it too much and then there was the whole point of him backing away from her. Which he never would.

It was the latter mostly, he decided. She had invaded his home, showed little to no shame over it, and the last thing he was going to do was show her how much her presence...rattled him.

"Keep talking, Ms. Shetty."

"Okay, *sir*. Getting to it now, *sir*."

"Don't be ridiculous," he said, somehow controlling the urge to laugh out loud at her cheekiness. Or maybe drag her close and teach her some discipline if she was going to do that anyway. He closed his eyes, wondering why his mind was going to these strange, forbidden places, especially around this woman.

"If you insist on calling me Ms. Shetty in that tone, which by the way reminds me of my history professor, I have to call you that. My name's Jia. How come I've never heard you use it?"

"I have no need to become that...familiar with you."

"And yet, you have no problem getting all chummy with the rest of my family."

"They do not…provoke me like you do." He stepped farther into her space, which was his to begin with, forcing her to look up at him. Though it wasn't by much. She was taller than most women and he didn't have to look down at her as if from some great distance, and he liked this too. He wasn't supposed to like anything about this.

Something else struck him all of a sudden. He scowled. "How did you get in here? The security is infallible."

"And yet, here I am."

"You better start spewing answers to my questions, Ms. Shetty, or else…" He grinned, and opened the contacts list on his phone. "I have a feeling telling your father about your recent stunt is a better punishment than jail for you."

A soft, imperceptible shudder went through her and she stared at him, eyes wide. For once, that rough, *I can take on the world no matter what* attitude she wore like a second skin fell off, revealing the very young woman she was beneath. She looked at him as if he'd hit her below the belt. And damn if it didn't make him feel guilty. "I'm calling your bluff. You didn't squeal on me the last couple of times, *Apollo*," she said, making him feel foolish for the thirty seconds of guilt and curiosity he had felt for her.

Something about the way she drawled his name, as if she'd said it in her head many times and with less sweetness than she used now, hit him in the pit of his stomach with a honey-like languor. "So you admit that it wasn't a mistake that Rina went to a different restaurant to meet me the first time, and that you nearly got tackled by my bodyguard the second time, and the third…time," he finally choked out on a swallowed laugh. Even he had found that third stunt enormously funny, with her using her brother's credit card that she'd filched from his jacket when she'd *accidentally* bumped into him and then gotten into trouble for making Jay Shetty's vein pop in his temple.

"Of course, I admit it. Not that I succeeded."

"What was the success criteria?" he said, suddenly curious.

"To make you despise our family enough that you'd leave Rina alone."

"And the recent episode where your sister burst into tears at the thought of moving to Athens with me?"

She flinched, as if she herself was in pain. "I wouldn't make her cry. Even to get rid of you." Then she brightened, "Wait! Clearly it put you off—"

"Not enough to break off the engagement. Rina, as your father explained, is gentle and completely overwhelmed by her good fortune."

The woman snorted. She actually snorted, probably spraying spittle onto his shirt.

Apollo refused to show, even by the twitch of his eyelid which was a hard thing to stop when he was pissed, that she was getting to him. "I assume that this…little stunt is to get my attention. So why don't you start with how you got in here in the first place?"

"I have been working at your hotel for the last month, cleaning suites. I studied the plans and figured out which elevator rides up here and the shifting schedule of your security. I made friends with the woman So-phia, the only one allowed to clean your penthouse. I stole her key card, got your schedule from Rina's phone and here I am." She said the last to some show tune he didn't recognize, her arms and hands gesticulating as if she were some great conductor.

He covered another step between them and now when that lush scent of hers wrapped around his body like a tendril of lust, he knew he was making a tremen-dous mistake. Still, he didn't back down.

Her big brown eyes widened and her shoulders trem-bled but she stubbornly stayed still. "Now that you've cost Sophia her job, tell me why you're here like an annoying pest."

"If you fire Sophia, I'll go to HR. I collected every document I could about how religiously on time she is, how many years she's worked here and how there hasn't been a single complaint about her. HR chose her for you because she hails from the same village as your father in Greece."

Apollo was struck speechless, having never met a worthier opponent. She had not only done her home-work but she'd done it because she didn't want an in-nocent to get fired for her reckless act. Definitely not a trait he expected of Jay Shetty's progeny.

Another reason he'd thought Rina was perfect for him. She lacked personality and smarts and the kind of cunning that should be rampant in Shetty blood. This one had it in spades.

"What do you want?" he said, wanting nothing more than to get rid of her.

"I came here to make you a proposal."

"About?" he said, his heart suddenly pounding in his chest as if he were once again standing in line for an interview as a junior draftsman in a big architecture firm, nothing but dreams and goals in his wallet.

"An exchange of sorts. You release my sister from your engagement in return for…"

He waited, knowing that the flash of panic in her eyes was all too real. And yet like a predator hungry for a slice of flesh—her flesh—some unknown thing in his stomach grew. It wanted to eat up all her fear and taste the wildness writhing beneath. It wanted to pull away all that attitude, all those things she covered her skin in and reveal the real her to his gaze.

Seconds piled into minutes and the tip of her tongue flicked out to lick her wide lower lip. "In return for me," she said, her chest rising and falling. "I came here to sell you on the idea that I would make a far better wife to you than my sister." A harsh, self-deprecating laugh escaped her lips. "I broke into this maximum-security gilded cage, risked another woman's livelihood, risked more than your usual contempt, to sell myself to the devil. That's my evil plan."

CHAPTER TWO

CALLING HIM THE devil was probably not the best way to convince Apollo Galanis that she was a better prospect than her sister but then when had Jia's plans ever gone according to script? Her entire life, including her conception into this world, had been ruled by Murphy's Law.

This brilliant scheme to impress her sister's fiancé with her smarts and cunning and guts had looked different in her head. He was a ruthless, ambitious billionaire who was determined to cut her father's small architecture firm into pieces. She'd convinced herself that a man like that would appreciate her taking this initiative.

Of course, she'd fallen asleep in his favorite lounger. And now as he watched her with those intense gray eyes, she realized what she'd left out in her calculations and it was a biggie.

Apollo Galanis was not some manageable, ordinary man she kept reducing him to in her head. It was both delusional and dangerous.

There had been this…sparkling, tense energy between them from the first moment. She'd pretended to be her sister, Rina, and chatted away about her intense and scorching sex life, hoping to put him off, while he had known that she wasn't Rina and played along.

At the end, after she'd made a flaming fool of herself by comprehensively describing the foursome she'd just walked out of, his mouth had twitched and her gaze had gone to the sudden, blinding beauty of his lips and he'd caught her watching and that had been that.

Since then, as much as Jia had tried to fill the space between them with her loathing of him and he with his contempt for her, there had been something more volatile in the mix. Something she had refused to acknowledge in the beginning, something that had kept her awake later, the very something that had finally led to this madcap plan. That the basis of her proposal was "this energy" between them made her face and neck hot, even with her skin damp and sticky.

At least, he hadn't laughed at her.

But as the seconds and his silence stretched, being laughed at felt better than his scrutiny.

"Show me your skills, then. Sell yourself to me," he said, walking away.

Jia blinked as bright lights came on, her body suddenly flush with humming energy, her brain chugging along painfully slow to the fact that he wasn't throwing her out.

When she turned around, he was sitting on the white leather couch, one arm spread out over the back of it, one leg over the other, his expression one of smooth, wicked humor that Jia wanted to slap off his face. He looked like he was the lord of something, *everything*, and she, a poor peasant come to present her pathetic case.

"I'm waiting. Clearly, you think yourself a better candidate than your sister. Sell me on it."

If his gaze had moved down her neck in that condescending way of his, that told her she was nothing but amusing entertainment, she might have lost it. Instead, he looked at her with that conviction that nothing, *nothing*, in the world could convince him to take her on.

And that…that arrogance filled her with renewed resolve. All her life, she had known little kindness and love and the little she had, had come from her sister. She'd do anything to stop Rina's ruin at his hands. Even if it meant courting her own.

"My sister is gentle, kind and…in love with our ex-con chauffeur. As heartless as you are, I'm assuming you would hate a woman whose affections for you are in doubt."

"Your sister's too nice to cheat on me once we're married and too gentle, just like you said, to give her marriage vows anything but full commitment. As for affections, those are fickle and I have no use for them."

Jia's mouth fell open.

"That's what you based this whole escapade on?" he said, mouth twitching.

"Partly, yes," Jia said, refusing to let him get to her. "I mean, I knew you were a ruthless, unemotional robot but hearing the proof from your own mouth…" She made a show of ticking off an item on her imaginary checklist. "I also took a little nice detour down your dating history on the good old web and from all the women you've dated—kudos to the diversity in your playing ground BTW—it's clear—"

"BTW?"

"By the way," she said, sighing. "Moving on, it's clear that you like bold, adventurous, dare I say, even ballsy women for your...partners. Rina's nothing like them. She won't even fight back if you..."

"Careful, Ms. Shetty. Just because I let you insult me doesn't mean you can attribute weaknesses to my character."

"You'll be bored within two days. Why are you so intent on having the most boring marriage in the world?"

"Boring marriages last."

"Wow, so you're really only going for quantity, not quality?"

"I still haven't heard one word about how you're a better candidate. Only disparagement of your sister."

She gasped, feeling outraged. "I'm trying to protect Rina and you from—"

"Tell me," he said, leaning forward, for the first time showing a sliver of curiosity. "Did Rina ask you to save her from this predicament or is this all an elaborately spun lie so that you could have me for yourself?"

"Of course she asked me. Like multiple times. In fact, she's been..." Jia let out an angry breath, realizing the blasted man had tricked her into admitting it.

Something almost like distaste curled his upper lip. But then, his lips always seemed to greet the world with that lick of contempt. "Look, my sister is..." she began, wanting to defend Rina but he raised a hand.

She was so shocked he was engaging in dialogue that her brain stupidly followed his commands. "Why are you a better bet? You and I both know you have something bigger for you to drop."

Jia shouldn't have been surprised that he had figured her out. But she couldn't play her ace just yet. "You and I have chemistry. And your plan to punish my father would yield a thousand percent more results if it was me you—"

He shot to his feet and moved toward her, and Jia's synapses gave out. That lizard part of her brain seemed to come awake, screaming, *Hot sexy man at twelve o'clock.*

She craned her neck, just slightly, to look up into his face when he left only a foot or so between them. God, he smelled like cinnamon and pine and reminded her of decadent winter evenings spent near her mom's feet while she knitted.

This close, she could see the lines of tiredness fanning out from Apollo's eyes. And even as it reduced him from that larger-than-life figure in her head, Jia didn't like seeing them. Didn't like knowing him at this level.

"That's an interesting observation. Care to prove it?"

"Prove it…how?" she said, her throat suddenly dry, and hating herself for taking a step back. She should have known the beast would play with her.

"Kiss me. Then we will know if you're really a better proposition than—"

She pressed her hand to his mouth. Something hot and feral came awake in his gray eyes, something she hadn't even been sure he was capable of feeling.

"Please don't—"

"You should know, Jia," he said, wrapping long fingers around her wrist and tugging her hand away from his mouth. "Every game you begin, I will play, and play to win."

Her name on his lips was a sweet threat. A reminder that she was playing a dangerous game, that she was letting this attraction go to her head. And maybe even handing him a weapon. And he was right. He was a master at this. "Fine. I'll show you my ace. But you have to promise that you'll grant me three wishes in the aftermath. Whatever I ask for."

"You're so sure you'll win me over?"

"Give me your word, Apollo. Three conditions for our deal in your language."

"How do you know I won't go back on them?"

"Because I just know," she said, hating the fact that she trusted him. How had that happened?

That little flicker of heat again in his eyes and then a nod.

Jia drew in a deep breath, even as fear spread its tentacles wide and far in her body. If she did this, there was no turning back. If she did this, she was tying her future—at least half a decade in the best-case scenario—to this man, who was bent on ruining her family. If she did this, her father was never going to give her what she'd desperately craved for years.

But it was the only way to protect Rina and the only way to stop her father from getting hurt by this man who would not hesitate when he discovered her father's lies. And while the thought of settling into unholy matrimony, even for a temporary period, with this man turned her inside out, it would at least serve as a break from her own life. Especially if Rina summoned the courage to stand up to their father and leave home.

"The plans for the new wing of that private library in Seattle, the low-income apartments out in Brooklyn, my brother, Vik…didn't design any of that stuff."

"It's his name on the blueprints," Apollo said, thunder in his eyes. "He accepted a bloody award for it. His face was on a magazine cover for…who? Who's the architect?"

"Me. I drew the initial plans. And the revisions after you requested them. And… I did all of them. So, there you have it. I'm the asset you want. You take me out of Dad's company and…it loses its prestige faster than you can cut it up. It won't win any more contacts moving forward." Something thick and sticky coated her throat and Jia had to swallow to speak past it. "You marry me, and take me away from the company, and you truly have won."

Apollo took one look into those big, brown eyes, saw the tears she blinked away in a quick flash and knew she was telling the truth. Fury gripped him, even as his usual rationale tried to wrangle it into control.

He shouldn't be surprised by further proof of Jay Shetty's duplicitous nature. Suddenly, all of the older man's attempts to keep his younger daughter away from Apollo made sense. He had assumed Jay was attached to Jia and he'd had no interest in the woman with her rough edges and vulgar stories and her constant attempts to draw him into a fight.

Now he realized how perfectly Jay had played him by

dangling his beautiful, perfect, dull-as-cardboard first-born in front of Apollo. But why rob his own daughter of her name and her accolades…why pass it on as his son's talent…?

"You studied architecture. Your brother on the other hand was thrown out of college," he said, having cast a cursory glance at her records when the PI he'd hired had dug up everything on the Shetty family.

Usually, he would never overlook the details just because it was a woman. But from the first moment she'd walked into the restaurant pretending to be her sister and let herself loose on him, Apollo had decided that she was of no significance to him, that she was no more than a buzzing fly.

She shrugged, her mouth clamped, all of that dark humor and the teasing taunts gone. Her admission had clearly come at a high price and she'd still done it.

Her claim was that she wanted to save her sister from the horrible fate of being married to him? But why put herself in his sights, then? Nothing about Jia Shetty made sense to his logical brain.

"Is this another game your father's playing?" he said, his voice full of irritation at himself.

She went to sit on the couch. Tucking her feet under her knees, she leaned back and let out a loud exhale. The maid uniform rode up on her thighs, revealing smooth skin on top of the stockings and another button popped on the bodice, revealing the curve of a breast. She thrummed with an artless sensuality he found irresistible. "He's going to hate me for spilling the family's dirty secret." He heard the slight quiver in her words. "You can be sure of that."

"Why are you going against your own family, then? Or is lack of loyalty a family trait, passed down in blood?"

Her bow-shaped lips flinched. "My father is playing a foolish game, thinking he can change your mind in three years. Thinking he can impress you with my talent at the helm. He doesn't realize how many things could be ruined by continuing this…feud. I'm trying to save everyone."

"Why?"

"What do you mean, why? You're here, having maneuvered yourself onto the board, because my father stole something from yours more than two decades ago, aren't you?"

"Not a small something," Apollo said, gritting his jaw. The die was cast and yet some part of him wanted to understand her. "Your family doesn't deserve—"

"That's my decision."

She looked up at him as he moved toward her, the lamplight throwing the long line of her neck into relief. Everything about her was achingly lovely, perfection stitched together painfully with a multitude of imperfections.

He should turn away from her and her proposal, turn back on the entire idea of ruining Jay Shetty, and yet, Apollo had never been so aroused, his interest engaged on many levels. Everything about her was a challenge, a lure and a promise and the extreme achiever in him wanted to unravel her on every level. And conquer her.

"Maybe all this is a scheme to tie you to myself?" She let out a throaty laugh, and the collar of her uniform shifted to reveal a little more of her tattoo. "Maybe

I'm stealing you from Rina because of my uncontrollable lust for you?"

For all her flippant taunts, she stiffened when he sat down on the coffee table in front of her, caging her between his legs. Elbows on his knees, he leaned forward until he could see the browns of her eyes widen into large pools.

"What are your conditions?"

Her soft gasp was a whistle through the gap between those front teeth, tiny beads of sweat over her bow-shaped upper lip. It took her several more breaths to focus on his words and he suppressed a smile at that. Maybe the lust thing wasn't just a bluff. Her gaze met his finally, a steely resolve in it. "You will not retaliate against my father for this."

"And?"

"You will divorce me after two years, after you've exploited everything you can out of me."

"I intend to marry only once in my life, Tornado," he said, making it crystal clear that he wasn't giving her up. Not when he was just discovering what a treasure she was on multiple levels. "Whether that's your spineless sister or prickly you, I will make it work. I'll relish your father's—"

"I'm already aware of your elaborate revenge scheme. But believe me, you aren't going to want me anywhere near you in a year, tops. I'm generously granting you two."

He didn't hide his smile then. And when her gaze skidded to his mouth with a near-comical helplessness, he felt punch-drunk with desire. "No."

"You promised," she said, almost stomping those combat boots on the floor, in something akin to a tantrum.

He raised a brow, thoroughly unsure of what to make of this woman-child creature. If his assessment of those designs was right, and he was always right, she was not only brilliant but innovative in her field at a young age. There was the fact that she was writing her life away into the enemy's hands to protect her undeserving family. Then this…outward toughness she projected—from how she dressed to how she talked and acted—then there was the quicksilver flash of fear coursing through her body and her trust in him. And he felt as if he was standing at the door of either his biggest victory or his doom. The excitement in his blood though, the sudden hum in his veins…it seemed to not care.

"You should have specified that it was about the marriage itself."

"Ugh, you're…"

"You think I can't tolerate you, *ne*?" he said, softening without wanting to or seeming like he was. "Leave it to time."

"Fine."

"You'll be expected to spend a little time in Greece every year," he said, purposefully making it vague.

Apprehension filled her eyes.

"Is that a problem, Jia?" he asked softly, pressing down hard on his curiosity. Now that he had her, a true asset if he'd ever known one, nearly locked up, he didn't want to spook her.

"My entire life is in New York."

"But you're willing to give it up for Rina, no? And to be honest, it doesn't look like much of a life to me."

"You don't know anything about me," she said, the protest without fire.

Instantly, he felt the need to soothe her, for more than the obvious reason. "And your last condition for me?"

"Oh, I'm saving that one for later. It's more in the lines of a wedding present," she said, feathery eyebrows wriggling up and down.

Apollo felt the most insane urge to grab her and kiss the insouciance out of her. He wanted to reduce her to nothing but sounds and gasps, to wrest some kind of control from her, to prove to himself that she and her sister were interchangeable.

Christos, the thought of a kiss had never aroused or riled him so.

When he didn't say anything, she stood up, even though there was little space between his legs. "The wedding," she said, looking down at him now, "has to be a quiet, city hall affair. I can do Thursday and—"

He shot to his feet too. "No, absolutely not."

They were standing close enough that her chest grazed his just so. "This is an arrangement, a boardroom deal. Do we have to dress it up as some big romantic affair?"

"Yes."

"Fine. Don't blame me if I disappear the day before the wedding and you find Rina walking toward you."

"Are you planning to?"

"My family isn't going to be happy about this. Not just *not happy*. They might do anything to stop me."

"Because you're your father's golden goose," he finished, finally understanding her point. She seemed to have no illusions about her value to them. And yet, every time she talked about them, something sad and desperate filled her eyes.

"And I come with the same stock options as Rina. You can have them after two years of blissfully wedded life."

Apollo had never sought to punish the man's children for his sins. Marrying Rina after Jay had dangled the stock in his face, especially after he'd discovered that she had the spine of a noodle and would serve well as a wife, had been simply another step toward his goal. But with this woman, it felt like she was turning herself into a willing victim for her family.

It left a bitter taste at the back of his throat.

She waved her phone in his face, the action and her general irreverence and her body language all nearly alien to him. "Text me when you have the license."

"I have the license. Only the name needs to be changed."

She pressed a palm to her chest, her eyelashes fluttering. "Oh, how romantic."

Just as she bypassed him, Apollo reached for her. She fell into him with a soft oomph, her thighs pressing into his. "I have agreed to all your conditions, *ne*? I have one too."

"I'm not giving you any more dirt on my father."

He grinned then and cupped her cheek slowly. "What a diabolical mind you have, Jia. I have something more personal in mind."

Her eyelashes fluttered rapidly, like butterfly wings, and her lips too. "What?"

"All this chemistry you claim there is between us, this uncontrollable lust you have for me… I would like a taste of it. After all, I switched my choice to you pretty fast. I need a reminder as to why."

"Why? You didn't kiss Rina after all."

He grinned. "And how would you know if I kissed your sister or not?"

Color rose to her too-sharp cheeks and she shrugged. But she didn't shy her gaze away. "I…asked her."

"Why, Jia?"

Her gaze flicked to his mouth like a liquid caress, going straight to his groin. "Every time I saw you together, it was like pairing a wolf with an adorable baby chick. I kept waiting for you to realize she was too sweet and good and docile for you, and I was…curious about how a man could burn up for one sister and kiss the other. So I asked her, again and again."

"I was burning up for you? Your confidence is interesting, if nothing else."

"It's a fact."

"That your attraction to me is real," he said, satisfaction strumming through him like an unchecked river.

"Yes," she said, an edge of defensiveness to the word. "It's chemistry. I won't be made to feel shame over it."

He wondered who had made her feel shame over it and how he could reduce them to ash. "I am beginning to see one big advantage to this union, then. And getting quite excited about it too."

Her gaze flicked to his crotch and then back up.

Christos, the woman was bold. "You sure your…hard-on isn't because of what I can do for you?"

He threw his head back and laughed, true enjoyment coursing through him. And her eyes on him, tracking everything, drinking everything in…was a shot of desire injected straight into his veins. "I do believe we have one thing in common, Jia. Refusing to believe in delusions."

"So admit the truth, then. Power is the thing that gets you off."

"In this case, no. I should very much like to fuck you, as soon as possible. Is that clear enough?"

Her only reaction was the slight widening of her eyes and the heavy rise and fall of her chest. "Pleasure before World Domination for Apollo Galanis? That's… an unexpected turn."

"Well, you are quite the package."

"If we do this…" she said, her palm coming to rest on his chest with a boldness that set his muscles to curl with need "…if you really want us to have an actual marriage with sex and all that, for however long it lasts, you have to get rid of your other…girlfriends or flings or whatever you call them. You have to get rid of Portia Wentworth, like tonight." Her palm slammed into his chest in emphasis, his latest convenient partner's name gritted out. "I won't share you, even if you're not actually mine in the true sense…"

Apollo caught her mouth with his, her fierce claim as much of an aphrodisiac as the rough pants of her breaths. She was midsentence and her mouth was open and he swooped in, his want as raw and visceral as he'd ever known it to be. *Dios mio,* her lips were incredibly soft and she tasted sweet and tart.

She made a soft sound into his mouth, both complaining and eager, when he grazed her lower lip with his teeth, didn't back away. If anything, her fingers wound tighter around his neck and she leaned into him a little more.

Apollo pulled her closer, the dip of her waist and the flare of her hips as he moved his hands lower a lush invitation. He grabbed her bottom, deepening the kiss. She pushed onto her toes and bit his lip. A rough groan escaped him, as her belly rubbed against his hard shaft. *Christos,* he couldn't wait to taste her everywhere, couldn't wait to reduce her to nothing but his name and her pleasure at his hands.

After what felt like no more than a few seconds, he pulled back, eager to see lust paint its fingers over her sharp features. Still clinging to him, Jia buried her face in his neck, in a gesture that made him feel…something. Her little hot pants pinging over his skin like music notes.

Then she was pulling away, running her palm over her belly, her chest rising and falling, her gaze rapidly scanning everything around them but barely touching his.

Arms folded, amused despite the deafening thud of desire in his blood, Apollo watched her with growing fascination. The woman was a puzzle and a present wrapped in one and he couldn't wait to unwrap her *and* unravel her.

She collected her cap, her handbag that had fallen

under the lounger, and after what felt like an eternity, faced him. Brown eyes danced with lust-heavy brightness. "So this is on?"

He grinned, tucking his hands in his trouser pockets to stop himself from reaching for her again. "Are you waiting for a romantic proposal?"

She made a face at him but there was something very practiced about it. Apollo wondered at how much of her toughness was armor and what it hid. "Given I proposed to you, that will just be another farce, no? At least, we have a good story to tell when it all burns down."

He refused to argue the point with her. "There will be a car downstairs to take you home. It's past eleven."

She looked surprised. "Don't need it. I'm used to taking care of myself."

"And I'm used to taking very good care of my assets," he said, without missing a beat.

Her shoulders rounded, even as she gave him a two-fingered salute. "Of course you do."

Standing in the empty lounge, Apollo stared after the elevator doors, twin pulses of excitement and unease knotting in his stomach. More emotion than he had felt in a long, long time.

CHAPTER THREE

A WEEK LATER, as he arrived at the Shetty mansion—an ugly showboat if he'd ever seen one, jutting out amidst the surrounding dense, thick woods like a sore thumb— Apollo could not believe that he had been married for two days.

He *was* actually married and it had only registered when he'd given the news to his mother. After years of begging/threatening him to marry and have a life outside of his work, she had been delighted.

Until he had told her that he had married the daughter of the man who had ruined her husband, who had broken their family in ways they hadn't healed from.

But Mama was too gracious to voice her dislike. His sisters had jumped on the call and complained that he had deprived them of a celebration. It had been months since he'd returned to Greece, so he promised to bring his wife home and let his sisters throw them a grand reception.

His wife, Jia.

He couldn't help testing the fit and shape of those words on his lips, couldn't help the flare of intense satisfaction of such a complex woman bearing his name.

He wondered if the novelty of her numerous edges and contours would be enough to keep his interest aflame for an entire lifetime. Like showing up at the Manhattan city hall for their civil wedding in a lacy white silk tank top without a bra and skinny black jeans and fuchsia-colored stiletto heels.

With tiny diamond studs at her ears and dark red lipstick her only adornment. The thick, wavy strands of her gold-burnished brown hair had been hanging loose to her waist.

She had looked sensational and stunning and sensual enough that men turned to stare as she walked toward him. He had spied a thin, fragile gold chain when she'd neared him, a single, tiny sapphire pendant shimmering against her golden-brown skin. And as she played with it, turning it round and round while they signed the forms, Apollo knew that it was a talisman.

She had so bravely caught his interest away from her sister, achieved her goal, openly admitting to being attracted to him, laid down conditions for this marriage, and yet, she was nervous and alone and so…painfully young.

The whole time until the registrar announced they were married and they walked into the October sunshine, she had been waiting for someone. When he inquired, she made a show of looking like she didn't care. Then she admitted that Rina had said she might come.

Tenderness and something more twisted through Apollo, emotions he didn't want to feel, especially for his new bride. He still wasn't sure of her motives, and he didn't want to forget she was her father's daughter.

She was an important acquisition. And he did need her healthy and functioning for the next part of his plan to come to fruition. Feeling uncharacteristically indulgent, he'd asked her where she wanted to have their wedding breakfast. And she, of the infinite surprises, had demanded a pretzel from a street cart.

Contrary to his expectations, he'd enjoyed the salty, buttery pretzel, chased by a grape soda and then, her lips stained purple from the sugary drink, the tip of her nose pink in the cold, she'd asked him if he intended to kiss her again, with noisy New Yorkers flowing around them without breaking stride.

Apollo had broken his natural distaste for PDA and kissed her. She had tasted like salt and sugar and everything in between. It was a miracle he had been able to break away from her, instead of dragging her up to his penthouse and ravishing her to his heart's content.

He was absolutely going to enjoy the passion simmering between them but he wouldn't let it control him, couldn't let his fascination with her distract him from almost two decades' worth of planning.

And now, two days later—more than enough time for her to have broken the news to her family—her silence was beginning to weigh on him. He was breaking his promise to her that he'd let her spend another month on this side of the pond, but after three unanswered calls to her cellphone, after she'd promised him to be available, and this strange unease in his gut, he'd had enough.

It was time to collect his asset.

He got out of his chauffeured car to find the illustrious Shetty family sitting out on the lawn, looking as if they were posing for a photoshoot featuring one of America's richest families.

Except Jia.

Something about the picture bothered Apollo and it had been the same every time. Either Jia usually ran around taking care of logistics or stood outside the circle the other three formed.

Rina got to her feet as Apollo neared them, as did her father, though a bit slower. Her brother, Vik, lounged in his chair, his legs spread out far and wide—all useless posturing. Apollo had instantly disliked him at the first meeting six months ago. Now, knowing that he had willingly passed off Jia's hard work and talent as his own, his assessment was spot-on.

"Where is she?"

Rina paled at his tone while Jay's mouth flattened. "You had no right to turn her head. My lawyer's preparing annulment papers even as we speak and if I were you—"

"But I would never be you, Jay," Apollo bit out softly. "I would never steal intellectual property from a man I called friend and benefit from it while his family struggled. Apparently, stealing IP and passing it on as one's own is a family trait."

A paleness emerged beneath his skin. Hurriedly, Jay threw out an arm to stop his son, who'd shot to his feet.

"I could have you both in prison in an hour for IP theft. But Jia, probably the smartest of you lot, made a deal with me. As for an annulment, there will be no cause for that after today."

The man flushed a deep red.

"Where is she?" Apollo repeated.

"She's…unwell, Mr. Galanis," Rina said, "or she—"

"So unwell that she couldn't answer the phone? Or is she saving one of you from another mess?"

Rina blanched. "It's just that—"

"Already missing me, darling?" came a soft, husky voice from behind him.

Apollo turned to find his new bride a few feet away, dressed in a black lace top and black jeans, her hair in a messy bun on top of her head, her expressive eyes hidden behind wraparound shades.

Whatever unease he had felt didn't dissolve at seeing her. If anything, it intensified. Reaching her, he snatched the shades off her face. A deep, black-and-blue bruise shone under her left eye, stretching sideways toward her cheekbone where she had two butterfly stitches.

Rage swept through him. Was this the reason she had so readily made a deal with him? To escape from this?

Her eyes flared with apprehension at whatever she saw in his face and she took a step back. It was enough for Apollo to steady himself. One hand on her hip, he gently pulled her closer. Something in him calmed when she came without protest.

He ran the pad of his thumb under the bruise, careful not to touch the painful-looking boundary against unmarred skin. "What happened?" he said softly, loathing the presence of their audience, wishing he had never let her come back here.

"I tripped and landed my cheek on the leg of a table."

"Hmm…right after we got married too," he said, not missing the practiced, neat explanation. "This is the reason you wouldn't answer my calls?"

"Rina took me to the ER and it took forever. I had

to get stitches and then I had the worst headache for hours. I popped a couple of sleeping pills and slept for, like, twenty hours straight."

Apollo didn't push it, even though she wasn't telling him the complete truth. One of the two men behind him were responsible for her bruise. If he pushed her, she would only double down on her lie. And he wanted her to trust him. "Why didn't you text me?"

"I didn't realize my phone battery had died. This morning, you kept video calling me." She made a tsk-ing sound, leaning closer. Her fingers played with the buttons of his shirt, and every swipe of her fingertip against his throat tightened the knot of desire in his gut. "The last thing I wanted was my new husband to see what a frightful sight I was and return the merchandise. I was feeling sad enough that I didn't get a proper wedding night."

Despite his simmering rage, Apollo's mouth twitched. There was something almost adorable when she put on that hot-for-him act. He couldn't wait to discover how much of it was real. "You're a horrible flirt. Fortunately for me," he said, just to tease her.

"Hey! You're just not used to women coming on to you freely, are you? My generation believes in owning our desires. I foresee a lot of this age gap causing problems in our married life," she finished with a sigh. "It could count as 'irreconcilable differences' when we—"

Apollo shut her up the only way he knew, and the only way he wanted to. He caught her mouth with his, and she was surprised enough that she gasped.

It was their third kiss and the fact that he was keeping count like a teenager betrayed more than he cared to admit. But not enough to stop him from deepening it when she opened up with a soft moan. *Christos*, she was sweet and hot and he was regretting not taking her back to the penthouse immediately after their wedding. Her father wouldn't be threatening him with annulment and he would have had the chance to explore this fizzing need and bring it under control.

He gentled himself when she panted, even as his arousal heightened by the weight of her pressed up against him. For all her outward toughness, she was a skinny, almost fragile thing in his hands. Her fingers fluttered over his jaw and instantly, the kiss changed tenor, became softer, sweeter, as if she could magic out of it what she needed.

When she pulled back with another soft sigh and hid her face in his chest, Apollo wrapped his arms around her in what he would call a tender embrace. Which was another first for him because he wasn't the man women flocked to for tenderness and understanding.

Her tight knuckles drummed against his chest as she looked up. He saw a flash of anger in her eyes, directed at herself and him, before she cursed. She hadn't wanted that kiss to happen in front of her family.

Because she'd painted a picture of the suffering in store for her as his wife? Or because she felt exposed at her clear attraction to the family's enemy? Or because she had a whole new scheme cooking in her cunning brain and he'd disturbed it by showing up ahead of time?

Dios mio, the sooner he took her out of this place and from among them, the better for both of them. He could stop feeling like a caged animal at the mercy of its base desires and return to the rationality he knew and needed.

He rubbed his palm over her back, marveling at the wiry, lean strength of her body. Marveling at his attraction to a woman who was such a study in contrasts. "Say goodbye. We're leaving. Now."

She looked up, confusion clouding her sparkling brown eyes. "Now? You said I had six weeks."

"I didn't realize that you needed a keeper."

She stiffened, reminding him of his older sister's cat. "It's an accident, Apollo. Just a bruise."

"Do you really want to get into what it is now, *matia mou*?"

Her mouth turned down at the corners. "Give me at least until tonight."

"You have fifteen minutes and it's more than enough to collect your various electronics."

She pushed back from him then, mistrust shining in her eyes. "Not to say a proper goodbye and it's—"

"Now, Jia," he said, letting her see the temper he was tamping down. "Before I forget all my promises or that I still owe you one."

She straightened, shutting down whatever little vulnerability she had shown him. "If I'm using that one, it can't be half-assed."

He regarded her with an outside calm, even as he knew what she would ask. "What's the full condition, then?"

"I don't want to talk about this ever again."

He didn't need to ask her what she meant. He didn't

give his assent nor did she ask for confirmation. If she trusted him that much already, that was her problem. But no way was she getting what she wanted this time.

She belonged to him and he would destroy the man who had lifted a hand against her, whoever it was.

All through the flight to Athens, Jia kept wishing her husband was truly the closed-off, ruthless monster she'd made him out to be in her head all these months. A villain full of nefarious intentions and cutthroat tactics could have served her so much better.

His calling her his "asset," his telling her father that there would be no annulment after tonight, his demand that she leave instantly at his command…all of it pricked like a thorn stuck under her skin. But it was no less than what she'd expected. He was a powerful man used to getting his way and she was an important pawn.

Just because he'd gotten angry over her bruise, or kissed like he meant to soothe her…didn't mean much. The fortunate thing was that all her life, beginning very early on, she'd had a taste of everything but real love. Oh, her older sister, Rina, had been kind to her and loved her—even when it invited their father's annoyance—but it was the same emotion that she showed a puppy that Vik had tormented when they'd been kids.

Her father's begrudging acknowledgment and a little affection had come *after* she began showing real talent in architecture, after she'd won several contracts for the company, *after* she had repaid his generosity in letting her mother keep her.

Until then she'd been only a reminder of his wife's infidelity.

So Jia knew not to mistake Apollo's rage at her bruise for anything more than basic human decency, or his concern as anything more than another reason to hate her family. His demand that she leave her family behind was nothing but his need to make sure "their deal" was completed ASAP.

She was a willing pawn at worst, and an important asset at best. And in between, a weapon to be used against her father. Hopefully, her actions would count toward nullifying the last. Of course, her father had been furious, muttering that she'd ruined everything, ranting about an annulment.

Now, as she whiled away the hours on the jet, sitting across from Apollo, with a low buzzing ache at the back of her head that wouldn't let her sleep, Jia wished she could enjoy the flight. Wished she could ignore him as easily as he was ignoring her.

Through the drive to the private airstrip and the two hours into the flight so far, he'd barely looked at her, his dark mood hanging over the luxurious space like a thunderous cloud.

"Do you need medical attention, Jia?"

Jia sat up at the sudden question. Every time he said her name, it felt like a caress and a reprimand rolled into one. And while she wasn't going to go out of her way to please him, she didn't understand his animosity. She'd handed him everything he'd wanted on a platter without making any demands. What was his problem?

"I'm perfectly fine," she said, flicking an imaginary

dust mote from her jeans. Clearly, he had been watching her the whole time.

"You keep rubbing your head and your neck."

"I'm a little out of sorts," she snapped and sighed. "You did drag me away from my family and my things and…"

"Your precious collection of lacy silk blouses and dark denim?"

"Exactly," she said, not letting the smile that wanted to bloom touch her lips. He wasn't allowed to be grumpy one second and then charm her the next.

He stood up and before she could take in a rushed breath, loomed over her, filling her field of vision. With his shirt unbuttoned to reveal olive skin at his throat, his corded forearms sprinkled with hair and his gray eyes focused on her…he was incredibly intimidating, to say the least.

She'd been confident they would lead separate lives for most of the year. Given he traveled a lot and would want her to continue her work for the family firm. She hadn't expected to be around him so much so soon.

Something about him made her feel unbalanced. Which was why she'd played offense and admitted her attraction to him. Better to own it than let him turn it into a weapon.

He extended his hand toward her and that bubble of tension around them tightened. "Come."

After staring at it for a few seconds, she placed her hand in his with a tremble she couldn't hide. He pulled her up and shuffled them toward the rear cabin, telling the flight attendant that they weren't to be disturbed.

Jia flushed at the idea of the entire flight knowing what they were up to, and when dampness bloomed between her thighs, she flushed a little more. God, a one-word command from him and she was melting like an ice cream cone on a summer day.

You told yourself you'd enjoy this, remember, a voice whispered and she scoffed. She had done that. Out of this whole miserable deal—for which one party hated her and the other didn't trust her—hot, fun sex with the sexiest man she'd ever known was the one highlight she'd imagined could happen.

Theory was one thing and reality a whole other.

She was trembling by the time he closed the privacy curtains on them. What if she didn't please him? What if he was…?

"Take off your clothes," he said, once they were inside the luxurious rear cabin.

"What?" she said, whispering the word past the deafening pounding in her ears.

"Your clothes, I want them off. Do you need help?"

A sliver of mockery had crept into his voice and it made her spine straighten. That little twitch at the corner of his mouth…it reduced him to earthly dimension, made him look deceptively adorable.

Rolling her shoulders back in a conscious movement, Jia shook her head. "No, I don't."

She licked her lips, searching for a reason to ask for the lights to be dimmed or to just put this off for now. The twinkle in his eyes said he was expecting her to do just that and damned if she was going to let him box her like that.

"I thought you were very excited for all the sex we were going to have," he added, sitting down at the edge of the bed and loosely caging her between his legs. With his hands pressing into the bed, head tilted up, he looked like an emperor assessing his latest gift. "Don't tell me all of that was a pretense to trap me."

Jia's heart gave a thud against her rib cage. "Of course not," she said, swallowing past a swarm of butterflies in her throat. It was so much easier to make bold statements than actually be bold in front of him in such an intimate setting. "But I was expecting some foreplay at least."

"My eyes on you won't turn you on?"

Heat streaked her cheeks. "I don't know," she said, opting not to lie.

"You're of the generation that likes to try everything, *ne*? So let's see if stripping for me does anything for you."

Her mouth twitched at how cleverly he used her own words against her. She played with the lacy hem of her tank top, without meaning to be coy. His gaze slid there and away. "And you? Ordering me around turns you on?"

He grinned then, and somehow it felt more real than anything she'd seen in his expressions. As if she'd caught him by surprise once again and he liked that. A lot. "Not simply ordering you, Jia. But seeing you fight the instinct to give in definitely turns me on. It's quite…alluring."

How easily he read her…

He raised a brow, his arctic gray eyes sparkling. "But

I don't want to develop a reputation as a miserly husband. I'll give you as much foreplay as you need, if this doesn't work."

Jia took her blouse off and then shimmied out of her jeans, which was quite the feat with him looking on, because they were tight and she wasn't full of grace, like him. She stood in front of him in a strapless bra that pushed her small breasts up and matching panties in blush pink, her pulse going haywire all through her body. His gazed moved over her like some kind of laser pointer, with such leisure that she felt swirls of heat everywhere it landed.

A tiny flare of heat in his eyes when it stayed on her tattoos—her half sleeve with a bird flying out of a cage, the one on her lower belly, right above her pubic bone, of a heart, was the only sign that he liked what he saw.

Goose bumps erupted on her skin.

"Turn around," he said, packing a catch and a command, in just those two words.

She wished she didn't like how it pinged over her skin, how it made dampness bloom between her thighs. But God help her, she did. She liked the little lick of heat in his eyes, how his gaze lingered over her tattoos, the way the space around him seemed to crackle with tension. She even liked the taut set of his shoulders as if he was stopping himself from pouncing on her.

Pounce away, she wanted to say, but the words never left her throat.

When she didn't budge, he did a rotating motion with his index finger, his nostrils flaring.

Legs trembling, she turned. When his fingers landed

on her hip bones, and he gently tugged her back, she thought she might faint at the dizzy pleasure that claimed her. His warm breath coasted over her back in arousing trails. She could feel his gaze run up every dip and curve of her flesh, up the long, toned length of her legs to her buttocks barely covered in pink panties, lingering on the butterfly tattoo over her lower back and then up toward her shoulder blades where she had a small one of a starling. His scrutiny was thorough and intense enough that her breath shallowed out.

Slowly, she turned back, her own skin feeling two sizes too tight, anticipation inflating her chest.

Another sweep from beneath his lashes and then he gave her a nod. When she met his gaze, whatever desire she'd imagined seemed to have melted away, leaving a cold indifference. "Glad to know you aren't hurt anywhere else."

"What?" she murmured inanely, past the pinprick of hurt ensnaring all her senses. Then goose bumps rolled all over her bare skin. Her arms shook as she managed to stop herself from wrapping her arms around herself. She was not ashamed, of her body or of the desire she felt for him.

"I needed to make sure you do not have any other bruises," he said, coming to his feet.

"So you made me strip? Under false pretenses?" she said, thanking the universe the tears she felt crawling up her throat didn't coat the words.

"Would you have told me the truth if I asked?"

She opened her mouth and closed it, like a fish gasping for air on land. A draft from some hidden vent in the cabin blew over her skin, making her shiver. Before she could reply, he was in her face again, crowding her with his broad frame, draping the duvet around her shoulders with a gentleness she couldn't abide.

Jia shook it off, merciful anger coming to her aid. "I'm not some…victim you have to rescue."

"No? Because I'm beginning to wonder if your eager proposal wasn't an escape hatch."

"That would only work if I mistook you for a hero, Apollo. But you aren't. So please, don't let it go to your head."

"As long as we're—"

"Far from being a hero, you're a villain, to prey on my family's company, on my family. To use my desire for you to mind-fuck with me is only another step."

His chin tilted down, a flash of anger in his own eyes. But with a control that was miraculous to watch, he tamped it down. "I didn't mind-fuck you."

"No?"

"I used what I had in hand to achieve what you won't give me. How do you think I've crawled up out the muck your father left us in to where I am today. If that makes me a villain, then yes, I am one."

"Whatever it is that you're imagining about my family, about me, is not true," Jia said, losing her temper.

Fingers on her jaw, Apollo tilted her chin up with such gentleness that tears scratched at her throat. *This is pity*, she chanted in her head but something in his eyes, or her projection of what she wanted it to be… made it so damned hard not to see it as more.

"So your father or brother didn't cause this?"

"No one punched me. I wouldn't have let it go so far."

His fingers tightened infinitesimally, brackets of tension around his mouth. "Did one of them cause this, Jia?" he repeated.

She leaned forward until his exhale stroked her lips, until she could see into the fathomless gray of his eyes and imagine drowning there. Until she could feel the tension emanating from his hard, solid body. And his mouth…a tightness pinched it that had nothing to do with his perpetual grumpiness.

He had played with her, but it hadn't been without cost to him. And Jia needed that equalizer between them more than she needed air. She stepped back and faced him, her body still shaking with anger and unmet need. "You have no rights to my secrets or fears or wants. Whatever little trust was there between us, you've broken it."

He released her. "I see that I've made a mistake."

"What…what do you mean?" she whispered, already missing his feather-like touch.

"Rina *was* the right choice for me."

It was meant to hurt and so automatically, shouldn't, but God, it did. How foolish was she?

She tried to shake it off, used to that kind of casual rejection all her life. When she looked at him though, her belief that he meant to hurt her faltered. He truly believed her sister *was* the better choice. Or that they were interchangeable, except for her talent. And while there were any number of real, valid reasons Rina was a better choice for any man, she wasn't a masochist to try and find out his.

"Of course Rina's the better choice," she said with a scoff.

"As for gaining control of your talent, I could have done it through the board in a year or two anyway. You distracted me," he said, almost to himself.

The admission soothed the little hurt he'd dealt seconds ago. God, the man was giving her whiplash. Or her reaction to him was doing it. "What will you do? Return me with the packaging and the tag intact? Get an exchange deal?"

His mouth curled in distaste.

An uncontrollable shiver went through her again.

"As villainous as I am," he said, magicking a robe out of somewhere, and with firm but gentle movements, pushing her arms through the hole, "I protect my assets at any cost." He tugged the silky flaps closer and tied the sash at her waist, like he was dressing a recalcitrant child.

His gaze found hers and it was like two stars colliding somewhere in the cosmos, leaving an explosion and rubble behind. Only it was in her body. "Especially valuable ones. Even if it's from themselves."

Jia glared at the exit long after Apollo vanished. Shoving her legs roughly into her jeans, she cursed him and herself. She didn't need his damned pity or his honor. And, really, he'd done her a favor by…playing with her desire. He'd shown her that, for him, it was only another form of currency, another weapon.

At least now it wouldn't be hard to resist the damned man.

CHAPTER FOUR

APOLLO STOOD IN his private office and watched as the junior architect team surrounded his wife, peering over her modifications to his initial designs for an eco-resort in one of the Aegean Islands. Her enthusiasm and wit made them swarm to her like bees to honey and it had been so since day one. His staff didn't know he was watching them from within his office and never before had he felt the need to.

He was not a man given to impulses, detours and illogical actions but ever since he'd seen her snoring in his favorite armchair, every rule he'd lived by was suddenly moot.

In the weeks since they'd arrived in Athens, he still hadn't told his family that he and his shiny new bride were here. It wasn't a conscious decision or even the strangest thing he'd done either.

Jia had looked exhausted when they'd arrived at his penthouse in Athens late into the night. Without sparing him a glance, she had moved into the guest bedroom and closed the door.

He wasn't used to having women in his personal space and while a part of him had been relieved that she wasn't going to encroach on his, a part of him felt increasingly restless with each passing night, knowing she was under the same roof. He wanted her next to him, beneath him, where he could explore all those tattoos day and night.

Now that she'd taken it away, he realized how charming and addicting her easy honesty could be. He hadn't slept well in days now, the fact that he'd hurt her sitting like a weight on his chest.

Which was illogical in itself.

He'd never once cared about how abrupt and aloof he came off to his partners. Work had always been his number one priority and it should be now too. And he was damned if he apologized for something he'd had to do. Better she learn that there were some things he wouldn't tolerate.

To break the ice, he'd brought her into work that first morning, into the offices of his architect firm and introduced her as his latest hire and not his wife. He had a reputation for drawing talent from all over the world.

He'd been eager to see her in action, to see if she was truly as good as she'd painted herself to be. And in the meanwhile, she would thaw and realize that it was ridiculous to freeze him out when he was looking out for her. That he'd give her what she'd so brazenly demanded if only she admitted that he was right.

Now, three weeks later, Apollo had to concede that she was as stubborn as him, if not worse. Not once in three weeks had she smiled at him or let loose one of her sarcastic comments that put him on edge, or brought up their deal in any way.

If anything, watching her parade in his designer shirts—he'd no idea when she'd filched his stuff—and booty shorts that showcased her long legs and round ass as she cooked breakfast every morning, or those silk slips in the evenings while she played video games in his living room, was slowly driving him out of his mind.

He'd never before cohabitated with a woman, so the experience was unique enough. But wanting a woman's attention and being treated as less than a dust mote was…something else.

Even the shopping spree he'd forced on her on day three by inviting a team of designers with their latest couture collection hadn't thawed her. Usually, it was what he used when his sisters got upset with him. But, instead of enjoying the experience, Jia had simply chosen skinny jeans and lacy tops in different colors, added a couple of work jackets when the stylist commented that her lacy tops might not be suitable for work attire. The whole thing had been done in thirty minutes.

For a woman who wore the same thing over and over, her stuff took over his home. Hairpins, earrings, bottles of dark nail polish and chocolate wrappers…he couldn't walk out of his bedroom without seeing her plastered all across his home.

At work though, she was polite and direct, forever calling him Mr. Galanis in a saccharine sweet tone that grated. With everyone else, her smiles, her words, her actions…were genuine. Enough to turn him into a grumpy bastard with his staff.

If there had been any doubts about her talent, she'd ground them into dust. She wasn't just brilliant but innovative, with a fresh outlook toward how living and working spaces should and would look for a younger generation. She had not only fit in well with the team, but in the short time frame of three weeks, she'd made herself its locus.

Everyone swarmed to her—men and women, old and young—and Apollo knew she was an asset on many levels. And yet that word felt cheap and reductive. He wondered what it said that she had sold herself to him as such and that he had taken her on as such.

A sudden burst of laughter brought his head up. One of his brilliant young hires—though Jia was the youngest—a man named Paulo from Italy, had his hand on her shoulder and whispered something into her ear. The more he wanted to go out there and pull Paulo's hand away from Jia, the more Apollo resisted the urge. It would only embarrass her and the team. *Christos*, he was thirty-nine years old. He should have a better handle on his baser instincts.

She hadn't even asked him why he'd hidden the fact that they were married. Instead, she'd simply gone along with it and the lack of protest bothered him even more. Was this how Jay had treated her too and she'd simply given in to keep the peace?

The idea of her not fighting him and his dictates made Apollo's stomach knot. As did the idea that she thought he was the same as her father.

Outside his office, Jia smiled at Paulo, replied in English and slipped out from under his hold. When Paulo would have insisted, she flashed her ring at him, a gentle rebuke on her lips. Paulo raised his palms, said something that made her blush and then with what looked like genuine regret, put distance between them.

Having had enough of gawking at her like some love-sick fool, Apollo reached for the door. Even the realization that she had somehow won this battle between them wasn't enough to stop him. He would eventually win the war, he told himself.

Right now, what he wanted more than winning was to kiss his wife until she couldn't ignore him anymore.

Summoned to his office, as if she was nothing more than one of his minions.

He'd never before singled her out during the day. Was he going to get rid of her already? Jia's stomach swooped. Around her, smiles wavered and encouraging comments multiplied. He'd been a demanding, irrational beast for the past week and they didn't even know the half of it.

With each step, Jia felt like a rabbit braving the lion's den. Worse, a foolish, horny rabbit who was ready to beg the lion to consume her whole. Because, damn... living with the man while not claiming wifely rights was like being shown an array of specialty doughnuts but forbidden from tasting.

In the first week, she'd seen it as a reprieve from him, from their arrangement, from her own roller-coaster wants and emotions. Even as an opportunity to prove her worth to him, because that's what this deal was about. Her work was the only reason she was Mrs. Apollo Galanis. His secrecy, while it had surprised her, had also been another reprieve, from his family, the media and the world.

In a way, he'd given her a gift she hadn't wanted or known that she needed.

His Grumpy Assness would no doubt take it away if he knew how much she enjoyed the carefree anonymity of being completely herself. *Of being only Jia*, with a chance to prove her mettle, to find a place among her coworkers by her own merit, to be free of patterns and needs that had been cemented over a lifetime. For the first time in her life, she wasn't her father's unwanted daughter, or a resentful brother's sister, or even a protective one, and didn't have to pussyfoot at work or home.

It was only now, away from home and New York, that Jia understood how much her family took up space in her head and her heart. And it was a harsh reminder that Apollo was no different from any of them, except that he was up-front about her value to him.

She'd have even counted the last three weeks as some of the best of her life, if not for the tense evenings and rife mornings with Apollo. Seeing him walk into the kitchen at the crack of dawn, his hair disheveled from sleep, his muscled chest naked, his pajamas hanging low on his hips, made him even more appealing. As if she needed the reminder that the man was sexy in every dimension. If it was power that rolled off him in Armani suits, it was an earthy, easy masculinity that dripped from him in casual clothes.

But she'd found a way to use those awkward, charged encounters to her benefit too. Especially once the thought snuck into her mind that he was hiding her from the world because he was ashamed of her. It wasn't quite a jump since he said he'd made a mistake in choosing her, straight to her face.

Their awareness of each other was bigger than either of them. So she flaunted herself in his oversize dress shirts—even after he'd bought her clothes—took over every inch of his precious penthouse and generally made herself impossible to ignore when he came home.

But she had no idea if any of her ploys to get under his skin had worked.

"Lock the door behind you," he said now as she entered his office, his back to her.

It sounded ominous enough that Jia did so with a mounting heartbeat. But no, he wasn't allowed to see how easy she was for him. Never again. She took a deep breath, and donned her armor before turning around. "Did I pass the test?"

He was leaning against the large mahogany desk, his long legs thrown out in front of him. His office was vast with two different sitting areas, and yet it was dwarfed by him. Tie and jacket gone, his unbuttoned shirt gave her a glimpse of a chest covered in whorls of hair. His hair looked like someone had run their fingers through it, messing it up. He looked like he could belong in a boardroom or a photoshoot, that easy grace radiating off him.

Any hope that he'd reached the end of his tether died when she met his crystalline gray eyes. He looked as inscrutable and unshaken as ever.

"What test?" he said in a voice that rumbled down her spine. It was the first time in three weeks that they were alone together, addressing each other, making eye contact. All the reassurances Jia had tried to tell herself that he wasn't all that irresistible melted away.

"These three weeks at work...you wanted to make sure I wasn't lying."

"I simply wanted to see how you work with a team."

"And?" she said, eager for praise.

"You let everyone's opinions into your head. A little more discernment and a little less people-pleasing would work better for your individual—"

"It's called being a team player," she cut in, ire dancing on her skin.

"Doesn't mean you let all these narrow-minded people dilute your vision. You're brilliant, Jia, and sometimes, you have to be ruthless to give it rein, to meet your full potential."

Whatever protest she'd been about to offer on principle died on her lips. Warmth and a dizzy kind of joy fizzed through her. "That's high praise from the enemy," she said, when she felt his gaze move over her mouth with an intensity that scorched.

"Is that how you still see us?" he asked, straightening.

"Enemies who've made a deal, yes," she said, pressing her palm to her belly, as if she could stop the flutters there. "Believe me, it's better that way."

"You're still angry with me, then?"

What the hell did the man want from her? Why did he care if she was? He'd made it clear that she or her finer feelings didn't matter to him in the big scheme of things.

He simply wanted the truth, Jia, whispered the soft, vulnerable underbelly she always tried to protect.

"Of course not." When he raised a brow, she gave him the truth. At least a part of it. "Let's say I'm not blinded by my attraction to you anymore."

"Because I used it against you?"

"Why ask me when you know all the answers?"

He rubbed a long finger over his thick brow, sudden tension emanating from his broad frame. "I ask because I don't have all the answers. And I don't like not knowing."

"I imagine that would bother the all-knowing Apollo Galanis." Sarcasm dripped from every word. "What is it that you don't get?"

"Why did it hurt you this much? By your own admission, chemistry is not a big deal."

She looked away and then he was there, too close. Her nostrils filled with his cologne and sweat, the air around her suddenly warm with his body heat. His fingers landed on her cheek again. It took everything she had to not lean into the touch, to not give herself over into his hands.

Two fingers became his whole palm. He clasped her jaw and tilted her face up. Warm lights flickered in gray eyes, reminding her of her favorite lighthouse on the bay back home. "Why?"

Something about the way he said the one word got under her skin. She licked her lips, willing her body to stay strong. "Everything else between us is for others. You and my father and Rina and the company and that decades' old revenge, all of it is tainted and twisted. But this attraction between us...it's mine and real and it was the only thing that kept me going."

Her breath became a balloon as she waited for him to push her away, to call her a sentimental fool, to remind her of the terms of their engagement.

Instead, his eyes searched hers, as if he wanted to plumb the very depths of her. His large hand spanned her jaw until the pad of his thumb rested against the pulse at her neck. She could feel its thrashing beat against his flesh, begging for something she shouldn't want.

"I should very much like to kiss you, Tornado. Now."

"To seal the deal now that you know I'm actually good? To keep me compliant enough so that I'll give it my all? To give me just enough to keep me panting—"

His lips fused with hers, and a shuddering breath left her, leaving trails of agony in its wake.

"Because you're right, and this is too good and too real to not celebrate," he whispered against her mouth and there was no turning back.

Jia rubbed her lips against his, and his hands wandered from her neck to her shoulders to her hips. He pulled her flush against him, her arms went around his shoulders, her fingers sank into his hair and he was kissing her as if he meant to devour her whole.

It was different, this kiss, rough and heavy with three weeks of desperate wanting.

He was different, and it showed in how he licked and nipped at her lips, how he demanded access and swept his tongue through her mouth, how he lifted her until she wrapped her legs around his waist as if it was a move they'd performed for years.

His unfiltered need stoked hers. His mouth at her

neck, trailing down to the valley between her breasts, made her breath shallow out. Jia writhed herself against his growing shaft, her mouth dry, her head dizzy with pleasure. He was hard and thick and she wanted more.

Pressing her back into the wall, Apollo rocked his erection into the cradle of her thighs, hitting the exact spot where she needed it. How she needed it. Her eyes nearly rolled back in her head at the pressure building, roiling. God, she might come just dry humping him like this and she didn't even care and…

Suddenly, the door to his private office flew open and four women of varying ages stood in the entryway, eyes wide in their faces.

"*Apollo!* Shame on you," said the oldest woman, and Jia wanted to sob because her release was flying away and her lower belly felt empty and abandoned and she thought she might never get the one thing she'd given herself permission to want from her husband.

Apollo released her legs from around his hips with a muttered curse, and still holding her, straightened her top and jacket with gentle care. Jia hid her face in his chest. His quick buss at her temple and harshly whispered reassurances made warmth curl through her. And she wondered, in that lust-heavy haze, if protecting her wasn't simply protecting his asset but something more.

Just a sliver more.

Just a teensy bit particularly-about-her more.

Her knees trembled when her feet hit the floor, but he held on, and Jia had the craziest thought that he would always catch her, no matter what. And the thought was both exciting and terrifying.

* * *

"Apollo! Explain this! At once!" the older woman re-peated in fractured English.

Jia snuck a quick look at him and was bemused to see a strip of dark color streak his cheeks.

She turned but remained behind him, reluctant to meet people who'd hate her on sight, just when she was getting used to him. There was no doubt who these women were.

"Hello, Mama. Hello, Christina, Chiara, Camilla."

When it became clear that Apollo wasn't going to budge from his place—he couldn't even if he wanted to for Jia was clinging to him like a jellyfish—his mother advanced into the room while one of his sisters closed the door.

"You arrive in Athens three weeks ago and don't even tell your family. You don't bring your new bride to meet us. And when I come into your office to give you a piece of my mind, I find you kissing some teenage…"

"Floozy," one of the sisters supplied helpfully.

Apollo's mother shook her head, and Jia's respect for the women grew, along with the hysterical chuckle in her chest.

"Kissing a work colleague, while already neglect-ing your bride?"

Jia giggled. Loudly and disgracefully, and even muf-fled into Apollo's muscled back, it sounded alarmingly flippant.

"The floozy dares to laugh at us, Mama," the one who seemed to be the oldest sister supplied in flawless English, looking truly angry. "This is what your son has reduced us to, our family to, in his pursuit of revenge, and what he has turned—"

"You were always one for drama, Camilla." Apollo finally spoke. He didn't desert Jia though. No, he pulled her from behind him, and wrapped an arm around her waist. "Mama, *this is* my wife, Jia. Jia, this is Mama and my sisters—all older than me. The one who held judgment is the middle one, Christina. The one giggling at us both is Chiara and the one spewing fury is the oldest, Camilla."

For long, awkward moments, Jia could do nothing but stare at them. They were all tall, with distinct, almost overpowering features, all cut in the same mold as their brother. And yet, where they all missed the mark of true beauty, something had come together just a little differently in his case, and the result was a stunning, gorgeous man.

Her man, if she let herself believe him.

"Very nice to meet you all," she said, "though I wish it was under different circumstances. That's why the inappropriate giggling."

His mother sighed while Camilla didn't look one bit mollified.

Jia tried not to crumple under her refreshed glare, which meant she was remembering who she was.

"Hello, Jia," his mother said. Kindness shone from her eyes as she moved forward, her gaze eating her up as intensely as Apollo's did. "I'm sorry for barging in and yelling at you. I didn't realize Apollo's wife was—"

"Barely older than a teenager," the one called Chiara supplied, mischief in her eyes. "All these years, Mama, we keep pushing mature, sophisticated women toward him and turns out Apollo has a taste for young—"

"I admit he's of a different generation than me," Jia rushed in, wanting to shake them as much as they were doing to her world, "but your brother's like…a stud and I've always been into that whole age-gap, smoldering alpha-hole thing, so it works."

Mouths fell open and hit their chests. Again.

Jia bit her lip, regrets flooding in. God, she'd always gone on offense when she felt cornered.

Chiara and Christina burst out laughing while Camilla's glare intensified. His mother's eyes twinkled. With pleasant surprise, Jia hoped.

"You are different from what we expected," she finally said.

"She's full of surprises," Apollo said, his eyes full of that wicked humor and a sliver of something that sounded like pride. No one had ever shown that emotion on her behalf. Jia felt like grabbing his face and kissing him all over again. Audience be damned.

"Why didn't you tell the staff that she's your wife?" Camilla said, clearly still spoiling for a fight.

Whether her ire was directed at her brother or Jia, she had no idea. But Jia didn't want the whole story about how their marriage was nothing but a deal to be exposed in front of these women. Clearly, they cared about Apollo and didn't understand his actions after all these years, any more than she did.

It wasn't that she wanted a good start with Apollo's family, not when she was going to leave, sooner or later. But she couldn't take more taunting, on top of everything her own family had doled out at the mere idea of this relationship. And that kiss, before they had been rudely interrupted, was as real as anything Jia had ever known in her life. Or more, even. She didn't want it tainted by everything else that surrounded it.

"That was my idea," she said, riding the impulsive train all the way. "I wanted to start work and bond with Apollo's team without any preferential treatment. Also, there's the fact that your brother's too much of a workaholic to take me on a honeymoon. This way, our first few weeks of marriage are both secretive and spicy. And just for ourselves."

They stared at her, as if she were an exhibit Apollo had checked out of a museum. It wasn't just that she was the enemy's daughter, but how she dressed and her tattoos and everything about her, Jia realized. She didn't doubt she was as different as possible from Apollo's previous…interests. The mere thought of them made her stomach knot.

"That kiss we interrupted was definitely something," Chiara added.

Jia blushed. Their mother shushed her.

"So you work here, Jia? And you plan to continue working with my brother?" It was the middle sister, Christina, this time. There was genuine curiosity in her question.

"I'm an architect, and, yeah, I plan to continue working with Apollo. It's one of the reasons he was so… moved to steal me for himself. On top of our crazy chemistry, I mean. We understand each other even in our work."

The words left her of their own accord and Jia real-ized the truth of them only then.

For all their age gap and enemy vibes, Apollo and she shared the same kind of vision for their work, for how they wanted to shape the world around them. For how they changed it.

Flushing, she turned to look at Apollo, who was frowning. As if she was putting out main character energy when she should be in the back with chorus.

She pinched his side, which was all rock-hard mus-culature and didn't really give into pinching, and then winked at Christina. "To be honest, I'm trying to make sure he doesn't forget what a delight I'm to be around twenty-four hours, seven days a week."

Christina stared at her brother and Jia for long mo-ments. After a while, she extended her hands to Jia. "Welcome to the family, Jia. I have a feeling you're exactly what my brother needs."

She kissed Jia's cheeks even as her statement rang hollowly through Jia's gut. If she let herself, she would see romantic crap in everything. Just as she was for-ever searching for the slightest hint of approval in her father's words and gestures.

Apollo's mother and other sisters followed suit, air-kissing Jia's cheeks. Talk moved slowly to their non-wedding in New York, the hurry for it, and inevitably to Jia's family and how Apollo was taking over the family company.

On that front, Jia couldn't summon even a fake smile. Around her, English morphed into Greek and determined to wait them out, she stood there, like a statue frozen amidst life.

But when her father's name came up and a flash of such intense hurt crossed Apollo's mother's face, all the armor Jia had cloaked herself in fell away. The sisters watched as the son and mother argued in rapid Greek and then joined in. Only Christina seemed to be arguing on his side. Finally, his mouth set into that arrogant tilt that no one could budge, Apollo stepped away.

Oh, why had he insisted on marrying one of the Shetty daughters knowing it would hurt his mother to even have the shadow of Jia's father touch her family? What did he hope to accomplish except fill them with doubts about her and himself? Would having control over her fate go such a long way toward appeasing his thirst for revenge? Why had Jia thought this would be as simple as bearing undeserved judgment and anger from his family?

Pain was something she was familiar with and it danced in his mother's eyes.

Impulsively, Jia reached out and took the older woman's hands. "I'm sorry that my very presence causes you such...anguish. For what it's worth, I apologize for all the pain my father caused your family. It was inexcusable and if I could change it, I would."

Stunned silence met her foolish declaration. Even the fiery Camilla, it seemed, had nothing to counter it with.

Jia tried hard not to look at Apollo. She couldn't bear it if he thought her statement was pandering to them or if he mocked and dismissed the sentiment itself.

Apollo's mother shook her head, one rogue tear running down her cheek. "Children are not responsible for their father's sins. Or their failures," she bit out.

Out of the periphery of her vision, Jia saw Apollo flinch.

The older woman gently clasped Jia's cheek and a soft exhale left her. "Christina was always the smartest of my children." The other three protested loudly. She laughed, wiped her cheek and, leaning toward Jia, whispered, "You're exactly what Apollo needs. Let's hope he doesn't realize it or he will…" She sighed.

Leaving Jia to wonder what she meant by it and why it felt so unbelievably good to be welcomed by his family when they should hate her on sight.

When they finally left—nothing short of Apollo's promises that they would be at the family home that very night had achieved it—Jia made to follow them.

Hand at her elbow, Apollo stopped her.

Pressing her forehead to the cool door, Jia refused to turn. She was feeling emotional, and the last thing she wanted was to betray something he'd consider ammunition in this battle of theirs. God, who'd have thought being married to the enemy would be this hard on her heart?

For a man who didn't deal in feelings, Apollo seemed to understand her reluctance to face him. His arms came around her waist gently and pulled her until she was plastered to him, chest to thigh. It wasn't a sexual embrace but neither did it feel like a transactional kindness. It was something in between, like their relationship itself, teetering between labels.

"I didn't marry you to punish you."

"No? Because from where I stand—"

She didn't finish her statement because his mouth was at her neck. He nibbled at her fluttering pulse and Jia melted into his arms, her muscles instantly loosening and tightening of their own accord.

"You were right. Whatever this started as, there's this very real thing between us, *ne*?"

"Is there?" she asked, arching her neck to give him better access. Dampness bloomed between her legs when he gently nipped the spot.

"Yes, Jia. Maybe I should have said this that very night you begged me to marry you and—"

Jia knocked her elbow into his gut and grinned at his surprised grunt.

"Or maybe at our wedding," he said, turning her to face him. His gaze held hers, something shimmering in it.

"Said what to me?" she said, hanging at the edge of a rope, desperately aching for something.

"I see you, Jia, and everything you are. And a little more that you hide."

Gratitude and something more joined the arousal in her limbs, making her dizzy.

Bending, Apollo pressed a kiss to the corner of her mouth, his large hand cupping her hip, as if he already knew all the nooks and corners of her body. "So, let's celebrate this with a real wedding night. Whenever you're ready."

His promise reverberated through her as Jia went back to her open cubicle and tried not to hear the frenzied whispers around her. For the next couple of hours that she lingered at work, no one would meet her eyes, or respond to her without looking at her as if she'd suddenly turned into a bug-eyed monster. Paulo, when she forced him to respond, couldn't get away from her fast enough.

The reprieve was over. His family knew, her coworkers knew and now, the whole world would know that she was Jia Galanis. And yet, as she repeated to herself a thousand times, and relived the moment when Apollo had looked into her eyes and admitted that he saw her, Jia didn't feel trepidation at all. If anything, she felt excited about this new, temporary relationship more than she ever had about a real one.

CHAPTER FIVE

APOLLO HADN'T MEANT to leave her to the curious, even aggressive in Camilla's case, clutches of his family. He had just decided to bring her home, right before they had descended on them en masse.

But after, even though he'd taunted her that he wanted his wedding night, he'd sent her to his family home with his chauffeur, claiming a work emergency. Long past midnight, he had returned to his penthouse.

Whatever he thought he was escaping by sending Jia away, duplicitously no less, smacked him in the face when he walked in. From the vast sitting lounge where she'd spread around her sketching papers to the kitchen where she'd abandoned spice tins and tea boxes and chocolate hampers, to the large media room where her video game equipment lay scattered about, she had already stamped the space with her presence.

The silence without her was different from the one with her, and he realized how companionable even that had become between them. As if they were an old couple, married for fifty or so years, easy with each other in everything, like his grandparents were. Even the bathroom—week two she'd begun using the one attached to his bedroom, claiming a woman needed the more luxurious one—didn't remain untouched. There was a box of tampons on the black granite.

He'd found her sobbing one evening, hair in a messy updo, pillows clutched to her chest while watching some old Bollywood flick. When he'd demanded to know what had upset her so, she'd stuffed more chocolate into her mouth and bit out that she always cried like that on her period and would he please leave her alone. He had sat by her, pretending to be absorbed in the colorful movie that he didn't even understand, and then fascinated when she started explaining the convoluted plot, forgetting her usual frosty silence.

None of his sisters had ever complained or sobbed or made such a mess of themselves on their periods, he'd thought. But then, when had he had time for any of them, either growing up or after their father had died. For all he claimed to do for his family, he'd had very little to do with his own for the past two decades. Something Mama hadn't missed pointing out in the three minutes they had talked to each other.

Several hairbrushes, a bottle of perfume and tubes of lipstick surrounded his sink, mocking him. He almost lifted the bottle of perfume to sniff it like some lovesick fool when he caught his reflection and stopped.

Walking back into the kitchen, he poured himself a glass of wine and then discarded it. Even the damned wine reminded him of her. Remembering Jia got headaches from red wine, he'd already asked his housekeeper to stock more whites.

Then as he moved through his bedroom shedding

his clothes and donning sweats, the source of his restlessness finally hit him.

I'm sorry for everything my father did to your family, she'd said.

No one could doubt her apology had been heartfelt, not Camilla. Not him. And yet, her words and her expression haunted him, holding up a mirror into which he didn't want to look.

He'd thought telling her that his marrying her wasn't meant as a punishment would be enough. But was that true of his intentions, or the impact it had caused on her life? Knowing her now, knowing how he'd uprooted her from her family, without even her familiar things, knowing he'd thrust her into the center of his family, knowing how prejudiced they would be against her, what was it if not punishment?

For close to two decades, he'd worked himself to the bone, neglecting his relationship with his mother and sisters, neglecting his own happiness and comfort, pursuing wealth and connection and power, with one goal in mind.

To ruin Jay Shetty's company and his peace as he'd ruined theirs. To push him toward despair as he'd done to Apollo's father. And along the way, he'd deemed it okay to include the old man's family. He'd known Rina didn't wanted to marry him but he hadn't cared much about it because all it took was for her to naysay her own father, right?

Not his problem.

But now, when he remembered the ache in Jia's face when they had all argued about her family as if she wasn't standing right there, her easy, blunt honesty and her apology as she faced up to what her father had done when she'd been no more than a child, her flirty answers so that the coldness of their deal wasn't exposed to his family... Apollo wondered at the sanity of what he had done. Wondered suddenly about all the possibilities of a future that he had stolen from Jia.

Did she have a boyfriend back home? A lover who was even now mourning her loss? What were her dreams, other than rescuing her useless family? Why didn't she work for some other company instead of letting her brother pass off her work as his own? Why the desperate effort to save a family who seemed undeserving at best and loathsome at worst?

He knew nothing of her hopes and fears. But more importantly, with the little he did know, Apollo didn't want to give her up.

She was Jay Shetty's daughter, she owned the stock that Apollo needed, and she was one of the most innovative young architects he'd ever met, and keeping her as his wife would be a lifelong, painful thorn in the old man's side. Especially since he would make sure that Jia shifted her allegiance completely toward him.

Anything less than complete surrender was unacceptable to him in his wife, on principle. But even more, from the woman he was fast becoming obsessed with.

All the fun, parties, peace and comfort, and even sex, that he'd given up in his twenties and most of his thirties, he would make up with her. The prospect of spoiling Jia and himself, of glutting himself on her, with her, breathed new life into his burned-out soul.

As he pushed his muscles beyond endurance on the rowing machine in the state-of-the-art gym—one place Jia hadn't invaded because she claimed she was allergic to sweat—he shifted his view of this marriage he'd insisted on.

Whatever he had taken away from Jia, he was sure, was small and pathetic enough that he could replace it. He'd drown her in wealth and recognition and laurels for her work, lavish her with gifts and luxury, so much so that all that fierce loyalty she showed her undeserving family would soon be his.

He would have all of her, and he would make her happier than Jay ever had and *that* would be the best revenge.

Two days later, it was midafternoon when Apollo stepped out of the chopper he'd called in at the last minute. Usually, he enjoyed the two-hour-long drive from his headquarters in Athens to the eco-friendly mansion he had built for his family nearly eight years ago.

It was one of his favorite projects, a contemporary but warm design set on fifteen acres of land—a gift to his mother. Although she'd never been as happy or receptive about the gift as he'd expected her, even needed her, to be. Neither did he forget that she wouldn't have even moved in if not for Camilla, who, after a nasty divorce that had left her with nothing, had wanted her boys to have a good life.

Christina, whose partner, Fatima, was a world-renowned artist and traveled quite a bit like him, had been the least challenging about accepting gifts from the wealth he had amassed. Among all of them, she was the outdoorsy one, and the idea of living on fifteen acres of land, surrounded by her family, held great appeal for her. Being the compassionate one, she was also the one who had tried to understand what had driven Apollo for so long, though she never quite supported him either.

Chiara, whose husband had failed at several businesses, had three children, and Apollo was more than happy to support her and her family.

And yet, he hadn't visited the estate more than twice, and not once in the last two years.

As he walked the gravel path heading up to the mansion, he felt a strange elation in his gut, as if his return this time was more significant than it had ever been before. Was it because he had finally reached his goal of defeating the man who had ruined his family's happiness? Or was it simply a need to see the woman who had occupied his thoughts for the last two days?

Whatever it was, Apollo decided he would accept the feeling, as another gift after his long struggle.

As soon as he crossed the threshold and walked into the large living area with its high ceilings and exposed beams, he heard her laughter—deep, husky and without reservation. Pleasure drenched him, a fist of need tightening his gut.

Sunlight streamed through the high windows, dappling the light furniture and dark hand-stained wood floors in beautiful contrasts. The scent of delicious food emanated from the open kitchen, where he could see his mother, Christina and Chiara fighting and shouting and slaving over the stove. Chiara's husband was chopping vegetables.

Apollo had to take a small detour to see past the pillars into the cozy great room. Up on the opposite wall, the huge plasma screen TV showed off some role-playing game in high-definition color. And standing behind the coffee table with controllers in hand were Jia and Camilla's sons on either side of her, whooping and squealing and shouting as they killed some many-pronged creature on the screen.

A short distance from them, caught between the kitchen and the living room, was Camilla, watching the trio with naked envy on her face. Apollo remembered his mom telling him that Camilla was having a hard time connecting with her sons, who were now sixteen, and were starting to ask more and more questions about their papa.

As if aware of Camilla's gaze on her back, Jia turned and beckoned his older sister, holding out the controller. One of Camilla's sons joked about his mother not knowing anything except handling a spatula in the kitchen. Jia paused the game and told him off with no hesitation.

Only then did Apollo allow himself to look at her properly.

His wife, it seemed, had an allergy to clothes and, *Christos*, he was determined to fix it. Cutoff denim shorts that covered her ass, thank the saints, but showed off her long, toned legs. Paired with a teeny-tiny crop top that left inches of flesh between the hem and the shorts, she looked like she could be an older girlfriend that one of his nephews was forever trying to show off.

Under the anime T-shirt, which Apollo realized belonged to his nephew, her colorful tattoos peeked out. Her hair was in a messy bun again. Stubborn strands kept falling into her face, which she pushed away with the back of her hand. Sunlight picked out the golden highlights in her hair, just as it shone on her skin.

She looked good enough to eat, and he was ravenous for a bite.

He walked into the lounge and landed a soft slap over his nephew's shoulder. The monster thingy that Jia had almost killed on-screen ate her little elf avatar in one quick gobble, while she watched horrified, unmoving.

His other nephew groaned and burst into broken English about how they'd almost had him and why had Auntie Jia suddenly lost focus.

Grinning, Apollo leaned his head over her still, tense shoulder and grabbed the controller from her. She jerked as if his touch scalded her. He threw the controller to his nephew who caught it with nimble fingers. Then Apollo grabbed her hand and tugged her behind him.

She stumbled once as they passed the enormous kitchen and his mother and sisters called out greetings to him. He waved at them, barely adjusting his stride.

When they reached the open, hanging stairs past the corridor, Jia seemed to come to herself and dug in her feet. "What happened? Where are we going?"

"Which one is our bedroom?" he said, going down one step so that he could look at her. The steps were made of wood and hung unsupported on one side, opening out into the other living room, while the glass walls on the opposite side gave magnificent views of the wild gardens outside.

Industrial-size pendant lights cast a soft glow as evening slowly gave way to pitch-black night.

"The big one with the attached suite on the second floor," Jia added almost automatically. "Your mother said they saved it for you and your wife."

"Perfect. Come."

"Why?" she said, watching him with wide eyes. Her mouth was soft and pink and reminded Apollo of how much he liked sweet and tart strawberries.

"There's something I would like to show you."

Doubt shone across her face. "In the bedroom?"

"Ne."

"And it can't wait?"

"Ohi."

"Well, I'm not in the mood to see anything. You send me here with them, ignore me for two days and then show up here, demanding I…pay attention to you? *No!* I was in the middle of a game and then Maria was going to show me how to cook this dessert I love, and Christina and I planned to watch a horror flick, and Chiara said she'd do my nails. I'm not pushing all that off because Your Arrogant Highness has decided he wants to show me something."

"Fine," he said, leaning closer. *Christos*, just the scent of her was enough to twist him into a mass of need. The red rose undertone to whatever she used…it had begun to linger on his clothes, around the sheets and towels, and damn if he hadn't begun to chase it all across his penthouse like a junkie. "I'll simply order them to not do any of those things with you until you attend to me."

"Attend to you? You're not my bloody—"

"I have a wedding gift for you."

Her eyes widened and her lovely mouth fell open. She was all lean, taut curves but her mouth...it was wide and lush and utterly sensuous. And he loved how she melted when he licked it, how she jerked when he nipped it. "You do?"

"Yes."

"And that's what you want to show me?"

"Among other things."

She blushed then and it was the most glorious sight Apollo had ever seen. Her gaze slipped to the small gift bag in his hands and then back to his eyes, via a lingering detour at his mouth. Her soft exhale coasted over his lips, taunting.

The little frown was back between her feathery brows and he swallowed an impatient curse. Only now did he understand what a distrustful creature she was. Just like him. "Why can't you show it to me in front of everyone?"

"I didn't want to embarrass you. But if you prefer—"

"No, they're already teasing me because I made up all that stuff in your office," she said, stepping down and then walking up with him.

He hid his grin. "*Why did* you make up all that stuff? Why hide the reality of what this is?"

"Your mother and sisters..." A soft, almost wondrous note entered her voice. "I could tell at one glance how lovely and kind they are. How much they adore you. My family already thinks I've betrayed them. There was no point in letting yours see what a monster you are."

"I thought I was a villain, not a monster."

"Interesting that you see the distinction."

He laughed and like clockwork, her gaze clung to his mouth.

"Tell me."

A breathy sigh. "A monster can't help acting on his instincts."

"Ahh... I'm growing in your estimation."

She shrugged, just as they reached the landing and then started up the second set of stairs. "This home... Maria told me you designed and built it. For her."

It was his turn to shrug.

"I spent the first day just exploring all the clever little nooks and crannies. Every inch of it gets natural light. And, oh, my God, that office on the ground floor... You used the wood from the trees that were cleared to make space for the home, didn't you?"

He nodded. "We used every inch of it that we took from the land."

Not even a sunbeam could match the brilliance of her smile. "It's the most beautiful home I've ever seen, Apollo. Like, if I was given a choice where to live the rest of my life, it would be here."

He was stunned enough to stare at her. This time, the pleasure that filled him was...different, almost insidious in nature, creeping and settling into places and pockets he hadn't realized were empty in him.

"What?" she demanded as he continued to stare at her. "No one can deny you're a brilliant artist. Although, you haven't done anything like this in the last few years, right?"

"Something like this?" he said, awed at this woman who so easily saw through to his burnout that no one, not even Christina, had seen.

"This place is kind of magical. Your latest designs are much more…commercial and soulless."

"Ouch," he said, laying a hand on his chest.

"Tell me about how the solar panels work. All the glass must make it cool in winter but I saw that there's no central heating."

It was the last thing Apollo had expected her to ask him. No one in his family had realized how special this project was to him. Which was why Mama's almost instant rejection and continued refusal had hurt so much. "My father was the one who did the initial designs," he said, finding his voice suddenly rusty.

Jia smiled, running her hands over the dark wood banister. "I thought it had an old-world charm to it. You know, I've looked at some of his plans for the eco-cabins they were designing back then. I found them in the archive's office…" She slowed down when he didn't respond. "My mother used to talk about him sometimes. I was curious enough that I went to the archives."

Shock suffused him enough that he simply stared. When a regretful look came into her eyes, he hurried on. "I didn't realize they were still there."

"She hadn't been exaggerating. Your father was… had a very unique touch."

He gave her a nod, unable to speak past the sudden lump in his throat.

"So this home…you modified the initial plan?"

Apollo told her, at length, as they walked up the second set of stairs. With each word he said, and each step they took toward their suite, and each memory he unlocked, some hard, petrified thing in his chest cracked wide-open. And he found himself breathing deep and long, as if he'd been only half-alive until now.

It was easy, and a strange kind of wonderful, to talk to Apollo about the design of the house.

Jia had never fallen in love faster or deeper in her entire life. It was as if the house was a physical culmination of all the dreams she hadn't even allowed herself to feel.

The high ceilings, the exposed wood beams and pillars, the open expansiveness of the plan…even the hand-stained hardwood floors and the lighting fixtures, every inch of it spoke of the attention and love he'd poured into the house. More than anything else, it spoke of the man and the beat of his heart.

Which had then made her feel foolish because Apollo Galanis had no heart and what was more proof than the fact that he'd not only kept her identity secret for three weeks among his staff, but then dumped her with his family, while he did God knows what for two days.

And now here he was, demanding attention, dangling a gift in front of her face just when she was determined to hate him all over again. Or better, become indifferent to him.

She walked into the vast bedroom suite, which had

glass for ceiling and three walls, enchanted by it all over again when she realized he'd fallen silent behind her.

"You like the house, then?" he said so softly that for a second Jia wondered if she was imagining the sliver of vulnerability in it. But his eyes remained hard and inscrutable. There she was again, projecting her own feelings into his words.

"I do," she said, wanting desperately to find that sliver again when she shouldn't. "Is there a reason you haven't let anyone photograph it?"

Leaning against the closed door, he shrugged.

Jia didn't miss that he did that when he didn't want to answer a particular question.

When he lifted the small bag in his hand, excitement beat a thousand wings in her belly. The unnerving intensity of his gaze as it swept over her, up and down, sent a shiver through her. "Is it a guilt gift or pity gift?" she said, brazening it out.

He cocked a brow, arrogance dripping from the very gesture.

"Guilt because you did something you shouldn't have in the last two days. Pity because you ignored me and feel sorry for me."

He threw his head back and laughed with such abandon that she felt helpless against the sensuality of it. A river of longing ripped through her. She stared at the corded column of his throat, the deep grooves around his mouth, the way his thick, rigidly cut curly hair flopped onto his forehead.

He looked…heart-meltingly gorgeous and he was hers, that foolish voice whispered. When his laughter died down, it still colored his eyes, making them warm and deep.

"Well, which is it?"

"I want no one but you, Jia. I'm committed to this marriage."

"So pity, then," she said, some unknown thing fluttering in her chest at the resolve in his eyes. "Not needed because, honestly, I like your family. I'd even say the appeal of this marriage increased tenfold when I count them all in the package."

He placed his palm on his chest, mock-flinching. "You don't like being ignored."

"I don't like that you control everything in this relationship."

"And yet, I wasn't the one who executed the Three-Week Frost," he quipped with a mock shiver.

"You made up a name for it?" she said, laughing despite her intention to stay strong.

"It was the coldest I've ever been in my life."

And now, she was the one melting...

He pushed off from the door with a deliberate grace that sent her heart thundering in her chest. It was ridiculous to flee because she wasn't scared of him but she took a step back. Eyes now a molten gray, he stalked her across the vast room. When her bare feet touched the cold wood past the rug under the bed, he took a detour to turn the fireplace on. Another thing she'd noted—how he took care of the smallest thing that caused her discomfort, how he was always watching out for her.

Then he was there, caging her against the dark wood

bookshelves, which lined the only wall that wasn't glass. "Jia Galanis…scared of a little gift?"

She squared her shoulders and tilted her chin. "I'm not scared of you or anything you do."

"Then open it."

She took the bag, made a face at him when he laughed at her trembling hands. Her heart decided to take on Olympic speed as she pulled out a dark blue velvet box. She wasn't a huge jewelry person but this was a gift. And she could count on one hand the number of gifts she'd received in her life. Most were before her mom had died when she'd been thirteen.

Slowly, she undid the latch on the box and there, nestled in a soft, velvety cushion was a thin, exquisitely made gold necklace with tiny, detailed leaves and a teardrop sapphire in the midst. It was exactly like the one piece of jewelry she'd coveted all her life but wasn't allowed to have.

Tears filled her eyes and a strange urgency beat at her. The necklace almost got twisted in her trembling fingers before Apollo steadied them. When he lifted it, to put it around her neck, Jia jerked away. "I want to put it back in the box before I…break it."

"Jia—"

"Put it back, Apollo," she said, nearly yelling.

"Okay," he said in a tender voice that threatened to break her apart. Then, as she watched like a vulture circling prey, he nestled it back into the box and closed the clutch.

Jia grabbed the box from him with a proprietorial jerk, opened her little backpack and shoved it inside.

When she straightened, he was at her back, crowding her with his broad, lean frame. His arms came around her waist, his large palms resting on her belly, and without her meaning to, without her permission, her body relaxed into his hold.

She allowed herself the luxury of his tender embrace for a few moments. "Where did you…how…"

"I asked Rina about your interests. She's feeling guilty enough that she stole into your father's locker and photographed it for me. I commissioned the piece. I was waiting to pick it up before I flew here."

She looked up sideways and his gaze caught her as easily as if she was a floundering fish. "Why?"

"I wanted to give you something that you would like. Giving you something that you'd never been allowed to touch was better. I didn't expect to make you cry," he added in a droll voice that didn't quite mask his concern.

Jia hesitated, reluctant to answer the hidden question. But he'd taken a step toward making this more than a cold, business arrangement, hadn't he? This gift and those words in his office…as much as it terrified her, she knew it was time she took a step too. At least, in her own head and heart. "That piece was my mom's. My father gave it to her. She wore it for special occasions only. She's…" her voice broke just at those two words "…she's the closest thing to my heart."

"Tell me about her."

She shook her head.

"Jia…"

"No. Some things are too precious to taint as ammunition between us."

He stiffened around her, his disappointment as visceral as the thundering beat of her heart. "Your wants and your fears and your dreams," he said, repeating the words she'd thrown at him on the flight. "You guard them as if they were a treasure."

But Jia didn't relent. Couldn't. "They are foolish and simple. Of no value to you."

"This was a horrible gift, then," he said with a scoff, releasing her.

Jia turned and fisted her fingers in his shirt, refusing to let him go. "No, it isn't. It's…the best gift anyone's given me. Especially since I know my father will never let me have the original." When he looked doubtful, she hid her face in his chest and breathed him in. He was solid and hard and warm, his heart thundering under her cheek. And now, she wanted to take a thousand more steps toward him. "I don't want to fight with you. Not after you gave me such a…special gift."

CHAPTER SIX

JIA THOUGHT HE'D push her away and the very prospect sent dismay curling through her. He'd called Rina, made the effort to find out what would please her, and then he'd had it commissioned, blasting through all the fake, false armor she'd draped herself in. It was more than anyone had ever done for her.

Maybe she was giving him too much credit for a little gift—she was that deprived of basic affection—but she couldn't help it.

After what felt like an eternity of her clinging to him, his fingers came into her hair. He roughly yanked the clip she'd used to put it up and his fingers circled her nape and then crawled up to tilt her face up to him. "I will have all of your secrets, Jia. Willingly, from you."

It was a promise and something more, but she didn't have the will to challenge him anymore. "You won't take what I more than willingly, wantonly offer," she whispered, and then on a dare, she went on her toes and dug her teeth into his chin. It was a possessive gesture but she didn't care. This was the most freedom and selfishness she'd allowed herself in her life and she wanted to drown in it. *In him*.

A gasp escaped her when he lifted her and deposited her on the desk.

"You're right. I'm a poor husband, *agapi*," he said, tugging at the hem of her blouse until he could pull it off her head. A sudden blast of cold air hit her skin.

Shock and arousal flooded her system, releasing a riot of shivers through her. His big hands cupped her shoulders, palms rough and abrasive, his body heat a sliding rasp against her front and his mouth...his hot, soft mouth was at her lips. Nibbling away the last of her defenses.

Jia's groan seemed to emerge from the depths of her being.

Apollo kissed her roughly, nipping and biting, barely letting her breathe while his hands drifted down from her shoulders to her back. Her strapless bra came loose and her nipples puckered.

Shivers overtook her, of a different kind this time, when he cupped her small breasts and the pads of his thumbs flicked at her nipples. Jia arched her spine, each little flick arrowing down straight to her core. When he pushed her with a hand on her shoulder, she bowed back as if she was made of nothing but elastic desire.

Steely eyes held hers as his tongue laved at one nipple and then the other, before he drew it into his mouth with rhythmic pulls. She jerked at the stinging pressure, slowly lapping over into shivering waves all through her. When she tried to rub her thighs, his thigh blocked the movement. She made a keening sound in her throat, her arousal winding and tugging concentric circles in her lower belly. Eager to do the same to him, she scooted forward on the desk.

She undid the buttons on his shirt roughly, until she could reach warm, taut skin. Holding his gaze, Jia stroked her palms all over him—the hard planes of his chest, the rough down of his chest hair and the ridged muscles of his stomach. With each stroke of her hands, the gray of his eyes deepened.

When her hand drifted to his crotch, he captured it, lifted her hand, and pressed his mouth to her wrist. Both hands arrested, Jia leaned forward and rubbed her bare breasts against his chest.

He groaned. The rough brush of his chest hair against her sensitive nipples was both torment and pleasure. His attention on the slide of their flesh, he released her hand. Jia snuck it down his abdomen until she could cradle his erection. With a rough grunt and a rougher curse, he rocked into her touch before he caught himself.

"You're cheating," he said, his hands caressing her breasts with such thoroughness that she forgot what she meant to do.

"All's fair in lust and war," she said, craning her body into his touch.

Grinning, he paid her back in full. As if he had all the time and energy in the world, he started all over again, trailing kisses down her jaw, between her breasts and down to her belly button and then back up.

He teased and tormented her nipples with his tongue, sucked them into his mouth, grazed them with his teeth until Jia was writhing on the desk, a mindless wanton made of nothing but nerve endings, spiraling and fragmenting. Her climax was a taunting mirage just out of reach. When his hand went to the seam of her shorts, she stilled.

He licked the shell of her ear, his voice a husky taunt. "If you're not ready for more, it's fine. But let me make up for ignoring you for two days."

She looked up, honey pooling in her veins. "They're all out there and can probably hear us. I couldn't face them if—"

"What do you think my sisters do with their partners?"

She blushed. "I…it's the middle of the day and—"

"All you have to say is 'not now,' *pethi mou*," he said with a tenderness that threatened to break her into pieces.

"No. I want this. I came prepared for this."

"That sounds like an exhausted, put-upon wife bracing herself for her marital duties."

She looked up and the humor in his eyes undid the sudden tension that seemed to have overtaken her. "No, I mean I was… I was looking forward to this. I started the pill before we left."

"But?" he said.

Jia thought he'd meant to say something else but changed tack at the last second. "No buts and ifs. I want this, Apollo. You have to give me a little control though."

His smile was wicked as he moved his hands in a *have at me* gesture. But the tension in his body was unmistakable. Suddenly, it didn't feel like she was the only one drowning. And Jia realized that that was the root of the problem.

His gift, horrible as he called it, had shifted the current between them and she felt as if she'd been splayed open for his benefit. Knowing he was as gone for this heat between them…made her feel better. Made her feel equal and wanted, at least on this surface level.

Pressing her mouth to the warm, hard skin of his chest, she busied her hands with the zipper on his trousers. His black boxers went next. Impatience coating her skin with a tremble, she barely pushed them past his hips when his cock popped out.

A fresh set of flutters began between her thighs. Wetness soaked her thong when she fisted his length and gave it a tug. His head thrown back, his chest heaving, Apollo looked like one of those stone sculptures she'd once seen at the MOMA. But warmer and harder and so…more achingly real than any perfect marble bust could be.

Jia increased the speed of her fist, acting purely on instinct and feeding on his reactions. She traced the slit in the head with the pad of her thumb and when it came away wet, she sucked the pad into her mouth.

Apollo let out a filthy curse. "Jia…you drive me wild."

"You taste…" Jia swallowed at the dark cavern of want opening up in his eyes "…like decadence and arrogance and all the filthy desires I never admitted to myself."

Fingers circling her nape, Apollo pulled her in for a near-brutal kiss.

Whatever little freedom he gave her, it seemed, was over after her outrageous little comment. A sudden puff of cold air against her folds told her he'd ripped her thong off. And then his fingers were there, coasting and stroking over her inner lips, draping her wetness all over. As she watched, her breath a shallow whistle in her throat, he brought his fingers, coated with her arousal, up and then painted it over her nipple. It was filthy and freeing and set Jia on a spiral she didn't want to stop climbing.

And then his mouth was on her nipple, sucking and licking, tasting her arousal and groaning, even as his fingers went back to her folds to resume their torture.

Assaulted from all directions by sensations, Jia felt like she was riding a crashing boat on rough waves in the middle of a storm. He was everywhere, his lips and fingers driving her out of her skin, setting a mad pace she couldn't follow, until he speared her with a broad finger and hit a particular spot deep inside her.

Jia jerked against him, her thighs a vise around his hand as her orgasm crashed through her, thrashing her this way and that. A sob escaped her throat, along with her panting breaths.

Apollo didn't relent.

His lips tugged at her painfully sensitive nipple and he kept the base of his palm against her clit as wave after wave settled into tiny jerks and languorous after-shocks. Fingers in his hair, Jia clung to him, clung to the clove and pine scent of his warm skin.

Her flesh cooled, but she wanted more. She wanted all of it. This was all she was allowed of any relationship in a long while and, God, this was all she was allowed to ask and want and own of *him* and she wasn't going to settle for anything less than claiming all he would give.

Even as her spine trembled and her thighs felt like she'd run a marathon, she straightened and caught his mouth in a kiss. While she hadn't allowed anyone to come close after her first and only disastrous relation-ship, she'd allowed herself kissing. And now she used every inch of her experience to tangle her tongue with his, to sweep it through this mouth, to bite and nip at his lower lip until she could feel his tension mounting. His touches became harder, deeper, his caresses wilder and rougher, leaving little divots in her willing flesh.

She ran her mouth down his jaw to his chest, peppering kisses and bites all over his taut skin. It was warm and salty and suddenly, she wanted to taste him somewhere else. She wanted his cock in her mouth, and him a little out of control. No, a lot.

She wanted him to lose it all.

His grip in her hair tightened when she wrapped her fingers around his cock and gave it rough, hard strokes. "Let me down," she whispered, skating her mouth down to his tight abdomen.

"Not today," he answered roughly, and then he was shoving her hand away, pulling her closer and rubbing the head of his erection all over her folds. The sight of him against her was erotic and intimate.

Jia braced herself on his hard muscles, her entire pulse centered there where he played with her.

"You're ready for me, *agapi*?"

"God, yes, Apollo," she repeated and before she could catch her breath, he entered her with one smooth thrust.

Jia jerked and stilled, like a fish caught on a bait. It pinched a bit. No, a lot, bordering on hurt. It had been so long and even then, it hadn't been all the way like this.

Slowly, the delicious soreness faded, breath by breath. Nothing in the world could equal being tethered to Apollo like this. She had a feeling of being utterly full and tight, and when she wiggled her ass on the desk, he shifted inside her and the pinch faded and a spark of pleasure sputtered through her.

Then it went out.

Chasing it, she thrust her hips and tested the fit again, and heard Apollo's rough grunt. And then she didn't have to do anything, because he pulled out almost all the way and stroked back in. Not as deep as the first stroke but teasing and taunting her with it. Trying what would drive them both to the edge.

And slowly, in tune with his thrusts, her own climb began all over again and they found a rhythm. Jia raked her fingernails down his chest, nipped at his flesh, clung to him like a rag doll as his thrusts gained momentum.

The desk banged against the wall and she, apparently, was quite vocal when it came to pleasure and Apollo's grunts were not quiet. When another short but powerful orgasm began to rip her into so many pleasure-filled fragments, she told him how good it felt, how much she liked it when he pinned her with his hips, and then, sweat dripping down his forehead and holding her gaze, Apollo mouthed a filthy word and shuddered when his own climax followed.

It was very late that night when, finally, Apollo was free to do as he pleased.

As Jia had predicted, they had been interrupted that afternoon, minutes after they had *finished* with loud bangs on the door to their suite. They hadn't even separated yet.

In his urgency to get Jia alone, he hadn't let his mother or his sisters tell him that they had invited around hundred guests to celebrate his and Jia's sudden union. A wedding reception, Mama had said with a glint in her eye, so that their extended family, long-standing friends and his grandparents could meet her wonderful, new daughter-in-law and bless this very real marriage.

He had been in such a hurry that he hadn't even noticed the staff putting up marquees and tables outside. The reason why they had all been so busy cooking, even with outside catering ordered.

While Apollo had fixed his clothes and responded to Chiara banging on their door with a catlike grin, Jia had disappeared into the bathroom and locked herself in. He hadn't seen her again until the evening when she descended the stairs behind a beaming Chiara.

Apparently, his wife had made a deal with Mama— in exchange for donning a dress and deserting her usual lacy tops and short shorts tonight, Mama would teach Jia how to cook.

To say he was stunned, by her negotiations with his mother *and* her look, would be an understatement. It was becoming clear that not only had she won them over in just a few days but his mother and sisters had already gained her trust. As if she was blossoming in a different way under their honest and yet tender care.

Still, as only Jia could, she retained her own style, and that little fact pleased him way out of proportion. For all the rigid requirements he'd held on to in his head for a wife for years, he wanted to change only one thing about the one he had now.

In a shimmery copper satin dress with flimsy straps and simple bodice that rippled like dark water when she came down the steps, Jia had looked soft and pretty as if she'd been tamed for one evening. And he liked that. Liked knowing that her true wildness was all his.

Only his.

Against the shimmery satin of her gown, her skin glowed and her tattoos stood out. The one at her collarbone, a bird in midflight, looked like it was fluttering its wings with how fast her pulse beat at her neck. Her hair pulled back and put up, called attention to the fine bones of her face, drawing out the fragility she hid beneath her tough attitude. Was that what her sisters and mother had already seen?

And had he, the arrogant fool, once thought her anything less than stunningly beautiful?

When she was almost to the bottom of the stairs, he noted the necklace nestled at her throat. The leaves and the pendant shone brilliantly against her skin, almost blending into the tattoo on the other side.

Catching his gaze on her neck, she smiled. A tremulous, hopeful one that he'd never before seen on her lips. He had never felt such feral satisfaction as he did at that moment, at seeing her sweet joy, knowing that his gift pleased her. Not his first million, not when he'd won multiple awards, not even when his goal of nearly two decades had finally been within reach.

The boisterous arrival of his extended family had saved him from examining the feeling too closely.

And now, as he walked up the stairs to his suite, he wondered at how that feeling still persisted, at how smoothly and irrevocably Jia seemed to fit into every aspect of his life.

He found her in the large claw-foot bathtub, in relative darkness except for a few beams of moonlight and a couple of flickering candles. The ceiling was all glass, which meant one could sit in the bathtub and view the stars. It was one of his favorite features in the house.

Candlelight and moonlight seemed to battle to bathe her silky skin in an ethereal glow.

As he closed the door behind him and leaned against it, her eyes opened. Shadows danced there and he wondered if the evening had exhausted her. His family could be a lot.

No, withdrawn, he amended, on second thought.

Why, he thought with a fierce protectiveness he had never known before. If someone had said unkind words to her because of who she was, they would face his wrath.

He had always wanted to provide for and protect his family, especially after Papa's death, but this was different. This feeling had its claws deep in his bones. Was it simply his new determination that he would own everything about her?

"Hey," she said, clutching her trembling lower lip between her teeth.

Pushing off from the door, he started unbuttoning his shirt. "Can I join you? Or would you like to play the tired-tonight-honey wife card?" he added, desperate to make her laugh.

She smiled and it just touched her eyes, pushing back the earlier shadows. "I thought that was when you wanted to avoid sex."

A lick of fire came awake in his veins as her hazy gaze swept over his bare chest and lingered over his fingers at the band of his trousers. He unzipped and kicked off those and his boxers. Her mouth fell into an O, on the wave of a soft, helpless gasp.

As if tuned into that husky pitch of her, his cock grew to stiff attention.

"So you're not averse to it," he said, grinning. Pleasure was a river dragging him along in its undercurrent and he didn't want to let up, not even for a breath.

"Not when you give it so good."

He laughed, desire and a strange kind of joy fizzing through his veins.

"Plus, I have been given loads of advice, from your grandmother to your aunts as to how to manage you."

"That sounds ominous," he said, sliding into the tub.

It took a moment for her legs to settle between his, her feet ending up on his thighs. He grabbed one and kneaded the high arch.

She let out a hiss of pleasure, head thrown back. Water droplets clung to her long neck, inviting his mouth to lick up. "Christ, Apollo, is there anything you aren't good at?"

She sounded so put-upon that he grinned. "Was anyone unkind to you? My aunts and cousins can be blunt and voluble."

"No, if anything, they were all extra kind and open. Like I said, giving me all kinds of tidbits as to how to manage you." She punctuated that by drawing on his chest with her foot. "Apparently, I have saved you from a horrible, loveless existence."

When he tracked his fingers up her ankle, she pulled back with a giggle.

"Then why the shadows in those beautiful eyes, *matia mou*?"

"What?" she said, startled enough that she slid a little lower in the tub.

Apollo used the chance to pull her to him. A little stiff, she came into his arms reluctantly as if she didn't dare trust him, even after the afternoon they'd shared. It annoyed him that she always held something of herself back. It was the very trust he wanted, was beginning to crave even in waking moments.

He would figure her out, he promised himself.

He settled her legs around his hips and she relaxed, her core pressed right over his shaft, and they groaned. He stole a soft kiss, liking her like this, all wet and soft and malleable. But he wasn't about to let himself get distracted.

"If no one was rude to you, why the sadness?"

She shrugged and hid her face in his neck. Her armor was showing holes, he realized, with that weird pride slash satisfaction.

"Jia?"

"I just…" Tears swam in her eyes when she looked up. She wiped them with the back of her hands and scoffed, the sound full of self-deprecation.

"Tell me, *parakalo*." Even that word, which he barely said to anyone, came easy with her.

A shuddering wet exhale shook her slender shoulders. "Your family is…like my dream family. They fight and argue and yell at each other, but beneath it all, there's this thread of acceptance and love."

She whispered the last as if the word might reach out and bite her. Then she cut her gaze away and he knew it was because she didn't want him to see it. "I couldn't help…wishing mine was remotely like that."

"My family is yours, Jia."

Her gaze was stricken when it met his, as if the very idea was impossible.

"You can let the old one go and embrace this one. Especially since they all adore you already."

"Spoken like a ruthless billionaire," she retorted but there was no bite to it.

When he grabbed her hips and rubbed her folds against his erection, she groaned. The hiss of pain beneath that sound poked a hole through his haze of lust.

"You're sore," he said, arresting her hips when she'd have repeated his actions.

"It's been a while," she murmured, her tongue lapping at his shoulder like a cat.

"How long a while?" he said, her mouth playing havoc with his control.

She looked up, and frowned. "Am I allowed to ask the same question?"

"About…three years. Don't even remember her name," he replied. "I've been busy—"

"With taking over my father's company," she said, nodding. Then she scrunched her brow. "Seven years and once, technically but not quite."

She never said "our company," he noted with a spark of anger on her behalf. "So I didn't pull you away from a young, ardent boyfriend?"

She rubbed her cheek against his and moaned when his stubble scraped. "It's a little late for that question."

He gripped her chin in his fingers, stopping her exploration. Willing her to meet his gaze. "Not an answer."

"Why all these questions now?"

"I'm curious."

"I've only ever had one boyfriend if you could call him that. I was eighteen, and we met in secret because my father wouldn't have approved. He was a musician."

"Ahh…the tattoos," Apollo said, his voice dry. That this old, far-gone lover had left such a mark on her made him intensely jealous.

Jia grinned and scraped her teeth against his chin, before peppering soft, warm kisses against his jawline as if she was mapping the contours of his face to memory. "Jax did encourage me to get that first tattoo. But the rest are all mine. A kind of rebellion, if you really want to know. My father hates them."

And yet, she sought his approval in other ways. Didn't she see that? "So what happened?"

"It never took off to last." Then she pulled back and searched his eyes. "You really want to know?"

"Yes," he said, grabbing her by the tight indent of her waist. "The sooner you tell me, the sooner I will give you what you want."

"That's sexual blackmail," she said, grinning. Then she sobered. "Jax…was a decade older than me. He wanted to travel the world. Travel and music were his passions and he wanted me to leave with him."

"That's quite an ultimatum to issue to an eighteen-year-old," Apollo said, immensely glad she hadn't left with him. But it also meant that her martyr-like need to save her family had not only been present then too, but it had alienated a man who might have cared for her.

Apollo didn't understand it; she was so smart, worldly and tough in every aspect of life. But with her leeching family, it was like she willingly put on blinders.

"He…changed his plans for me. Even got a job to show me that he could do boring nine-to-five. He waited for me to be ready for a lot of things. But when we actually started seeing each other regularly, all we did was fight. He thought I should move out, stop coddling Rina, stop…" A sigh rattled through her. "He thought my family was a shackle and that he was nothing but entertainment on the side for me. That last time it blew up, we were in the middle of it, literally. He stopped, dressed and left. Never looked back."

"Do you regret it?" Apollo asked. "Not leaving with him?"

This time, Jia hid her face in his throat again. "It's pointless to look back. And he should have known better than to ask me to choose him over them."

"Is that a warning, Jia?"

"You're a clever man, Apollo Galanis. You figure it out."

It provoked him to no end. Before, Apollo didn't want them to have her loyalty, because he wanted to be the victor in this little game. Because he wanted everything she had to give for himself.

But now he wanted her to see for herself how blind and undeserving her devotion was. How she had limited herself all these years, for them. That it was that very trait that had brought her to him…threw him into confusion.

He lifted her gently and slid his fingers to her center. *Dios mio*, she was wet and ready for him. "Should I remind you that you have thrown your lot in with me?" he said, finding her clit and flicking at the bundle.

She jerked and arched against him, the plump points of her nipples sliding deliciously against his chest.

"Do you need a reminder that your stock in the company in three years, your talent, your work, *you* are all mine?" he said, pumping one and then two fingers inside her.

Mouth lax, eyelashes fluttering, she threw her head back and let out a moan. His cock became painfully hard as her muscles squeezed tight around his fingers deep inside her.

"Or maybe you want to argue a little more about this and I should stop?"

She stilled and then in a violet fury of movement that splashed the water around them, cupped his cheek and took his mouth in a filthy, possessive kiss that said everything he had without using words. "All I want," she said, nibbling at his lips, "for myself is this—" something fierce and feral glowed in her eyes "—and if you deny me this, Apollo, if you take this away from me…"

"I won't," he vowed, cherishing how freely and easily she gave of herself here. How from the first moment, she had honestly and bravely faced this attraction. It was the most arousing thing about her—that fierce attitude and that honest, scorching desire for him. For now, it was enough. That she wanted this with that fiery need was enough. The rest he would have soon.

"Come for me, Tornado," he said, pinching her clit between his fingers.

She wrapped her fingers around his cock and squeezed, licking the shell of his ear.

"For tonight," she said, nipping at his earlobe, "can

we come like this? Together? Tomorrow, I'll be less sore—"

"This is all I've been thinking of all day, *agapi*. You falling apart for me. You not hiding anything from me."

And then they were kissing again, and their hands were everywhere, their bodies weaving together and retreating in the water, and Apollo thought he'd never been more eager and desperate, never tasted such bliss before.

Already familiar with his body and his want, she stroked him harder and faster. He gritted his teeth, fighting the oncoming wave. He wanted, needed, to push her over first.

She was writhing and twisting around his fingers, but her eyes, so wide and clear and penetrating, never left his. As if that was the thing that would send her to the edge she was seeking.

"This is going to get messy," she said, arching into his touch, and the stubborn thing that she was, she never let her own strokes falter.

Apollo grinned and laved at her lower lip. "I had a feeling about that when I found you snoring in my armchair."

She laughed then, and that's how they came together and came apart and Apollo wondered at how addictive this woman could become.

If she hadn't already.

CHAPTER SEVEN

SHE LOOKED LIKE a wraith, sweaty and feverish, amidst a cloud of navy-blue bedsheets. Stilling at the entrance to their bedroom, Apollo tried to work through the turmoil that had gripped him ever since she'd fallen sick.

In a mere two weeks since she'd fainted at work midday, Jia had already lost weight.

It didn't matter that the team of doctors he'd summoned had reassured him that it was a very bad case of chest infection. Or that his mother and sisters took turns tending to her and feeding her when Apollo had to leave her side. Which, to be honest, hadn't been much.

He wasn't the best person to nurse someone in such fragile health but the thought of deserting her when she was weak and vulnerable didn't even merit consideration. At least, Mama had convinced him to let the nurse he'd hired check on Jia every few hours, in case he missed any turn for the worse.

For the first time in his adult life, he was behind on deadlines for two different projects, his two assistants were constantly reminding him about the things he was pushing back, and one billionaire client, and an old friend, had jokingly threatened to cancel when Apollo had told him that he had no bandwidth to look at his design modifications. Apollo's reaction to that had been telling on many levels.

It felt like a personal affront to Apollo that she would fall this sick under his care. He and his entire family were all healthy as oxen so where had Jia caught this illness? Had he driven her too hard by having her work long hours with his team so soon after taking her away from her family? Had he demanded too much of her at work and in bed? Had she been unhappy? Shouldn't he have seen the signs that she was unwell long before she'd fainted at work?

When he sat by her, he felt restless, useless…and worse, helpless. Which he'd never been good at abiding. Still, a strange, horrible fear that she would slip away if he left had kept him glued to her side, night and day.

He didn't require a degree in psychology to understand that it reminded him of the time that Papa had started taking to bed at all hours of the day.

He had been crushed by Jay's deceit, devastated by having to sell most of their assets to pay off overdue bank loans. Had hated the fact that they'd all had to move back in with their grandparents. Nothing they'd done had stirred him from the fugue.

Mama had urged Apollo to concentrate on his own studies, that whatever Papa was going through was a temporary thing. The small malaise had lasted for months. Until one day, Apollo had found him lying still on his bed, his face pale and all his vitality gone, overdosed on painkillers.

And he, Apollo, had done nothing to help him. Which had set him on a path he hadn't budged from in two decades.

"Why do you look so angry?" The whisper-thin question from the bed jerked Apollo into the present.

Sweaty hair sticking to her forehead, Jia looked small and pale, as if the infection was doing its best to dim her. Except her eyes, which finally had that sparkle back. She raised her arm, smelled herself and then fell back against the sheets with a sigh. "You can come closer. I don't stink."

Despite the volatile mix of emotions churning through his gut, his mouth twitched. This was the spirit he had missed in two weeks, the Jia he was coming to see as the prize for all his struggle. The only prize worth winning and having and keeping.

Only a month and a half of marriage, and she had embedded herself under his skin, and he wasn't even sure if he wanted to pull her out. He'd blindly and arrogantly stumbled onto the best thing in his life and for a man who reached his goals on his own merit and strategy, it was unsettling as hell. Because what was the guarantee that it wouldn't be snatched away from him? Especially, since he'd done nothing to deserve her.

"Who do I have to thank for the latest sponge bath? I smell like my favorite red roses."

Without answering her, he pressed the back of his hand to her forehead. She was damp and sticky. "I think your fever's finally broken." His hand shook as he reached for the water glass, so great was his relief. In its wake, exhaustion hit him like a full body assault. Grabbing a straw, he dunked it into the water and pulled her up a little so she could drink it.

Her eyes stayed on his face as she sipped. *Dios mio*, how he had missed that playful, challenging, sometimes downright angry gaze on his skin…and sometimes so addictively open in its wanting.

Unable to help himself, he tucked a thick lock of damp strands behind her ear. He wiped a drop of water from the corner of her mouth, feeling his heart finally settle into a normal pace.

"You didn't answer my question."

"Which one?" he said, settling near her legs.

With a rough exhale, she pushed off the sheets, and looked down. The cotton top stuck to her skin and her shorts had ridden up all the way. Sitting up, she adjusted her clothes. "Who gave me the last sponge bath?"

He wrapped his fingers around her ankle, his gaze caught on a small red heart tattoo there. "How did I miss this one?" he muttered to himself.

"You're way too focused on my breasts. And another spot further south."

When he looked up, she was grinning. It sparked a chain reaction in his chest, some feelings known and acceptable, and some…downright debilitating.

"You owe me two answers," she said, her gaze sweeping over his face intently.

"I was the one who gave you all the sponge baths. You were docile as a lamb, for the most part. Though I can tell you I prefer you as you usually are."

"Mistrustful and argumentative?" she said with a self-deprecating laugh.

"Rearing to take me on," he added, running his thumb over the tattoo.

"Wait." Color flushed her sharp cheeks and it was a welcome sight. "You were present…when I couldn't walk to the bathroom, and the other day when I threw up…"

"All me."

She buried her face in her hands, groaning. Then she lowered her fingers. "And when I had that really bad dream and woke up thrashing?"

"I got into bed with you." And he had stayed with her for the rest of the night.

"You were here the entire time? The whole time," she said, her chest rising and falling as if she'd reached some impossible conclusion.

He felt insulted that she found it shocking he would look after her. What did she think he meant by *commitment*? And what did it mean that he couldn't make himself leave her side?

"Your fever was too high and you were delirious. The doctor said someone should be with you every minute. Plus, you've got your fingers stuck in half the firm's projects, so there wasn't really a point in me harassing the rest of the team for progress."

Pushing her hair away from her face, she sighed. "So you're angry that everything's backed up at work? That was quite the ferocious expression you had earlier."

It was the perfect out for Apollo to take. But then, he'd never harbored self-delusion. "I was frustrated. And I'm not the greatest at sitting patiently doing nothing."

"That's quite shocking to know," she said, sarcasm dripping from each word. "Why frustrated though?"

"No one can tell me, apparently, why you got so sick."

Her mouth slackened. And then she smiled. And

Apollo felt as if his entire world had turned upside down. "Apollo, there can be a hundred reasons why I got sick. And—"

"Yes, but the rest of us are well. Only you got sick. I don't like it. Nor was the speed at which you've been recovering to my liking."

"Oh, I'm sorry that I'm not recovering fast enough to please Your Grumpy Highness." And then, because she was Jia, she tossed a throw pillow at him. It hit him in the chest and dropped to the floor.

"Now I know you're truly on the mend," he said, getting up and walking toward the door. She'd need more than the broth she'd been surviving on to recover. Suddenly, as if a switch had been flipped, his entire workload slammed into his brain, claiming his attention.

"Wait, Apollo."

He turned to find her combing her fingers through her hair and pulling it into a knot. The action pushed her breasts upward, her nipples poking through the silk top. Her stomach looked even leaner than before. The desire to hold her gripped him like a vise but it wasn't just the base lust to claim, own and find that delicious edge. It was more.

Whatever she saw in his gaze, a flush climbed up her chest and neck. Like a newborn calf testing its legs, she got off the bed gingerly.

Apollo went to her just as she stumbled and she fell against him with a huff. And then her hands went around his waist, and she clung to him. "Thank you for taking care of me. Even if I cost you thousands."

"Millions, Tornado," he said, his voice strange to his own ears.

She dragged her teeth against his chest roughly, teasing and provoking him. And he realized a great big thing that he'd overlooked all this time. Willingly enough, she'd given him everything she'd had ever since walking into his penthouse.

Except now, he wanted the thing she thought she didn't have.

He held her loosely, sudden itching to get away from her. From himself in this state. But she was soft and warm and sweaty in his arms and he had missed her lithe body, her tart comments and how hard she made it to gain an inch of her trust but when she did…

"I take my vows seriously, Jia," he said, pressed a kiss to the top of her head and then walked out.

Jia stood under the double-jet shower after Apollo left and tried to make sense out of her knotted thoughts. Before they turned into feelings and wishes and hopes and foolish dreams.

But she was afraid that she was already too late.

The fact that Apollo hadn't left her to herself, the energy and hours he'd put into looking after her…she didn't know what to make of it.

He was a billionaire…he could have given her care over to any number of staff. Even his frustration that she wasn't getting better fast enough…had cloaked something far deeper. She was sure of that, even as she warned herself not to make it into a big deal.

Her mind spun in circles as she stepped out of the shower and looked at herself in the mirror. She'd lost weight just in two weeks and looked even more angular than usual. But her eyes, even sunken, held a glow, as if a small flicker of joy had been lit up within. Work life where she was noticed and respected, a family that offered unconditional acceptance and care, and a man who respected her and challenged her and then turned her inside out with his demands at night...

Wiping the steam from the mirror, Jia let herself speak and see the truth. For all that she'd been sick, she was happy within. A kernel of hope had taken root in her heart and it was already changing her. And she knew she could get addicted to the illusion of this happiness with Apollo. That if she wasn't careful, she'd fall into the trap of wanting more and more.

She needed to stay strong, like she had during her mother's illness even as she had realized finally why she fit differently into her own family. All her life, Mama had loved her, but the cost had been being good, being quiet, being the best daughter and sister Jia could be because Mama hadn't wanted her father to find fault with Jia. She had let it dictate every action and numbed the whispers of her heart.

Her arms shook as she pulled on sweatpants and she tried the warning in her head again. Like everyone else in her life, Apollo's approval and affection for her came with a cost. And yet, neither her heart nor her body believed it one bit.

A few days later, Apollo was finishing breakfast when Jia came down the stairs, her phone pressed to her cheek. It was cowardly but once he had known that she was on the mend, he'd fled to Athens and stayed at his penthouse. He'd dropped by this morning with the convenient lie that he needed her to look over some designs.

Now, her eyes blazed with anger when they met his, and her throat moved on a swallow.

Irritation flared through Apollo and it took all the willpower he possessed to not grab the phone from Jia and smash it into so many bits. He had no doubt who the caller was for he had dealt with the matter only last night. His wife's spineless sister, Rina.

The very idea that he had almost married her made bile rise through him. If not for Jia's fierce loyalty and courage, his life, right now, would have been very different. The realization grated on him.

"You...insensitive, lying bastard!" Jia said, running down the last two steps, fury dancing on her face.

Apollo shot to his feet and caught her as she tripped on a video game console and almost took to the floor. *Christos*, she felt breakable in his hands, all crackling fury and no substance beneath. Around him, his mother and sisters came to attention.

"Jia—"

"You promised you'd leave it alone, Apollo," she was yelling now, pushing at his chest with her fists. "It's the wish you granted me. But even that's not sacred to you. To think I was actually beginning to believe you and trust you—"

"Stop it, Jia." Apollo grabbed her hands before she could beat at his chest again. Tears filled her eyes. Alarm rang through him, making his words sharp. "You're going to make yourself sick. You've barely recovered and—"

A bitter laugh escaped her mouth as she roughly

wiped her cheeks with the back of her hand. "Oh, please, don't pretend as if you care."

"Jia, listen to me—"

"Apollo! What did you do?" his mother said, joining in.

Apollo gritted his teeth and prayed for patience he didn't have. The last person he wanted to discuss Jia's family with was his mother. She'd never understood his drive for reparation, *his madness for revenge* as she called it. He definitely didn't want her to know the particulars of his and Jia's marriage or all the ways in which her family used her.

It might have started as a business deal but their relationship had already morphed into something else, which he'd been struggling to make peace with. Damned if he was going to let his family see their marriage differently, see him differently, just when he was beginning to see the error of his ways.

"This is between Jia and me," he said, hoping they would take the hint.

When none of them budged, he met his mother's gaze. She looked miserable, as if Jia's pain was her own. All his sisters, even Camilla and his rowdy nephews, glared at him, ready to take him on if Jia only gave them the word. "Please," he said, addressing Mama, "trust me."

And this too felt like a rite of fire because he could see Mama struggle. Had he fallen so far in her estimation that she assumed he would hurt his wife on purpose?

Finally, she nodded and herded the rest of them out of the living room. He wrapped his arms around Jia and thanked the saints he didn't believe in that she didn't push him away.

"You promised you'd leave it alone," she repeated, subdued and stiff. "Instead, you had cops haul Vik away. You're ruining my family and I've lost the last chance with my father to..." She sighed.

So that's what had sent her into such a...temper? Had her father somehow pinned Apollo's actions on Jia? How did he think she would control a powerful man like him?

His chest felt tight, a painful kind of powerlessness clutching him in its hold. With every fiber of his being, he wanted to get rid of this hold her father seemed to have on her but he couldn't. He hadn't been able to stop the damage done to his father and it felt like he was in the same boat again.

This time, the obstacle was an invisible, intangible thing and if he pushed the matter, he would hurt the only innocent in all this.

"Your blasted brother nearly took your eye out. You shouldn't be protecting him."

"He just lost his temper," Jia said, pulling back. "He was...drunk and upset that I married you without telling them. We got into an argument and he was stumbling and pushed me. I fell against the edge of a table. That's the truth."

"He's a twenty-eight-year-old man," Apollo bit out. Just the image of her brother pushing her was enough to send him into a rage. "He should have better control of his temper."

"Maybe yes, but he doesn't deserve to go to jail for it and—"

"Did Rina tell you he pushed her too last week?"

"What?" Jia said, blinking hard. "She was crying and my father was yelling in the background—"

"He pushed her. They had to bring her to the hospital—"

"Is she hurt?"

"No, she insisted on going because apparently she's pregnant and wanted to make sure everything was okay."

"She told you all this?"

"Last night, between sobs," he said, dryly.

"She's…pregnant?"

"Yes. Which is why she shamelessly pushed you toward me. What little courage she might have, she used it up telling me she'd have just married me anyway *if* you hadn't interfered, and it felt awful that she'd let you take her place and, oh, please would I help her because your father was going to throw her out, and she found out from you that I wasn't the horrible monster she thought I was."

Jia rubbed her hands over her face, a ghastly calm taking place of the frenzy from before. "Vik…he adores her. He shouldn't—"

"Why is it okay for him to push you around but not your older sister who's supposed to look after you?"

"That's ridiculous," Jia replied and turned away, but not before he missed her flinch. All her fury was spent and he could see her withdrawing into herself, as clearly as if she was setting up brick walls around her.

"No, Jia," he said, grabbing her around the waist until she looked at him. "You started this, *agapi*, and I demand that you finish it. You and I both know Vik needs to learn a lesson, before he does something worse than getting drunk and pushing his sisters around. If your father had any kind of sense, he would let him rot in the cell and fear the consequences."

"Fine. I agree."

"Then please, kindly answer my question," he said, unable to keep his temper out of his tone.

"It's a ridiculous assumption."

"Jia—"

"How does it matter who looks after whom? You're the youngest but you take care of all of them, don't you?"

"My sisters don't take advantage of me. Mama hates everything I have done for the last decade but she would never sell me out to some stranger who might or might not—"

"My mom asked me to look after them, okay?" Jia burst out, her eyes flashing. "To keep them together. All my life, she begged me to be good and quiet and capable and strong...stronger than any of them. She said it was her fault that my father had become so hardened and soulless and she couldn't desert him and I shouldn't either."

"What weakness?"

Something like pure anguish danced in her eyes. It stole the breath from his lungs.

"She...she had an affair and I was the result. When she found out she was pregnant with me, she confessed everything. My father...loved her enough that he agreed to raise me as his own."

"So Rina would've followed in her footsteps if you hadn't saved her?"

She glared at him but didn't argue. Apollo wondered if that was progress. "I didn't…know until I was thirteen, when Mom fell sick. I finally understood why he was so…strict and unbending, especially with me. I promised her that I would be strong, that I would take on her responsibilities in her absence."

Suddenly, Apollo had a blueprint to every little thing that had thrown him about her from day one. The emerging picture only served to anger him. "So you'll forgive them anything? Forgive your father because he raised you as his own, even though, clearly, he expects you to pay for it?"

"He's never asked me for anything." She pushed her fingers through her hair, her gaze far off for a moment. "I… I did it willingly. And not everything is black-and-white, Apollo. Would you forgive me if I cheated on you?"

The very idea made him want to howl like a deranged person. "I'm not answering that because I know you won't." He had no idea where his faith came from. But it was there, unwavering and real, as solid as the house they were standing in. Stronger than any conviction he'd ever had before.

"The fact is he loved her enough to raise me as his. He gave me a home, an education, a family."

"But he continues to punish you for it."

"He's never said one unkind word to me my entire life."

"He pawned off your work as your brother's—"

"Because Vik was about to lose his job. We agreed that it would be a one-time thing. Even the black eye," she said softly. "He didn't know that Vik pushed me. I never told him that Vik loses his temper when he gets drunk. You can't blame him for something he's not aware of."

"Ahh…you have such little expectations of the people around you, *matia mou*. By that measure, our marriage should hopefully last a hundred years."

"At least he met my expectations, little as they were," she said, tilting her chin. "Unlike you."

Her silken thrust found a raw spot, one he wasn't aware existed. To be compared to that man with no morals and to come away wanting…felt like the worst kind of defeat.

But then, he was discovering a lot of things hadn't existed for him before this woman. And yes, some were to be expected because he had never been married before. But he was also aware of doubts where there was only certainty before and of a hundred little changes in his thoughts, in his actions.

He raised a brow, refusing to let her see his dilemma. Needing for her to come to him, to ask him for what she wanted. She unbalanced him so easily, that he was always looking for leverage in their relationship. He hated losing in the slightest, and the stakes were only increasing.

"You gave me three wishes. You broke the third one."

"What would you have of me, *pethi mou*?"

A flicker of warmth shone in her eyes before she rubbed her eyes with her fingers. The action reminded him of how painfully young she was. "Will you help Rina out please? For me?"

He sighed, even as he felt a contracting tightness in his chest. As if his heart was too big or his body too small to contain these…feelings she evoked. He couldn't explain it or banish it. Because he had tried to, when she lay in bed, all of her fierce vitality doused.

"I have," he said, loathe to make her beg when it came to her damned family. "Her lover has a job with the New York branch."

"Already?"

"You keep forgetting that I know you now, Jia. Maybe better than anyone else."

Something soft and vulnerable sparked in her eyes before she chased it away.

"Your third condition is for you to use," he said, knowing he was playing a very dangerous game. But then, he was a man who had taken big risks for the things he wanted. It was how he'd made a name for himself and millions for his family, how he'd risen to the top and become powerful enough to take on the man who had ruined his father. And this…this game he was playing with his wife and her as the prize, it was the biggest battle of his life. "*For you, Jia*. Not for anyone else."

"Good to know," she said, digging her teeth into her lower lip. She scooted closer, her fingers fisting his shirt in a possessive gesture that made his blood pound. "Although, anything I want from you for myself, I have a feeling you'll give it freely."

"Such faith," he said, gathering her to him. She was even more slender than before and yet, somehow, if he closed his eyes, he knew he would only see her gap-toothed smile, and her vibrant attitude and the soft vulnerability she rarely showed. But he was getting little slivers of it now. "You have to do something for me in return."

"What?"

"Get back to bed."

"I've just spent two and a half weeks there. And this recovery period is worse. I'm lonely—" faint color dusted her cheeks "—and I have all this sudden energy."

She looked so sparkly and cheerful that Apollo didn't have the heart to point out that it was because he had agreed to help her lying, cheating coward of a sister. If she let them, her family would suck the marrow out of her. "I'll ask Christina to join you and keep you company."

"No."

"Camilla, then."

"God, no. She'll make me drink that awful bone broth again."

"You need it."

"I know what I need."

"What?"

"You, in bed, with me." When he only watched her without replying, she pouted. "I mean, I adore your family, yes, but I want you."

His mouth twitched, despite his resolve not to give in. But he was angry and disgruntled enough with her, disturbed enough by her revelation about her mother and her father that he wanted to be persuaded. Seduced. Wanted. He'd never before in his goddamned life wanted to be wanted.

"Please, Apollo. You can bring me up to speed on that eco-resort in the Philippines."

"If I get in bed with you, we will not be discussing

architecture. I doubt we will be talking at all and you're too weak for that kind of activity."

"Of course I'm not weak. Especially if I let you do all the work," she said, wriggling her feathery brows. "I know you long for a wife who will willingly put up with whatever you do to her."

"That sounds like *your* fantasy, *pethi mou*. Not mine."

"What do you think I'm trying to tell you without actually saying it?"

"Maybe I won't understand until you beg me."

"You're mean."

"You're the one who called me names in front of my family. Now even they believe I'm a villain."

He didn't add that his mother already thought so. It hurt him, this unspoken rift between him and his mother, but he had no idea how to fix it. Until recently, he hadn't even wanted to. Though now, he saw that his restlessness of the past few years stemmed also from this disconnection between him and them.

Mama didn't understand his point of view and he definitely didn't understand hers. Neither did he forget that, in Mama's eyes, marrying Jia without knowing his nefarious intentions, which he was now glad Jia hid from her, was the only right thing he had done in his adult life.

"I'm sorry for that," Jia said, flushing. Rocking back and forth on the balls of her feet. "I...overreacted. I'll explain it to them. I'll tell them the antibiotics made my brain wonky. I'll tell them you're the best husband I could've ever asked for, that you keep me well stocked in orgasms. At least, until two weeks ago."

His destruction, he'd never thought, could come in the form of a woman. Or that he would willingly walk toward it. "Not enough," he said, bracing himself against her warmth as she pressed a kiss on his chest.

She stomped her foot and blew impatiently at a lock of hair that dared to caress her cheek. "I miss you, Apollo. Won't you please keep me company?"

He tucked his hands into his pockets, to stop himself from reaching for her. "Not nearly enough."

She exhaled roughly. "I miss…talking with you about work and our vision for the future and I… I miss your kisses and how you let me use you as a squishy when I'm deep in sleep and I'm horny for you and only you. I kept having these feverish dreams where I'm caught under you and I'm not even trying to get away as you have your way with me and those weird dreams were the only thing that made it worth staying in bed. So, my dear husband, won't you please pin me under you and have your wicked way with me?"

Apollo had no idea if she'd said anything past that or if he'd replied at all, because all he could hear was the thundering whoosh of his desire in his ears and all he could feel was the weight of her slender body in his arms as he carried her up to their bedroom.

CHAPTER EIGHT

IT WAS LONG past midnight and Jia thought her bones might crumble to dust if she so much as moved her little finger. But even sated to the point of exhaustion, she couldn't fall asleep.

Apollo had been extra ruthless and demanding and insatiable since she'd slowly been gaining her strength back. There had been a near-frenzy to how he had made love to her, as if he had to make up for the time they had lost when she had been ill. As if he had worried about losing her.

Which was ridiculous because it had been an infection. Even that looked like a blessing given it had shifted something between them. Within her.

Admitting to the promise Mom had asked of her had provided a strange relief and rearrangement of facts in her head. After so many years, she thought of those days when Mom had been sick and everyone had been devastated and Jia had been at the center of the storm. She wondered how confused and scared her mom must have been to extract such a promise from a thirteen-year-old.

Had she ever truly loved Jia? Or had she only seen

her as one mistake that she had to make up for, for the rest of her life?

It had taken Apollo's relentless probing to make her question the patterns that had been set a decade ago.

Now this new experience of intimacy with him. A whole week of glutting on him, and not just sex either. He had taught her how to play chess in bed and she had taught him how to binge-watch reality shows—though the workaholic that he was didn't have a natural talent for it. They worked briefly on some design modifications because Apollo had shockingly enough taken the week off, talked about the charity projects he had put aside a decade ago because he hadn't the resources to see them through.

He demanded so much from her that she could imagine living in a different galaxy where *she* was the sun and he some orbiting planet. No one had ever wanted to know how she'd gotten every scar on her body, the meaning of her tattoos, or what her deepest dreams were and why she kept them locked tight.

One evening, he'd flown them to visit a large, and by that she meant *vast*, plot of land that he had bought two days prior.

He was building a new house there and would like her input for its design, he'd murmured when Jia had prodded him through sleep-heavy lids. Irritatingly enough, she had tired far too soon on their outing and had been almost drifting to sleep. Now she had a feeling he'd whispered the truth because he had thought her out of it.

A house for their family.

It was a commitment she'd never expected from this relationship, never dreamed of from this marriage when she'd broken into his penthouse in New York.

The prospect of that dream, of letting herself see that far into the future, made her heart dance far too fast in her chest, coated her skin with slick sweat.

God, despite her best intentions to safeguard her heart, she wanted it all. To belong to him, to build a new life with him, to root herself to him and the house he wanted to build for them…meant hoping and wishing and praying that he would always want her with the same intensity. That he would always see the value in having her in his life. That someday, he wouldn't see a mistake when he looked at her, like her Mom always had.

And that kind of faith in him and herself… Jia didn't know how to build it, much less hold on to it. She'd never been shown how.

When her rational mind showed her the prospect of leaving him behind one day, as if to protect her, her heart raced. Her limbs shook. She pushed herself up on her elbow, to better drink in his haughty, rough-hewn features.

His dark hair was graying at the temples and his mouth, relaxed in his sleep, was lush and wide. The column of his throat, the defined musculature of his chest and abdomen, everything about him screamed hardness. And yet, he could be so incredibly tender with her.

In sleep, he looked like the man he'd buried deep under his motives and ambition, the man who hadn't deserted her for a minute when she'd been sick. The man who would do anything for his family but somehow found himself outside of the tight unit.

Jia hadn't missed the distinction.

His mother and sisters loved him and yet, she'd sensed the painful rift, especially between his mother and Apollo. And ever since she'd caught snippets of its source, she finally saw beyond the machinations and the thirst for power to the tormented man beneath it all. Her heart ached with the need to take away his burden, to make him see what kind of man he was outside of this revenge that had consumed two decades of his life.

Giving in to the urge, she traced the bridge of his nose with the tip of her finger and then the bow-shaped curve of his upper lip.

Such little expectations of the people around you, he had said, mocking her.

And it had been easy to follow that edict. Except now, with him. Beneath his obvious anger toward her brother and father, beneath his very righteous belief that here was another way her father was a villain, had been something else though. Something more.

It was such a tempting illusion that Jia fell back against the bed, shaking.

A large, rough palm landed on her belly before long fingers traced the curve of her hip with a possessive familiarity that made her breath come in little pants. "Not tired enough for sleep?"

"I'm…restless tonight." She was standing at a crossroads, and her heart wanted to go one way and her mind another. One way lay the rational, no-risk, empty life she'd always lived and the other way…lay the possibility of infinite happiness. "Confused," she added, feeling this uncharacteristic urge to bare all of herself to him.

"About?" he said, a grave tone to the single word.

"About myself, you. And us." Each word ripped her out from under all the shackles she had bound herself with. Released her into a new terrifying world. But she couldn't stay put anymore, not after tasting this joy with Apollo.

"What about us?" He practically growled the words at her.

"Why do you want to build another house when we can live in this one?"

"It's a fresh start." He replied readily enough that she knew he had been thinking of it too. "For us."

Or a fresh start for him?

The words he didn't say danced between them, shocking Jia with their vulnerability.

Because this house was tainted with his need to prove something to the world? Because it was tied to the shadow of a man he had not let go of? Because he was finding himself in a new place with her, and wanted to let go of old things like revenge and reparation?

Excitement skittered through her. "If I sign over my stock in my father's company to you tomorrow, instead of three years later as he and you agreed on, will this all be over?"

Delaying the stock transfer was the one thing her father had asked of her when Apollo had given her ten minutes to leave. The one thing she'd promised herself she'd never do.

And yet here she was, ready to betray the man who had raised her.

He only raised you. He wasn't really a father.

She heard the cruel words in Apollo's voice.

The idea took root in her head and was already spreading its gnarled whispers all over, solidifying. What if she could give Apollo what he wanted and this was over? What if it meant a real fresh start for the both of them, and not just a shiny new house? What if it meant there were no conditions hanging over their relationship?

Behind her, Apollo stiffened. Sudden tension swathed them, as if forming their very own bubble. "What?"

"It would bring you controlling percentage in the company, yeah?"

"Yes."

"It's what you wanted all along?"

"Yes."

"If you promise that—"

"He will never forgive you."

"Someday, he will realize that I protected him, that I did only what was best for them. But for now, it will be over."

"He will never realize that, never give you what you're seeking."

"What I choose to believe is my prerogative, *ne*?" she said, imitating his gruff tone. "So, tell me, will it be over?"

"Will what be over?"

"Your…revenge. This pursuit of his destruction."

"You're not signing your stock over to me. What I want will be mine, soon."

"Yes, we've established that, Apollo. And really, I'm just…"

"Just what, *agapi*?"

"I'm thinking of what I want my life to look like in a few years. Thinking of what *I want* for the first time," she said, giving free rein to the emotions sitting like a tight fist at the center of her chest. It was easier when she wasn't looking into that unfathomable gray gaze and wondering if she'd one day drown. "I haven't ever, you know. Thought about what I want, where I want to live, how I want to work and—"

"Let me know when you figure out the specifics."

"Why?"

"So that I can give it to you."

Jia shivered at the steely resolve in those words. Apparently, there was no doubt in his head that he wanted to be married to her for the distant future.

She didn't know what to make of that certainty. Was this chemistry and compatibility enough for him? Did he truly think they could last a lifetime with their pasts so murkily tangled and their foundation built on a cold arrangement? "That's an ambitious promise," she finally said, running her fingers over the coarse hair on this forearm.

His laughter spread ripples on the back of her neck. "You married a man for whom nothing is impossible. I thought you understood your commitment to me."

She could feel his frown like a burn on her cheek as he fully turned toward her, almost angry that her emotions, and she, dared to not follow his dictates. And that made her smile. Because underneath all the ruthless bluster and grumpy dictates, her husband hid a heart of gold.

One hairy, muscled leg thrown over hers, he pulled her closer, and his mouth descended to her neck. That spot where once he kissed her, she lost all reason and logic and self-preservation.

She arched her neck as his teeth grazed the sensitive spot, dampness blooming between her thighs, as easily as if flipping a switch.

"All this talk of your restlessness has made me restless. Only one thing would cure it," he said, each word pinging over her skin.

"It's always only one thing with you," she said, stretching into his touch.

"I want to be inside you," he said, laving the bite with his tongue. Breathing the words into her skin. "Now. Say yes, *agapi. Parakalo.*"

When Jia might have turned toward him, he stopped her, one arm crisscrossing between her bare breasts, and the other hand coasting down her side, waist to hip to thigh, finger slowly creeping across her lower belly. Tiny trembles began to skitter across her flesh like ripples on water.

"You're distracting me and it won't..." she whispered, but the thought never fully formed as he dipped his fingers into her folds.

She jerked as he pinched her clit, and traced every inch of her aching flesh until her wetness coated his fingers, and then he told her how it felt when he was inside of her, and how she clenched tight when she thought he might retreat, and how he thought it couldn't get better when he came inside of her but it did. Every single time, it got better.

Words and fingers and lips...he used them all to drive her out of her skin.

She wanted to protest—she wanted to talk to him—but God, the man was enormously talented and Jia moaned as he speared her with two fingers.

"I don't like it when you don't fall in with my plans, wife."

"You don't want a wife. You want a doll who'll play along and be your... Oh."

His mouth was at her nipple, licking, sucking and nipping. Jia had never lost a battle this willingly and this fast.

"No, Tornado," he said, withdrawing his fingers, leaving her empty, lost. "I want *you*, only you, willing and happy and amenable to my plans."

"Come inside me, Apollo," she said, those words propping her up for now, "and I will fall in with any plans, please."

As if all he'd needed was her assent, he lifted her leg and probed her wanton, wet flesh with the head of his cock and then he was thrusting into her from behind and Jia thought she might be the exploding sun itself.

It was a sore, tight fit with a delicious burn in this position but she didn't want to be anywhere else. She didn't want anything else. She felt engulfed by him and she loved it.

Hands kneading and cupping her flesh all over, keeping her still and soft for his tender assault, Apollo set a merciless rhythm, pounding into her. The slap of their flesh, the erotic tussle of their breaths, the words he whispered into her skin…pleasure suffused every inch of her. Their bodies slipped and slid together as if made for each other, racing toward a pinnacle she'd want again and again.

It was only after their climaxes nearly broke them that Jia realized she'd tried to put everything on the line for him. And he hadn't wanted it.

CHAPTER NINE

SHE CAME TO him at dawn, dressed in a thick robe that hung off one smooth shoulder and fell to her ankles. *His robe.*

He hadn't been hiding precisely. But after he had tired her out, desperate to control her, own her, bind her to him, whatever restlessness had chased her seemed to have transferred to him.

It was her offer to sign over her stock to him. Mere weeks ago, the same offer would have been a prize he'd counted as his final win. Now, with his feelings all twisted up about her and his own part in where they were, it felt like a…curse. A gut punch.

Even as he'd lain there boneless and sated, her offer had niggled and pricked.

Why had she offered that to him when it was the only thing of any value she possessed? Did she crave her freedom so much? Was it such a chore to be married to him? What was there for her back in New York except a family that would chew her up for all she was worth and spit her out given half the chance?

He had felt unsettled enough, unwanted enough that he found it unbearable to stay near her for one more second. For all she tried to buy her way out of his life, she clung to him in sleep, her legs and arms all coiled around him.

That feeling of not being enough struck some deep, primal part of him that he had forgotten existed.

It was the same thing that had haunted him after he'd found Papa unmoving, the same thing he'd tried to escape by pouring himself into climbing the corporate ladder high enough to own it.

And yet, after all that he'd done to get to this place now, that he could once again be haunted by that feeling…threw him. He wanted to run from it, hide from it, go back into bed and work himself out on Jia until they were both exhausted again and she made no foolish offers to get away.

But he was not a fool, and he knew not to outrun the same problem in the same way all over again.

So he was sitting at his desk in the large airy study, the oncoming dawn a distant pink splash in the horizon. For a moment, he considered telling her to leave him alone. But the words stalled, drowned out by his need to hold her, to have her near.

"You need your sleep," he said, tempering his tone somehow, intensely disliking the knowledge that he could hurt her with one wrong word.

It was a dangerous power to have, because he hadn't met a kind that he didn't wield in the end. Not even Mama's utter dislike of him had broken his taste for it, once he'd had it.

Hands clamped on the sash of the robe, she walked to him, instantly fitting herself in between his legs, as if she belonged there.

"You're not happy about my offer." She pushed her hair behind her ear, confusion writ in her gaze. Her frown cleared. "No, you're angry about my offer. Why?"

He looked past her and the glass wall into the inky night beyond. Every memory today seemed to bring him back to the helplessness he'd struggled with after Papa's death. *Dios mio*, he'd had many sleepless nights, just like this. "What's your condition for it?"

"Are you sure that I have one?" Her expression was somber now.

He nodded.

"Finish this revenge of yours. Let them be. Let yourself be."

He scoffed. "I should've known."

Her eyes flashed but she corralled her temper and it was a sight to behold. "Rina told me earlier that Vik *is* facing the consequences. She's moving in with her chauffeur. With you having controlling stock, my father can't afford the delusion anymore that he can come back from this. He has lost everything, Apollo. You have won. So let it be," she said, clasping his cheeks and tugging until he looked down at her. Her eyes were wide, brimming with an emotion he couldn't read. "I ask it for you too. So that you can be free."

He pulled away from her so fast that she almost stumbled. But he caught her, then released her. "I do not need any favors, Jia," he said, stubbornly. "At least nothing that's not part of our deal."

She joined him at the chaise longue, hands folded primly in her lap. "I have spent enough time with your family to realize that your father's death wasn't…a natural one. To understand that your need to pay for his loss has caused a rift between you and your mother. I know you enough to see that this revenge has cost you even more than it has cost my father."

"Sleeping with me for a few weeks doesn't make you an expert on me."

If he thought she'd be hurt, he was wrong. Her chin tilted up, a combative expression entering her eyes. "And yet you were right about me. You made me doubt if my mom even saw me as anything but a mistake she had to make up for. You made me wonder if she molded me into this...pushover for the rest of my family as part of her reparation to him. You made me realize that maybe he never truly loved me as he did Rina or Vik. If the mind-blowing orgasms you dole out have given you that much insight into me, why shouldn't I have the same?" She smiled then, and it was the most breathtaking sight Apollo had ever seen. His chest ached to be in its presence and ached more anticipating its absence. "Plus, like you said, your sisters are blunt and voluble."

He clasped her cheek, the need to touch her ever present. "Is it me you want to free from the past or yourself from the present?" The words fluttered between them, dripping with his vulnerability.

She frowned. "I don't understand."

Her confusion was genuine enough that some deep longing in him settled. "If you think I'll release you from this marriage because you sign over your stock—"

"I didn't think that," she said, tapping the side of her head. "After all, as we both know, the real asset is my brain. At least, until you're addicted to my body—and my mouth," she said, licking her lower lip, "and then that becomes the real asset."

He grinned, suddenly feeling light as a feather. It was another new feeling in the box he was collecting of them. And the realization that maybe, just maybe, she truly meant for him to be free, as well as her own father, filled him with awe and that dissonance again.

What did he do with such a woman? He was running out of deals and conditions and contracts that he could use to bind her.

He sat down on the chaise longue next to her and she instantly leaned her head against his shoulder, utterly unaware of how her every touch and kiss and caress unmanned him. "Is it true that you...found him?"

"He was cold when I touched his hand."

She took his hand and laced their fingers and clasped him so tight that he felt the crust of ice around his heart melt. He hadn't talked about this with a single soul, not even Mama. And suddenly the words came easy, as if all these years, they'd been waiting to be released. "I was... so angry in those first moments. I could only think of myself and how he had abandoned me when I worshipped him. He was my hero. That he didn't think I, or any of us, were enough to hold on to, to find a way to move forward. And the only way I could escape that feeling was to channel all that rage into action, toward the right man."

"I can't imagine how hopeless he must have felt after losing so much. But he did abandon you, Apollo. It's okay to love him and still be angry with him over that." When he let her words soothe him, she scoffed. "Says the woman who craves her father's approval even though she knows she'll never get it," she added with a flippancy.

"All I have fed for nearly two decades is that rage and it has burned everything else down. I'm a stranger to my own family. Mama has never understood that rage, that drive to make your father pay, the need to amass so much power and wealth that no one can ever make me feel like that again."

Only to learn now that no power or wealth could buy him this woman's loyalty.

"But you're here now, with them," she said, coming into his lap like Camilla's cat, demanding to be pet, and vined herself around him. "And you could begin again. All they want is a word from you to build that bridge. All they want is to know that the boy they know and love is still there beneath the ruthless billionaire."

Apollo didn't miss the wistful note in her words and tightened his arms around her. Neither did he miss the fact that his mother's sudden approval of him was mostly due to this complex creature he had married, which had come about by her design and his greed. The fact that his fate could have been so much worse didn't sit well with his need for control.

"So what do you think of my offer? Can you get the paperwork ready?"

"No," he said instinctively, without even examining the source of it. "I don't want to take those stock options away from you. Not yet," he added to keep her dangling.

"But that means you still—"

"Leave it, Jia. You have solved enough problems for him."

"I told you, Apollo. This isn't about him."

"Excuse me if I don't believe that you can break the pattern of a lifetime in a moment, *agapi*."

Within a blink of an eye, she was out of his arms and halfway across the study, fury radiating from her.

"You're being childish," he called out, wanting to chase her and pin her down under him like a predator. He was beginning to feel like that was all he'd want for the rest of his life. To have her writhing under him, biting at him with her tart words, softening in those moments when she let down her armor enough to trust him.

Her eyes glowed in the soft light of the lamp as she halted at the doorway. "If you want us to be locked in this…arrangement forever, fine." She was almost out when she paused, her throat bobbing up and down. "But then I want nothing to do with the house you build. I'm not leaving this house and I'm definitely not starting a…"

Whatever she saw in his eyes, she swallowed the rest of her words. Something unbearably sad flashed across her face before she turned away.

Apollo thought she might have said, *So much for a fresh start for you and me.* But he was damned if he begged her to explain any more than he already had. Or stay in his life willingly. He had already cornered himself into a weaker position and the uncertainty of it picked at him night and day.

He had married her as part of the deal she herself had struck and he would be a poor businessman if he let her change the terms of their deal now. And he wasn't done with her father, as she had so naively assumed.

CHAPTER TEN

JIA WALKED UP to the second-floor open terrace that looked out into the turquoise sea and took in a deep breath of fresh air on the unseasonably warm day. It did little to calm her stomach that afternoon.

She'd been feeling queasy all day but she'd kept it to herself. Apollo, with his usual bullheadedness, would've sent her back to bed and she'd miss seeing the house that his firm had custom-designed and nearly finished for a seventy-year-old Arab tycoon.

It was the first house they'd designed together. Granted, near to completing it, Apollo had been stuck in some aspects and Jia had helped make a few modifications. And now, there it stood carved into the side of a hill. The expanse of blue sea and green hillside working perfectly to encapsulate the all-white home.

Jia wasn't usually a fan of the modern contemporary designs that lacked all warmth and color, and rejected natural elements like wood and fabric. Solely depending on steel and chrome, they looked like geometric cubes.

But here, in this house, the sharp, flat cube design had no flourishes. Only white walls and glass, which served to highlight the lush, natural landscape around it. A rectangular pool at the front of the house reflected sunlight like jewels on its blue surface.

It was a perfect escape for anyone who wanted to get away from the hustle, the perfect destination for a small family to spend the weekend. God, she was beginning to think like Apollo Galanis's wife, with thoughts of summer homes and island destinations. When she didn't have a single nickel to her name.

It had never bothered her before. All she'd lived for was to win her family's approval, to somehow contribute to their well-being. Only last week, she'd learned that the stock she owned in her father's company had shot up meteorically. Not unconnected to the formal press release that Apollo Galanis was taking over the firm.

Weeks after she'd made the offer to sign it over to him, Jia still didn't understand why he didn't take her up on it. How long could she bear to have the shadow of the past color their relationship?

Joy tingled on her lips when he kissed her, danced through her body when he made love to her, was beginning to shine like a flame in her chest when he looked through a crowd or coworkers or his family for her. When he spotted her, those little crinkles appeared at the corners of his eyes and his mouth curled up. Everything around them dissolved, leaving the two of them alone in the entire universe.

Even knowing the truth of the trauma Apollo had faced when he'd discovered his father's body and everything that had followed, Jia couldn't find it in herself to hurt her father anymore. If that made her a sentimental pushover, so be it. It wasn't like she was faring any better with Apollo. In a mere two months, she had shifted her loyalty to him without any qualms.

Absentmindedly, she took a sip of the champagne. It coated her throat with a slick bile, threatening to bring up the little she'd managed to eat at breakfast. Bad enough that her period was due any day now and...

Jia quickly checked her calendar. Shock jostled her stomach a little more as she looked at the colorful numbers. She'd had only one period since she'd arrived in Greece and that was nearly nine weeks ago, when they'd still been in Athens. Her legs trembled as she came down the stairs to the main level.

Was she pregnant?

Having a baby with Apollo was the last thing she'd ever imagined, when she'd struck the deal with him. But the thought of not having the baby filled her throat with fresh bile and she nearly tripped on the way to the bathroom.

Large hands held her hair back as she emptied her stomach, whispering reassurances, holding her when her knees buckled.

Jia washed up, doing her best to avoid looking at the large circular mirror and meeting his watchful eyes. If she did, he would know. And if Apollo knew, he would be...happy. She knew that as surely as her racing heartbeat.

A house for us and the family we might have.

Closing her eyes, Jia leaned into the hard warmth of his body behind her. His corded forearm clasped around her waist with utter gentleness. "I'll have the chopper ready in five minutes. You should have told me you weren't feeling well."

Tears filled Jia's eyes and she trembled with the effort to hold them back. She'd have to take a pregnancy test, yes, but she knew. Especially since she'd been told that antibiotics could mess with the pill.

Slowly, shock gave way to crystal-clear clarity.

"What's wrong, *agapi*? Where does it hurt?" Apollo said in a voice she'd never heard from him.

But she couldn't say anything because the thing she did want to say was the biggest truth of her life. She wanted to stand at the highest peak, and scream into the sea and the sky that she had fallen in love with him.

She was in love with her husband. And with this baby, *their baby*, which was probably no bigger than the size of a tiny worm right then.

And she was in love with how precious their life together that he kept showing her tiny, taunting glimpses of, could be.

She was in love with a man who was obsessed with making her father pay for his sins and in the process, refused to feel anything else, a man who considered her an asset. A man who in the pursuit of that revenge had even alienated his own mother.

"Jia, look at me. *Parakalo*."

It was the *please* that did it, full of his own desperation, that reminded her that he did care for her, but just not in the way she wanted him to.

She turned around and threw herself at him and cried like she'd never done before. How could he be the storm that was wrecking her and still also be the only harbor left to her?

God, she couldn't bear the weight of loving Apollo without him loving her back. She didn't want to spend the rest of her life locked in a marriage with a man who would always see her last name first, or her brains and now the fact that she was his child's mother.

Would he ever want her for herself, even as he built castles for their now very real family? Would he love her as she longed to be loved, as she loved him?

And if she stayed, she would be trapped and miserable, unable and unwilling to give him up. But could she leave him and raise this baby alone? Would he even let her? Or would she be ruining a bright present in search of a future that didn't exist?

"Enough, Jia," Apollo was whispering into her temple, his hands moving over her back in a frenzy, a rough bite to his words. "You will make yourself sick and I will not allow it. Enough, *agapi mou*. Whatever it is, I will fix it."

The scent of him filled her lungs and instantly her body calmed, as if it knew him better than her mind did. Even better than her heart.

Jia clung to him, took solace in his words, even though she knew it was only temporary. "I'm scared, Apollo. I…"

"Of what, Jia?"

She buried her face in his neck—her safe space. Here, she could feel his steady pulse and breathe in the pine and clove scent, and know that with those arms around her, she wouldn't be lost.

His hands moved over her, kneading and pressing, gathering her so tight to him that she felt like she might break apart. His mouth was at her temple, warm and soft. "Shh... Tornado. You're with me and I won't let you go."

And when he lifted her in his arms, and walked through the house that he'd built and carried her to the roof in front of all the staring guests as if she were precious, as if nothing else mattered, Jia wondered if she could be brave enough to do the one thing she'd never done in her entire life.

For Apollo, could she hope? For this baby and the life they might build together, could she trust in herself that she was worthy of his love? Could she stay and love him as she wanted to?

Apollo watched Jia as she half-heartedly riffled through the design folders he'd brought in from the firm, at her request. From playing video games with Camilla's sons to cooking with his mother, to her work, everything she did these days was with half a heart, her mind a million miles away.

Something was wrong, ever since that day two weeks ago when they'd been visiting a client's home in Andros Island. He had never seen such panic in Jia's eyes and even now, if he closed his eyes, her expression haunted him.

To this day, she wouldn't tell him what had made her cry as if her heart was breaking.

Oh, she pretended that everything was good, but he caught that haunted look in her eyes when she thought he wasn't watching or when she forgot to keep her armor up. He also didn't miss how her moods fluctuated from happiness to sudden sadness, like a shroud dimming her spirit.

The only place where he had her completely, where he knew only his touch ruled her, was in bed. She was as desperate to be touched and held and consumed as she'd been before and if it wasn't for that intimacy that tethered her to him, he might have lost his mind by now.

He was getting there slowly though, seeing the constant shadow in her eyes, wondering what he could do to fix it, wondering how he could get the old Jia back.

He'd even hounded Rina about the cause, wondering if her family was at the root of her problems, as always. Rina had not only come up empty, but finally showed a little backbone by asking him if he'd considered that he could be the source of Jia's pain.

Jia married you because she had no choice, Rina had pointed out, with sudden acidity, and the doubt had been planted.

Jia was unhappy with him, with their relationship, and he had no idea how to fix it, for all he'd promised her he would. Asking her had got him nothing but evasion.

I've given you everything, Apollo. There's nothing left, had been Jia's sarcastic taunt when he'd probed. And then, like a child seeking approval from an adult they'd alienated, she had clung to him that night.

"You're worried about her."

Apollo turned to find his mother next to him, holding up a cup of dark coffee in one hand. Just the scent of it told him she'd prepared it the exact way he liked it. The realization arrested his childish impulse to snub her offer.

He hadn't even been aware of her presence in the kitchen, so caught up he was in watching Jia. For once, all his sisters and their broods were busy elsewhere and the house was eerily quiet.

With nothing else to do, he took the coffee mug and turned away.

"Will you not talk to me, Apollo?" Mama said, her words heartbreakingly soft.

He shrugged, a sudden patina of grief and anger clinging to his throat. For so long, they had been at odds with each other. She had been critical of everything he had done, and he hadn't cared enough to mend the direction of his life. And now, when he'd achieved everything he'd set out to own, when the world was at his feet, this rift with his mother was still an open wound.

Was it too late to mend it? Did he even want to?

The moment the resentful thought came, he found the answer. Of course he wanted to build a bridge to his mother again. But he didn't know how. Just as he didn't know how to help Jia.

"I'm still your mother, Apollo, even if you have conquered the entire world," she said, rebuking him with the same thoughts.

She came to stand next to him and her subtle sandalwood perfume came to him. A river of longing opened up, touched by memories of baking with her in a tiny kitchen, of hugging her and feeling so secure, of…seeing her strong face break into terrible sobs when she'd seen Papa's body, of how long she'd spoken to him that night about how it wasn't his fault. That Papa had loved them all, but he hadn't been strong enough.

"You tried very hard that evening, after I...found him," he said.

She frowned, an instant shadow of grief touching her eyes. A long sigh then. "You were always your Papa's son. I knew how much you adored him and I also understood how betrayed you must have felt. Because I felt the same."

The mug clattered onto the tiled counter with enough noise to wake the dead, but across the open space, sitting in the living room, staring at something in the distance, Jia didn't even stir.

Apollo pressed the heels of his palms into his eyes, the past and present combining and separating as if in a science fiction movie—one Jia had made him watch. "I felt so...helpless and angry."

His mother, so tiny and small beside him, wrapped her arm around his waist and squeezed. "I wish I had helped you in a better way to—"

"No, Mama. You were right when you said that he could have been stronger for us. None of us wanted the wealth he lost or needed it. We would have moved into a hut with him and still been happy. He didn't see that, didn't realize the value of that and I..." his breath came in shallow pants "...I chose a path that made me lose you too."

"But you have not lost me, or your sisters, Apollo," she said, her voice steely in its resolve. "We have all been here, waiting for you. And you haven't lost the kindness that was so much a part of your Papa's either. All the good parts are still there."

"I am not so sure."

Mama covered his hand on the countertop. "You're admitting defeat, Apollo?"

He laughed and examined his hands. "I'm admitting that everything I have done so that I never feel help-less again…doesn't work. All the wealth, all the power I have amassed are no use to me when I want to…"

"What?" Mama said, following his gaze to the woman in the living room. The woman he realized held his heart in her slender, tender hands. "Tell me."

"Something is wrong with her."

It came to him slowly, as if he was moving through a fog, that his mother wasn't surprised. "In what way?"

"She smiles but there's a shadow. She talks but it's different. She clings to me at night, but it's as if she's running away from some great sorrow. She will not tell me what it is and I'm afraid that she's slipping from my fingers. I'm afraid that there is nothing in the world that I can do to fix this for her."

"I have seen what you speak of, Apollo. She's quieter than she usually is. Maybe she's homesick?"

Apollo turned so fast that his neck hurt. "Did she say that to you?"

"She has been talking a lot about families and how they come to be. She asked if I had been happy with your father. She's been begging Camilla and Christina to talk about children and families and how they knew if they were ready."

Was that simply it, that she missed her damned family?

"I wondered if she…"

"She, what?" When his mother hesitated, Apollo grabbed her hand. "I'm going mad trying to figure this out."

Her soft gaze lit on his face, carefully scrutinizing every inch. "Why?"

"Why what?"

"Why are you so worried?"

"Because I've pulled her away from her entire world, her family, her friends and she's mine. Because I…"

Because he was in love with her and he would do anything to make the world right for her again. Except let her go, he added to himself.

Maybe it wasn't love, then. Maybe it was something else. Maybe it was his need to control this too. Wasn't love supposed to be selfless and grand and divine?

He felt the opposite, like there was a storm brewing in his stomach. Like he'd never know certainty in anything ever again.

"Please, Mama."

"I wondered if she…" hesitation danced in her eyes "…is pregnant."

It felt like he had been slapped so hard that the echoes of it rang in his ears. Every inch of him stilled.

"When Camilla asked gently, she said you two are not planning for a family and…"

The rest of his mother's words drifted away as Apollo moved past her to the stairs. He took them three at a time, his heart thrashing around in his chest like a crushed toy.

All her stuff lay in half-open cosmetic bags or in

haphazard piles in the drawers in the bathroom. He rifled through her handbag and her jewelry box and her pen case and her...

He found the discarded pill sheet first, sitting innocently under a pile of underwear. And in another drawer, a pharmacy receipt for two pregnancy tests. He didn't have to see the tests themselves to know that his mother's guess was right.

Jia had been sick that day when they'd been touring the client's house in Andros Island, had had no appetite for days after and she had been so panic-stricken because she... She was pregnant.

With his child.

Their child.

A child she'd never planned for, and had made it clear enough times that she didn't want with him. A child whose very conception had made her sick at heart. A child she was keeping a secret from him, over whom she was turning herself into a shadow.

Did she hate the idea so much, enough to want to... leave him?

It felt like a crack reverberated through his heart, the thought was that painful.

And in that moment of utter confusion and anguish, Apollo knew. In that moment when he had to face the possibility that Jia wanted to leave him, he knew.

It was as solid and real as the house he had built for his mother. As real as the anger he had finally allowed himself to feel against his father for abandoning them. As real as the hope he'd been nurturing for weeks now.

Dios mio, he was in love with his wife and he had

no idea how to sit with that knowledge. When he knew that she was only in his life because he had forced her hand. When he knew that anything they had shared, anything they had created together, like this precious child, had been an accident of his path, not her choice.

He sank to the floor and clutched his head in his hands, feeling like he had hit the bottom of the world. Still, the crash was unending. But even through the panic pulsing through him, there was a pinprick of awe at this new emotion swirling through him.

He was in love and he had never known anything more terrifying or more wonderful.

CHAPTER ELEVEN

THREE WEEKS AFTER her discovery, Jia had come up with a hundred different plans for how she could tell Apollo and discarded them all. Her period had always thrashed her about like a ship caught in a storm, and it seemed her pregnancy was going to be more of the same. Despite that, she'd forced herself to consider the ugly prospect of leaving him with a clear mind.

What kind of a future would she be providing for her child? Apollo had helped her shed her rose-colored lenses about her family. She would be all alone in the world with a tiny precious baby to care for.

That was, assuming Apollo simply let her go.

Abandoning his pregnant wife was something he would never do.

And if she stayed…would things get better? Could her love simply wither and die if she didn't nurture it? Could she one day forget that it even existed, flickering like a live flame inside her chest? Would it be so bad to make a family with him knowing he admired her, respected her, even cared for her, in his own way?

When the questions became too much, she floated through her days in a strange limbo. Like a flesh wound on her finger hidden away under layers of gauze, so she only felt it when she had to use it. Then it became a pulsing throb of pain.

Nights were easier to get through.

Especially like now, when she was in bed and waiting for Apollo to join her. She'd spent the whole day with so many doubts that all she wanted was his brand of possession.

In the dark intimacy of their bedroom, she forgot everything. In their bed, with his hard, warm body tangled around hers or pinning her down into the mattress as he drove them to sweet release, or as he cradled her from behind and drowned her in his caresses making sweet love to her, it was easy to imagine that Apollo adored her as much as she adored him.

A sudden ping on her phone had her scooting up on the bed. It was a text from her sister.

Reading it made tears prick her eyelids—what didn't these days?—and laugh at the same time. But beneath the joy that Rina was getting married and the acceptance of her sister's long, heartfelt apology, a dark envy lingered. If Rina, who'd always let their father and brother intimidate her, who'd never gone against the grain even in thought, could find true love, why couldn't Jia?

With uncharacteristic frustration, Jia threw her cellphone across the bedroom. It landed with a loud thump on the rug. God, what was she turning into? It was almost as if the pregnancy and her love for Apollo were releasing all the petty and intense but valid emotions she had caged inside all her life.

"Jia?" Apollo stood under the archway to their

bedroom. "Did you just throw your phone across the room?"

"Yes."

"Feel better?"

"No."

With moonlight coming in through the glass walls behind him, every angle of him was limned lovingly as if she herself had crafted him with her hands.

A broad chest, strong shoulders, tapering to a thin waist and abdominal muscles that she rubbed herself on without shame…he was everything she'd never even had the nerve to imagine. Just the sight of him made her heart flutter with dizzying pleasure, her body come alive as if it had been sleeping for years.

Powerful and yet kind beneath the grumpy exterior, a man who was a hundred times worthier than the man she called father…

Was he hers? Could he be hers forever? Was her love enough to sustain them?

Suddenly, Jia knew what she had to do. Her happiness, her spark for life, her very joy itself was already bound to this man. How could she leave him? She had spent all her life serving her undeserving family, hoping to earn a smile, a pat, approval from a man who didn't even see her.

How could she do anything less for the man who had seen her messy, chaotic self from the first moment and only found it fascinating? For the man who had only tried to protect her when he thought she was being harmed, the man who encouraged her to scale new career heights, the man who was always telling her to never dilute her vision, to never lessen herself for anyone, including him?

A sudden rush of energy filled her at her resolution. Her lips curved. Her body thrummed with fresh need that wasn't just about escaping her worries, but with new appreciation, for her own desire and for him.

"Jia?" Apollo said her name again. Only this time, it was heavy with frustration. With...pain even. He thrust a hand through his hair, making it stand up every which way.

Coming to her knees on the bed, Jia extended her hands to him. "Will you hold me, Apollo?"

He threw the towel he'd been holding and reached her in seconds with those long strides. Whatever she'd asked of him, however unreasonable she'd been with her own indecision, he'd held her through it, through the storm, without complaint. Without making her feel like she was a burden.

Even her own mother had thought her a burden at one time.

Jia threw herself at him, shuddering with relief brought on by her decision. It was right. She knew it in her bones.

His skin was warm, his muscles tense and hard as he wrapped those steely arms around her. She laid open-mouthed kisses on his bare chest, leaving little dents with her teeth, loving the rough bristle of his chest hair against her skin. The lacy top she'd worn rasped against her beading nipples, making the torment a thousand-fold.

"You're shaking, *matia mou*," he said, his mouth at

her temple. "*Again*. Jia…" her name was both a mantra and a curse on his lips "…this…whatever this is needs to stop. We can't continue…you can't…"

"I know. I know," she said, looking up.

His eyes caught her, trapping her in the midst of a maelstrom. A shaft of fear pierced Jia at what she saw there, even though she couldn't put a name to it.

"I'll do better, Apollo," she said, just as she had once promised her mother, so desperate to please and matter and love. But tonight, this promise to her husband wasn't borne out of that same desperation. This promise was different. It moved through her like a rich, fertile sapling spreading its branches, planting roots deep inside her.

This wasn't just for a reward or for approval or to earn love. As if anyone ever had to.

No, she wanted to make him happy. She wanted to please him, make him laugh, make him see who he was beneath all the layers he'd covered himself in. She wanted to love him as well as he loved her, even if he never said the words.

She stroked her palms over his shoulders, loving the tight stretch of his skin over muscles. Loving that she already knew his flesh so well. "You've been very patient with me and I've been an awful employee and an even more awful wife but I swear I will—"

"You think that's what I care about?" he said, roughly tugging her up, until she looked into his eyes. He looked tormented. Unraveled, like she'd never seen him before. Angry, yes, but afraid too. And she'd never seen that in Apollo's eyes. "That you're not performing at peak efficiency at work? Or that you haven't behaved like however a proper wife is supposed to act? Do you think so little of me, Jia?"

He hadn't raised his voice but there was an edge to it that had her searching his face for answers. Alarm punched through her. He was right.

She'd been like one of those gothic heroines Rina was always reading about, walking around dark, edgy moors with tears running down her cheeks, her hair in a disarray, waiting for someone to save her. But she'd already saved herself, with Apollo by her side.

She just hadn't known it. Worse, she'd been so deep in her head that she hadn't wondered how it must have looked to Apollo. Clearly, he had been paying attention to everything she'd done and not done.

"No, of course not. But I know it's not easy to live with a moping mess of a—"

"So what? How do you plan to suddenly not be that... woman?" His fingers were digging into her shoulders, not hurting but not gentle either. "What magical potion will you take to just transform all of a sudden?"

"I have been thinking of magical potions in the past week too. One I would sneak into your morning coffee so that I could have my wicked way with you, so I could make you give me everything I want. Whatever I want." She moved her hand between their chests, grinning like a loon. "Made for each other."

The cold frost in his eyes broke, and his mouth twitched. "You are insane."

"I know there's no potion, Apollo. I just made a decision, is all."

His hand snuck under her top, and his palm felt abrasively delicious kneading her hip. "You don't need one with me. You could simply ask."

"And you would give it to me?" she said, feeling feverish and elated.

"Anything."

She rubbed herself up against his chest, and groaned when her nipples peaked to hard points. "Before I tell you how I plan to leave behind that gothic heroine in the making..."

Distracted by the play of his muscles, she ran her finger down his pecs, over his hard stomach and over the seam of his sweatpants, and down, over the shapely outline of his growing cock. Need twanged between her thighs and she rubbed them for relief.

How could she have forgotten how real this heat between them was? How could she have forgotten that they had made this child, *their child*, in an act of complete surrender to each other?

It had to have been that afternoon after she'd barely recovered. When she'd screamed murder at him and he'd solved her problems for her in the flicker of a second. When he'd carried her to their bed in the middle of the afternoon and coaxed her to drink her soup and then made love to her as if he'd been starved for her. With the afternoon sun warming their already damp skin, it was the first time Jia had wondered about a future with him.

How could she have even imagined for a second separating him from their child?

"Jia?"

She looked up, colored at his scrutiny and went for his lips. He grunted with surprise when she bit his lower lip, nearly drawing blood and then when he let her in, she kissed him roughly, chasing his tongue, letting him take all her breath and her beats and all of her want. All the things she wanted to say to him and couldn't, she poured into her kiss, hoping he would understand, hoping he would see how crazy she was about him.

His fingers tightened in her hair as he took control of the kiss. And the tenor of it only intensified.

He was angry, Jia realized as he nipped at her lower lip. He gripped her jaw with tight fingers holding her just so for his assault, then dragged his teeth down her jawline and over the arch of her neck, as he came back for her lips like a drowning man reaching for land. Over and over again.

When she gasped out a rough breath, he pulled back. "You're like glass in my hands and I'm being even more rough than usual."

"No," Jia said, grabbing his hand and bringing it to her cheek.

"You have never lied to me before."

"I'm not now," she said, heat streaking her cheeks. "You were rough. But I want rough with you, Apollo. I want whatever brings you to your knees."

Holding his gaze, she cupped his cock and squeezed him over the sweatpants, just the way he liked. A short grunt escaped his mouth before his fingers arrested her roving hand, and tugged it up. She flattened her palm against his chest, and scraped her nails over the taut muscle there, wanting to leave deep gouges in his skin.

God, loving him was making her bloodthirsty.

"Tell me first."

She placed her cheek next to her palm, eager to hear his heartbeat. It was a thundering whoosh against her ears. "I want to feel you move inside me. I want to… lose myself in you."

His fingers were at the nape of her neck, crawling upward and cradling her head. "I cannot believe I'm saying this. But you can't use sex as an escape or as manipulation. Whatever is good about it will be lost then."

She looked up, feeling both shame and shock. "I didn't…" She held her answer as she looked into his eyes. The pain there stole her breath. Had she hurt him? Had she been so blind that she hadn't seen what she was doing to him? "I wasn't using it to escape or to manipulate either of us. I just needed the reassurance that things between us can be good."

"They won't be if you hide from me."

She swallowed at the soft thrust, so close to the truth, and nodded. "I'm trying, Apollo. I really am. I needed to know that there was more than just an arrangement between us. More than—"

"So what suddenly caused the good mood, then?"

She pouted at his commanding tone. "Can't we have sex first, please? And no, I'm not using it for anything. I want to celebrate you and me and…what better way?" When he only continued to consider her with that thick-lashed gaze, she sighed. "I will even go down on you and do that thing I've been preparing to do for three weeks."

"Tempting offer, *agapi*," he said, running his knuckles over the gaping neckline of her top. "But no."

"I just don't want us to fight and then—"

"Then don't do the thing that would make me mad and lead us to fight."

"God, now you sound like the grumpy beast you were when we first met. Fine! At least we can have angry sex then."

"Jia…" he said, elongating her name, telling her he was at the end of his tether.

"Rina's getting married. I want to be there for the wedding."

For just a second, Jia thought she saw him flinch. But why would he?

"When?"

She also had a feeling that his first impulse had been to say no and that he'd barely stopped it. "Next week. God knows where Vik is and my father's definitely not attending. I don't want her to be alone."

"You were alone for our wedding."

"I asked Rina but…"

"Right, you didn't want anyone to see you going under the guillotine, even though it was for them."

"First of all, it was a choice I made. So please stop calling it that. In fact, when things are better, I want to have a different…" God, was it any wonder he was looking at her as if she'd lost her mind? She was doing this all wrong. "I'm not going to spend the rest of my life being bitter about what they have done or not done for me. Especially now that Rina has apologized for 'being naively useless' and wants to start our relationship over. Even my father texted asking how I was, and he never ever texts."

He raised a brow. Jia had the fantastical thought he looked like some apex predator waiting to pounce at the slightest hint of weakness.

"I just want to go for a short trip and I feel like I need to see them and…" Again, she swallowed her words. It was getting harder and harder. There was so much she wanted to tell him but…she knew the timing was wrong. And she needed just a little bit of courage. Courage she was hoping she'd find after one look at her old life. "I'm a little homesick, Apollo. Is that so hard to understand?"

The tension in his features eased just a bit and Jia knew she hadn't imagined his flinch earlier. "We will leave in a couple of days. *If* you continue to be well."

"If I continue… Wait, you…you'll come to New York with me?"

"Is that a problem?"

"You hate my family. If she sees you at the town hall, Rina will probably faint straightaway."

"That's her problem, no?"

"But this is…" She straightened and pulled back, feeling a sudden snap of tension coil around them. Tight enough that her breath shallowed out. "Why does it sound like this trip is conditional on your coming?"

"Why is it conditional if I just want to attend my wife's spoiled sister's wedding?"

Jia fell back on her haunches and stared up at him. There was a curve to his mouth that mocked her. It wasn't a sneer but it was there sure enough. That part of her that was used to going on offense flared up but she fought the impulse.

Something *was* off with him and she had a feeling in her gut that she was responsible for it. And she had this overpowering need to soothe it, to soothe *him*.

"When we left after the wedding, it was in such a hurry. You barely gave me any time and every assumption I made about you, and this marriage and about us…it's been turned upside down. I just…want to see my old home, my family, my life as it was before, with this new lens I have now. I want to say goodbye to my mom for the last time. I…"

Apollo stepped back from the bed, his jaw tightening with each word she said. "You can do all that with me by your side."

The tautly stretched cord snapped. She jumped from the bed, that sudden energy she wanted to use up driving him to the edge, fueling her anger. "This is ridiculous. You do realize that I don't actually need your permission to leave, right?"

"And if I *ask* you to not go without me?"

She threw her hands up in frustration. "Why are you being so…stubborn? I've played along with everything you decided from the moment I stepped into your damned penthouse and I'm truly asking for one thing. One thing for myself, that you already promised me and you're acting as if you don't even trust me to—"

"I don't. I don't trust that you will return."

His words were so hollow that Jia wondered if she was imagining them. But one look at his tight mouth told her she wasn't. Her stomach made an alarming swoop. "You don't trust me to…return? You think I'm using this trip as an excuse to…" She rubbed a hand over her chest. "What? Leave you? Run away from you? How can you say that?"

"You're pregnant. Pregnant with my child, *our child*. And you haven't said a word about it. You've turned yourself inside out, you have made yourself sick, you don't eat, you don't sleep, you…stare up at me with those eyes at night. *Three weeks, Jia!*" The more agitated he became, the quieter his voice got and each word landed like a stone pelting her flesh. "You have known for three weeks and you have made me watch you torment yourself. I've never felt so powerless and this is counting that I found my father's dead body." He drew in a sharp breath, and paced around the bed, like a caged tiger. Tension poured out from every inch of his body. "And now, suddenly, you make this one-eighty today. You tell me things are going to change. You tell me to give you one last thing. How do I know you'll return? How do I know you won't take my growing child with you and disappear? Can you honestly tell me that you didn't consider it for one second?"

Jia opened her mouth and closed it, feeling a cold fist in her chest, spreading like a crack in ice over a lake.

He'd figured it out. Of course he'd figured it out. God, how stupid was she? What had her fear and cowardice brought them to?

Instead of telling him the truth, instead of sharing her fears, instead of having faith in the best thing that had ever happened to her, she'd broken the little, tenuous trust that had formed between them. "I did think that. But that's because—"

He flinched, and stepped back. As if she was a thing

that could harm and hurt him. And Jia's heart broke alongside his. "And yet you throw it in my face that you don't need my permission? Of course you don't need my permission to go anywhere or to see your damned family. But if you're leaving me, with my child in your belly, have the courage to say it to my face."

"I'd never have run away like that," she said, willing him to hear the conviction in her voice. "Never. But leaving you, yes, I considered it. And discarded it, all in a minute. Not telling you was…" she said, getting off the bed.

He stared at her as she walked toward him as if she was his nightmare come alive.

"Killing me. If you saw the torment, you know the reason now. I wanted to share it with you, I wanted to make plans with you, I wanted to tell you that…"

He clutched her wrists when she wanted to wrap her arms around him, and stared down at her, some dark, hungry thing in his eyes.

It was his faith in her, in them, flickering out, Jia realized, on its last breath. All along, it had been there, brilliant and alive and she had nearly doused it with her fears and foolishness.

"But you did not," he said, releasing her. As if he couldn't bear to touch her. "Every moment of you not telling me, every breath felt like torture. Like torment. And then all of a sudden, you say you have a solution. You say you will be better. You want to leave for bloody New York. What do you think that leads me to believe?"

"I know. And I'm so sorry, Apollo. I wanted that trip to be a goodbye to the old me, the stupid, scared, pushover me. I wanted to come back to our life, to this life with a free, fresh perspective. I wanted to beg my father to—"

"I don't want you to have anything to do with your blasted family."

"I don't want anything from them either," Jia said, her own voice rising now. "Why do you think I've been pushing you to forget about this damned revenge? Why do you think I offered to sell my stock to you even though it was the one thing I swore to myself I wouldn't do?"

"I don't want your stock. I told you—"

"How can you not see how that makes me feel? I wanted you free of this obsession with him, with that company. I wanted us free of the thing that brought us together. I wanted a fresh start with you. And I knew seeing them and my old life would only show me how far I've come. Would give me courage."

He shook his head and Jia knew he wasn't listening. That her hiding the truth had taken him out at the knees. That his feelings for her, the very feelings she'd been afraid he didn't have, made it possible for her to hurt him.

He pressed the heels of his hands to his eyes, a rattling groan making his powerful body shake. "You should have told me that you're pregnant. You had so many opportunities, so many nights, so many—"

"I was scared that when you found out about this pregnancy, you would want me only for the baby. Never for me. I wanted you to want me for just myself, Apollo. And I'm sorry that I made you doubt me, that I..." Jia closed her eyes, wondering if she'd left it too late. If she'd burned down the little trust between them completely.

When she opened her eyes, he was gone. And that felt like a body blow to her.

After what felt like an eternity of waiting for him to return, she went back to the bed, grabbed the pillow and buried her face in it. Only a faint whiff of his scent was left in the fabric.

Fear clogged her throat, but she forced herself to breathe past it. She spent a few minutes talking to the bean in her belly, that their papa was angry but that she'd sort it out. All she had to do was wait out his very justified anger and tell him how much she loved him. At least she knew her own heart now.

She wanted a life with him, this wonderful, aching, real life with him. And she hoped he'd give her a chance to prove it to him. Because she knew now, beyond doubt, that he was happier than he'd ever been before, with her, that her pain had hurt him too, and that he loved her, even if he wouldn't admit it for the rest of their lives.

She had to have faith enough for the both of them.

CHAPTER TWELVE

AFTER A WHOLE week of Apollo not returning to the family home, or returning her calls, Jia decided she'd had enough. Yes, she'd hurt him, but couldn't he give her once chance to explain it? See it from her point of view? Understand that it had been her desperation to matter to him that had led her to hiding the truth?

Only now, when she was more rational, did she understand how deeply she'd hurt him. He expected her to abandon him like his father had done. And that was what she'd have done if knowing him and loving him hadn't changed her on a cellular level.

And maybe the only way to prove to him how much he meant to her was to leave this life and come back by her own choice.

And no matter what the state of her relationship, she wanted to attend her sister's wedding. She wanted a chance to build a new kind of relationship with her sister, who was doing her best to make amends.

So one bright chilly morning, Jia booked a flight, packed her bag and came downstairs to find Apollo's mother in the kitchen.

If she hadn't already cried enough to last a lifetime, she'd have fallen apart in front of this kind woman who even then had looked at her with nothing but understanding. Maria had wrapped her arms around Jia, kissed her temple, and gave her advice about how to combat the nausea and to take care of herself on the long flight.

She ran her hand over the dark wood of the banister, a bright glow of conviction in her heart.

This was her home, her family and her life with the man she adored with every breath. She wasn't abandoning it just when she'd realized how precious it was.

A day after Rina's wedding, Jia returned to their family home to collect a few things from her bedroom. Except for some books, keepsakes, and one large photo of her with her mom and Rina that she'd blown up and framed, she added the rest to a trash pile.

It was both fortifying and sad that she didn't need or want anything more from this home she'd lived in all her life. Everything that mattered, everything that she needed, Apollo had already given to her, a hundred times over.

She taped up the small cardboard box and brought it down to find her father, Vik and Rina waiting. For her.

For just a second, Jia wished for Apollo's presence so much that it was a physical ache in her belly. But no matter, she reminded herself, because he was there in her heart.

Rina strode to her side, hugged Jia and announced in that timid whisper of hers that she had a new job as a receptionist at a dental office. Jia had never been happier for her sister. Clearly, Michael was a great influence.

Vik, on the other hand, had a beard, dark shadows

under his eyes and looked like he'd had a rough last few months. "I shouldn't have a laid a finger on either of you. Drunk or not," he said stiffly.

Jia nodded.

Her father, hands tucked into his coat pocket, looked as smart and stylish as he always did. But there was a beaten-down look in his eyes that made Jia wonder what new plague Apollo had unleashed on him. For so long, she'd done everything in her life to please this man. She'd yearned for one word of affection, for one hug, for one kind glance even.

"Is he treating you well, Jia?" he asked her, as if reading from a script he'd been asked to learn by rote. And suddenly, she wondered if this stilted, awkward reunion was all Apollo's doing.

Jia laughed, through the tears pooling in her eyes. "He's…good to me."

"About your stock," her father began.

"I don't want it," she said, shrugging. "I'll sell it to you for a dollar. Just tell me where to sign."

"I was about to tell you that it doesn't matter what you do with it. *He* already has controlling stock. He's had it for weeks now."

"What? How?"

Rina bit her lip, carefully avoiding their brother's and father's gazes. "I sold mine to him. Paul and I had nowhere to go and Dad had fired him. So I called Apollo and asked him if he wanted to buy it."

"My own daughter, selling out behind my back," Father said, with a flatness to his tone. It almost felt like… acceptance. Even regret maybe. "Not that I have ever done anything to earn any loyalty from either of you."

"What?" Jia asked, her mind reeling. "And he agreed?"

"Yes," Rina said, smiling. "He paid way over the market price. When I tried to protest, given he's your husband and I might need his help again, y'know," Rina said, winking in a very un-Rina way, "he said he needed this to be over. And then he turned around, appointed Dad the CEO again with some conditions, got Vik out of jail and—"

"When?"

"In the last couple of weeks. But he's not the controlling stock owner. You are," her father said, something almost like a smile twitching at his lips.

Jia had to reach for the pillar to steady herself. "What?"

"He said the only reason he wasn't also sending me to prison, for stealing from his father, for treating you with such…neglect was you. And the condition that he imposed was that I—"

"You treat me like a daughter you care about. As if I'm not the walking, talking symbol of your wife's infidelity," Jia said, giving voice to the words she'd wanted to for so long.

His father blanched. "I was wrong, Jia. On so many levels. And I'm here willingly to make any amends I can. I planned to fly out and see you even before Apollo began another level of upheaval in the company." Her father stared at his hands, and his mouth pursed. "I didn't realize what I had in you until I had nothing else."

Jia wanted to believe him. While he had never loved her as he should, he had never lied to her, or said a cross word to her either. And she did see the glimmer of truth in his eyes now. But, suddenly, his affection, his amends didn't matter much. Maybe she was just as good as Apollo at keeping grudges but right now, she had no bandwidth left to heal this particular relationship.

She simply nodded in his direction, bid her brother goodbye and left her childhood home with her happy sister by her side and a box full of memories.

Her heart was so full to bursting that she thought it might explode out of her chest. He had written the company he'd worked so hard to own into her name, he'd looked after them despite everything, had even forgiven the man he'd hated for years.

If there was a teeny pinch of doubt about his love for her, Jia had none now.

Jia had meant to fly out the same evening but when she'd gone back to the luxury hotel room she'd booked herself into, on Apollo's card, she found that she was exhausted. Every inch of her wanted to go back to him, to their bed, to their room, to that beautiful house where she'd discovered how much she loved him.

But after she'd showered, changed into one of Apollo's T-shirts that she'd carefully packed in her bag, and crawled into the large, luxurious king bed, sleep never came.

She turned and tossed for a couple of hours, then, finally sat up and ordered room service. Lunch had been a salad with Rina at one of their favorite places and she'd passed up dinner in pursuit of sleep.

When a knock came mere minutes later, she grabbed a robe, tied it and opened the door. To find Apollo standing there, his coat jacket on his arm.

Shirt buttons undone, a thick stubble on his jaw and his eyes wary with dark shadows cradling them, he looked rough and twisted inside out and somehow... incomplete. Exactly like she did.

Shaking from deep within, she opened the door wider and simply stood aside. Sudden, intense energy swathed what had felt like a vast space.

Jia watched as he threw the jacket on one of the chairs, paced the sitting lounge and then, after what felt like an eternity of seconds, came to face her. She, not having budged an inch from when she'd opened the door, pressed herself against it. She didn't feel fear, obviously. But something else. Something primal and so real that she felt dizzy under the weight of it.

"If you're angry that I came to New York anyway, let me explain," she started.

He shook his head. "I knew you would two minutes after I left our bedroom. And I've never, not even in that first moment, ever wanted to change who you are, or how you love so wholeheartedly. You're like a blazing sunset, *matia mou*. It was never... I wasn't trying to tell you that you couldn't see your bloody family. If you want, I'll arrange for them to—"

"I know that, Apollo. I also know that I broke the little tenuous trust you placed in me."

"Little and tenuous, *agapi*? The sky itself couldn't contain the trust I have in you. The love I feel for you."

Jia trembled, and fought the sob rising up from her stomach, through her teeth like some great storm. But he stole that away too, filling her with shock when he went to his knees in front of her. "I'm sorry. I never

ever meant to hurt you. I... I wanted you to love me. I wanted you to choose me for nothing but me. And I lost myself in that."

He leaned forward and pressed his mouth to her belly. "The thought of losing you and this baby and this..." a serrated growl left his mouth, his massive shoulders trembling like an evergreen bending under a gale "...turned me into that powerless, helpless monster again."

"Only I get to call you that. And after everything you did for my family...thank you."

"Thank you, Jia. It wasn't only for you, *ne?* It was for us." Then he looked up and Jia cradled his cheeks and she thought she might faint at the love shining in his eyes. "You have released me from a prison of my own making. And suddenly, all I have is this overpowering, all-consuming need to adore you and love you and kiss you for the rest of our lives. Will you let me, Jia? Will you marry me again because I cannot imagine my life without you?"

Jia nodded and fell to her knees. He caught her and kissed her, and that sob she'd tried to hold off so hard broke through anyway.

Which of course made her grumpy husband very angry. He shot to his feet with her in his arms, brought her to the luxurious bed and held her in his lap, and clasped her jaw with a firm grip she loved. "No more tears, *agapi. Parakalo.* I can't bear to see them. I adore you, *yineka mou*, and if you continue to neglect your health, you will force me to—"

"I won't," Jia said, hiding her face in his throat.

"And will you take better care of yourself? Will you eat?"

"I want to eat," Jia said, giggling into his skin. "It's your little bean that uses my stomach as its very own washer and dryer."

Apollo looked up, stars and tears in his eyes, his palm covering her belly with a gentle reverence. "You're happy about this, then?"

Such anguish flickered through the question that Jia had to swallow before she spoke. "Yes. Absolutely. I want this, with you. I want to have at least two more and I want us to love them as much as we love each other, and play with them, and hug them and teach them how to build castles. But more than anything, more than even this, Apollo, I want a life with you. I want to love you and be loved by you. Forever and ever."

"All of it, and so much more, it's all yours, Jia. I'm all yours."

She buried her face in his chest and clung to him while he pressed tender, reverent kisses up and down her temple, jaw and neck.

Finally, after what felt like hours but was mere minutes, her heart settled. Especially when he pulled her under him and began to lavish her with kisses and promises.

EPILOGUE

THREE WEEKS LATER, as afternoon gave way to early evening, Jia tried her best not to steal a glance out the bedroom's window at Apollo's, no, their family home.

While she'd spent most of the afternoon napping and daydreaming and drooling over Apollo's sweatshirt that she'd wrapped around herself—because he'd been gone for the last three days arranging her surprise—Christina came in to help her get ready.

Which wasn't really necessary. Yes, Jia was showing, because the bean was growing at a steady, good pace, but Apollo's sisters and mom and he himself, of course, treated her like she was the first one in the entire galaxy to give birth.

Anticipation fluttering through her, she pulled on loose jeans and a lacy, flowy top that flared from under her breasts to still give her a nice shape. The top was a shimmery ivory silk with pearl beading along its neckline, a gift from Chiara. Jia had laughed when she'd opened the package, because Apollo's sister finally seemed to have understood that she was never going to get Jia to wear frilly, over-the-top dresses.

In the week since he'd told her, Jia hadn't asked Apollo what the surprise was and it had come at extreme risk, since no one in her life had ever taunted her with one. But, knowing that getting this right was really important for her everything-must-be-perfect husband in this new, fragile, overwhelming stage of their relationship, she had stopped trying to coerce various family members into spilling the secret.

When she came down the stairs, her eyes widened. The entire house had been lit up with soft fairy lights and was overflowing with extended family and friends—most she was beginning to recognize now. Uniformed waiters weaved around the crowd with serving trays filled with champagne and other drinks. For a split second, Jia thought she'd seen her father and sister but she was being pulled along.

Congratulations and cheers surrounded her, with that great-aunt and this uncle interrupting them on their way to the backyard. Standing at the entrance to the patio, Jia spied the large white marquee. And past the white marquee, following the cleared walking trail, an arch had been set up with lilies and white roses curving around it, along with twinkling lights. Behind it was the gentle lapping of the ocean and above her, a canopy of stars, as if the sky itself had decided to put on a show.

No, as if it had been commanded to put on a show by her grumpy beast of a husband.

Breath hitching, Jia walked down the steps, only to find that a path had been made up of red rose petals toward the arch. As if someone had orchestrated it by magic, every single guest settled into their chair.

"Jia?"

She turned to find her father, trying his best to not crowd her.

"May I give you away, please?"

While their relationship would never be the one she'd imagined, the new one—mostly repaired and forged by his efforts—was not bad. Tears filling her eyes, she nodded. And on the way, she spied her sister, her eyes bright and shining.

And there, at the end of the small path, standing in a black Armani suit that made him so gorgeous that her knees buckled, was Apollo. Jia forgot everything, everyone as she stared up at him.

She could feel his eyes travel down her length and he laughed as they lingered on her top and jeans. When his gaze swept back up, pausing just for a second on her chest, to her hair, pleasure suffused her. "Will you not come to me, Jia?" he said, extending his arm out to her. But even the darkness couldn't mask the hoarse tremble in his voice.

"You should have told me what you were planning," she whispered, beyond overjoyed.

"And have you show up in some frilly dress that's not you? I adore you as you are, *pethi mou*. And I wanted to give you a wedding under the stars."

Jia breathed hard, awed again by this man who heard every sleepy wish and dream she mumbled about. So, she went to him, her heart already given over to him.

"You take my breath away, *yineka mou*," he said, lifting her knuckles to his mouth and pressing a soft kiss. "And nothing, nothing, in the world has ever rendered me so."

And now she could see his face that she adored so much—that high forehead, and the arrogant thrust of his nose and those wide, thin lips that had kissed and caressed every inch of her in desire and affection and... reverence.

Then she turned to look out over the grounds and he was behind her, his arms coming around to rest on her belly again. He was going to do that a lot, Jia realized. Their guests laughed at their unconventional behavior but then they didn't know that she was the one who had proposed this marriage to the man she adored.

"You're ready to marry me again, then?" Apollo murmured in her ear.

"Yes, please. Now," she whispered and then with her hand in his, she followed him toward a life that she knew would never be lonely or empty or unloved. Even past the contract deadline.

* * * * *

Did you fall in love with Contractually Wed*?*
Then why not try these other fabulous stories
by Tara Pammi?

The Reason for His Wife's Return
An Innocent's Deal with the Devil
Saying "I Do" to the Wrong Greek
Twins to Tame Him
Fiancée for the Cameras

Available now!

VOWS OF
REVENGE

JULIA JAMES

MILLS & BOON

Memories of happy holidays in the Highlands
with my family.

CHAPTER ONE

DAMOS KALLINIKOS STOOD beside the excavation's director, Dr Michaelis, looking out over the site, paying only cursory attention to what was being said to him about the work being carried out around them. He was not here because he was interested in Bronze Age settlements on this remote island in the Aegean—though the good doctor thought he was—and nor, indeed, as he had trailed quite deliberately, because the Kallinikos Corporation might be interested in sponsoring the dig. No, his interest was completely different.

His lancing gaze went out over the site's excavators, many on their knees in the dusty earth, inching their way deeper with trowels and infinite care, some going back and forth, taking photos of finds or carrying them, with even more care, to the tables set out under the shade of olive trees around the edge of the site.

So, which one was she? She wasn't one of the females on her feet, so she must be one of those kneeling. He'd never met her in real life, but the photos he'd had taken of her by his investigators were clear enough. As clear as the résumé they'd provided him with of her particulars.

Kassia Bowen Andrakis, twenty-six years old, English mother, Greek father. The mother he knew nothing about, and cared less—the opposite was true for her father. Yorgos Andrakis was a very familiar figure to him indeed. He was one of Greece's wealthiest men—and one of the most unpleasant. Damos had met him enough times to have that reputation confirmed.

But he didn't care about his personality—only about his latest business venture.

And the means Yorgos Andrakis was using to secure it.

Damos's expression hardened. Well, Andrakis would not succeed. The company he was aiming to add to his acquisitions was, in fact, going to be acquired by himself. Cosmo Palandrou's freight, transport and logistics business was ripe for takeover. Despite Cosmo's inept handling of what he had inherited, resulting in strikes and disaffection amongst his badly treated workforce, which had led to client contracts increasingly being cancelled, there was a significant amount of untapped value in the business—once it had competent management at the helm.

Damos had plans for its expansion too—capitalising on the large number of currently under-exploited prime site depots, developing new markets and maximising the synergy with his own marine-based interests. Oh, yes, there was a lot about Cosmo's business that he wanted.

But so did Yorgos Andrakis.

Andrakis, though—as usual with all his acquisitions—wanted to buy it cut-price, so that when he broke the business up, as he would, for that was his way with acquisitions, plundering them for what he could strip out, he would maximise his profits.

Cosmo, however, was driving a hard bargain with Andrakis—he wanted more, and the 'more' that Andrakis was prepared to offer him, according to Damos's sources, was right here—digging in Bronze Age dirt.

Kassia Andrakis. The daughter Yorgos Andrakis was

planning to marry off to Cosmo in order to get hold of Cosmo's company. The bride-to-be who would make Cosmo a son-in-law to Yorgos Andrakis. A win-win all round.

Except that Damos had other plans for Kassia Andrakis…

His eyes narrowed. He'd just spotted her. She'd looked up momentarily, wiping her brow with the back of her hand under the hot sun, before resuming the careful twisting of her trowel around something she seemed to have found. Yes, that was her, all right—it tallied with the photos.

He let his eyes rest on her a moment. Did she know of her father's intentions for her? If she did, she surely could not be a fan. No woman would be. Cosmo Palandrou shared Yorgos Andrakis's abrasive, repellent personality, and physically he was just as unattractive—overweight, with pouched, close-set eyes, flaccid jawline and a slack mouth.

No, Kassia Andrakis could scarcely want to be Cosmo's bride.

But there was something Damos was going to ensure she *did* want to be—something that would stop Andrakis's scheme in its tracks, leaving the way clear for Damos to scoop up Cosmo's company himself.

Because Cosmo Palandrou was going to discover that Kassia Andrakis was the very last woman he would want as his bride…

He turned to the excavation's director.

'Fascinating,' he murmured. 'Could we take a closer look, do you think?'

Kassia Andrakis was getting to her feet. In her hand, Damos could see, was a shard of pottery. The timing was perfect.

Damos nodded towards her. 'Is that something just uncovered?'

Without waiting for an answer he started to stroll forward. Towards the woman he wanted to meet—the woman who was, although as yet she absolutely no idea of it, going to become his next mistress…

Kassia felt sweat trickling down her back and between her breasts. Her tee shirt was damp with it, and her cotton trousers grimed with dirt from where she'd been digging. She studied what she'd just uncarthed—definitely a piece of a stirrup jar, once used for storing olive oil, over three millennia ago—then carried it carefully across to the table for initial cataloguing and identification.

'Ah, Kassia—what have you got there, hmm?'

The voice of the director of the excavation made her look up as she approached the table.

She opened her mouth to speak, to tell him what she'd found, but no words came. Her eyes had gone, as if pulled by a magnet stronger than that at the earth's core, to the man beside Dr Michaelis. He was completely out of place in his pale grey expensive business suit—top dollar, she could see at a glance—with his dark burgundy silk tie, high-gloss black shoes and gleaming gold watch around his wrist. He looked as though he'd just walked out of a board meeting.

But that wasn't what was making her stare. It was the fact that this man, whoever he was—tall, lean and impeccably groomed—was, quite simply, the most incredible-looking man she had ever seen in her life…

Damos put a smile on his face. Just the right amount of a smile. But behind the nicely calculated smile his thoughts were racing.

So, this was Andrakis's daughter. Well, anyone looking less like the kind of woman he usually consorted with he could not envisage—she was the very opposite of glamorous. But he made the necessary allowances. She'd been kneeling in the dirt, in the heat, so he could hardly be surprised at her flushed face, the smudge of dusty soil on one cheek, and the hair liberally sprinkled with dust too, working its way loose untidily from the tight knot clamped at the back of her head. As for what she was wearing...

Damos's cataloguing was thorough—and ruthless.

A sweated-out shapeless tee in a singularly unlovely shade of mustard, and baggy cotton trousers with dirt on the knees in mud-brown. Feet stuck into worn trainers, also covered in dust and dried soil. Figure tall and gangly—impossible to tell more under those shapeless clothes, and quite probably that was just as well.

No. Kassia Andrakis, standing there, flushed and awkward, looking grubby and messy in her drab and dusty work clothes, with her shoulders stooped from kneeling, did not present an alluring image.

Can I really go through with this? Have an affair with this unlikely woman?

The question was in his head before he could stop it. Then his mouth tightened. His personal opinions of her as a female were irrelevant. She was a means to an end—that was all. And in pursuit of that end—which was lucrative and therefore a worthwhile one to him—he was prepared to put himself out.

As he was already doing.

He put a questioning expression on his face now. 'Will you show us?' he invited.

For a moment the woman he'd bestowed his smile upon did not move. She'd already frozen when she'd looked up from the shard cradled in her hands to see him standing there, beside the excavation's director, and now he could see she looked like a rabbit caught in headlights. Just before it was turned into mush on the road…

Well, maybe that was a promising sign, at least. Not that it surprised him. Without vanity, life had taught him ever since his teens that women liked what they saw when they looked at him. Even before he'd made his money that had been so. Now, with money made, the problem was more to keep them at arm's length. Though of course he enjoyed making his selection of those whose company he decided was most useful to him—and most pleasurable.

As 'new money'—very new indeed—he knew it did him no harm to be seen with a well-known face on his arm, so he liked to select women already in the public eye, from actresses and TV personalities to models and social-ites. All beautiful, all glamorous, all alluring. All of whom loved basking in the limelight and knew just how to do it. Women who knew, too, that being seen with him was good for them—their egos as well as their careers. No woman ever objected to an affair with him.

His eyes rested unreadably on this woman who—how-ever unlike any of her predecessors she looked, and the very antithesis of glamour—was going to be next in that line. She would not object either—he would make sure of it. She would enjoy being his mistress.

But first he had to get her there…

She still had that rabbit-caught-in-the-headlights blank expression, and to it was now added a stain of hot colour across her already flushed cheeks that Damos knew had nothing to do with the baking heat of the day.

As if belatedly realising she could not just stand there and stare at him, she gave a start. 'Er…' she said, as if speaking coherently were utterly beyond her.

Her director came to her rescue. He peered forward at

the grimy shard. 'Let me see—a shoulder, definitely, and judging by the curve the original would have been at least twenty centimetres tall. Did you see the rest of it?'

Damos saw Kassia Andrakis's eyes switch to her director, but it was as if it were an effort—as if there were weights on them.

'Um... I think so—well, definitely more fragments. A bit of the pouring lip and some of one of the handles.'

Her voice was distracted, and that high colour was still in her cheeks.

It didn't suit her.

Damos flicked his eyes away, back to what they were supposed to be looking at.

'Is that some kind of decoration I can make out?' he asked, as if he were interested.

'Yes,' enthused Dr Michaelis.

He started to wax lyrical about the kind of ceramic decoration prevalent at the time, and Damos listened politely until the director ran out of things to talk about.

Damos turned his attention back to Yorgos Andrakis's daughter. 'So, can you show me how you go about getting the rest of the pieces out? I take it you have to go carefully?'

He saw her swallow, clearly still ill at ease.

'Um...' she said, then glanced uncertainly at her director.

He took charge immediately. 'I'll get this piece photographed and listed,' he said, deftly removing the shard from her hands. 'You show our visitor how we work.'

He seemed keen that she should do so, and Damos knew why. He was a prospective sponsor—whatever he wanted would be immediately offered.

Damos saw the colour deepen in Kassia Andrakis's face.

'Er...' she said, visibly hesitating again.

Her vocabulary was not large, it seemed, so Damos helped her out.

He took her elbow. 'Do show me,' he said. 'It's all quite fascinating.'

A look came his way—not one he expected. At first he took it for surprise—and then something more suspicious. He countered it by bestowing upon her a smile—a bland one.

'I've never visited an archaeological excavation before,' he said smoothly.

She stepped away slightly, so he had to let go her elbow.

'Why are you here now?' she posed.

There was something new about her—something… guarded. He didn't want it there. He wanted her open to him. Susceptible.

'I might be interested in sponsoring one,' he remarked, starting to head towards the trench she'd been working at.

'Why?'

Her question followed him. He looked back casually.

'It's tax deductible,' he said.

Her expression changed again. Tightened. If she was going to say something he wouldn't let her.

'Why disapprove? Wouldn't you rather excess profits from business were used to do something for the country—the community?'

He stepped carefully down into the shallow trench, mindful of his handmade shoes and his bespoke suit.

'OK, so show me what you do.'

He was aware of heads turning to see what was happening—aware, too, that he was getting attention from another female, a full-figured blonde. But he simply smiled blandly again, then hunkered down next to Kassia Andrakis.

'Mind your shoes,' he heard her say sharply. 'The dust gets everywhere.'

'Thank you for the warning,' he murmured.

He picked up her discarded trowel and held it out to her pointedly. She took it, but he sensed her reluctance.

'I really don't know why you're interested...' she said, resuming her kneeling. Her voice wasn't as sharp now, but it was still not exactly enthusiastic. 'You don't need to know or see the nitty-gritty to sponsor a dig. No need to get your hands dirty,' she said, and her voice had tightened again.

He got a look from her. One that told him, plain as day, that being hunkered down in a shallow trench, on a dusty dig on a remote island, in no way matched with a man wearing a ten-thousand-euro suit and five-thousand-euro handmade leather shoes.

He met her look straight on.

'My hands have been dirty in my time, believe me,' he said.

He hadn't intended that edge to be in his voice, but he heard it all the same. And there was an edge inside him too. That this daughter of one of Greece's richest men, born herself into wealth, however much she was slumming it now, should presume to criticise him as she was so obviously doing...

She dropped her eyes, fixed her grip on the trowel. She pointed the tip at an uneven piece of undug earth.

'There's likely to be something under there,' she said. 'But you have to be very careful. Like this.'

She gently teased at the hard, dry ground with the tip of the trowel, picking up a nearby bristle brush with her other hand, and whisking away the loosened baked soil. As she did, Damos could see the convex curve of pottery revealed.

'This,' said Kassia Andrakis, 'is the first time sunlight has been on this piece of ceramic for over three thousand years.'

There was something in her voice—something that made Damos look at her. He wondered what it was, and then realised. It was a word he'd never spoken—but he knew what it was.

Reverence.

She was looking down at the humble piece of pottery as if it were a holy icon.

'Three thousand years,' she said again, and that same reverence was still there in her voice. 'Think of it—think of that age…so long gone. A world as vibrant as our own, with international trade routes, art and civilisation, learning and discovery…'

She looked across at him. It was the first time, Damos realised, she had actually made eye contact with him. He also realised the unflattering rush of colour to her cheeks was gone, and that her eyes were grey-blue, with almost a silvery sheen.

She gestured across the site with her trowel and went on, her voice not so much reverent now as impassioned. 'This place—all of it—is just a minute fraction of that world. A world that came to a catastrophic end three thousand years ago. So much is lost from that time—which is why we *must* do what we can to preserve what is left.'

Damos frowned. 'Catastrophic?' he echoed. He felt his interest piqued, which surprised him.

She nodded. 'Yes, the collapse of the Bronze Age all over the Eastern Mediterranean happened very suddenly. The population crashed…sites were abandoned. Living standards plummeted. It was a dark age—a very dark age.'

He got to his feet. 'Tell me more,' he said. 'Tonight. Over dinner.'

He didn't wait for her reaction, simply climbing out of the

trench and walking towards Dr Michaelis, who was over by one of the tables. Dr Michaelis looked at Damos hopefully.

'Fascinating,' Damos said. He paused a fraction. 'So much so,' he went on, keeping his voice smooth, 'that I'd like to ask your young colleague—' he nodded back towards the trench '—to expound further. This evening. Over dinner.'

Dr Michaelis opened his mouth, then closed it again. Then a shrewd look—surprisingly shrewd, given his ingenuous enthusiasm previously—entered his eye. It was, Damos could see—and knew perfectly well why—tinged with surprise.

Not at the invitation.

At the person invited.

If it had been the voluptuous blonde he wouldn't have been so surprised.

Damos decided it was time to deflect both surprise and speculation.

'I know Kassia's father,' he said, giving a slight smile. 'He mentioned to me that I might encounter her here on this latest dig she's involved in.'

It was a lie, but that was irrelevant. And anyway, he did know Yorgos Andrakis slightly—they moved, after all, in the same affluent plutocratic circles in Athens.

Dr Michaelis's expression cleared. This was a suitable explanation for what his wealthy visitor and hopefully prospective sponsor had just put to him.

'Ah, of course,' he said genially. 'Now,' he said, 'is there anything else that I can tell you, or show you, that might be of interest to you? You have only to say!'

Damos smiled politely. 'Thank you, but what I have already seen is very impressive. I shall give your worthy endeavours very serious consideration. I am glad I had this opportunity to call by. I'm en route to Istanbul, on business, and this was a timely deviation.'

He held out his hand, let Dr Michaelis shake it in farewell, and turned to go. As he neared the cordoned-off perimeter he glanced back. Kassia's voluptuous blonde colleague, he noticed, not with any surprise, was covertly watching him. Kassia Andrakis, he saw, was not. Her attention was focussed right back on digging. Not on him at all.

A glint showed in the depths of his eyes. Kassia Andrakis might be ignoring him now—but for all that there was only one place she was going to end up.

His bed.

It was just a question of getting her there...

Pleased with his progress on that front so far, he headed back to his waiting car, parked on the dry, dusty lane leading through the overgrown olive grove beyond the dig. He got in, glad of the air con. Then, sitting back, he reached inside his jacket pocket, took out his gold monogrammed pen and a silver, monogrammed case, withdrawing a business card from it. After casually scrawling what he wanted to say on the back of it he handed it to his driver.

'Take this down to the female in that first trench. Not the blonde—the one with the mustard-coloured tee shirt.'

He sat back, eyes half closed, contemplating the next step in his campaign of eventual seduction. Dinner on his yacht would be the first step. And then... Well, he would have to see what would serve him best. A lot of money was riding on it—for himself.

As for Kassia Andrakis... She would enjoy her affair with him—women always did and she would be no exception. Why should she be? He would ensure her time with him was pleasurable, and she would enjoy his attentions.

She does not look like she's used to much male attention...

He felt himself frown slightly. There was something… troubling…about Kassia Andrakis. In the normal course of events she was not the type of woman he'd pursue—academic and studious, instead of glamorous and publicity-hungry. But because of his ambition to thwart her father's plans for her to his own advantage his focus of necessity must be on her.

His frown deepened. Yes, he had to make allowances for the fact that she'd been working all day long in the heat and the dust, so would hardly have been looking her best… There was a questioning look in his half-closed eyes now. And yet she seemed to be almost…self-effacing. Was that the word? About herself and her appearance. Flustered at even the most innocuous of attentions from him. She was tall, and yet her shoulders were hunched—maybe not just from kneeling, but as if she were trying to hide her height. And her straggly, tugged-back hair, covered in dust and needing a good wash, did absolutely nothing for her either.

It was as if she could not care less. Her awkward manner had been obvious. His expression changed suddenly. Until she'd made that impassioned plea for preserving the antiquities she was excavating. Then her eyes had lit, making him notice them for the first time…

Grey-blue, with that silvery sheen…

He frowned very slightly.

Intriguing—and quite at odds with the rest of her…

His ruminations about Yorgos Andrakis's daughter were interrupted by his driver returning, getting back into his seat, gunning the engine, driving off.

Damos put Kassia Andrakis and his plans for her out of his head, and took out his phone to check his messages.

CHAPTER TWO

KASSIA SAT ON the bed in her little room in the *pension* she and others in the excavation team were staying at. She was staring at the back of the business card that had been handed to her by a chauffeur in a peaked cap that afternoon. A chauffeur of any kind—let alone in a peaked cap—was, to put it mildly, out of place on an island like this. But then the man who'd had the card delivered to her was totally out of place.

His handmade suit and shoes...his silk tie, gold watch—the whole caboodle!

But now at least she knew who he was.

Damos Kallinikos.

The name on the business card meant nothing to her, even though Dr Michaelis had told her he'd said he knew her father—hence inviting her, rather than him, the dig's director, for dinner this evening. Or that was what both Kassia and her boss could only assume, for there was certainly no other reason for singling her out. She wasn't the type of female who got asked to dine by drop-dead gorgeous men for her own sake—she knew that well enough.

As for the company Damos Kallinikos headed, according to the printed side of the business card, she'd never heard of that either. New money, by the sound of it. New money springing up in Greece after the financial crash in the first decade of the century, which had ruined countless lives and provided an opportunity for those canny and ruthless enough to take advantage to scoop up some bankrupt bargains.

It was what her father had done, she knew—boosting his already considerable wealth by snapping up businesses that had gone under in the crisis at rock-bottom prices. And he'd scooped up another round only a few years ago, when the global pandemic had hit, all but destroying Greece's vital tourist industry during those lengthy lockdowns that had immobilised the world, sending yet more businesses struggling. From deserted hotels to abandoned, unsellable, untransportable inventory, he'd turned their loss into yet more profit for himself.

Was that what this Damos Kallinikos had done too? Even if he hadn't, she could still hear his voice saying *'tax deductible'* as if in justification for caring about his country's treasured past. But she could hear Dr Michaelis's hopeful voice as well.

'Kassia, I do hope you will accept his dinner invitation and do your best to persuade him to sponsor us, so we can have a second season next year. Chatting to this man over dinner may well just swing it for us.'

She gave a sigh. Well, she would do her best—though she wasn't comfortable about it. Oh, not about pitching for sponsorship, but for a quite different reason.

As she sat on her bed Damos Kallinikos was vivid in her mind's eye—and so were his drop-dead good looks. Looks that had sent the colour flaring into her cheeks.

She made a face. What on earth did it matter that Damos Kallinikos looked the way he did? A man like that would not look twice at a woman like herself—someone totally lacking the kind of appeal that females like Maia, for example, possessed. Her mouth twisted. Hadn't her father drummed that into her all her life?

The sneering echo of her father's voice stung in her memory.

'Look at you! You're like a piece of string! A stick! Not even a decent face to take a man's eye off your stringy body! Your mother might have cost me a fortune to be rid of her, but at least she had looks!'

She sighed inwardly, accepting the truth of her father's criticism. Her mother was petite and shapely, with china-blue eyes set in a heart-shaped face and softly waving blonde hair. Kassia's own lack of looks were a constant cause for complaint by her father.

'No man will ever want you for yourself! It will only be for my money—for who I am, not you!'

That was his regular accusatory refrain.

She silenced the sneering voice. She was never going to let herself get sucked into her father's scheming, and to that end she should be grateful that her plain looks ruled her out of it. Had she looked like Maia, her father would be touting her all over Athens and beyond. Marrying her off to whoever would be most valuable to him as a son-in-law, making use of her to his own advantage.

As it was, thankfully, he'd all but written Kassia off, telling her to busy herself with her digging in the dirt and to keep out of his way, except for on those few unexpected occasions when he summoned her back to Athens for some social event where he wanted a daughter—even one as un-prepossessing as she was—at his side for some reason. She always obeyed such summons, for she knew her father had got himself made a patron of the provincial museum she worked for, and would make difficulties if she refused.

She stared down at the business card in her hand. This was another summons. In black scrawl on the back Damos Kallinikos had simply written:

The marina, eight o'clock.

She gave a sigh, wishing it were Maia who was being summoned—the girl had already expressed her envy at Kassia getting to spend the evening with the drop-dead fabulous Damos Kallinikos...

Impatiently she got to her feet, heading for the shower. Time to get on with getting ready for the evening ahead. Best not to think about it. Even more, best not to think about Damos Kallinikos—let alone his drop-dead fabulous looks. They were nothing to do with her, and she was the last person he'd ever be interested in in that way.

Yes, definitely best not think about him...

Damos glanced at his watch. It was just gone eight. He was standing on the foredeck of his yacht. Behind him a table had been laid for two. The yacht was moored at the far end of the marina to afford him more privacy. Privacy in which to start the process of seducing Kassia Andrakis.

How would she present herself this evening? Though she was no couture-clad socialite, as Yorgos Andrakis's daughter she would obviously know how to dress the part for an evening on a private yacht. So would she have done her best to glam herself up, or not? He had a gut feeling it would be 'not'. And a few minutes later, when he saw her appear in the marina, he knew he was right.

As she approached the foot of the quay he saw she'd changed out of her work clothes. But only, it seemed, to put on a fresh pair of wide-legged trousers—cotton and dark blue, cheap from a chain store—and a loose-fitting cotton top in a slightly paler blue. The worn, dust-covered trainers had been changed for flat canvas slip-ons. Her hair was brushed, and not straggly now, but still confined into an unflattering tight knot at the back of her head. Not a scrap of make-up adorned her face. She looked clean, neat and tidy—but that was about it.

He gave a mental shrug. He was not put out by her lack of effort to dress for dinner with him on his private yacht. After all, so far as she was concerned this evening was merely an extension of her work, nothing more. Yet even so...

Is there any other reason she makes so little effort with her appearance?

Damon's gaze narrowed slightly. Few women didn't care about their appearance in some respect. So why didn't Kassia Andrakis? Perhaps, though, the clue was in her surname. Had she been a high-profile beauty Yorgos Andrakis would doubtless have made use of it—so maybe she just preferred to keep a low profile?

His mouth thinned. Low profile or not, dressing down or not, Yorgos Andrakis was nevertheless ruthlessly planning to make use of her for his own ends.

As are you, yourself...

He silenced the thought. Yes, seducing Kassia Andrakis was in his interests, but nothing would happen that she did not want. And he reminded himself again that he would make sure she enjoyed their affair. Yet a flicker of something he could not name hovered a moment. He dismissed it. She was coming up to the yacht's mooring, looking up to where he stood by the prow.

'The harbour master told me this was yours,' she announced.

Damos smiled in a welcoming fashion. 'Indeed, it is. Come on aboard.'

He indicated the gangplank, a little way down the length of the yacht, and she went to it, stepping up to the deck, glancing around as she did.

'She's a new acquisition,' he said blandly.

'Very nice,' said Kassia Andrakis politely.

'Thank you. Not to be compared with your father's, of course.'

That got a reaction.

Her expression tightened. 'His is a ridiculous monstrosity!'

'A trophy yacht?' Damos nodded. 'But the helipad must certainly come in useful for speedy arrivals and departures, should the occasion arise. However, each to his own, and I prefer something a little more modest.'

Kassia's expression stayed tight. '*Modest* is relative,' she remarked. 'All yachts are trophy yachts.'

'Rich men's toys? I agree.' He smiled, refusing to take offence. 'Now, come and have a drink on this particular rich man's new toy.'

He indicated the foredeck, where one of his crew was waiting to serve drinks. Kassia moved forward, looking about her. She seemed tense, and Damos wanted to put her at ease.

'What may I offer you?' he asked politely. 'Champagne is often *de rigueur* on yachts—however modest! But perhaps you would prefer something else?'

'An orange juice spritzer, if that is possible,' came the answer.

'Of course.'

Damos nodded at the crew member, who disappeared below deck, to reappear shortly with Kassia's drink in a tall glass, and his own martini. His crew knew what he drank at this hour of the day, and he murmured his thanks as he took his glass, handing Kassia's to her.

'We'll dine in fifteen minutes,' he instructed, and the crew member nodded and disappeared again.

Damos came and stood beside Kassia—but not too close—as she sipped at her spritzer and looked back across the marina. It was busy, but not full. A couple of upmarket restaurants were positioned to take advantage of the moored yachts, and were doing a healthy trade. The lights from the marina and from the vessels moored, as well as the green and red harbour lights, all danced on the water, and the tinkling sound of furled sails and masts moving in the light breeze, and the deeper sound of hulls tapping against the stone moorings, added to the atmosphere.

'There's nothing like a harbour,' Damos said, looking around, his tone relaxed, trying to encourage her to do likewise. 'It's a haven from the open sea, but also a portal to that sea—to the voyages beyond. A harbour is a place of promise and opportunity. Now and down all the long ages past—and ages yet to come.'

He saw her turn her head to look at him. He smiled down at her.

'Too fanciful for a hard-nosed businessman who only sees archaeology as a tax-deductible instrument for greater profit?'

She didn't answer, but he got the impression she was studying him. Covertly, yes, but she was making some kind of assessment. Not reaching a conclusion, though. Wariness radiated from her—as it had that afternoon.

He took a meditative sip of his martini, looking out to sea past the harbour wall with its ever-blinking green and red lights.

'So, what kind of seafaring did they get up to in the Bronze Age?' he asked.

After all, that was what this evening was supposed to be about—expanding his knowledge of her field, so as to decide whether to invest in the work.

'It was extensive,' she answered. 'Right across the Mediterranean. Trade was widespread. As you probably know, the copper for bronze is plentiful in this region—Cyprus, of course, is named after the metal itself—but the tin needed to make bronze had to come from further afield.'

Damos could tell from her voice that she was somewhat stilted, and he focussed on drawing her out. Sticking to the subject she was most interested in—the one she believed he'd invited her here to discuss—he asked another question.

'How did they navigate in those days?' he posed.

'It's not my speciality,' came the answer, 'but if you're genuinely interested I can point you towards those who have made it theirs.'

There was sufficient inflection in her voice for Damos to know that she personally doubted that.

'In general, the Mycenaeans—and the Minoans and all the East Mediterranean peoples of the time—knew nothing of the compass, so they steered by the sun and the stars, and by the known distance from the shore plus speed and heading.'

'Dead reckoning?' put in Damos. 'As ever, right up until the eighteenth century, determining latitude was not so much a problem compared with determining longitude. That took highly accurate time-keeping—not available to the ancients. What was boat-building like in those times?'

'Boats were round-hulled, with square sail and oars which would one day develop into the famous biremes and triremes of the later Classical period—the battle of Salamis and so on. Sails, I believe, were considerably more limited than in later times.'

'Yes, it needed the development of the lateen sail—triangular in shape, but more difficult to operate—to allow vessels to sail much closer to the wind,' commented Damos.

She looked at him, clearly curious now. 'You know a lot.'

Damos gave a slightly crooked smile. 'I grew up in Piraeus and went off to sea as soon as I could. Working on merchant ships and crewing on the trophy yachts you so despise. It was the latter experience,' he said pointedly, 'that inspired me to be rich enough one day to buy my own yacht.'

'And now you do,' she said dryly, sipping at her spritzer.

He shook his head. 'No,' he said.

'No?' Kassia looked at him again. 'Is this only chartered?'

'No—as in, no, I don't only own my yacht—or charter it. I own a fleet—both leisure and merchant marine.'

'Oh,' she said. 'That's your money, is it?'

He smiled. 'Some of it.' He nodded along the line of the marina with its moored yachts. 'At least two of those are mine—chartered. Of course, like your father, my business interests are diverse. Ah!' He changed his voice, turning his head. 'Dinner arrives,' he said.

He held out one of the two chairs set at the table and Kassia sat down before he took his place as well. He exchanged some pleasantries with his crew members, who set down the dishes, placed a wine bottle in the chiller on the table, and discreetly retired.

'Do you eat seafood?' he enquired politely. 'If not, there is a vegetarian alternative.'

'No, that's fine,' came the answer.

She started to help herself from the central platter, piled high with prawns, calamari and shellfish, and Damos did likewise, adding leaves and salads to his plate, as did she. She didn't pick at her food, he noticed. So many of the females he consorted with visibly calorie-counted. Kassia Andrakis didn't look as though she did—or had any reason to. Despite her loose-fitting clothes, he could see she was definitely slender, not fulsome in her figure.

He eyed her through half-lidded eyes. She might be downplaying her appearance, but her slenderness was appealing, and now that he had more leisure to peruse her across the table, he could see that her face—still without make-up, but no longer flushed and dabbed with dusty soil—was fine-boned. Was that the English side of her? he wondered.

He found himself wanting to see if he'd just imagined that silvery sheen in her eyes when she'd enthused about her work. His half-lidded eyes moved their focus, and he also found that he wanted to know what she might look like with her hair loosed from its confining, studious knot.

What she might look like without any clothes at all...

His veiled gaze rested on her a moment longer. Had she obviously dressed herself up to the nines, glammed herself up for him, he might well have ventured, over a leisurely dinner and increasingly intimate conversation, to speculate that the night might end with her going down to his state-room to spend the night with him.

A woman who was interested in him that way, and in whom he had made clear a similar interest from himself, would have given signs of it—indicated that she found his attentions of that nature welcome to her and invited more of them. Until a mutual understanding of their respective willingness to take things further had been arrived at.

Kassia Andrakis, dressed down and unadorned, was showing no sign at all that she expected dinner with him to be anything other than what it purported to be. True, she was no longer flustered and awkward, as she'd been at the dig, but nor was she showing any visible awareness of him as anything other than a potential sponsor. No sign at all that she found him attractive as a man.

Should he be put off by that? He dismissed it out of hand. However composed she was being now, her initial reaction to him at the dig had been sufficiently revealing to him—

he had no need to doubt it. But right now he wasn't even trying to get her to see him in that way. Coming on strong to her at this stage would be crass.

Worse, it might arouse her suspicions.

Because there was one thing he was discovering about Kassia Andrakis and he was clearly going to have to take it into account. She was no idiot. Oh, not just because she was a professional archaeologist, who obviously knew her stuff inside out, but because right from the start he had seen that she was perfectly prepared to assess, judge and downright challenge him on his apparent interest in her field and his declared intention of considering sponsoring it.

Disarming her wariness—and the assessing acuity she directed at him—was going to take some finessing.

His veiled gaze rested on her a moment.

He'd known from the start that Kassia Andrakis was nothing like the women he usually consorted with—and not just because the only reason for his own interest in her was her father's business plan and his own plans to thwart Yorgos Andrakis by the method he'd selected. No, Kassia Andrakis was different from his usual type of female in *herself*, not just in the circumstances of who she was and why. And therefore she had his attention—more so, he was finding, than he'd originally assumed.

Seducing her, he was starting to realise, was not going to be a simple case of showering flattering compliments upon her. She was a woman unused to receiving them and he was a man whose sexual interests were usually blatantly targeted at glamorously beautiful females. No, a far more subtle approach was going to be needed to disarm her—charm her into his bed.

A disquieting glint showed in the depths of his veiled gaze. *It will be a challenge...*

The glint in his eyes deepened. And challenges were something he always found satisfying to achieve.

After all, his whole life had been a challenge. He had challenged the poverty into which he'd been born, changing it through determination, ambition and a hell of a lot of dogged hard work into riches.

So, he mused consideringly, keeping his speculative gaze on her as she ate, maybe Kassia Andrakis was not his usual type of woman, and maybe she was dowdy and unglamorous, and maybe her calm composure was showing no sign at all of responding to his masculinity, but for all that there might be something more enjoyable about seducing her than simply getting the result he was set on.

His thoughts coalesced. It might even be enjoyable for itself…as a challenge he would relish.

He was looking forward to taking it on.

Quite definitely…

That glint was back in his eyes, and he felt a sense of enticing anticipation…

Kassia was just beginning to feel her edge of acute wariness dissipating. Maybe she was getting used to Damos Kallinikos. He was being polite and making conversation, continuing to tell her about his time crewing on rich men's yachts.

'In some respects it was tougher than working on merchant ships,' he said dryly. 'Because you were on call twenty-four-seven, and rich men can be very demanding employers.'

She nodded, making a face as she did. Her father was inconsiderate of anyone who worked for him, and he would never dream of thanking them or showing any appreciation of their work and efforts.

She let her eyes rest on Damos Kallinikos for a moment across the table. She'd already noticed that he said please and thank you to his crew members, and passed the time of day with them pleasantly. That was to his credit, surely?

Her eyes flicked away again. She was conscious that she was not looking at him very much, or for very long—and she knew exactly why. Even though he was not, of course, focussing any kind of masculine attention on her—that was par for the course with her and men—that did not stop him being ludicrously good-looking. Whatever it was that made a man attractive, Damos Kallinikos had it in spades—and then some.

And then some more—

She dragged her thoughts away. No point assessing him in that respect. No point thinking how lethally attractive he was to her sex, with the way his dark hair feathered across his brow and his long eyelashes dipped down over those wine-dark eyes, or how his mouth curved into a half-smile that was tinged with a caustic humour as he regaled her with a particularly capricious demand by a yacht owner.

Their main course was being presented to them—chicken fillets in a wine sauce with saffron rice—and she got stuck in. Absently she lifted the wine glass that Damos Kallinikos had filled, and took a mouthful.

'What do you make of it?' he asked her.

'It's very good,' she said politely—because it was. 'Not that I know much about wine,' she went on. 'What is it?'

'A viognier varietal,' came the answer. 'One of my vineyards has been experimenting…developing a vine that grows well on the volcanic soil here in the Aegean. I'm glad you like it.'

Kassia glanced at him. '*One* of your vineyards?'

'Yes—wine is one of the sectors that I can invest in with

pleasure as well as profit in mind. And I have a particular interest in developing domestic wines. Greek wine should be better known internationally.'

'The blight of retsina?' Kassia rejoined dryly.

'Indeed—though retsina has its place. As do, of course, wines produced locally, entirely for local, low-cost consumption.'

Kassia gave a wry smile. Faint, but definitely a smile—her first of the evening, she realised with a little start.

'On excavations we don't run to more than the local table wines and beer of an evening.'

He looked at her, and she could see curiosity in his expression.

'How do you manage the adaptation?' he asked. 'You are Yorgos Andrakis's daughter—and yet you work digging up broken pots from the dirt.'

She paused a moment, then answered, choosing her words carefully.

'I don't spend much time in Athens—or in being Yorgos Andrakis's daughter. Besides,' she went on, 'I'm not always on excavations. Out of season I'm based at a provincial museum. I spend time studying our findings, cataloguing them, writing them up, contributing to papers, going to conferences—that sort of thing.'

'Not exactly a jet-set lifestyle,' Damos Kallinikos said mordantly.

She shook her head. 'Not my scene,' she agreed. She looked across at him. 'And, since I have no head for business, the only thing for me to do as Yorgos Andrakis's daughter would be to go to parties and spend his money and be "ornamental". But...' she took a breath '... I am not "ornamental", so I'd rather do something useful and dig for broken pots in the dirt and catalogue them.'

He was looking at her now, and there was something in the way he was looking across the lamplit table that she found unnerving. She didn't know why. But it was unnerving, all the same. To stop it, she took a quick mouthful of her wine, and another mouthful of her tender and delicious chicken, and then quite deliberately moved the conversation on.

'Speaking of digging up broken pots—what was it that you wanted to know about our excavation?' she asked. 'Fire away with the questions—after all, it's what I'm here for.'

'So you are…' Damos Kallinikos murmured.

For just a moment that unnerving look was in his eye again—then it vanished. As if it had been cleared away decisively.

'OK, well, let me pick up on something you mentioned to me this afternoon,' he said. 'You said something about the collapse of Bronze Age Civilisation. I didn't know it had. Why did it—and when?'

Kassia felt herself relaxing—and engaging. This was familiar territory to her.

'The "when" is pretty well attested by the archaeological evidence—around 1200 BC or thereabouts. The "why" is more controversial and contentious.'

She reached for her wine again—it really was a very good wine after the table wines she was used to on digs.

'We can see that sites were being abandoned—the great palace complexes, like the most famous at Mycenae—and the population crashed. Linear B, the script of the Mycenaeans, all but disappears, and written Greek doesn't reappear until the adoption of the alphabet from the Phoenicians, in about the tenth century or so BC. The powerful Hittite empire in modern-day Turkey disappears too, and trade plummets in this post-Bronze Age period—though there is evidence of huge demographic changes, either from new arrivals, or from those economically displaced. It's the era of the still mysterious Sea Peoples, raiding and invading, and it's also the most likely time for the legendary Trojan War—'

She drew breath and plunged on, warming to her theme, running through the various possible causes of the collapse—from old theories about newly arriving Dorians from the north to current theories about climate change and the development of iron technology changing the balance of power and warfare. She was in full train, explaining the differences in smelting copper and tin to bronze, and the higher temperatures needed for smelting iron, when she stopped dead.

Damos Kallinikos had finished eating and was sitting back, wine glass in one hand, his other hand resting on the table. His eyes were half lidded, and she had the sudden acute feeling that she was boring him stupid.

She swallowed. 'I'm sorry. It's fascinating to me, but—'

He held up his hand. 'Don't apologise. I asked the question and you answered. I'm spellbound.'

For a moment she had the hideous feeling that he was being sarcastic. But then he leant forward.

'Your face comes alight when you talk with such passion,' he said.

His eyes met hers. Held hers.

Kassia couldn't move. Not a muscle.

Damos wanted to punch the air.

First contact.

First real him-to-her contact.

And all over the collapse of Bronze Age civilisation...

Well, so what? Whatever it took to bring her alive in the way it had just showed in her face was fine by him. Just fine.

Because, however it happens, I need to make personal

*contact with her—make the connection that can eventually
lead to where I want it to go.*

His eyes went on holding hers for a moment longer. As
they did, he felt something go through him—something
unexpected.

Was it the way her face had lit up and, yes, even in the
soft light bathing them on the deck, the way that he'd caught
that silvery glint in her eyes…?

It was doing something to him…

But it was time to back off—which was all part of the
subtle approach that he knew was going to be necessary
with her.

'You know,' he said, injecting just the right amount of
humour and sincerity into his voice—both of which, he
realised, he felt quite genuinely, 'if you intended to make
a sales pitch for getting me to sponsor the dig, you've just
made it.' He looked at her wryly. 'Doesn't it ever strike you
that it is…unusual…to be so passionate about something that
has not existed for over three thousand years?'

There was open curiosity in his voice. Kassia Andrakis
was like no other woman he'd met, and the novelty of it was
catching at him.

'I don't know,' she answered slowly. 'Maybe because it's
a…a continuum. Like I said this afternoon, those people
back then—however long ago it seems to us—were just
like us. Living their lives as best they could. Just as we do.'

His wry look turned into a wry smile. 'That's not a bad
way to live—then or now. Living our lives the best we can.'
Damos heard his voice change. 'It certainly fuelled my determination not to stay poor—and to enjoy all that comes
my way.'

He held her gaze for another moment. He put nothing
into it of flirtation, nor any intimation of it. He wanted only

to keep this moment of contact going. It was something to build on.

Then he glanced towards the wine chiller. 'Speaking of enjoying all that comes our way…this wine will go to waste if we don't finish it.'

He casually refilled her glass, and then his own, replacing the depleted bottle back in its chiller. He'd exaggerated the predicament of the wine—any leftovers would, he knew, be consumed below deck by the crew. One of the perks of the job, and something he was perfectly happy with.

He wanted to keep the atmosphere light, and so, taking another mouthful of his own wine, he sat back again.

'Does your work ever take you to Istanbul?' he asked casually. 'I'll be heading off there tomorrow.'

Kassia shook her head. 'I've visited Hissarlik—the site of Troy—in my time, but I have never made it to Istanbul.'

For a moment Damos considered inviting her to go with him, then set it aside. That would be premature. No, better just to use this evening as prep for planning his next encounter with her. Though where and how were yet to be decided on… One thing was definite, though. When he moved on in his seduction of her he did not want it to be in Greece, and certainly not in Athens. It needed to be kept private—very private. Until, with his goal in sight, it suited him for it to become very public knowledge…

Especially to Cosmo Palandrou.

There was a dark glint of anticipation in his eye. Because that would be the moment when he would have outmanoeuvred Yorgos Andrakis. Spiking his guns completely. Andrakis would have nothing to offer Cosmo—nothing that Cosmo would accept.

Damos's face hardened. No, Cosmo Palandrou would never want Yorgos Andrakis's daughter as his bride…

Not once he knows—and all of Athens knows!—that she's been my mistress...

Because for all that Cosmo might swallow Kassia being a dowdy archaeologist, not a glamorous trophy socialite, providing she brought with her the promise of the Andrakis riches, he wouldn't stomach marrying a blatant cast-off of another man—and Damos Kallinikos at that. That would stick in his craw...would be an affront to his ego and self-esteem...and Andrakis's bid for his company would be dead in the water.

Leaving the way clear for me.

But he wasn't there yet. First he had to get Kassia Andrakis into his bed.

He brought his thoughts back to where they needed to be to achieve that end. How to build on where he'd got with her so far and take it to the next base.

'Do you travel much for your work?' he asked now, in a conversational manner.

'I go to conferences outside Greece sometimes. My mother lives in England, so a UK conference is a good opportunity to visit her.'

Damos paid attention—this was useful intel. He made a mental note to check out any likely UK-based conferences coming up on her subject that she might be likely to attend.

'Your parents are divorced, I take it...?' He trailed off, though he knew the answer perfectly well from his dossier on her.

'Yes, she's English and now remarried—unlike my father. Neither had any more children.' She made a face, half humorous. 'I don't think my mother wanted to ruin her figure, and my father didn't want to risk another hefty child maintenance divorce settlement!'

Damos knew that wry expression was back on his face.

'All rich men fear being married for their money. I've certainly become a lot more popular with women since I made money,' he heard himself saying, and wondered why he was saying it.

He frowned inwardly. Should he have said that? And why say anything about himself at all? This evening was about drawing Kassia out, exploring how best he could achieve his aims for her.

He saw she was looking at him now, but not unsympathetically.

'That's understandable,' she commented. 'Even I—if you can believe it!—get attention paid to me simply because of my father!'

Damos relaxed. This was better—she was revealing things about herself, not making him reveal things about himself.

'Why "if you can believe it"?' He infused just the right amount of uncomprehending curiosity into his voice.

He got a straight look and a straight answer. 'Why else would they pay attention to me?'

She gave a short laugh, but it was without resentment. It was infused, he thought, with wry resignation if anything. And there was that air of indifference to her own appearance that he had picked up on from the start—as though it was just not important to her.

There was a glint in her light eyes as she went on. 'Not everyone, Mr Kallinikos, is sufficiently fascinated by Bronze Age Civilisation as to want my company for dinner!'

This was approaching thin ice, he thought—time to move the conversation off it. But gracefully…and perhaps with some humour at his own expense to deflect the moment.

'Or as keen to find a good tax haven for this year's profits, don't forget!' he said lightly.

He got one of her wry half-smiles in return, and was satisfied.

He returned to a subject he wanted to draw her out on. Herself.

He found himself frowning inwardly for a moment. She had been so upfront about not expecting men to be interested in her. Was that a good sign or a bad sign as far as his prospective seduction was concerned? It definitely meant he had to tread carefully, or her suspicions would be aroused.

Yet that was not his only reaction to her dispassionate disclosure. Surely it was sad that she wrote herself off the way she so obviously did?

No woman should do that.

His own voice cut short the thought. 'So, did you grow up in England?'

'Mostly, yes. I went to boarding school, and then university. I've always spoken Greek, though, and that's helped, of course, with my career.'

The crew were appearing, clearing away empty plates, replacing them with dessert.

'What can I tempt you with?' Damos invited.

He'd ordered a good range, from a sumptuous gateau St Honoré in towering choux pastry, to more frugal fruit and cheese.

Kassia made a face—she was definitely more relaxed with him, Damos could see, and he was highly satisfied with that. He was making good progress...

'It has to be the gateau,' she said. 'How can I possibly resist? But then I'll be virtuous and have some fruit afterwards.'

He laughed, cutting her a very generous portion of the towering dessert, spun with caramel and oozing cream, and then watching her start to tuck into it with relish and clear enjoyment.

It set a new thought running…

A woman who enjoys the sensuous pleasure of a rich dessert can enjoy other sensuous pleasures…

But that was a good way off yet. For now, it was just a question of continuing as he was doing—getting her to relax in his company, rounding off dinner with coffee, and then escorting her off the yacht to return her to her *pension* and her colleagues.

A good evening's work and a good base to build on. And time for him to consider his next move. And when he had he would act on it decisively, effectively. The way he always did in life.

She will be in my bed, and my plan will have succeeded.

It was a satisfying prospect.

He let his half-lidded contemplation of her sensuous enjoyment of the luxurious dessert linger a moment longer than it needed to, as into his head came again the thought that seducing Kassia Andrakis, so totally unlike any female of his considerable experience, and so completely oblivious of what he intended for her, would provide a distinct and novel challenge to pursue and achieve.

Not only because it would open the way to the lucrative business acquisition he wanted to make.

But for my own enjoyment…

A glint came into his veiled gaze. A glint of anticipation…and promise.

Yes, a satisfying prospect ahead indeed.

All that was required now was to plan his next move.

Kassia lay in her bed in her room but could not sleep. The evening she'd just spent kept playing inside her head. It shouldn't—but it did.

It shouldn't for one obvious reason. She'd had dinner with

Damos Kallinikos solely to encourage him to sponsor the excavation—nothing else.

And yet it was hard—impossible—to put it out of her mind and go to sleep. Even though there was obviously no point in dwelling on it.

Because what would be the point of remembering how it had been to sit out on that foredeck with Damos Kallinikos, feeling the low swell of the sheltered harbour water beneath the hull, with the stars high above, the warmth of the night air, the scent of the flower arrangement on the table and the glint of light on the glasses filled with chilled white wine? And what would be the point of remembering talking with him, hearing the timbre of his voice, responding to his questions, feeling that half-lidded glance on her, knowing that if she let her own eyes settle on him they would simply want to gaze and gaze...?

No point at all. No point, she told herself sternly, in doing anything but reminding herself that a man with looks like his—looks that had reduced her to flustered silence when she'd first set eyes on him that afternoon at the dig—was way out of her league—stratospherically out of her league. Oh, he'd been polite, and civil, and he'd conversed easily with her. But she had to face it squarely on. A man like him was not going to think anything more of her beyond the reason he'd invited her to his yacht.

She'd been wary about going in the first place, but as the evening had progressed she'd relaxed more. The fact that he was so totally out of her league had made it easier, in a strange way. The kind of women he would take a personal interest in would be as fabulous-looking as he was...ritzy and glitzy and gorgeous.

Not like me.

For a second, fleeting and painful, she felt a sudden longing in her. Oh, she knew she was nothing much to look at, and she accepted that undeniable truth about herself—had even said it straight to Damos Kallinikos's face. And yet for a few searing moments protest rose in her.

Oh, to be possessed of the kind of full-on glamorous beauty that would make Damos Kallinikos look twice at her...

More than look at her...

She crushed the longing down. There was no point wishing for what was impossible. No point at all.

And no point replaying in her head the evening that had just passed.

Damos Kallinikos had briefly entered her life, and tomorrow he was sailing on to Istanbul.

And she would be going back to digging in a hot, dusty trench.

She'd done what Dr Michaelis had asked of her—made a successful pitch for sponsorship, as Damos Kallinikos himself had told her. All she could do was hope it was enough to make him follow through with it. As for the man himself—there was no reason for their paths to cross again.

None whatsoever.

So what he looked like, and what she looked like, and what she might long for or not long for, or even think about him, remembering the evening that had been and was now gone was, she told herself yet again, completely pointless.

With that final adjuration to herself, she turned on her side, closed her eyes, and determined to sleep.

CHAPTER THREE

DAMOS RELAXED BACK into his first-class airline seat. His mood was good. His generosity in making it known to Dr Michaelis that, yes, he would indeed sponsor next year's season, had been rewarded when, after he'd made a carefully casual enquiry after Kassia Andrakis, the excavation's director had told him she was currently in England, visiting her mother. Damos had noted with decided interest that she was going on to Oxford afterwards, for a conference.

It was exactly the intel Damos had wanted.

And now he, too, as it happened, was also headed for that very city…

It had been nearly three weeks since their dinner on his yacht, and he needed to make his next move. Yorgos Andrakis, so his information on that front was indicating, was definitely softening up Cosmo Palandrou, spending time with him and paying him attention.

For a moment Damos frowned. Yorgos Andrakis might want to marry his daughter off to Cosmo, but why would Kassia co-operate? After all, she had her own career, and she didn't seem interested in being a fashionable socialite, so why would she do what her father wanted and marry a man almost as repellent as her own father?

His frown deepened. Not many people stood up to Yorgos Andrakis—maybe he would simply bully and browbeat Kassia until giving in was easier than opposing him? In which case...

In which case, having an affair with me that puts Cosmo Palandrou off her totally will actually be to her benefit. As well as mine.

It was a reassuring thought.

The flight attendant pausing by his seat to enquire what he might like to drink distracted him. He glanced up at her. She was blonde, good-looking, and it was obvious to him that she liked what she was seeing too. He smiled, but it was a perfunctory smile only as he gave his order.

For now there was only one female who was the focus of his thoughts and his attentions.

Kassia Andrakis.

And it was time to get to second base with her.

Kassia gazed up at the plaster replica statue of the two-metre-high *kouros* looming over her in the Ashmolean Museum. She always liked to look in at the Ashmolean whenever she was in Oxford, and it was a pleasant way to while away the afternoon before the opening dinner of the conference that started on the morrow.

She was glad to be in England—not just for a conference, where her old professor would be giving a presentation, or because she'd spent a few days seeing her mother, but because it was a welcome change of scene for her.

For all her determination, putting that evening on Damos Kallinikos's yacht out of her head was proving more difficult than it should. Of course it was pointless to dwell on it—she kept telling herself that robustly—but for all that it would replay in her mind at odd moments, bringing it vividly into her thoughts again. Bringing *him* vividly into her thoughts again...

Which was ridiculous, as well as pointless. It was nearly three weeks ago, and Damos Kallinikos had been and gone from her life.

A voice behind her spoke.

'This must be my lucky day—the perfect person to expound to me on this monumental youth.'

Kassia froze. Disbelievingly, she turned. As if she had conjured him from her very thoughts, Damos Kallinikos was standing there.

'What on earth…?' she heard herself say. Incredulity was spearing in her—and also something quite different from incredulity…something that made her breath catch in her throat. 'What are you doing here?'

Damos Kallinikos smiled. 'The same as you, it seems. Admiring this very handsome chap.'

'But what are you doing in Oxford at all?'

There was still incomprehension in her voice, she knew. And incomprehension might be uppermost in her, but it was not her only reaction to what she was seeing. Her pulse had given a hectic kick, and not just from surprise. She felt suddenly breathless.

'Oh, I've got some business here,' he said, his voice casual. 'What about you?'

'A conference,' she said mechanically. 'It gets going this evening—at a pre-conference dinner—then runs tomorrow and the day after.'

She was still fighting down surprise—and that other, completely irrelevant reaction to seeing him again. Fighting down the urge to just gaze at him…helplessly and gormlessly.

'More Bronze Age, I take it?' Damos Kallinikos was asking conversationally.

She nodded abstractedly. 'My old professor is giving a presentation on Mycenaean battle tactics.'

She got Damos Kallinikos's wry smile. 'Yet more I haven't a clue about,' he said. His glance went past her to the gigantic *kouros* behind her. 'Just like this guy. So, tell me about him. Why's he smiling like that?'

She turned sideways, between Damos and the *kouros*. 'Oh, that's the famous Archaic smile. It's on loads of statues from that era—between the Dark Ages that followed on from the collapse of the Bronze Age, to just before the Classical Era proper in the fifth century. Statuary in the Archaic period was very static—probably deriving from Egyptian styles. Just the left foot forward... Greek sculpture only really took off in the fifth century—'

She was gabbling, she knew she was, but shock—and so much more—was still overpowering her.

She felt her arm taken.

'Fascinating,' Damos Kallinikos murmured. 'So, what else has this place got? I only wandered in as I'm staying at the hotel opposite.' He guided her towards some display cabinets a little way off. 'What's this lot in here?' he asked.

Mechanically, Kassia started to expound upon and explain the contents, amplifying the descriptive cards. Her head was reeling. How had Damos Kallinikos suddenly turned up like this, out of the blue, in the Ashmolean Museum, of all places? How come he was here in Oxford on business at all, when she was here for a conference? And how come he just happened to be in the museum when she was?

Well, coincidences do happen, she thought helplessly. *However unlikely, sometimes you did just bump into someone you never expected to.*

He was still listening to what she was telling him, distracted though she knew she sounded, but when they'd exhausted two more display cabinets he held up a hand.

'That's it—you've hit the limit of my brain capacity! Time for tea.'

'Tea?' Kassia said blankly, as if he'd suggested something she'd never heard of.

'Yes, afternoon tea. My hotel does a very good one, so I'm told. Come along—you must be parched after that ancient history lesson you've given me.'

Once again she felt her arm taken, then she was being guided up the stairs to the entrance level, and out into the fresh late-summer air.

'That's my hotel,' Damos Kallinikos said, pointing across the road.

Kassia was not surprised—it was the most expensive in Oxford.

He guided her down the broad flight of shallow steps from the museum to the pavement, and then across the road. Kassia was still trying to make sense of what was happening…encountering Damos Kallinikos again, totally unexpectedly. And why he was bothering to spend time with her.

She tried to rationalise it in her head. Well, why shouldn't they have tea together? They did know each other, albeit slightly, and he had, after all—so she'd heard from Dr Michaelis—agreed to sponsor next year's season. Maybe that explained his asking her more about the ancient world?

Yet as they settled down to be served it was not antiquities that Damos asked her about.

'Do you know Oxford well?' he posed.

'Not very well, no,' she answered. 'Only for conferences, really.'

'This isn't your old university?'

She gave a self-deprecating laugh. 'No, nothing so lofty! I went to a north-country uni—decidedly redbrick.'

He frowned. 'Redbrick?'

'Just about any university more modern than Oxbridge,' she explained dryly.

'Oxbridge?' He frowned again.

'Short for Oxford and Cambridge,' she expounded. 'One is either Oxbridge or one is not,' she went on, even more dryly. 'I'm definitely *not*. But I do get to go to conferences here sometimes.'

He looked at her. 'It sounds very elitist.'

She could hear an edge in his voice. Condemnation.

'All of academia is elitist, really, if you think about it. An ivory tower. It's a privilege to be part of it—even if I'm only from a humble redbrick or a provincial Greek museum. Speaking of which,' she went on, 'Dr Michaelis is delighted at your decision to help fund next season's dig.'

'Well, I hope he's thanked you for your sterling efforts to that end over dinner that evening!' came the reply.

'I didn't really do anything,' Kassia said awkwardly. 'Just bored on about the Bronze Age.'

'It was,' said Damos Kallinikos, 'far from boring.'

His eyes—dark, thickly lashed, and with an expression in them that did things to her heart rate—were resting on her for a moment, and to her dismay Kassia felt her cheeks flush with colour. To her relief, the waiter arrived, setting down their repast. It was lavish in the extreme, with savouries, scones, jam and cream, and sweet pastries.

Kassia's eyes widened.

'I'll never manage the conference dinner tonight if I eat all this!' she exclaimed humorously.

'Looks good, doesn't it?' Damos agreed cheerfully. 'Get stuck in!'

Kassia did—it looked too good to resist. And then she realised the waiter was setting down not just a teapot, but two glasses of gently fizzing sparkling wine.

'To celebrate,' Damos said, handing her one and lifting his own.

'Um…celebrate what?' Kassia asked, confused.

He smiled across at her. 'Afternoon tea,' he said. 'One of the great contributions to civilised life!'

Kassia laughed—she couldn't help it. And nor could she help feeling her cheeks colour again, just because of the way Damos Kallinikos was smiling at her.

Oh, dear God, but he was just so…so…

Descriptive words failed her—and were quite unnecessary. Because the colour in her cheeks, and the skipping of her heart rate, the sense of effervescence in her veins, was telling her just how strongly she was reacting to seeing him again.

I thought our paths would never cross again. That he'd been and gone from my life. And now…

Now here she was, totally unexpectedly, totally out of the blue, having afternoon tea with him in Oxford's best hotel…

As coincidences went, running into him like this as she had, it was beyond amazing.

'Cheers!' said Damos Kallinikos, clinking his glass lightly against hers, smiling across at her with his warm, wonderful smile.

She took a sip of the sparkling wine, feeling suddenly light-headed, dipping her eyes. Whatever extraordinary coincidence had caused Damos Kallinikos to step back into her life, even if just for afternoon tea, she was very, very glad of it.

It was definitely worth enjoying.

* * *

Damos set down his glass and reached for one of the delicately cut sandwiches. Satisfaction was filling him. Kassia had accepted completely that there was nothing more behind their encounter than sheer coincidence, just as she'd accepted his invitation to afternoon tea.

She clearly welcomes meeting me again, and is happy to spend time with me.

Second base had definitely been achieved. Now it would be a question of building on it. OK, so for the next couple of days she'd be occupied at the conference, but after that…? Time to put himself in her diary.

'What will you be doing after the conference?' he asked. 'I think you mentioned over dinner that you visit your mother when you're in the UK…?'

Kassia reached for a savoury tart and started to eat it delicately. Damos surveyed her through half-lidded eyes. Though she was neatly dressed, the long-sleeved top and trousers she was wearing were very unexciting, he found himself thinking. She was still not wearing any make-up, and her hair, though again very neat, was simply pulled back into a knot on her nape.

Why does she not make more of herself?

His gaze rested on her assessingly. He had been prepared for her lack of chic, but he still wondered at her apparent complete lack of interest in fashion or her appearance. His gaze lingered for a moment. And yet her bone structure was good, and there were those light, almost silvery eyes, and her slender figure showed itself off in her delicately sculpted collarbones and the elegant length of her forearms.

Her reply to his question distracted his thoughts.

'I spent a few days with her before I came to Oxford,'

she was saying. 'She lives in the Cotswolds, so not too far from here.'

'Very scenic, I believe, the Cotswolds,' Damos commented.

He knew more about her mother now—he'd had her checked out. She was remarried to a retired industrialist, enjoyed a plentiful social life, and holidayed a lot. Just how much communication she had with her ex-husband he wasn't sure, but he could not risk it. Could not risk word of his forthcoming affair with Yorgos Andrakis's daughter getting back to Athens.

Fortunately, his sources had indicated that she was likely to be taking off for an annual late-summer holiday at her husband's villa in Estepona, in southern Spain, so she should be off the scene shortly. That would fit in nicely with his own planned timing.

'I don't know much about this part of England,' he went on musingly. 'Apart from Oxford itself, and the Cotswolds, what else is worth seeing? I ask because I've business in London late next week, so I've some days free for sightseeing here. What do you recommend?'

'Um…it depends what you like,' Kassia replied.

She sounded awkward again.

'Oh, the usual tourist things,' he said airily. 'What about grand stately homes? England is famous for them, after all.'

'Well,' she ventured hesitantly, 'Blenheim Palace is only a few miles out of Oxford, if you want to stay local.'

'Sounds perfect,' he said, taking another savoury and starting to demolish it. 'Why don't you show it to me?'

'Me?' She looked taken aback.

'Yes, we could make a day of it—after your conference.'

'Er—um…' Her hesitation was palpable.

'Do you have something else planned?' he posed.

She might, for all he knew. Presumably she had friends in England. She might have arranged to see them while she was here, as well as her mother.

'No…no, not really,' she replied awkwardly. 'I might visit an old schoolfriend, but not till next weekend.'

Damos smiled encouragingly. 'Good,' he said, and started on the scones.

He was past second base and things were going just the way he wanted them to. He spread cream and jam generously on his cut scone, took a hearty bite, and with his free hand indicated the remaining delicacies.

'Eat up,' he said cheerfully. 'And tell me all you know about Blenheim Palace. Now that we'll be visiting it together…'

Kassia sat in her seat at the conference, but her mind was not on the presentation. It was back on having afternoon tea with Damos Kallinikos.

Damos Kallinikos, who had turned up out of the blue, in Oxford, taken her off to tea at his hotel, and then lined her up to visit Blenheim Palace with him the day after tomorrow.

Why?

That was the question in her head. Why did he want to spend more time with her? Accosting her at the Ashmolean might just be explicable, with reference to his decision to fund Dr Michaelis next season. But taking her to tea? Going off to Blenheim with her?

It didn't make sense.

I'm the last kind of female a man like him would spend time with.

She knew that for certain now. Back in Greece she'd been unable to resist the temptation of looking him up on the Internet—and what had leapt onto her screen had not been his business affairs, in which she was not really interested anyway, and besides he'd already told her it was marine and shipping and so on, but what interested the tabloids and celebrity magazines. And that was, quite definitely, his social life. A social life which always seemed to involve him having a beautiful female draped on his arm. She'd counted at least two women familiar from the TV, one of whom was a fashion model, and another two who were well-known socialites in Athens. What they all had in common was the fact that they were show-stoppingly beautiful and glamorous...

And if there was one description which would never be used of herself it was that.

Just as she had in her bedroom after that dinner on his yacht, she felt a wave of sudden longing go through her. Oh, to be capable of looking glamorous—beautiful—show-stopping—stunning!

But it was hopeless. She'd always known that.

Her father had spelt it out brutally, with his sneering criticism of her gangly frame, and even her mother, far more kindly, had sighed because nothing she ate ever seemed to give her any curves or stop her growing so tall. On top of that, her hair was mouse-coloured and hung limply if loosened, and her eyes were too pale, her lashes likewise. So she'd never bothered trying to dress fashionably, never bothered to do anything with her lank hair, never bothered to wear any make-up.

But then in the world she lived in none of that mattered. Academia might be an ivory tower, as she'd remarked to Damos the day before over tea, but in it you were never judged on your looks.

After all, she thought, it was not as if she never dated. She had as a student and still did—fellow archaeologists and academics—only it was never with anyone remotely in Damos Kallinikos's league.

She gave a sigh. She must stop thinking about him. Yes, it was unlikely that he wanted to spend a day visiting Blenheim with her, but maybe he just preferred to have some kind of company, and someone who was English and knew a fair amount about history in general. Anyway, she'd agreed, and that was that.

We'll spend the day there, see the palace, then he'll drop me back in Oxford and wave goodbye.

Paths diverging again.

And Damos Kallinikos would be out of her life, and she wouldn't see him again.

Again.

'Now, that,' Damos said, 'is impressive!'

He gazed at the huge bulk of Blenheim Palace, now revealed in all its massive glory after their walk from the car park.

'It is,' Kassia agreed.

She still couldn't quite believe that Damos had followed through on his casual suggestion that she accompany him here—and yet here she was. He'd picked her up in a hire car—a very swish one—from outside the college where the conference attendees had been staying. She'd felt shy at first, and awkward, as they'd headed out of Oxford, but Damos had been relaxed, and clearly putting himself out to put her at her ease.

In return, she would do her best to be a helpful guide for the day, she told herself firmly.

'Didn't you tell me over tea the other day that it's the only non-royal palace in England?' Damos asked her now, as they strolled into the huge and impressive Great Court in front of the grand entrance, along with the many other visitors the palace attracted.

'Yes—though ironically it's sometimes used in films as a substitute for Buckingham Palace!' she replied.

'Remind me why it's got a German name,' Damos said.

'It's named after the first Duke of Marlborough's most famous victory, at the Battle of Blenheim, in Bavaria in 1704. England and Austria were fighting the Bavarians and Louis XIV of France. It was designed by John Vanbrugh and took over ten years to build. It's so large that apparently the first Duchess, the infamous Sarah Churchill, bossy confidante of poor Queen Anne, hated it. She complained the kitchens were so far from the dining room the food was always cold!'

Damos laughed, turning his head to look at her. 'You know all this stuff without even consulting the guide book—it's amazing!'

She made a self-deprecating face. 'Well, I guess history overall is my subject, really—if you like one period you like lots. I've been here before, too, when I was a schoolgirl. Though not since.' She glanced sideways at him. 'It's good to come again—thank you for inviting me,' she said politely.

'Thank you for accepting my invitation,' he responded promptly.

There was a glint in his eye. She could see it.

'I can tell you not that many females of my acquaintance would think this a fun day out!'

She looked away. No, the kind of women he ran around with—those beautiful and glamorous TV personalities, models and socialites—wouldn't be seen dead playing tourist like this. Her thoughts flickered. It wasn't the kind of outing a man like him would be likely to enjoy either, she'd have thought. It didn't exactly compare with sailing around on his private yacht... *One* of his private yachts, she reminded herself tartly.

But maybe I'm just overthinking it. OK, he's rich now, but he wasn't born to it, so he probably doesn't think it beneath him to be a tourist. After all, I don't think it beneath me—and I was born to wealth.

Not that she lived that kind of life. She far preferred the low-profile existence she had—working as an archaeologist, having as little to do with her father as she could. Most of the time he let her alone, but from time to time he summoned her to Athens to play her role as his daughter, such as it was, and attend dinner parties, functions—that kind of thing. Her father made it clear to her on such occasions that she was not to put herself forward, but to be meek and docile, and not bore people with all her 'archaeology nonsense', as he called it.

'It's bad enough being saddled with a daughter as plain as you,' he would say dismissively.

She would have preferred not to be summoned, but was mindful that her father had made himself a patron of the museum she worked at—to defy him would be to lose that patronage, she knew. So, since he didn't often want her in Athens, going along with his demands didn't seem too onerous an obligation, although she was always glad when it was over. Her father was not pleasant company...

Of her two parents, she far preferred spending time with her mother—not that her butterfly of a mother, affectionate though she was, ever had much time for her in between her constant social engagements and flitting abroad on holidays with her husband. Kassia was fond of her mother, and indeed her stepfather, whose stolid patience was a good foil for his flighty wife, but she didn't see a great deal of them.

It had been good, though, to spend a few days with them on this visit, before they'd headed out to Spain.

'OK, where are we going first?'

Damos's question interrupted her thoughts.

'Can you face a tour of the palace?' she asked. 'The state apartments are as impressive as the exterior.'

'Why not? Then we can explore the grounds afterwards.'

They made their way to where the tours began. Inside, Damos gazed around the magnificent rooms appreciatively, and gave a low whistle.

'That first duke certainly made good for himself!' he murmured admiringly, pausing to take in all the splendour.

'He got to the top from relatively humble beginnings. He was very ambitious—as was his wife,' she commented dryly.

'There's nothing wrong with ambition.'

The acerbic note in Damos's voice was audible. Kassia looked at him.

'Without ambition, hard work gets you nowhere,' Damos said. 'With it, anything can be achieved.'

'I… I suppose it depends on what you want,' Kassia said cautiously.

She had a feeling she was hitting Damos Kallinikos on a nerve. Maybe one that was still raw, given his own rise from humble beginnings. He was looking at her with an expression in his eyes she hadn't seen before.

'You're second-generation wealth, Kassia,' he said. 'Oh, you may work diligently in your career, but you have that cushion of wealth behind you all the same. It gives you a sense of security, of expectation, that you are scarcely aware of.'

She swallowed. 'I know I've had a privileged upbring-ing, but I try not to exploit it.'

A short laugh came from him. She did not hear any humour in it. Only vehemence as he spoke, biting out the words.

'Privileged, all the same. You've never felt the hunger of an outsider. University was out of the question for me. You said to me at the dig—I remember it quite clearly—that I wouldn't want to get my hands dirty. But I've done my years of hard manual labour, believe me. While you were enjoying the luxury of higher education, paid for by your father, I'd been working since I was fifteen on the docks—crewing on private yachts and merchant marine, working to make money, save money, give myself a financial base and make something of myself, haul myself up the ladder rung by rung. It isn't easy starting from scratch. It takes determination and, yes, ambition—and I've got both, or I would never have achieved what I have.'

Kassia was silent. Her father, too, was ambitious and determined—ruthlessly so. Seizing every and any opportunity to make money, boasting of how he'd built himself up from nowhere by snapping up ailing businesses driven to the wall during Greece's prolonged financial crisis fifteen years earlier at rock-bottom prices. He'd done it again during the more recent pandemic. Then he'd sacked as many employees as he could, stripped out any valuable assets, and run the businesses at the least cost and greatest profit to himself, before moving on to his next acquisition. He was probably working on another one right now—he usually was.

'I apologise. I didn't mean to speak so critically.'

Damos's voice cut across her darkening thoughts, no longer vehement now, and she was relieved. Surely there was no reason to think Damos Kallinikos as ruthless as her father? But then, where did the balance come between ambition and ruthlessness?

'Please,' she responded immediately, 'I didn't mean to condemn simply being ambitious, or wanting to make money. It's just that my father...' She hesitated, then went on awkwardly, 'Well, you must know his reputation for ruthlessness in business, riding roughshod over people, making use of anyone he can to achieve his ambitions—'

She broke off, not wanting to compare Damos to her father. Wanting to think better of him.

'Whatever your father's business practices are, Kassia,' Damos said tightly, '*I* made my money honestly.'

For a moment she met his eyes full-on, knowing there was a troubled look in her own. Then she looked away, blinking. She felt a brief touch on her arm. Damos was speaking again, his voice lighter now, but still pointed.

'Let's change the subject—not spoil this very pleasant day. So...' he took a breath, making his voice warmer '... what's this next room?'

He guided her forward into an adjoining chamber as magnificent as the last one. They were all magnificent—a breathtaking enfilade, with doorways ornamented, walls bedecked with tapestries and portraits, floors richly carpeted, curtains heavy and silken, furniture gilded and ornate, tables laden with silver and priceless porcelain.

'Not exactly homely,' Damos said dryly.

Good humour was back in his voice now, and Kassia was glad. Relieved. She made her tone of voice match his.

'Well, these are the state apartments, so they are designed for showing off grandeur and opulence! I'm sure the current Duke has a wing or whatever, for himself and his family that is far cosier,' Kassia replied.

'That's reassuring,' Damos observed. 'These massive rooms are OK in the summer, but everyone must freeze in a British winter!'

Kassia laughed. That moment of friction between them had been uncomfortable, but it was over. She could relax again.

'English country houses of the time were infamous for being freezing, however many fireplaces they had! I believe it wasn't until the impoverished aristocracy started marrying all those American dollar princesses at the end of the nineteenth century that things like central heating were installed.'

'Dollar princesses?' Damos posed.

'American heiresses to all the new money being made in the USA at the time. They arrived in Europe to snap up titled husbands in exchange for their huge dowries. Consuelo Vanderbilt was one. She married the Duke, the cousin of Winston Churchill, whose own mother, Jenny Jerome, was another dollar princess.'

'Tell me more,' said Damos, and Kassia did.

She was much happier talking about such things than touching on how Damos Kallinikos had made his money and hoping it wasn't anything like the way her father had made his. Her father was the most ruthless man she knew, stooping to any level to increase his wealth.

I don't want Damos to be like that—to be anything like him!

Why, she didn't want to question—except she knew that she wouldn't want anyone to be like her father.

And why should Damos be like him? There are plenty of decent ways of making money—hard work, high achievements. No need at all for him to be as ruthless as my father...

State apartments all viewed, as well as Winston Churchill's birth room—surprisingly modest, as Damos pointed out to her—they made their way outdoors. The warmth of the day wrapped around them, and Kassia felt her spirits warming too.

'Lunch?' suggested Damos.

Kassia nodded.

'Let's sit outside, and decide where to go next,' he went on, leading the way to one of the several eateries Blenheim offered—this one with outdoor seating in a courtyard leading to the gardens beyond.

They chatted amiably over a light but tasty lunch of soup and a sandwich for her, and traditional English sausages, mash and gravy for Damos, which he ate with relish. They rounded off the meal with coffee and a selection from the bakery.

'It's nice that you don't feel the need to calorie-count,' Damos said, and smiled as Kassia finished off her rich brownie.

She made a face. 'One of the perks of being a piece of string!' she said lightly.

'String?'

She gave a little shrug. 'It's what my father always calls me. A piece of string.'

Damos's eyes narrowed. 'Tell me,' he said, 'you're taller than he is, aren't you?'

Kassia looked surprised. 'Well, yes—but then I'm taller than a lot of men. You're one of the few exceptions—' She broke off, not wanting to be too personal. 'My mother, by contrast, is petite,' she went on. 'She always says—'

She broke off again.

'She always says…?' Damos prompted.

Kassia gave another shrug. 'She always says she thought I'd never stop shooting up. That I must take after her grandfather.'

Into her head came her mother's familiar next words.

'Of course, for a man it doesn't matter, being so tall…'

Her mother would have loved her to be petite and curvaceous, as she herself was. To be pretty and ultra-feminine simply for Kassia's own sake. Her father, by contrast, had she been possessed of such beauty, would have doubtless touted her off in fashionable circles and probably tried to marry her off to someone he could make use of. Another businessman…a politician—it wouldn't have mattered who to her father, so long as the marriage benefited himself. Her own preference would have been irrelevant to him.

At least her lack of looks protected her from that kind of pressure. That was something to be grateful for, she thought ironically. Except that now…

She gave a silent sigh. A man like Damos Kallinikos was used to having only beautiful and glamorous women at his side, and she knew that for the first time in her life she would have loved to be in that league. She sighed again. She was yearning for something that was impossible…quite impossible.

She became aware that Damos was looking at her speculatively, with a look in his eyes she hadn't seen before. She wondered at it. But then it was gone.

He picked up his coffee cup, draining it. 'Time to hit the gardens,' he said. 'How about starting with the water terraces? They're the closest.'

'Sounds good.'

Kassia smiled. She was glad of the change of subject—talking about herself had made her feel self-conscious, and not in a good way. Exploring Blenheim's glorious gardens would be far more pleasant.

They made their way out of the courtyard and took the path leading to the upper water terrace, adjacent to the west front of the palace. It was certainly impressive, and they wandered leisurely along the paths around the ornate stone ponds. Kassia paused for a moment to trail her fingers in the cool water, and Damos did likewise, having turned back the cuffs of his shirt beforehand. Kassia tried not to let her gaze linger on the lean strength of his wrists, or the square solidity of his hands. Hands, she supposed must have hauled up sails and set rigging and done any amount of hard manual labour in their time.

Now, though, an expensive watch snaked around his lean, strong wrist.

'Don't let that get wet!' she exclaimed warningly.

Damos glanced at her. 'Waterproof to three hundred metres,' he said. 'I could wear it scuba diving if I wanted.'

'Do you?' she asked, perching herself on the wide stone rim of the fountain. 'Scuba dive, I mean? Not wear a zillion-euro watch while you do it.'

'No,' he said. He perched himself beside her. 'I haven't the time.'

'That's a shame. Now that you've made money, could you not relax more?'

She'd meant what she'd said. But her thoughts went back to what he'd said about ambition. Maybe he felt he still hadn't made enough money? Maybe he was determined to be richer still? Was he still chasing his next achievement?

A sideways look came her way. 'Isn't that what I'm doing now? Relaxing…taking time out to be a tourist?'

Kassia smiled. 'Well, maybe it will help give you a taste for relaxing more—taking your foot off the business accelerator.'

He didn't answer, only idly laced the water between his fingers. For a few moments longer they went on sitting there, side by side, hands casually stirring the water, hearing birdsong all around them, other visitors wandering past, sunshine bathing them all.

She gazed about her at all the splendour of their surroundings in the summery warmth. This day had come out of nowhere…being here with Damos Kallinikos who, for whatever inexplicable reason, seemed to want to spend it with her. But she wasn't going to question it. All she was going to do was simply enjoy it…

Damos levered himself to his feet. 'Shall we check out the lower water terrace now?' he posed.

Kassia stood up, and they made their way off the upper terrace.

'Apparently, the fountains on the lower terrace are in the style of Bernini's fountain in the Piazza Navona in Rome,' Kassia remarked.

'Have you been to Rome?' Damos asked casually.

He wanted to keep all his conversation with her casual. He'd been unnecessarily intense on the house tour, sounding off about how hard he'd had to work to get where he was today. His own assertion echoed in his head now.

'I made my money honestly.'

Well, it was true, he thought defiantly. He *had* made his money honestly—he had never cheated, or undercut, or been underhand. When the time came he would make Cosmo a fair offer for his business—once he'd disposed of Yorgos Andrakis's attempt to snap it up, using his own daughter to do so.

Just as you are doing.

The words hung in his head, making him suddenly uneasy.

He dismissed them.

It would stop her father using her, he retorted instantly. And nothing her father wanted would be in Kassia's interest—certainly not being bullied and browbeaten into marrying Cosmo Palandrou.

Whereas what I want is, in fact, in Kassia's interest.

And not just to protect her from her father's ruthless ambitions.

Her words over lunch came back to him. He'd wondered why she did not make more of her appearance, but now he was pretty sure he knew the answer. His mouth tightened. He'd take a bet that Yorgos Andrakis, powerfully built and physically imposing, well used to overbearing other people with his abrupt and hectoring manner, did not like it that his own daughter dwarfed him—it would put his back up straight off. And it sounded as if her mother simply made her even more self-conscious about her slender height.

His glance went to Kassia, walking beside him. She wasn't hunching her shoulders, he noticed. Presumably because he was taller than her and she didn't need to? Her now straight back and shoulders gave a graceful sway to her body as they strolled along...

'A couple of times,' Kassia said.

Damos realised with a start that she was answering his question about whether she'd visited Rome.

'The remains of ancient Rome are very splendid, but they're a thousand years and more later than my period.' She smiled.

'Yet two thousand years ago from the present day?' he commented. He frowned deliberately. 'History does seem to occupy an inordinate length of time,' he said ponderously.

She laughed, and he liked the sound of it.

'And on that profound note,' he said, lightly and self-mockingly, 'shall we head down towards the lake?'

'That would be nice,' she replied politely.

He gave a laugh. 'We don't have to if you don't want to—there's a lot else to see.'

'Well, it's your day out, after all,' she answered. 'I can

come here any time, really, whenever I visit my mother, but you might not be in this area again.'

'True,' he murmured.

Truer than she realised…

I'm only here at all because I am in pursuit of you.

And his pursuit of her was for a very specific reason…

He'd said, back there on the upper water terrace, that he was taking today out to relax, but he'd spoken disingenuously. If he had to file this day—this entire trip to the UK—under anything, it would not be 'leisure'. Making up to Kassia Andrakis was serving a business purpose—a clear and unambiguous one.

His glance went to her as they strolled along the winding path leading them towards the lake, his gaze veiled. Yes, he'd forged this acquaintance with Kassia Andrakis for one purpose only.

But is it only one?

The question was in his head, and he could not dismiss it.

Or deny it.

Was his intention to have an affair with her simply a means to thwart her father's plans for her in respect of Cosmo Palandrou? Was it really the only reason he was spending time with her? Or was another reason making itself felt?

Because he was enjoying the day, he realised. Enjoying this leisurely ambling around this magnificent place, seeing the spectacular fruits of one man's towering ambitions. He was enjoying the ease of the day, enjoying feeling as relaxed as he was, and enjoying thinking about something quite other than what usually dominated his thoughts: his endless business concerns.

I'm enjoying being with Kassia.

She was so very different from the women he was used to

consorting with. True, if it hadn't been that she was Yorgos Andrakis's daughter he knew he would not have bothered to know her at all. But now that he did…

I like her. I like her company, her conversation. I like her courtesy and her consideration and her knowledge of things I know nothing about, which she makes interesting and easy to enjoy.

And he knew there was something else he liked about her. The fact that she was not indifferent to him.

Oh, he wanted her to be responsive to him—that was essential if he was to have the affair he planned with her. But now he found he wanted it for reasons quite different from that purpose. Reasons he had not expected at all when he'd first engineered an encounter with her. Reasons he knew he had to acknowledge.

Even if she were not Yorgos Andrakis's daughter I would want her to be responsive to me…

His veiled gaze rested on her as they strolled along, chatting about things that seemed easy to chat about, such as the way the gardens had been laid out and what else there was to see. But as it rested on her, he frowned. There was something about Kassia Andrakis that he did *not* want.

I don't want her thinking about herself as she does—with that dismissive criticism of herself, as if she agrees with her parents' verdict on her—as if she sees nothing amiss in the way she remarked, on my yacht, that men only make up to her because of whose daughter she is. I don't like the way she thinks so little of her looks and her appearance.

He did not like that at all.

A sense of irony struck him. Kassia's background might be privileged, but her self-image was anything but. Determination speared through him, and he realised he had just taken on board a new sense of purpose. To reveal to Kassia the beauty that could be hers...

For his own sake, yes—he was honest enough to concede that point—but for something he hadn't thought would matter to him. Now it did.

For her sake too.

CHAPTER FOUR

KASSIA CLIMBED INTO the passenger seat of Damos's hire car and buckled up as he settled himself behind the wheel. Her eyes flickered sideways as he pulled his own seat belt across him and gunned the engine. So, they were heading back into Oxford, where he would drop her off, and then tomorrow she would set off to the Midlands—she'd arranged to stay for a couple of days with an old schoolfriend.

Then she'd probably fly back to Greece.

Taking memories of today back with her. Good memories.

Because today *had* been good—very good.

Spending it with Damos.

Once she'd disciplined herself not to keep stealing glances at him, not to be too aware of just how incredibly attractive he was to her sex, she had settled down to enjoy his company. He'd been easy-going, interested in what they'd talked about, and good-humoured, with a ready smile and a ready laugh. After the lake they'd gone further afield, across the splendid south lawn, exploring more of the vast grounds and gardens, finishing off with coffee at yet another café on the huge estate.

'Tired out?' Damos smiled across at her as they eased their way down the imposing drive towards the main road.

'Good exercise.' She smiled back.

It was only a few miles back into Oxford, so this, she knew, was the end of her day with him. She'd be saying goodbye to him and this time it would be permanent. No more coincidentally running into him again. Oh, he might, perhaps, show up at next season's dig, just to see what his funding might have turned up, but that was about all. Possibly, too, when she was next summoned to Athens by her father, for whatever reason, she just might see Damos around. But he'd doubtless have some glamorous female draped over him...

She felt a pang of sadness well up in her—or something like sadness. She wasn't sure what. All she knew was that she didn't want the day to end.

Just why that was she didn't want to think about. Because what would be the point? She wasn't glamorous, or beautiful, and Damos Kallinikos had only been being friendly, sharing today with her as a convenient but passing companion, for want of anyone else—that was all.

'Well...' he turned on to the road leading back to Oxford '...if you're not too tired, I've another favour to ask you.'

He threw a glance at her, and Kassia looked at him with questioning surprise.

His eyes went back to the road.

'The favour is this,' he said. 'After my meeting yesterday, while you were at your conference, it seems I have an invitation to one of the colleges this evening. It's some kind of shindig—is that the word in English?—where former students who are now influential in the world of business and politics and so on can be wined and dined. Presumably with a view to encouraging them to spend their money and exert their influence on behalf of their old college. My business contact here is one such former student, and he has got the Master to give me an invitation as well.'

His voice took on a sardonic tone.

'It seems one does not have to be an old student to be considered potentially useful to the college providing one has money—even foreign money, like mine. That said, the evening could potentially be useful to me, too, as my business contact tells me that a government trade minister whom it would be helpful for me to know personally will be attending. So…' He glanced at her again. 'Would you be prepared to be my plus one for the evening?'

Kassia looked at him. 'But surely you'll be the guest of your business contact?'

He shook his head, his eyes back on the road. 'Not really. The invitation is from the Master, and it includes a plus one of my own.' He looked at her again as they paused for the traffic lights by the Oxford ring road. 'It would be good if you would perform that office.' He made a slight face. 'It would just make the sociability of it all that much easier.'

His tone grew sardonic again

'As I'm sure you'll appreciate, nothing so vulgar as business or money will be mentioned—this is all about networking, socialising, making introductions and so on. It's a social investment, I suppose—and my arriving with a plus one would play to that.' He paused again. 'What do you say?'

Strange feelings were going through Kassia. It was happening again. A man she barely knew—or, to be fair, had barely known before today—was now making a point of inviting her to spend time with him. But why?

Obviously, as she knew perfectly well, it was not for any of the usual reasons that a man might invite a female out— that thought wasn't even in the running. But did he really want to extend the day they'd spent together into an evening together as well? It seemed he did. And, yes, she could see why—up to a point…

He was speaking again.

'And it's not just any plus one, Kassia. This is your world—academia. You're at home in it in a way that I am not, even though it could prove useful to me in a business sense ultimately. You'll be at ease at an Oxford college social event.'

'I never went to Oxford,' she objected.

'You work in academia—that's my point.'

'In a very junior capacity—'

'Stop making objections!'

There was humour in his voice, but there was something else as well. She could tell. It was determination. He wanted her to say yes. It would suit him for her to do so.

'Look…' he went on. 'On my own, I'm just some self-made Greek business guy, only knowing the world I come from, only knowing the English businessman who arranged this invitation for this evening. With you at my side it would give me something else as well. I've no idea if their professor of ancient history, or whatever, will be there tonight, but just the fact that you can talk on equal terms with other academics—even if you're just a junior one—will help oil wheels. Like I say, this is your world, not mine. You'll be at home here, and that will help me. So, will you come along?'

What he said made sense. OK, so she wasn't an Oxford graduate, but she could hold her head up robustly enough. She'd just been a conference delegate here—she was, in short, *bona fide* in the world he was entering this evening.

But then a real objection hit her.

'It's going to be black tie, isn't it? These formal things always are at Oxford. If so, I haven't got any evening clothes with me,' she said.

The smartest outfit she'd brought with her had been for the pre-conference dinner—a day dress she'd worn with a jacket and low heels. Nothing good enough for a black-tie affair.

'No problem. We're still in time for the shops,' said Damos. 'I'll head for the shopping centre and drop you off. Will that do?'

'Um…yes, thank you,' she said.

'Good. That's settled.'

Satisfaction was clear in Damos's voice.

He crossed the ring road, heading into the city. Beside him, Kassia sat, wondering what she'd let herself in for. But she knew from the way her heart rate had quickened that, whatever the reason Damos Kallinikos wanted her to come with him this evening, she wanted it too.

I don't have to say goodbye to him. Not quite yet…

And her heart rate quickened again.

Damos's mood was good. Very good. He minutely adjusted his bow tie as he gave himself a final glance in the mirror in his hotel room. The car would be here soon, to drive him the short distance to the college hosting the event this evening. He would meet Kassia at the entrance—the college she'd been staying at for her conference was almost next door, so she'd said she'd walk.

He wondered what she'd be looking like…what kind of evening outfit she'd got for herself. But, judging by what he knew, he didn't hope for much.

He was right to do so.

When, some fifteen minutes later, he saw her waiting under the stone arched entrance to the college, he gave an inner sigh. The matronly dress she'd bought for herself did absolutely nothing for her. In a dull shade of dark green, it had a high round neck, a bodice that looked ruched in a bunchy way, and was tightly long-sleeved. Beneath the ruching it dropped widely to her ankles, looking as if it were a size too large for her. Her hair was still in its knot on the back of her head, and she still had not used any make-up.

Frustration stabbed through him, laced with determination. He would change Kassia's low self-image of herself… make her realise her potential… But not tonight. Tonight was about getting to third base with her.

He smiled warmly as he came up to her. 'Dead on time,' he greeted her. 'Excellent.'

'Well, I'm right next door after all,' she replied.

They walked forward under the archway, nodding at the college official on duty. A reception table was set out just beyond, and Damos gave his name and hers. Beyond, in the grassy quad, guests were already gathering. The evening was warm, and the clink of glasses and the chatter of conversation reached across to them. Around the edges the ancient college guarded this central area, in one corner of which a string quartet was playing.

'Shall we?' said Damos, holding his arm out to Kassia.

She hesitated slightly before placing her hand on his sleeve, but then did it anyway. Damos looked around him. The college was incredibly atmospheric in the evening light—the golden stone of the buildings, the dark green of the quad's pristine lawn, the strains of classical music wafting over the space… As they neared where the other guests were gathered he saw that several tables with white linen tablecloths were laden with glasses and bottles, serving staff behind them.

'Now, I do think on a quintessentially traditional occasion such as this clearly is that champagne is in order,' Damos said, and smiled, accepting a glass from one of the servers and handing it to Kassia.

She made no demur, and he took a glass for himself as

well, strolling on with her on his arm. She wore some kind of perfume, he noticed—nothing heavy, but something light and floral. It mingled, he thought, with the scent of jasmine descending from climbers festooning one area of the college walls.

'Ah, there you are!'

A voice hailed him, and the man who was his business contact here stepped out of a knot of people. Introductions were made and, just as Damos had foretold, Kassia was quite able to hold her own as she was introduced to college dons, answering questions about her own specialist field and then moving the conversation on. Canapes circulated, along with more champagne, and Damos relaxed into the occasion.

At some point he was duly introduced to the Master who—again as he had foretold—was more than happy to make the acquaintance of a wealthy guest, albeit a foreigner. The Master then introduced him to the government minister, and pleasantries were exchanged, potential future contacts made which might well prove useful at some point. And then there was a general move into dinner.

'High Table,' murmured Kassia, glancing around the ancient dining hall, panelled and resplendent, as they took their places once the Master, dons and the ministerial guest of honour had taken theirs and a long Latin grace had been intoned. 'We had nothing like this at my northern redbrick!'

She spoke humorously, but Damos looked at her. 'Do you wish you had been a student here?'

She shook her head. 'I didn't apply,' she said cheerfully.

'Why not?' Damos frowned.

'Because I knew I wasn't Oxbridge material, and so did my teachers. It doesn't bother me,' she said with a smile. 'I've always accepted my limitations—including intellectual.'

She shook out her napkin and draped it across her lap, pouring herself some water and replying politely to a remark addressed to her by one of the other diners. Damos let his eyes rest on her, her words resonating in his head. A new determination fired in him—there were some limitations she should not accept. He did not want her to. They were holding her back.

Holding her back from responding to me as I want her to.

Because he could tell that she was doing so. Oh, she might be far more at ease in his company now—their day out together at Blenheim had seen to that—and she'd lost any last trace of awkwardness or hesitation with him, but she was still treating him as if she were holding back from regarding him as anyone but a pleasant companion.

Yet the signs were there that that was just not so. There were too many tiny but telltale giveaways. The way she moved away from him slightly if he was too close…the way she threw little glances at him when she thought he would not notice…the way a faint colour would run into her cheeks if he held eye contact with her too long.

He knew the signs.

But what he definitely wasn't doing was responding to them. He wasn't coming on to her in the slightest. Not yet. If he did, she'd shy away. He knew it with every instinct. No, all he could do for now was continue as he was, making himself pleasant, easy company for her, enjoying the evening. And it was certainly an evening to remember.

Kassia was clearly enjoying it too, with the candlelight playing on her face as the courses were served, the wine was poured, and all the arcane rituals observed—including having everyone remove themselves to another panelled room to partake of a second dessert, comprising cheese, sweetmeats, fruit and choices of port, liqueurs and sweet wines. Damos couldn't decide whether to be impressed or amused...

'Hang on to your napkin!' Kassia whispered. 'We're supposed to mingle with new people now.'

They did, one of whom was a classicist, and Damos held back and let Kassia engage with him happily on a comparison of Mycenaean, Homeric and Classical Attic Greek. She was in her element, he could see, and that same silvery glow was in her expressive, grey-blue eyes as he'd seen when she'd enthused about the broken bits of pots she spent her time uncovering.

He sat quietly and watched. Even in that dress that did nothing for her, with her severe hairstyle and unmade-up face, there was still something about her...something that made him want to go on looking at her. Hearing her voice... Being close to her...

He realised he was being addressed by the classicist, who was asking him if he, too, were an archaeologist.

He shook his head. 'But I've agreed to sponsor Kassia's museum's dig next season, if that exonerates me,' he said, and smiled.

'Oh, indeed,' came the reply. 'I would keep quiet about that here, though, if I were you. Archaeology is an expensive business, and always hungry for funding! You'll be plagued to death if word gets out!'

Damos gave the expected laugh, but his thoughts were sober. He had sponsored Dr Michaelis's excavation not out of the slightest interest in archaeology, but for the sole purpose of engineering an introduction to Kassia. Moving in on her. Lining her up to clear the path for him to acquire Cosmo Palandrou's logistics company. It would significantly enlarge his own business interests, increasing his own wealth yet more, the way he'd striven to do all his life, from poverty to riches, in order to fulfil his driving, relentless ambition...

Yet somehow, here and now, with Kassia beside him in this historic, atmospheric panelled room at this ancient Oxford college, having spent the day with her among the baroque splendours of Blenheim in the heart of England, that all seemed very far away.

But I am only here with her to drive my purpose forward. That is my only reason for being here at all.

He must not forget it. Whatever his thoughts about Kassia now, they did not obviate his intention in that respect. Yes, he might have come to be drawn to her, irrespective of who she was, but for all that she remained Yorgos Andrakis's daughter—and it was for that reason alone that he had an interest in her.

Then tell her.

The words were in his head out of nowhere. Stark and bare. Impelling.

Tell her. Tell her what you suspect her father is up to. Tell her that the sure-fire way to stop him in his tracks is to let Cosmo Palandrou see you are involved with her. Just tell her that. It's all you have to do.

But if he did...?

More words came. Words he could not silence, or dispute, or deny.

How do you know what her reaction will be?

He didn't—that was the blunt answer.

She might not believe him...might think he was exaggerating...might dismiss it out of hand. He could feel tension tighten across his shoulders as he drove the logic forward. And even if she didn't—even if she did credit what he was telling her—why should she go along with his method of disposing of her father's plans? She might think it quite unnecessary—might believe that all she had to do was tell her father she didn't want to marry Cosmo. And maybe, for all his bullying ways, Yorgos Andrakis wouldn't succeed in pressurising her to do his will.

But he'll keep that from Cosmo for as long as he can. He'll drag things out...tell Cosmo she'll come round...keep him hopeful. And that means Cosmo won't be open to any other offers including mine. And while it drags on other buyers might get wind of what's going on, see that Cosmo's company is vulnerable and start to circle too. And then there'll be a bidding war, pushing the price up.

He drew a breath. No, the surest way to outmanoeuvre Yorgos Andrakis and make the way clear for his own bid for Cosmo's business was to spike his guns. By making Cosmo not want to marry Kassia at all—putting him off completely by the means he'd determined on right from the start. Getting to Kassia first himself, thereby putting Cosmo off for good—the way he was already doing.

His eyes rested on her. She was sipping her sweet wine and still discussing Ancient Greece with her fellow academic. Damos was all too darkly conscious that she was oblivious to what was going through his head. To the decision he was coming to—the only safe one to make.

He felt himself steel.

It's just too risky to tell her.

And there was no need to, he reminded himself tightly. No need to do anything other than what he was already doing. Keep going on the path he had selected.

It was working, and it would go on working—right to the end.

And by then...

Kassia will be mine.

He felt his thoughts soften, his eyes lighten, the tension

in his shoulders ease. He joined in with the conversation again, taking a refill of port as it circulated, feeling its richness mellowing him even more. The evening wore on, and he knew he was enjoying it—not just because of being here, but because he was sharing the evening with Kassia.

He said as much to her as, with the guests finally dispersing, they strolled across the quad.

'Are you glad you came?' he asked. 'Because I am—very glad. It wouldn't have been the same without you.'

His smile on her was warm.

'It was a unique experience,' she answered, her voice just as warm. 'Thank you for taking me.'

'It was,' he assured her, 'my pleasure.'

And that, he knew with certainty, was completely true. *She made the evening for me...*

It was a thought to warm him—much more than thinking about Cosmo Palandrou or Yorgos Andrakis and all that went with them. He set that determinedly aside, turning instead to Kassia.

'I'll walk you back,' he said.

He hadn't bothered to order another car—the distance to his hotel was not far, and the college Kassia was staying at was next door.

At the entrance, he paused, looking down at her. She was wearing heels, but very low, and her shoes, he'd noticed with the same condemnation he'd reserved for the dress she was wearing, were serviceable rather than elegant. She was still a few inches shorter than he was, though, and she was looking up at him perforce.

In the dim light he thought he saw something move in her eyes. On impulse, he reached for her hand. He lifted it to his mouth, grazing her knuckles lightly...so lightly. He felt her hand tremble in his as he straightened. He smiled down at her. A warm, encompassing smile.

'For me,' he said, 'it's been a memorable evening—quite an experience! And a great day out seeing Blenheim too. Thank you for making both so special.'

He released her hand and looked down at her a moment longer. She was gazing up at him, lips slightly parted, and there was something in her eyes he had not seen till now. Something wide and wondering.

Almost, he started to lower his head to hers. Then he halted. Instead, he glanced through the entrance to the college where she was staying. The night porter was visible at his desk, clearly able to see them. Damos took a step back.

'Goodnight, Kassia,' he said, still holding her eyes. 'Sleep well. And, again, thank you…'

He turned away, heading back down the road. He had the distinct feeling that Kassia had not moved. That she was watching him walk away from her. As if she did not want him to.

It was good to know. Very good. For reasons he did not entirely wish to acknowledge. Conflicting reasons…

He gave a shake of his head. But those reasons needn't be conflicting—that was the beauty of it. He could want Kassia for herself and for the reason he had set out to want her in the first place.

There is no conflict between them.

He kept the words in his head, walking on back to his hotel. It was time to think of what his next step would be. It would be his home run…

Making Kassia his.

CHAPTER FIVE

KASSIA LET HERSELF into her room, still in a daze. On her bare hand she could still feel the light…oh, so light imprint of Damos taking it in his and kissing it. Such an old-fashioned gesture—and yet now she could understand why Victorian maidens had swooned over it.

For just a moment she let herself relive it, feel again the warm clasp of his hand, the cool touch of his lips…

She gave herself a mental shake. She had no business reacting like this, she told herself sternly. No business wanting to read anything into it.

Deliberately, she moved her eyes to the mirror over the chest of drawers, made herself look at her reflection. Really look.

No, she had not turned into some fairytale princess whose hand a man like Damos Kallinikos—God's gift to women if any man was ever rated so!—would be kissing for any romantic purposes.

I'm still exactly the same as I always have been and always will be. Whether I'm in evening dress, or day wear, looking smart or looking casual, it makes no difference at all.

Whether her father told her brutally and viciously, or her mother sighingly and sympathetically, it did not—could not—alter what she was seeing in the mirror. What she had always seen…all her life.

She turned away, blinking a little. Damos Kallinikos had kissed her hand because he was being *gallant*—that old-fashioned Continental term for old-fashioned courtesy. He would have done as much had she been an old lady of eighty.

She took another breath, steadying herself. There was no point yearning to be some imaginary glamorous beauty like the kind Damos Kallinikos usually hung out with, because she wasn't. And that was that.

With a lift of her chin she reached her hands behind her back, unzipping her gown. She'd bought it in a rush, given the shortage of time, but it had served the purpose. It wasn't glamorous in the least, or even elegant—but then nothing in her wardrobe was.

She made herself ready for bed, regret pulling at her. Regret that the day was over. She would treasure the memory of their day out at Blenheim, and then the entirely unexpected bonus of the evening just ended. Treasure the memory of being with Damos...

It was strange, really, she thought. She and Damos came from such different backgrounds, led such different lives, yet they seemed to get on well together. Once she'd lost her sense of awkwardness with him, and once she'd got her quite irrelevant, if totally predictable female reaction to him under firm control, she had been quite at ease with him.

As she climbed into bed memories of the evening and of the day were still filling her head, vivid in her mind. She lay back, letting them play. Such lovely memories...

She frowned slightly. There had been only one jarring moment—when he'd talked about ambition, defending it, justifying it. Regret at her own reaction plucked at her.

I have no right fearing it has made him like my father. You can be ambitious without being ruthless...without mak-

*ing use of other people for your own ends. Damos wouldn't
do that.*

She turned out the light, settling down to sleep. Regret
was filling her now for quite a different reason. Because
her brief time with Damos was now well and truly over.
Definitely over.

It was time to go back to her own life—time to let Damos
Kallinikos and her brief encounter with him slip into the
past.

Damos was driving to London, his mind occupied with considering his next move with Kassia. He knew she was visiting a schoolfriend for the next couple of days. He'd texted
her that morning to wish her a pleasant weekend, and to
thank her again for the previous day. But she'd also mentioned, when he'd made a carefully casual enquiry at some
point during the day, that there was no pressing need for
her to get back to Greece—that she still had annual leave
accrued if she wanted to take it.

Damos definitely did want her to take it—with him.

But how to achieve it? How to get her to accept from him
what he wanted her to? Accept that he wanted more from
her than casual company—much, much more.

His brow furrowed and there was a sardonic twist to his
mouth. He was not used to having to work to get a woman
to accept his interest in her. He'd gone as far as he could in
taking his leave of her last night, and his deliberate hand-
kiss had made her tremble. Would he have kissed her if the
porter hadn't been able to see them? Would that have convinced Kassia of his intentions?

What he needed, he knew, was to get past her defences—
the barrier she lived behind. The barrier of her self-deprecating image of herself.

I need to change her mindset...change the way she sees herself...so I can change the way she sees me...

But how to achieve that?

His thoughts ran on as he cruised along the M40 towards London. He had some business to attend to there, but his main focus was going to be Kassia. It needed to be. Reports from Athens were indicating that Yorgos Andrakis and Cosmo Palandrou were definitely getting together... spending time with each other. Cosmo had apparently been a guest aboard Yorgos's mega yacht—absently Damos recalled Kassia's pungent criticism of it as a monstrosity—and they'd been seen lunching together a couple of times as well. Yorgos was moving things along.

And so must I. I have a limited window of opportunity.

He had the weekend in which to come up with a sure-fire way to seize it.

And by Sunday he knew just what he was going to do.

It would work perfectly...

Just perfectly.

Kassia was out in the garden of her mother and stepfather's house. It was manicured to within an inch of its life, with pristine flowerbeds, a clipped lawn, and an azure swimming pool glinting to one side. The pool looked tempting, even in the slightly cooler temperatures the weekend had brought after the run of hot weather. She would have a dip later.

She was here on impulse. An impulse she didn't quite want to admit to. It had been good, spending the weekend with her friend, but now she was at a loose end. Really, she should head back to Greece—there was nothing to keep her in the UK. But she was conscious of a reluctance to do so—conscious of a reluctance to admit the reason for her reluctance.

She wanted there to be something to keep her in the UK. Or rather some*one*. She knew she was being stupid—ridiculously so—and she knew it was pointless to be so stupid. Knew there was no reason—*none*—for thinking that maybe, just maybe, Damos might get in touch again.

Because why should he? She'd been convenient to him in Oxford—pleasant enough company for Blenheim, useful in her own way for the college dinner. But now he'd gone to London, as he'd said in passing that he would be, and given absolutely no indication that he expected to see her again at any time. That he had any interest in seeing her again.

She gave a sigh, and then gave herself a mental shake. This was absurd. There was no point hanging around like this. Her mother and stepfather were happily on holiday in Spain, and although they were fine with her staying at their Cotswolds house, what on earth was she here for all on her own?

It was pointless—just as pointless as staying on in the UK.

She reached for her phone. She would check the flights and book one for tomorrow. Then she'd text Dr Michaelis to say she'd be back at work this week and defer the rest of her leave till later.

She was just about to search for flights when an incoming call flashed up on her phone.

She froze. It was Damos.

Damos kept his voice smooth. 'Kassia. Hi. How did your weekend go? Well, I hope? Whereabouts are you now? Do you still happen to be in the UK?'

She took a moment to answer.

He felt himself tense.

'Um…yes. I'm at my mother's house. But she's not here.

She and my stepfather are in Spain. I'm just…well, just about to book my flight back to Athens.'

'Do you have to get back?' he asked.

Again she took a moment to answer, and again he felt himself tense.

'Er…no, not really.'

Damos felt his tension drop a level.

'In which case, I'll come right out with it. Could I possibly persuade you to do me yet another favour?'

He kept his voice light—deliberately so. She was back to sounding awkward again, and he wanted that gone. Wanted her to relax with him. But there was something else in her voice too. Something that his masculine senses were indicating that he definitely wanted to be there.

She is glad that I have phoned her.

'It's a bit of an ask,' he went on, 'but I need another plus one. You were so kind last week, to be that at the college dinner, and I was wondering if I could prevail upon you a second time.' He paused. 'Let me explain.'

She didn't say anything, so he went on. He needed this to sound plausible—genuine.

'I'm in London and, rather like in Oxford, I've been invited out of the blue to an evening affair.' He made his voice dry, and deliberately humorous. 'It seems that wealthy Greek businessmen are currently in high demand! Anyway, as in Oxford, it would be good for me to arrive with a plus one. So, I'm afraid I immediately thought of you.' He made his voice humorously apologetic now. 'What do you say? It's the day after tomorrow. You'd enjoy it, I'm sure—it's at the Viscari St James, up on the roof garden, so we must hope it doesn't rain.' He paused again. 'What do you say? Can I persuade you to rescue me yet again? I don't want to hassle you, but I'd be really grateful. Of course, if you don't want to I understand completely, and can only apologise for importuning you.'

It was a classic negotiating technique—putting something forward, then seeming to withdraw it.

'It isn't "importuning" me,' she responded. 'Only... Well...um...if you really think...?'

He moved in for the close. 'Kassia, thank you! I'm so grateful. OK... What would be involved is this: I'll send a car for you, the day after tomorrow, then there will be the evening function and a night at the hotel. Of course I'll be covering all expenses. Would that suit? I can't thank you enough. I'm just going to need the address of your mother's house...'

He had it already, but she would not know that.

She gave it to him, somewhat falteringly.

'Great,' he said. 'Look—do forgive me—there's an incoming call from Athens that I need to take. I'm so sorry. But, Kassia—*thank you*!'

He rang off. There was no incoming call, but he didn't want her having second thoughts. He put his phone away, crossed to the sideboard in his hotel suite, and poured himself a beer from the fridge. Relief was filling him. She might have turned him down...might have had other commitments. But she hadn't. She'd agreed to what he wanted.

The ice-cold beer slid down his throat as he took a long draught of it.

And what he wanted was to see her again. As soon as he could...

Oh, he wanted her to fall in with his plans—wanted all of that—but he wanted more, too. A lot more...

He took another, more leisurely draught of his beer.

Of that he was quite, quite certain. Because against all his expectations, all his assumptions, Kassia Andrakis had become more than just a means to an end. She was an end in herself. A very desirable end.

When she had become so, he didn't know. Sometime during that day at Blenheim, or that evening at the college dinner. Sometime when he'd found himself reacting against her downplaying of herself, her passive acceptance of herself as someone men would not be attracted to, when all along...

I know I can show her herself differently, teach her to think well of herself, not ill.

And now he had the opportunity to do just that. The perfect opportunity. It could not have worked out better.

He smiled to himself, finishing his beer, and set aside the empty glass, anticipation filling him. And impatience.

He wanted Kassia with him already.

The rest of the day, and the whole of tomorrow, stretched glaringly, emptily, frustratingly ahead.

CHAPTER SIX

KASSIA LOOKED OUT of the window of the car—a sleek, black expensive model—which had arrived that morning at her mother's house and conveyed her to London. But not to the Hotel Viscari. She looked out again, puzzled. The chauffeur had pulled up against the kerb and was now opening her door. She got out, surprise and confusion in her face. They were outside a famous and very expensive department store in Knightsbridge.

What on earth...?

Her phone buzzed and, still confused, she got it out of her bag to answer it.

It was Damos.

'Kassia? Don't move. I'll be there in a moment.'

Even as he spoke she saw him coming out of the store. Striding towards her. As she saw him she felt her pulse give a kick. She tried to crush it down, but it was a kick all the same.

One she knew she must not feel.

Because from the moment Damos had hung up the phone the day before yesterday she'd known she should have said no to him. Her reaction to his call had told her that—warning her in the way her pulse had quickened, the way gladness had warmed through her just at hearing his voice again. It was pointless to react like that when she was just not the kind of woman a man like Damos Kallinikos would ever think of in the way that she or any other female would love him to…

She sighed inwardly. Yet she'd said yes to him all the same. Said yes because it would be another chance to see him again when she'd thought she never would. How could she have turned it down, pointless though it was? Pointless though it could only ever be?

But now, as he strode up to her, a smile slanting across his face, she felt that betraying kick in her pulse come again, felt her gaze cling to him. And she knew that she was glad— so glad—to have said yes to him. And if it seemed odd— unlikely, even—that he didn't have anyone better than her to invite tonight, given that this was not provincial Oxford but the metropolis, where surely he must know more people…well, she just didn't care. There might be all sorts of reasons she didn't know about as to why he found it more convenient that she should accompany him tonight, and she knew she did not want to question it. Only to be glad of it.

Her own face broke into a warm smile in response to his and she knew her heart rate was quickening. Just seeing him again was a thrill. He was looking a million dollars, in a business suit that sheathed his tall, lean frame, and his dark eyes were as warm as his smile, doing such things to her composure…

He came up to her, greeted her, his voice as warm and welcoming as his smile, and then turned his attention to the driver.

'I'll be about five minutes,' he said.

Then he took Kassia's elbow. His touch was light, but it only added to the hollowing out inside her as he guided her towards the store's entrance.

'Damos, I don't understand. What are we doing here?'

She knew there was confusion was in her voice, as well as that hollowing in her stomach, that kick in her pulse.

He paused, turning to her. 'What I didn't get a chance to tell you on the phone,' he said, 'was that this affair tonight is themed. Thirties Art Deco. Guests are asked to dress accordingly. I've ordered a thirties-style tuxedo for myself, but you'll need something appropriate too. Don't worry...' He smiled reassuringly. 'It's all taken care of. I just have to hand you over, and the specialists here will do the rest.'

He guided her inside the store, towards a bank of elevators.

'But I brought the dress I wore to the college dinner...' Kassia said helplessly.

Damos shook his head. 'Not nearly Art Deco enough,' he said, mentally casting the frumpy green dress into the nearest bin. He ushered her into an elevator. 'All the styling will be taken care of, and of course I'll be covering the cost. All you have to do,' he said, his smile warmer than ever, his eyes warmer still, 'is relax and enjoy.'

Kassia felt breathless—for so many reasons. At seeing Damos again...feeling the warmth of his smile on her...the warmth of his dark eyes on her. But for more as well. She was being whirled away...taken over...by Damos...

The elevator soared upwards, making Kassia feel even more breathless, and she was still breathless when the doors sliced open and Damos ushered her out, towards a very elegantly dressed middle-aged woman who had clearly been waiting for them to emerge.

The woman smiled at Kassia. 'If you would care to follow me, madam...?'

Kassia looked helplessly at Damos. He smiled again.

'See you later,' he said. 'The car will bring you and your overnight bag to the Viscari when you're ready.'

He lifted a hand in farewell and stepped back inside the elevator. The doors sliced shut, and he was gone.

Slowly, feeling her heart thumping idiotically, Kassia went after the elegant middle-aged woman to her fate.

I'm having a dress fitted…a nineteen-thirties-style dress. That's all, she told herself.

But that was not all at all…

Damos stood gazing out of the window of his suite at the Viscari. The rooftops of St James's were beyond, the royal palace was just visible, and there were glimpses of St James's Park as well in the early-evening light. One hand was curved around a whisky glass, the other was plunged into the pocket of his trousers. They were a slightly wider cut than he was used to, and the jacket felt and looked different as well—more waisted, with a satin shawl collar, and it was worn over a white backless waistcoat with a vee-shaped notch. His cufflinks were gold—a new purchase for the occasion—and the wings of his shirt points stiff with starch.

But his thoughts were not on his thirties-style evening dress. They were on Kassia's.

It was just perfect that this affair tonight was Art Deco styled—it provided the perfect reason why Kassia should not be in charge of her appearance…the perfect opportunity to indulge her with a makeover.

Anticipation edged in him and he took a mouthful of his whisky, enjoying the fiery warmth of the choice single malt. He did not have long to wait now. The stylist had phoned through to say she was on her way.

He clinked the ice in his glass, suddenly tensing. He had plans for tonight—plans that would bring to fruition what he had set out to achieve since first getting wind of Yorgos Andrakis's intentions for Cosmo Palandrou—and for his daughter. By tomorrow morning those intentions would be ashes. Because by then Kassia Andrakis would not be anyone Cosmo Palandrou could ever want as his bride.

He felt his fingers grip the whisky glass more tightly. Into his head came the words that had come to him over dinner at the Oxford college.

Tell her—tell her how her father wants to use her for his own interests.

And yet again came his negation.

It was too risky…her reaction too uncertain. Not just for her father's plans for her. For his own.

His expression stilled for a moment, becoming shadowed.

There was one risk above all that he knew he was not prepared to take. Not any more.

I don't want her thinking I only want to make her mine to thwart her father's plans.

That might have been true once—but no longer.

I can't have her thinking that.

The certainty that that was not something he could risk filled him. And that, he knew with equal certainty, was why he wanted…needed…her to think differently about herself. To see herself differently. So that his seduction of her—his wooing of her—would be accepted by her for its own sake…for hers and his.

The shadow left his expression. Soon—any moment now—he would have his proof that that was not just possible but irrefutable. Being styled, gowned and adorned the way she would be tonight must show her, once and for all, that she had no need at all to accept the self-imposed limitations which she felt so unnecessarily she had to live by.

I will change all that for her—so that she can know without doubt or any reason not to believe it that I desire her…

And that is all that will be needed for us to be the lovers we shall be...

He felt himself relax, easing his shoulders, taking another mouthful of whisky. He turned his head to the rosewood pier table set opposite the sideboard in the suite's reception room, his eyes going to the thin, flat box delivered by secure courier a short while ago.

The final touch for the evening.

His phone pinged and he glanced at it. It was a text from the driver of the car collecting Kassia, telling him she had just arrived. He knocked back the last of his whisky, setting the empty glass on the sideboard, putting away his phone.

In moments, Kassia would be here.

Hungry anticipation speared through him.

He could not wait to see her...

Kassia edged cautiously along the wide back seat of the car that was pulled up outside the Viscari and carefully—very carefully indeed—stepped out. Behind her, the chauffeur touched his cap politely, shut the car door, and got back into the driving seat to pull away again. Kassia realised the doorman was also touching his top hat to her, instructing a bellboy to fetch her bag and convey it to her room, and holding open the wide glass front door of the hotel for her to enter.

Carefully—very carefully indeed—she walked into the foyer.

She was in shock, she knew. Had been in shock since the stylist, surrounded by the bevy of assorted specialists who had been at work on her for three endless hours, had gently turned her around to face the floor-length mirror in the private changing room.

Kassia had stared. So *much* had been done to her. Way before the dress fitting itself. She'd been whisked into a salon to have her hair washed, and a colour rinse put in, then skilfully snipped—not to shorten it, but to trim and shape it. Then some kind of rich product had been smoothed into it, so that now it had been blow-dried it felt no longer lank and limp, but lush and glossy, glowing a deep chestnut.

And it hadn't stopped at her hair. All sorts of peels and wraps and heaven knew what had been applied to her face and throat, until her skin had felt like satin. Her eyebrows had been shaped, her lashes tinted, and then the manicurist had started work on her hands, smoothing in velvety creams and applying nail extensions and dark red varnish. Then had come the face make-up—and finally had come the gown.

Her breath had caught as one of the assistants had brought it in. Its silky, silvery folds had slithered over her head, over the soft satin camisole and stockings into which she'd been helped, and her feet had been slipped into shoes whose heels were higher than anything she was used to.

And when it had all been done, she'd gazed at herself in the mirror.

She had felt disbelief filling her, and shocked amazement—and beneath and above both of those something else. Something that had made her glow from the inside out...

She'd felt her breathing quicken, her pulse quicken, and she could feel it still now, as she walked carefully on the high heels she wasn't used to across the grand marble-floored foyer—busy at this time of the day—looking around for the elevators.

A member of the hotel staff stepped forward.

'May I help you, madam?' he enquired politely.

Kassia murmured the suite number Damos had texted her.

'Of course. This way, if you please.'

She was ushered into a waiting lift, emerging moments later into a wide, thickly carpeted upper lobby, off which suite doors opened. The staff member led her towards the one marked ten and pressed the intercom. A moment later the door buzzed open and he was ushering her inside, withdrawing as Kassia stepped through.

She was in an elegantly appointed reception room and Damos was standing by the window. Looking right at her.

Not moving.

Completely and absolutely still.

But from across the room Kassia could see in his eyes something that suddenly, gloriously, made the glow inside her blaze...

Damos could not move. Not a muscle. it was impossible even to think of doing so. His entire being was focussed on his gaze, on what he was seeing.

For an endless moment Damos just went on staring. Then: 'You look *sensational*!'

No other word would do. A surge of triumph went through him. He crossed towards her, taking her hands, his eyes alight.

'I knew—*knew* it was possible!'

His eyes worked over her. He thought of the way he'd last seen her. In that concealing, shapeless, doing-nothing-for-her shop-bought dress, with her hair in a stark knot on top of her head and her face bare of make-up.

It was a thousand miles away from the woman who stood there now—a thousand, thousand.

Her evening gown was in a distinctive thirties style, cut on the bias, completely slinky, with narrow shoulder straps, and it pooled at her ankles. It was made of some kind of shimmering, silvery material that reflected the silvery sheen of her eyes—eyes which skilful make-up had now deepened and enhanced. Mascara lengthened her lashes, her cheekbones were sculpted by blusher, and her mouth—oh, her mouth!—was enriched with lush, dark red lipstick. He glanced down at her hands held in his, and saw that it matched her newly manicured nails.

As for her hair—its nondescript light brown had been coloured to a rich chestnut and it was loosened, finally, from its confining knot to sweep, lush and long, around one bare shoulder.

And her figure...

A rush of renewed triumph went through him. Finally he was seeing what her dowdy clothes had so obdurately concealed from him. Her fantastic, slender, racehorse figure, delicately sculpted, graceful and long-limbed.

His hands tightened on hers for a moment.

'I can't get over it,' he said, still sounding stunned. 'Kassia, I can't *believe* you were hiding all this!'

He saw a tremulous smile form at her lips.

'I... I didn't know I was hiding it,' she said.

He gave a laugh, swiftly lifting one of her hands to his mouth, and then the other, then lowering them again.

'Well, one thing is absolutely for sure—you are *never* hiding it again!

He led her forward, releasing one of her hands, admiring the way her walk was swaying now, courtesy of her four-inch heeled silver evening shoes. He turned her towards the mirror over the pier table. Still holding her hand, he looked at their reflections, side by side. He heard her breath catch. Saw her beautiful eyes glow more silver.

'Total thirties Hollywood,' he said. 'The pair of us! We just need to be in black and white!'

Kassia's eyes met his in the mirror. That intense glow was still in them.

'You look amazing yourself,' she said.

Her eyes lingered on him, and he felt another surge of triumph go through him.

'We definitely both look the part,' he agreed. 'Oh, Kassia…' His voice changed. 'I just can't get over how sensational you look!'

'Me neither,' she said. She gave a laugh as tremulous as her smile had been. 'I'm in shock—I know it. I just didn't realise—'

She broke off, and Damos picked up her words. 'But I did, Kassia,' he said. 'I realised that you simply believed your parents' verdict on you. But don't you see?' His voice changed again. He wanted, *needed* her to understand. 'They judged you by their own standards. Think about it… Your mother is petite and full-figured—you said so. And that, obviously, is the look that drew your father to her. It's the look he likes. But you, Kassia, are like a thoroughbred racehorse!' He gave a laugh, low and triumphant. 'Tonight,' he said to her, 'everyone—and I mean *everyone*!—is going to think I've got the latest supermodel on my arm!'

He squeezed her hand lightly, then let it go. Triumph was still surging through him. He'd wanted so much for Kassia to see herself differently, to be freed of that self-deprecating self-image she'd lived with. And now she was—because surely she could not deny what her own eyes were telling her. It would be impossible to do so—the evidence was right there. And he could tell she was beginning to get used to it, to accept it. She was still gazing at her reflection, glowing at what she was seeing, partly in disbelief, partly simply looking alight with delight.

'Let's have a drink before we head up to the roof terrace,' he said now. 'We've plenty of time. What can I pour you?'

Her gaze dropped from her own reflection as if reluctantly. 'Oh. Um…if there's wine later, then probably just another OJ spritzer is best now.'

'Coming right up,' Damos said, crossing to the sideboard and deftly pouring her a long glass, handing it to her, fixing himself a non-alcoholic mixer. He'd already had a whisky, and alcohol would be flowing tonight. He didn't want to drink too much…

Because there is only one way that I want this night to end.

His eyes went to her again as they clinked glasses, their gazes entwining. He felt his pulse kick…saw the sudden flaring in her eyes…felt his pulse kick harder.

He felt desire creaming in him and he knew, with a surge of triumph that was the strongest yet, that finally Kassia would accept that desire. Would believe it possible.

She cannot deny the beauty that is hers. The beauty that glows in her eyes has been revealed not just to me, but to her.

As he clinked his glass to hers he could see that belief taking a stronger hold yet in her. She was throwing little glances at her reflection, and he saw how doing so brought a curve of delight to her lips, intensifying the silvery sheen of her eyes.

'To tonight,' he said now, his voice low. 'To a wonderful evening!'

Silently he added his own coda.

And to an even more wonderful—wondrous!—night together.

Because one thing was for sure. Tonight, without the slightest doubt, was the night she would become his.

He only had to let his gaze rest on her, drink her in, to tell him why he was so determined on it.

Because any other outcome right now seemed quite, quite impossible…

This feasting of his gaze on her, on all the stunning beauty that she herself could now finally believe in, would this very evening release her to him.

Kassia was in a dream. A dream of disbelief and delight... delight and disbelief. But disbelief was impossible—every glance at her reflection told her that.

And more than her own reflection was the look in Damos's eyes as he gazed at her.

It was the look she had longed to see but never thought to. Had thought it pointless to yearn for. Never thought it possible.

But now...now it is.

She felt her heart rate give yet another skip, her breath catch yet again.

Now, thanks to the hours of grooming and pampering and adorning, she could hold her head up and know with the wonderful, heady delight inside her that no longer did she have to hopelessly, resignedly envy that parade of svelte, glamorous beauties the Internet had shown her draped all over Damos Kallinikos. Now she was one of them...

I truly am! I can see it for myself. Staring me in the face...

Her glance went to the mirror again, confirming it. How could it be otherwise when she was in this incredible gown, with her hair, her face, all telling her that now she was just the kind of woman Damos Kallinikos would want at his side?

She felt wonder course through her, hearing his words again. Could it really be that simple? That she had never believed she could look as she so obviously looked now just because her style of beauty was not her parents'? She had just accepted it—accepted their verdict and never tried to do anything with herself, never seen the point of it.

Realisation speared through her. It had taken Damos to see it—to see what she herself had not been able to and to get her to see herself differently.

And he's seeing me differently too...

She knew he was. She could see it in his eyes, in his gaze. A little thrill of new awareness went through her. It was telling her that now he was not seeing her simply as a pleasant companion for a day, an evening...but as someone much more. Wonderfully, thrillingly more...

And if having Damos smile at her had been able to make the colour run into her cheeks simply because they were enjoying their day together at Blenheim, or their evening at the Oxford college, now there was a new warmth in his eyes, a different warmth, and it was as if she, too, could have the same warmth in her own eyes. For the same reason.

I don't have to hide it any longer...conceal it—deny it.

She felt a shimmer deep inside. Felt her breath catch. Delight lit up within her—more than delight, oh, deliciously more. She smiled. She could not help it. The smile played at her mouth and she was dazed with it...dazed with the glorious new knowledge shimmering through her.

Damos was setting down his glass, picking up a flat case lying on the pier table, flicking it open.

'Sensational though you are, you need just one more adornment,' he said.

Kassia's eyes widened. Inside the case was a glittering loop—a single strand diamond necklace—and two equally glittering brooches in distinctive Art Deco style.

'They're originals from the period. I hired them for tonight,' he told her.

He picked up the brooches, holding them out to her, and Kassia took one, turning towards the mirror again to fasten it very carefully at the base of one of the evening dress's straps, and then do likewise with the other.

'And now the necklace,' said Damos.

He was standing behind her and he lifted the glittering strand into his hands, bringing it forward to loop it around her throat, carefully smoothing aside the fall of her hair. The stones felt cold on her skin—but his fingers, deftly fastening the necklace, were warm.

That deep, delicious shimmer inside her came again.

He stood back, his hands resting lightly on her upper arms, his palms warm. She could catch the tang of his aftershave, could feel his hands lying so devastatingly on her bare arms.

The shimmer inside her intensified as they gazed at themselves reflected in the mirror in front of them.

'How incredibly beautiful you are, Kassia,' she heard him say.

His voice was a husk, and his eyes…oh, his eyes…were drinking in her reflection. As she was drinking in his.

She felt faintness drum through her. Did she sway? She didn't know. Knew only that Damos was bending his head towards her, dipping it to the curve of her bared shoulder. The sweep of her hair was heavy around her other shoulder as she felt his mouth graze her skin softly, sensuously. The touch of his hands was so light…

She felt weakness wash through her, her eyelids dipping.

He straightened, and a slow, intimate smile curved his mouth as he held her gaze again in their reflection.

'My beautiful, beautiful Kassia,' he said.

And in his voice, warm and husky, was surely all that she could ever have longed to hear and never thought she could.

But she did tonight. Oh, tonight—thanks to the incredible, fantastic transformation that had been wrought upon her—she knew that the reflection of that other woman in the mirror was truly herself...all her...

And it was a wonder beyond all wonders that it should be so...

She held his gaze in the mirror, her eyes twining with his. The breath was stilled in her lungs.

And then Damos was letting his hands fall from her, holding out his arm to her in a stately fashion.

'Time for our evening to begin,' he said, and his smile reached to her, warm and inviting.

Her own smile answered his. Just as warm. Just as inviting.

She placed her crimson-tipped hand over his sleeve.

'Oh, yes...' she breathed. 'Oh, *yes*...'

Damos strolled forward. The rooftop garden of the Viscari St James was *en fête* indeed. Lights glittered from the perimeter trees, glowed from the undergrowth, festooned the paved terrace in front of the glass-fronted, glass-roofed restaurant to one side of the space.

'It's like fairyland!' Kassia exclaimed.

Her hand was still resting on his sleeve, and he could feel her leaning on him slightly. Maybe those four-inch heels were taking some getting used to. Or maybe she was a little nervous?

As they'd emerged on to the roof terrace level, already thronged with guests, he'd felt her tense for a moment. Maybe she was self-conscious about her sensational new appearance? She was certainly drawing eyes—just as he had said she would. Heads were turning as they walked out into the warm evening air to take in the amazing roof garden.

Whatever the reason, he liked the feeling of her leaning on him, letting him support her. They were, he knew, perfectly matched as a couple. Even in heels she was still a tad below his height, and so incredibly slender, her racehorse figure sheathed in the fantastic gown skimming her body, her bare sculpted shoulders a work of art in their own right.

A sense of possessiveness fused through him and he drew her little more closely against him. She was here, with him, for this evening.

And for the night ahead.

Because there could be no other way to end the evening...

Certainty filled him. Never had he been more certain, more sure, that *this* was what he wanted most in all the world.

Kassia—with him.

How far we've come...

His thoughts reached back to his first glimpse of her, crouched down in that trench, head bowed over her work, teasing out that bit of broken pottery in her baggy, dusty work clothes, her face flushed with heat and dabbed with earth, her hair clamped to the back of her neck, with loose, damp strands around her face. How little he had thought of her then except as someone he must engineer an acquaintance with...get to know without having the faintest interest in her personally. Simply because she was Kassia Andrakis.

How totally different it was now.

Totally.

Oh, she was Kassia Andrakis still, but as they stood together, admiring the scene before them, the only thing he cared about was that she was Kassia.

He felt desire course through him again as he caught the scent of her perfume, felt the warmth of her tall, graceful body half leaning against his. Filling his senses.

A server was circulating with trays of drinks, and he helped himself to two flutes of champagne, passing one to

Kassia, who took it, bringing her gaze from the roof garden back to him. Their eyes met and melded.

'To a memorable evening,' Damos murmured, clinking his glass gently against hers and then lifting it to his mouth. She did likewise, almost in an echo of his gesture. They were still holding each other's eyes.

It seemed to Damos that suddenly everyone else around them had vanished…

Then a voice broke the moment.

'Damos! Good to see you. Very glad you made it.'

A couple were coming up to them—the Cardmans, London acquaintances of his, through whom he was here tonight.

He greeted them smoothly, introducing Kassia to them, and the Cardmans to her in return.

'Charles is in shipping too—a yacht broker,' he said, explaining the connection.

Charles Cardman's wife turned her attention to Kassia.

'Have you known Damos long?' she asked.

She was probing—it was pretty obvious to Damos.

'Not very,' Kassia answered with a polite smile, unfazed by the question.

'What brings you to London?' Charles Cardman asked conversationally.

'I was in Oxford for a conference and bumped into Damos there. He very kindly asked me along tonight. It's quite amazing, this roof garden! I've never seen it before, and it certainly takes the breath away.'

'Conference?' Valerie Cardman probed.

A good few years younger than her husband, she was nevertheless older than Kassia. She was very good-looking, but Kassia was outshining her hands down. Maybe Valerie Cardman did not like that, thought Damos a touch cynically.

'Oh…um…yes—Ancient Greece,' Kassia said politely. 'I'm an archaeologist.'

Charles Cardman gave a bark of laughter. 'I thought archaeologists were all fusty, musty and dusty!'

'Not this one,' Damos supplied smoothly.

He changed the subject, asking Charles something about the business. Valerie Cardman focussed on Kassia, and as Charles answered his enquiry Damos heard her asking where she had got her retro-style gown.

He heard Kassia name the department store, adding, 'Damos kindly sorted it all out for me. I hadn't got anything suitable with me. It's incredibly slinky, isn't it? I don't know how those Hollywood actresses managed to breathe— I barely can! Yours is gorgeous—like that fabulous one with feathers Ginger Rogers wears in that movie when she and Fred Astaire are dancing together out on a terrace by moonlight. And you've got her amazing figure too! I'm all up and down—not in and out!'

Covertly, Damos glanced at Valerie as he chatted to her husband. Valerie was preening.

'That's exactly the effect I was after!' she exclaimed, pleased. 'Tell me, do you dance? There's going to be dancing later—not modern stuff, but proper ballroom dancing.'

Kassia shook her head. 'Not in the slightest,' she said ruefully. 'What about you?'

'Oh, I used to be a professional dancer,' Valerie said airily.

'How wonderful! No wonder you're channelling Ginger Rogers tonight!' said Kassia.

With a start of surprise Damos heard genuine admiration in Kassia's voice, and he heard Valerie laugh, pleased.

'How she ever did those amazing routines in high heels I just don't know,' Kassia was saying now. 'I can barely walk in these heels, let alone dance in them! With my beanpole height I'm far more used to flats and being...' she gave a laugh '...just as fusty, musty and dusty as your husband says! This is a real night out for me.'

'Oh, you get used to heels—and to dancing backwards,' Valerie was saying airily. 'It takes core strength, though. And good balance.'

'I can imagine... And it must need so much training and discipline.'

'Years,' agreed Valerie.

'And talent,' her husband put in at this point, smiling benignly at her.

His wife laughed, pleased at the compliment.

Conversation became general, and Damos realised that Kassia was getting on with Valerie in a way he had just not envisaged.

Maybe I'm only used to women competing with each other...seeing each other as rivals.

Kassia wasn't like that—and he could see she had effortlessly disarmed Charles Cardman's wife just by being natural and friendly. She'd got on just as easily at the college dinner, too, adapting her conversation to whoever she was talking to, male or female. Asking them questions... showing an interest.

Most of the females he was used to going out with were only interested in themselves, he thought mordantly. Kassia was completely different...

It was yet another reason for liking her, and for liking being with her. And he acknowledged that her interest in other people, in subjects he had never bothered to care about, had been steadily broadening his own horizons, too.

In the long slog of the years it had taken him to turn himself from deckhand to wealthy businessman he had been tunnel-visioned. Concentrating on one subject only—making money, and then making more money. It had absorbed his life, and everything had been dedicated to that end—dedicated to improving things for himself. Even his romances, such as they were, were always with women who could play to that purpose, add to his image of success and wealth. Whether he liked them or not had never been relevant to his spending time with them.

His eyes shadowed for a moment. When he had first engineered his encounter with Kassia that had been his attitude towards her, too. She herself had not been important—only whose daughter she was. Thoughts moved within him—thoughts he had never experienced before. He had targeted Kassia Andrakis for a very clear purpose of his own that had had nothing to do with either her looks—or lack of them—or her personality. Had she been the very opposite of natural and friendly he'd still have done what he had—and even if the makeover had not been as amazing as it so dazzlingly was.

For a brief moment a frown creased his forehead, as if things were colliding inside him. Confronting each other. Then he shook his head mentally, clearing them away and clearing his expression. He no longer felt that way about Kassia…as if it was only who she was that was important to him.

I've changed.

For a moment it hung there…that simple statement that somehow wasn't simple at all. That was somehow significant…important.

But he did not yet know how he had changed—how it was important…

His eyes went to Kassia, still talking to the Cardmans about ballroom dancing and what they might expect later on, Her beautiful eyes were alight, her face animated. Something swept through him, powerful and strange. Something that he did not recognise, did not know. He knew only that it seemed to be possessing him...taking him over...

Charles Cardman turned towards him, breaking the moment. 'What about you, old chap? How's your foxtrot?' he asked genially.

'Non-existent,' he admitted, mentally refocussing with an effort. 'I can probably manage a waltz, but that's about all.'

'Ah, but what tempo?' Valerie challenged. 'Fast or slow?'

'Does it make a difference?' Damos asked, taken aback.

'Oh, yes!'

She launched into technicalities, and Damos held up his hand.

'I'm lost already! I'll just have to lumber around and do my best.' He threw an apologetic look at Kassia. 'I'll try not to step on your toes as well!'

'You'll both be fine,' Valerie said reassuringly. 'Charles and I will dance with each of you first and give you a quick lesson. Charles isn't at all bad for an amateur,' she said fondly, patting her husband's arm approvingly.

Damos smiled, thanking her, but he knew it was not Valerie Cardman he wanted to take into his arms to dance with—it was Kassia.

To feel her in my arms...to hold her...embrace her. She, and she alone, is the only woman I want in my arms. And in my bed. The only woman...

And again that strange, powerful, unknown feeling swept through him.

Possessing him...

CHAPTER SEVEN

KASSIA SMILED DREAMILY as Damos ushered her into the lift.

'What a wonderful, wonderful evening!' she exclaimed.

She meant it—totally. Little fragments of evocative classic songs and melodies from the nineteen-thirties were playing in her head. She hummed aloud now, still smiling. Beside her, Damos gave a low laugh.

She glanced up at him, her eyes and her face aglow. 'Thank you so much for bringing me. I wouldn't have missed it for the world!'

'My pleasure,' he said promptly, and he smiled at her in return.

In her high heels she was very nearly at eye level with him, and it felt strange. At least, she thought wryly, she'd got used to walking in the heels. And dancing too.

Her smile grew dreamier. She'd told Valerie she couldn't dance and it was true. Certainly she hadn't been able to compete against the older woman's professional skill and flair, which had been such that, once the band had struck up after dinner, and the wide doors had been opened to the terrace beyond, the other dancers had given her and her husband all the space they needed to show off their moves.

But the Cardmans had insisted she and Damos take to the floor as well, each of them, as Valerie had promised, taking a dance with them. So Kassia had tentatively danced with

Charles, even though she was a good head taller than him, and accepted his instructions.

She had been aware that her attention was on his wife, in Damos's arms, similarly instructing him. Aware, too, that she did not like to see Damos with another woman...

When the number had ended and another had been struck up it had been a waltz, slow and beguiling. Charles had released her, and Valerie had released Damos. As Damos had turned to Kassia she'd felt a sudden tremor go through her. She'd all but frozen, rooted to the spot as one of his hands clasped hers and the other curved around her waist.

'Put your free hand on my shoulder,' he'd said encouragingly, and gingerly...oh, so gingerly... Kassia had done so, gazing helplessly at him.

Her eyes had gone completely wide, and she'd felt every fibre of her body tensing. To be in Damos's arms like that...

Then the music had swept into its full melody—and Damos had swept her away.

Into heaven. Just...heaven...

The same melody was in her head now, and on her lips, as she gazed dreamily at Damos.

What was happening to her she didn't know—hadn't known since he had swept her across the dance floor, turning her around, and around, and around as they glided away. What her feet had been doing she hadn't the faintest idea—she only knew what her heart rate had done. It had soared like a bird in flight...up, up and away...

She'd felt herself leaning back as they'd turned around the floor, and his hand at her waist had been supportive, and protective, and so much more. So much more than simply the firm clasp of his hand holding hers. So much more than the slight, but oh-so-potent smile he'd bestowed upon her as his eyes had rested on her face, their long lashes half veiling them, but never for a moment concealing what was in them…

She was still floating on air, floating off to heaven…just floating and floating.

The elevator stopped and the doors opened. Damos was ushering her out. His key card was in his hand and he was sliding it into the lock of the door to his suite. And she was going in…not even thinking to ask about her own room… not thinking at all…

Not realising that Damos was closing the door behind him…turning her towards him…and taking her into his arms…

Her mouth was silk. Her lips satin. His own lips only grazed lightly, so very lightly. He was using all his self-control to keep it like that. His arms were around her waist, hands on the rounded swell of her hips. As he lifted his head from hers he smiled that same half-smile he'd used on her as he'd taken her into his arms to dance with her. His eyes poured into hers.

'You have absolutely no idea,' he breathed, 'how much I have been aching to do that.'

She was looking at him with dilated eyes…eyes that had turned as silvery as her gown. There was wonder in them, and more than wonder. She was looking at him in such a way that there was only one thing to do—only one.

He kissed her again. And this time the lightness could not hold…could not withstand his own desire. Desire that she had inflamed from that first stunned silence as she had walked towards him, her hidden beauty finally revealed to him. Desire that had been building achingly all evening.

Dancing with her had been both bliss and torture—but now the latter was gone and only the former could exist.

And bliss it was.

His hands tightened on her hips and instinctively he drew her closer to him as his kiss deepened. She yielded to both— and it was all he wanted. Her mouth opened to his, and in her throat he heard her give a little helpless moan. It inflamed him more...

Did she realise just how she was arousing him? Well, she would know soon—it would be impossible to deny. And he had no wish to deny it—no intention of doing so. No intention of doing anything at all except what he had been wanting to do all evening.

Her hands had lifted to his shoulders and he could feel, deliciously, the fingers of one hand sneaking around the column of his neck, spearing into his hair as his kiss deepened yet more. And against the wall of his torso he could feel, even more deliciously, her beautiful, shapely breasts...peaking.

Was she aware of that? Well, she would be soon...very, very soon.

He drew back, breathless, his gaze still pouring into hers. 'Come,' he said.

His voice was low, husked, and filled with his own desire. He reached to lift her hand away from his nape, clasping her loosely by the wrist as her other hand fell away and he freed her from his own grasp. For one long, lingering moment he let his gaze feast on her as she gazed back at him, eyes wide, pupils dilated, lips parted and bee-stung, her face filled with wonder and bemusement and so much more.

His mouth curved into that half-smile and he led her to his bedroom.

And to his bed.

Her gown fell from her in a pool of silver at her feet. Beneath she was wearing only a satin camisole and wispy briefs. A confection of lace was all that was keeping her sheer stockings on her thighs. She'd heard Damos's breath catch as he'd slid down the zip at the back of her gown. She could not move—and why should she? For heaven was here, in his gaze upon her.

Desire blazed in his eyes, melting her with its heat. He said something in Greek, too low for her to make out the words. Besides, her blood was singing in her ears, her heart pounding in her breast. Then, abruptly, he was kneeling, and she realised he was unfastening the straps of her heeled sandals. She stepped out of them, her hand automatically going to his shoulder to balance herself. Then his hands were lifting…lifting to where her stockings were fastened. He undid them and one by one…silkily, gorgeously, arousingly…slid them down her limbs, freed her from them. Only then did he get to his feet again.

'Your turn,' he said.

And that half-smile that did such things to her was at his lips again.

She reached forward, sliding her hand between his jacket and his shirt, moving it up to his shoulder, easing his jacket from him. He caught it as it fell, tossing it carelessly aside to a nearby chair where it hung loosely. Then he lifted her hands to his tie. Carefully, a little frown of concentration on her face, she pulled at the ends, feeling it come away. Then, while her hands were there, she slipped the top button of his dress shirt. And then the next one. And the next…

Sliding her hands under the fine lawn of the dress shirt to the warm, smooth wall of Damos's strong chest beneath, she let her hand splay, easing across languorously. She gave a sigh of pleasure…

As if it had been a signal his hand shot up, fastening around her wrist, and then, without Kassia quite understanding how, he was sweeping her up into his arms and lowering her down upon the bed. He was ripping the rest of his clothes from him. Waistcoat, shirt and tie and all the rest joined the jacket.

Instinctively, she shut her eyes. Damos fully clothed could set her pulse soaring—but Damos *un*clothed...

She felt the mattress give as he came down beside her and heard a low laugh come from him. He leant over her and she opened her eyes again, to look into his. They were looking down at her with a glint in them which was half humour and half something quite, quite different...

'Oh, Kassia—so shy?'

She gazed up at him wide-eyed. Her heart was beating tumultuously, the blood was singing in her ears, and she was filled with wonder...a dazed, almost disbelieving state of bliss. And yet...

She gave a crooked smile.

'I... I think I am,' she answered.

His mouth dropped to hers. Gently, softly. Briefly.

'Leave it to me,' he told her, his voice warm.

Kassia did just that...

And Damos took her to paradise.

Took her there with a slow, seductive touch.

He explored her body with lips and palms and the exquisite expertise of the tips of his fingers, which found every most sensitive, erotic point of her body...

Slowly, sensuously, he ensured she felt every moment for its maximum pleasure. He eased from her the silky camisole, exposing the sweet mounds of her breasts, their peaks cresting as he circled them lazily, arousingly...oh, so exquisitely arousingly... He was teasing, and lingering, and then... Oh, how could it feel so good, so exquisitely delicious, as his mouth lowered first to one ripened breast and then the other and his tongue flicked at her straining, hard-crested nipples until she wanted to cry out with it.

Then, still holding one engorged breast beneath the soft kneading of his palm, he lowered his attentions. His mouth glided down from the shallow vee between her breasts to the flat plane of her abdomen, fastening his other hand around one hip. His mouth glided lower…and lower yet…

The hand at her hip moved to the wisp of her panties, easing along their waistband, gliding them from her body, then returned to where his mouth now was…

A moan broke from her, and she felt her thighs slacken of their own volition. He eased his hand between them, returning his mouth to her bared breast. And from breast to vee a flame started, running through every vein in her body. A flame that was in the tips of his exploring fingers as he reached to find the delicate tissues at the heart of her femininity.

A gasp sounded in her throat and her hands moved to close over his shoulders, to splay out across the nape of his neck. At her breast, at her feminine core, his ministrations drew from her such sensual delight, such an intensity of pleasure, such a deliciously, achingly mounting arousal as she had never known was even possible…

She moaned again, thighs slackening yet more, head turning on the pillow. An ache was building in her—a yearning, a craving—and the incredible, unbelievable sensations he was drawing from her were impossible to endure. It was impossible not to want more…and more, yet more…

Her blood was surging, engorging, swelling and ripening, exciting and arousing, quickening and intensifying. Her vision was dimming, blurring… The world was dimming, blurring…

Because nothing existed…

Nothing at all except…
This.
This, this, this…
This moment, this now, this absolute, total *now*, was sweeping through her, dissolving her, making her molten, liquid, sweeping through her, pouring into every cell of her body, lifting her, lifting her…
Oh, sweet heaven…
Impossible that she should be feeling what she was feeling. Impossible that such pleasure, such bliss, such gorgeous, gorgeous melting, such heat and sweet, sweet fire should be burning through her… Sweeping on and on…endless and consuming…

And then, before she could even become aware of anything else at all except what was possessing her, what she was possessed by, Damos was lifting away from her, lifting away his mouth and his palm and his gliding fingertips. Instead he was lowering himself over her, one hand cradling her beneath her hips, raising her to him as her whole body flamed yet more blazingly. His body fused with hers, filling her, engorging her, melding with her, and around him her body, completed now by his possession, pulsed and melted.

She clung to him, her hands around his shoulders, bowing up towards him as she cried out. He did too—a hoarse tearing of sound—and she knew with the scything knowledge that was in her thighs, tightening against his, to hold him, keep him there, just there, where her body was pulsing against his, drawing him deeper and deeper yet, making her cry out again and again…

She knew that for him, too, it was as it was for her…

Possession and passion…slaking and sating and never, never letting go…not her of him or him of her…

She held him within her, holding him in the cradle of her

arms, wrapping his strong, hard body in hers, holding him and holding him even as their bodies cooled and stilled...

She was dazed, breathless, and her heart was hammering yet, pounding within her—echoing, she knew, with a kind of exultation, the pounding of his own heart, beating against hers.

He lifted away from her a little, his torso only, and she felt him drop a shaky hand on her still-flushed cheek, smoothing it softly, gazing down at her with an expression in his eyes that made her breath catch.

'Kassia—'

Her name—that was all—and it was all she wanted to hear.

A smile curved across her mouth, wide and tender and embracing. 'I don't think I'll be shy next time,' she said softly, her gaze clinging to his, that smile still playing on her lips.

A crack of laughter broke from him.

'Dear God, Kassia, if this was you being *shy*...'

He swept her over to her side, still in her embrace, so that his own embrace could tighten. Their thighs tangled now, as they slipped from each other, and he was kissing her now—not with passion, for passion was exhausted, but with a kind of sealing of what had been between them... and a promise, too.

Kassia felt again that catching of her breath in wonder and wonderment. It was a promise of all that was yet to come before the night was over...

Damos lay drowsily and contentedly, Kassia tight in his arms, as daylight finally pricked its way into the room, edging around the drawn curtains. Amazement still possessed him. After the first time he'd set eyes on her, crouched in that dusty trench, could he ever have thought to this moment now? To how it would be for him? For her…?

Yet again that strange, powerful emotion swept through him. He did not know what it was—knew only that it possessed him. Filled his being.

Idly, languorously, he smoothed his hand over her hip as she lay cradled against him. He let his mouth softly kiss her shoulder, snuggled into his, as memory of the night that had just passed played in his head.

A night of passion—oh, such passion!

Kassia had made love without inhibition. He smiled reminiscently at his saying to her, *'If this was you being shy…'* She had given of herself without stint, with an ardent desire that had more than matched his own, that had had her body…her beautiful, slender body…clinging to his in her ecstasy. An ecstasy that had come time and time again…

Perhaps remembering that right now, while she lay cradled against him, was not the wisest thing… The feel of her body tight against his own was having an effect on him that, as full wakefulness came over him, was increasingly impossible to ignore.

His lazy smoothing of her hip moved forward, reached towards the vee of her thighs, and his mouth at her shoulder started to glide, to taste the delicate line of her throat, to tease…to arouse. Even as he himself was aroused…

She stirred in his arms, a little sigh breathing from her, as he nestled the hand at her vee into the contour of her body, trailing his mouth up from her throat to catch at her lips…

His own arousal was growing…intensifying. She was waking too now, half turning in his arms, her mouth moving to his, tasting and teasing, her thighs slackening. Her body was still pressing back against his…knowingly, sensually. He gave a low laugh, luxuriating in her effect on him, and his kiss deepened, no longer teasing and tasting but probing, possessing. And she answered in kind, turning fully now, so that the engorged tips of her already ripening breasts grazed his chest, arousing him yet more.

He gave a growl, sliding his hand around her hip once more to pull her against him, so that the full strength of his arousal was tangible. His thighs moved over hers in possession...his of her...hers of him. Their bodies were fusing yet again, desire crescendoing. He felt her back arch, her thighs strain. Her head was thrown back, the heat of her shuddering climax flushing her skin, her hair a wanton tangle on the pillow as her head threshed from side to side and she cried out with abandon. Then his own moment was upon him, and nothing else in the world existed except Kassia—this amazing, incredible woman who was his...

In a way he had never known she could be.

CHAPTER EIGHT

KASSIA STOOD NEXT to Damos, gazing out over the loch in front of them, a dreamy expression in her eyes. Had she ever dreamt that life could be so wonderful? No, she never had—it would have been impossible that she could ever have dreamt it so. Because never had she dreamt that a man like Damos could be in her life.

But the very expression 'a man *like* Damos' was wrong—it was Damos himself she had never dreamt about.

How wonderful he was! Just wonderful! And since that *wonderful* night she had spent with him her life had been transformed. Transformed into blissful happiness.

She turned to look at him now, her gaze drinking him in. He was standing beside her on the beach, binoculars pressed to his eyes, watching a large bird soaring over the forested far shore, behind which the ground rose upwards to a high, rounded ben.

She felt her heart give a little skip, the way it always did when she looked at Damos.

Is this really real...me being here with him?

That first morning, surfacing from that wonderful night, it had seemed almost a dream to her. But it was a dream he'd made real—was making real every day.

They'd spent all that first day together in his suite—in his bed—dining in as well. It had been another whole day until they'd surfaced.

'Let's get out of London,' he had said. *'I want you all to myself—somewhere miles and miles from anywhere.'*

Kassia couldn't have agreed more. She wanted Damos all to herself as well.

The Highlands of Scotland fitted the bill perfectly. Here, standing on the stony little beach, with the dark water of the narrow loch lapping gently near their feet, the only dwelling for miles around was the place where they were staying.

A castle—a genuine Scottish castle. Theirs for a whole fortnight.

It was only a small one—a solid, stone-built keep, set back from the loch's edge. It had an imposing entrance hall upon whose walls was a fearsome display of weaponry, a gracious drawing room with a cavernous fireplace and comfortable tartan sofas, an elegant panelled dining room with an oak table and furniture, and upstairs a bedroom with a four-poster bed with velvet hangings, and cosy sheepskins on the polished wooden floor.

The castle might be ancient, but it came with modern plumbing and central heating—and a married couple, the MacFadyens, to cater to their needs.

Kassia had texted Dr Michaelis from London, and told him she was going to take her annual leave after all, then headed north with Damos, on wings of wondrous happiness.

Was she wise to run off with him like this?

Her words to Valerie Cardman echoed in her head, after Valerie had asked her if she'd known Damos long.

'Not very long...'

That first dinner with him on his yacht, for the sake of his funding next season's excavation, then a day out at Blenheim, an evening dining at the Oxford college, and then the Art Deco dinner-dance at the Viscari.

That was all, really. Barely three days.

Yet here she was, plunging into a glorious, wonderful, ecstatic affair with him.

How well do I know him—I mean, really know him?

She heard the question in her head. Heard it and discarded it.

'It's an eagle—I'm sure of it!' Damos exclaimed.

Kassia was glad of the diversion to her thoughts.

'I think eagles keep to the high ground, don't they?' she said doubtfully.

'Well, it's swooped down from the ben, then,' Damos persisted. He lowered his binoculars, turned towards Kassia. 'Why *are* Scottish mountains called bens?' he asked.

'No idea,' said Kassia. 'We must look it up. It's probably Gaelic. I do know what a Munro is, though.'

'A Munro?'

'Yes, they are the mountains that are over three thousand feet—around a thousand metres or so—named after the Victorian mountaineer who first climbed them all. It's now a tradition—to bag a Munro!'

Damos looked interested. 'Could we bag one?'

'We'd need some decent kit,' Kassia said. 'I think there are plenty that don't actually need to be climbed, as such, but even walking would require proper kit. Idiots still go up in trainers and tee shirts, and then slip and fall. And then the weather turns and Mountain Rescue has to be called out.'

'We'll buy all the right kit,' Damos pronounced. 'It must be sold everywhere in Scotland. Then we'll drive to Inverlochry and load up with everything we'll need. Are you up for it? Bagging a Munro?'

Kassia's eyes rested on him. For Damos she would bag every Munro he set his sights on. Climbing them with him at her side would be bliss...

But then everything with Damos at her side was bliss.

'But not today. Today is just a getting-to-know-this-place day,' he said. He looked around him. 'It really is pretty good,' he said approvingly. 'A loch all to ourselves…a castle all to ourselves. And sunshine too.'

'And midges. The curse of the Scottish summer!' Kassia laughed. 'It's better here by the loch, I think. The breeze is keeping them away.'

'We can have a picnic lunch here,' Damos said.

Kassia groaned. 'How can you think of lunch already, after that gargantuan breakfast Mrs MacFadyen loaded us up with? Not so much a full English as a full Scottish. You put away at least two kippers and half a dozen Scotch pancakes—and that was even before you tackled the bacon and eggs and toast and marmalade!'

He turned back to her. 'I need to keep my strength up,' he said.

He dropped a kiss on her mouth. As he drew back, his eyes were glinting. They were the colour of the dark, peaty loch water, Kassia thought, as she gazed helplessly back.

'And so do you,' he murmured wickedly. He kissed her again. 'Glad we came?' he asked.

Her eyes shone as she answered him. 'Oh, yes,' she breathed. 'Oh, yes.'

Her questions—questions she did not even want to ask—evaporated into the clear Highland air. Perhaps she had known Damos only a short while, and perhaps she was being swept away by him, by her own happiness—but how could she argue against it?

And it wasn't just the sensual ecstasy she found in his arms.

That first day with him, after bumping into him like that, out of the blue in Oxford, surely had been a sign? And the easiness between them, when she had never thought there could ever be anything between them—surely that told her there was a connection there? Something that went beyond the heady delights of the nights they spent together?

We can talk together, laugh together, be together. And it feels so right, so natural...as if it were meant to be...

Surely all that was a sign that what was happening between them was good? That she could trust it. Trust Damos—and trust this wonderful, blissful happiness...

'Good,' he said, and there was satisfaction in his voice. Then he pointed towards the end of the little beach. 'There's a path there. Shall we see where it leads? Work up an appetite for lunch?'

He set off, and Kassia followed. The path was wide enough, threading between the shoreline and the spruce and birch, to afford easy going along its mossed surface, even in the trainers she and Damos were wearing. For anything more demanding, let alone bagging a Munro, they would definitely need proper walking boots.

They got them the following morning, after driving into the local town—a good twelve miles away from their remote castle—together with a fearsome array of mountain-proof gear that Damos insisted on. Kassia smiled indulgently. He was so enthusiastic she hardly liked to point out to him they were unlikely to need quite so much.

The shopkeeper was perfectly happy to cater to his foreign customer's very expensive enthusiasm, and as they finally left, piling umpteen bag-loads into the back of the four-by-four Damos had hired when they'd landed at the airport on arrival, Kassia smiled fondly.

'You,' she said, 'have made that Scotsman a happy, happy man!' Her expression sobered. 'I just wish you hadn't bought so much for me, though, Damos.'

He shut the tailgate with a slam.

'How could I bag a Munro without you? I wouldn't even know what one was, for a start! Now, all that kitting up has made me hungry. Where shall we have lunch? How about over there?'

He pointed across a cobbled square lined with solid granite buildings towards an ancient-looking pub.

They walked towards it together, Kassia slipping her hand into Damos's, knowing how right it felt. How very right it felt to be with him. She felt a glow inside her. However much she might have rushed into this affair with Damos, it was something she was going to trust.

Because I know I can.

Damos's brow furrowed in concentration. Duncan MacFadyen, the husband half of the castle's married couple, was teaching him how to cast a fishing line. It required focus, and just the right amount of flexibility in the wrist.

'Aye, that's right, your grip's fine. Now, lift back, and—'

The line shot forward, arcing across the water. Damos, like his tutor, was standing calf-deep, wearing waders, in the shallow, fast-flowing river.

'Och, not bad…not bad, laddie,' said Duncan MacFadyen. 'Now, reel it in and try again. Watch for those low trees, mind, or they'll tangle your line in a gnat's breath!'

Damos did as he was instructed. His focus was absolute. But then, when his mind was set on something, when he saw a goal he wanted to achieve, he went after it until he had it in his possession—whether it was skill at fly-fishing, or…

His thoughts were diverted for a moment. Behind him, curled up on a groundsheet and tartan rug on the bank, he knew Kassia was sitting, half reading, half watching him, enjoying the pale Scottish sunshine, batting away the midges.

Kassia—her name was sweet in his head. Sweeter than he had ever imagined it would be. But then, how could it not be? She was all that he wanted, and this remote spot in the Highlands was the perfect place for her to be with him. It gave him Kassia all to himself, far away from anyone else. His thoughts were shadowed for a moment. Far away from Greece, where word might get out of their being together. His eyes darkened as he thought of her father and Cosmo Palandrou. Then, deliberately, he pushed them both aside. That whole business was for later—not now.

The shadow left his eyes. Now was for Kassia, for his time with her, for their time together.

And how good it was…how very, very good. Every single moment of every single twenty-four hours.

He felt his breath catch with searing memories. By night, Kassia's passion for him swept him away. She was as ardent in his arms as that very first amazing night. She gave herself so totally to him, so completely—and he returned it in full. Never had he known how it could be…

And by day? Oh, by day there was hour after hour of good times, one after another.

They had bagged their Munro, duly kitted out, making a day of it. They'd chosen an easy one, unused as they both were to hill-walking, ascending up through larch forests to emerge on to the heather and head up to the peak, where they'd hunkered down out of the keening wind to eat their sandwiches and the obligatory Kendal Mint Cake, looking out from their lofty viewpoint over the glories of the Scottish Highlands spread around them, mile after mile.

The next day, needing a rest, they'd set off in the four-by-four to explore the area, driving past brooding lochs and forest-covered slopes, all ringed by heather-covered mountains. They'd stopped for lunch at a wooden lodge, both of them braving haggis and neeps—Damos smiled in recollection—before driving on to seek out a towering waterfall plunging down from the heights, sending myriad rainbows dancing over the spray.

Yesterday Duncan had taken them out on their own loch in a motorboat, exploring the far shore, cruising the length of it, while he regaled them with bloodthirsty tales from Scotland's warlike history, of feuding clans and invasion from both the Vikings and the English. And today Duncan was initiating him into the mysteries of fly-fishing…

'Och, laddie—did I not warn you?'

Duncan MacFadyen's admonishment made Damos realise that he'd let his thoughts wander and his second cast had, indeed, caught the low-hanging branches on the far side of the river. Disentangling it took Damos some time, but he had learnt his lesson and refocussed his attentions. After another half-hour he was doing distinctly better, and Duncan was saying they might try for a fish after lunch.

Lunch was taken seated on folding chairs around a table that opened up from the boot of the four-by-four, which was drawn up near the riverbank for the occasion. As ever, Mrs MacFadyen had done them proud, with a hot raised crust venison pie, poached salmon scallops, root vegetable salad, and fresh-baked crusty bread with salty Scottish butter and tasty Scottish cheese, all washed down with local beer for him and Duncan, and cider for Kassia.

Their repast finished with a 'wee dram' that Duncan produced from the silver hip flask kept about his person.

Damos downed his in one. Kassia choked over hers.

'Oh, good grief!' She looked at Damos and Duncan. 'How on earth do you cope with that?'

Duncan chuckled. 'Practice, lassie, just practice,' he said. He turned to Damos. 'Ye'll be wanting to visit our local distillery, mind. They've a fine single malt—aye, verra fine indeed. Take a bottle or two back with you to Greece. And if it takes your fancy you can buy yourself a cask, keep it here to mature. There's many a rich man does just that.'

Damos's eyes glinted. That might be a good idea. He went into a detailed discussion with Duncan about the excellence of the local whiskies and then, a second and final sampling of Duncan's flask done, went off with him to try his luck with a salmon.

He looked about him as he waded back into the water. This was good, this day—very, very good. The sun, the scenery, the salmon—and Kassia.

What more could he want right now?

Greece, Athens, Cosmo Palandrou, Yorgos Andrakis and any thought of outmanoeuvring them, helping himself to Cosmo's logistics empire and taking it from under Yorgos Andrakis's nose, seemed very far away.

Irrelevant.

And supremely unimportant.

Kassia's hand hovered over the chess board. She was deeply uncertain over what her next move should be. She could hear the rain pattering on the drawing room's leaded windows. The fine weather had turned, although the MacFadyens had said it was only a summer squall and would blow out overnight. Until it did, the drawing room was a cosy retreat, with the log fire roaring.

They'd kept indoors all day, except for an extremely bracing—and brief—expedition in gumboots and macs to the edge of the loch. Damos had huddled into his waterproofs, but Kassia had laughed, letting the rain wet her hair, and being buffeted by the wind—which had not been cold, only gusty, whipping up the waters of the loch and bowing the birch trees.

Damos, less used to British weather than Kassia, had endured it for five minutes, then called time, heading back to the castle.

She'd gone with him willingly, glancing sideways at him to where raindrops had caught his eyelashes, making her own heart catch as well. As it did every time she looked at him.

She stole another glance at Damos now, still hesitant about her next move. Chess was not her thing. She could never plan or plot ahead sufficiently. Damos—who had, so he'd told her, learnt chess on long sea journeys when he was a deckhand—was way better than her at it.

An enigmatic smile was now playing about his mouth as her fingers hovered indecisively, first over her bishop, and then her knight.

'I wouldn't, you know,' he warned. 'You'll lose your rook if you move your bishop, and you'll expose your queen if you move your knight. Here, this is safest...' He reached to advance one of her unused pawns. 'Now your other bishop can threaten my other rook. Except—'

His hand moved to his own pieces, and before she realised it he'd moved his knight to guard his rook, which then gave his bishop free run at her king.

'Check,' he said.

'Oh, grief—what do I do now?' Kassia said in dismay.

'You move your bishop to intercept mine and protect your king—which will likely lose you your bishop, but...' he pointed out '...it then lets your knight threaten my queen.'

She sat back, pretty much lost. 'I just don't think I've got the right kind of mentality for this,' she confessed. 'I can never see more than one move ahead—if that.'

Damos smiled pityingly. 'Foresight is essential—and planning ahead. And not just in chess, of course. In life, too. It's about spotting unexpected opportunities, if they present themselves,' he went on. 'And then moving to exploit them.'

She frowned. '"Exploit" is not a pleasant word.'

He gave a shrug. 'It just means use,' he said.

'Precisely,' she answered.

He shook his head. 'There's a difference between using opportunities to one's advantage and using people to one's advantage…making use of them.'

'I suppose so,' she allowed.

Her thoughts strayed back to that exchange with him at Blenheim, over the implications of another word—*ambition*. Like 'exploit', and 'use', 'ambition' was another word she was wary of, associating them too much with her father.

But Damos is nothing like him! she retaliated.

He would never make use of other people to his own advantage. Hadn't he told her, that day at Blenheim, that he'd made his money honestly? She should trust that declaration—he would never do anything underhand, exploit others, take advantage of them, use them for his own ends. Her thoughts darkened. Totally unlike her father, who never bothered with people he could not make use of, or who were not useful to him.

She was glad that at that moment there was a knock on the door and then Mrs MacFadyen was coming in, wheeling an old-fashioned wooden tea trolley. Yet again she had done them proud, with fresh bannocks, potato scones, toasted tea cakes and an array of jams and rich butter. If that left any room, there was a plate of crisp shortbread and a freshly baked Dundee cake, glistening with cherries and laden with almonds.

Damos was rubbing his hands in happy anticipation, praising her efforts and thanking Mrs MacFadyen enthusiastically with his ready smile. The stout, middle-aged Scotswoman was no more immune to Damos's charm than any female, and bridled with pleasure at his fulsome compliments.

'Och, get away with you!' she told him, bustling from the room.

Kassia smiled affectionately at Damos. She tried to imagine her father even thanking Mrs MacFadyen, let alone bothering to compliment her.

He and Damos are complete opposites—totally different in character.

She couldn't even make allowances for their differences arising from the origins of their respective wealth. Both men were self-made—her father and Damos—but there the similarities ended. Her father was ruthless, always using other people for his own ends—if he could, he'd have used her, his own daughter. She knew that bitterly well.

Damos is nothing like him—nothing!

It warmed her to think so.

'OK, what is that phrase in English? Are you going to "be mother"?' Damos was asking her.

And, again, it was a welcome interruption of thoughts she did not want to have.

She reached for the teapot—silver and elegant—and filled their cups—fine porcelain. The renting of this castle was not coming cheap, that was for sure. As well as the castle itself, furnished with antiques and luxuriously appointed, there was the lavish fare provided by Mrs MacFadyen, as well as the 'extras' on offer from her husband.

She and Damos had already ticked off fly-fishing and boating on the loch, as well as putting their four-by-four through its offroad paces on a tough, unmade track into the forest. Damos had driven—with Duncan to guide him—and obviously enjoyed it hugely, while Kassia had hung on for dear life. Duncan had taken them bird watching, too—Damos had been smug about finally spotting a golden eagle soaring way over the mountaintop—and even deer stalking, though both she and Damos had made it clear that they were just going to stalk, not shoot. Kassia was conscious that that was somewhat hypocritical, considering the delicious venison dishes that appeared at the dinner table…

As for dinner—Mrs MacFadyen did them proud there, too, every night, and Damos and Kassia responded accordingly. Though they dressed down for their activities in the day—their newly bought walking kit was seeing a lot of use—at night Kassia delighted in dressing the part for Damos. He put on his tux, and she the pale blue chiffon evening gown he'd insisted on buying her in London—along with an array of well-cut co-ordinates that flattered, rather than concealed, her tall figure.

Now, with the wonderful new confidence in herself that Damos had released in her, she knew that for the first time in her life she could really enjoy wearing fashionable clothes, making the most of herself instead of the least. And to that end, every night here in the Highlands, she made up her face for the evening and dressed her hair elegantly, glowing inside as Damos's admiring eyes rested on her.

Then she would take his gallantly proffered arm and walk down the imposing flight of stairs beside him, sweeping into the drawing room for pre-dinner drinks and then taking their places at either end of the polished oak table in the adjacent dining room, laden with silver and crystal, shimmering in the candlelight. There, they would await the arrival not of dinner, but of the piper who would announce it. He was Duncan's nephew, and he would march into the dining room in full Highland regalia, the music of the pibroch filling the room.

After he'd retired, dinner would follow hard on his heels. With vintage wines, rich dishes and traditional Scottish desserts, they dined sumptuously—Kassia had swiftly become a fan of Scottish raspberries, heather honey, toasted oatmeal and whisky cream whipped up into cranachan.

And finally, after heading back upstairs, her hand once more on Damos's arm, she would be escorted to their bedchamber. And there, with a sensuous skill that sent her into helpless meltdown every time, he would let his fingertips glide over her skin, arousing, touch by touch, all the sweet, sweet fire that he always so wondrously elicited from her and set glowing in every tremulous cell of her body.

To make her his.

Consummately, consumingly his…

And he is mine—oh, he is mine.

Because he was. Surely he was? How could it be otherwise when every night she held him as close to her as he held her to him? His heart beat against hers; hers beat against his. As if it could never be any different.

And in those precious hours—in the sweet, slow watches of the night—how could she not think, hope, believe what every passing day, every passionate night, was telling her.

I am falling in love with him.

Was it wise to let it happen? To give herself up to all that she was feeling? To give herself up to the tremulous, uncertain, but oh-so-longed-for hope that Damos might be falling in love as well? Did she…could she…dare to hope…?

CHAPTER NINE

DAMOS FROWNED. Kassia was having her morning shower—he could hear the water splashing—and he was using the time to catch up with his business affairs. Athens was two hours ahead of the UK, and the morning there was well advanced. Most of the updates he was receiving were routine, but the one that was currently bringing a frown to his forehead was not.

Things were on the move between Cosmo Palandrou and Yorgos Andrakis, so his sources were telling him. The director of a well-known firm of corporate accountants who specialised in mergers and acquisitions, and were known to have been previously engaged by Andrakis on such matters, had been seen arriving with his team at Cosmo's company HQ. Andrakis was clearly having due diligence done.

And there was more. Andrakis had been reported as lunching with the senior partner of a law firm specialising in inheritance and marital contract law, giving weight to what Damos was sure Andrakis had in mind for Cosmo and his daughter.

Damos closed down his laptop, still frowning. But not because it was clear that Andrakis was moving in on Cosmo Palandrou. Because two worlds were colliding.

The world of Kassia, here with him in this idyllic Highland retreat, so wonderful to him, so special, theirs and theirs alone.

And the world of his life in Athens—his business life, that had driven him all his life.

He set the laptop aside, getting to his feet and walking over to the bedroom window, with its breathtaking view out over the loch and the forest and mountains beyond. The fortnight with Kassia was flashing by…day after glorious day, night after passionate night.

I don't want it to end.

The assertion was in his head, almost audible and crystal-clear. He heard it again, more clearly still.

His gaze rested on the vista beyond, his thoughts running. His time here in the Highlands must end.

But not my time with Kassia.

The words were as clear as the Highland air around him. And their imperative just as clear.

There is no reason for it to end.

Why should it? Why should his time with Kassia not continue when they were back in Greece? Oh, once—long ago now, it seemed—he had assumed that the affair he was going to engineer with her would end once its purpose had been achieved. But now…

Now it was absurd to think that.

He felt his mouth tighten, made himself think of what he'd just read about Andrakis and Cosmo Palandrou. For an instant he wished it all to perdition—wished he knew nothing about it, knew nothing of what they were planning and scheming. He consigned his own whole damn plan to perdition as well. He wanted nothing to do with it any more—nothing to do with his plan for getting hold of Cosmo's empire.

Then he drew in a breath—a sharp one. Forced his brain back into the gear it normally operated in, the well-oiled channels it was used to. Acquiring Cosmo's logistics business made perfect sense. It would provide an expansion and a synergy for him that would significantly increase his own reach, bringing in handsome profits after he'd knocked the ailing business into shape and had it properly managed.

That hadn't changed.

His mouth tightened. And nor had the fact that Andrakis was going to try and use his own daughter to get hold of it first.

Unless...

Unless I spike his guns.

Using the method he'd envisaged from the first.

It's all I have to do.

That was the beauty of it—the simplicity.

A question forced its way into his head. He didn't want it to, but it did all the same.

And is it still that simple?

He felt his jaw tighten, his eyes resting on the surface of the loch, its waters dark and impenetrable. Just as were his thoughts.

He brought them to the surface. Saw them clearly.

Yes. Yes, it was still that simple. All he had to do was show Cosmo that Andrakis's daughter was not available to be his bride—just as he had planned from the off.

It really is that simple.

And because it was so simple there was no reason not to stick to it—not to go ahead with it...go through with it.

For a moment longer his gaze went on resting on the dark waters below, as if there were currents moving deep below the surface that had not previously been there, stirring deep waters in unknown ways.

Then, abruptly, he turned away, not wanting to think about it any longer. The day stretched ahead, and they were planning on heading off further afield, doing more sightseeing—this time towards the coast and Dunrobin Castle—for the day was fine and sunny.

He could hear that the shower had cut out, and shortly afterwards Kassia was stepping into the bedroom, wrapped in a towel, her hair pinned up loosely on her head, tendrils falling damply around her face. She looked effortlessly beautiful—bare shoulders, long legs, slender body.

He crossed to her, with a familiar glint in his eyes and an even more familiar tightening in his loins.

'That,' he told her, and he could hear the husk in his own voice, 'is a very dangerous thing to do, Kassia. If you want us to set off sightseeing in good time.'

His hand reached for where she'd knotted the towel over her breasts, gently easing the knot loose.

She caught his hands. 'Damos, no!' she laughed.

His eyebrows rose. 'No?'

'Yes! As in no,' she said firmly, stepping away from him. 'Breakfast will be waiting for us!'

He gave her a considering look. 'Hmm, tough choice… One of Mrs MacFadyen's gargantuan breakfasts versus making passionate love to you.'

She laughed again. He liked to hear the sound, and answered it with a laugh of his own.

'OK, breakfast wins. But…' he held up a hand '…don't think I won't claim making passionate love to you when we get back this afternoon!'

She blew him a kiss, but kept her distance.

Damos knew why—and knew, with a sense of deeply masculine satisfaction, that she would have been just as happy to defer breakfast a while…

'It's a date,' she promised, and her eyes had a glint in them that matched his own.

She turned away, fetching fresh undies from the chest

of drawers and a smart pair of trousers—nothing baggy any more, Damos thought with satisfaction—and a stylish cotton top to go with them that skimmed her breasts and shaped her slender waist. Brushing her hair out, she clipped it back with a barrette. Its new rich colour still held, catching the sunlight.

He watched as she applied a little mascara, a trace of lip gloss, but nothing more. There was appreciation in his regard. Oh, when she went for the full works—face, hair and gown—she could look sensational, just as he'd told her that evening at the Viscari Art Deco dinner-dance.

But she does not need to—not for me. Just to see her like, this is enough…more than enough.

Just being with her was more than enough.

And he had no intention—none—that he should not be with her…

OK, so their time here in the Highlands was coming to an end and soon they would be returning to Greece. But there…

I'll get the business of Cosmo and her father out of the way, dispose of it, and then focus entirely on Kassia.

It was a pleasing prospect—a very pleasing one indeed. *Kassia and me—me and Kassia…*

Again, as he had that very first night with her in London, he felt the strange, powerful emotion sweeping up in him that he could not identify. He only knew that it was possessing him.

Body and soul…

'Well, it was certainly a magnificent place,' Kassia said, as they headed back to their very own castle—a mere scrap in comparison with the vastness of Dunrobin Castle, another ducal residence, this time of the Duke of Sutherland. 'Such a pity about the Highland Clearances, though.' She gave a sigh. 'So ruthless…'

Damos steered the four-by-four along a road threading through dramatic scenery. 'Sheep were simply more profitable than crofting,' he said.

'So that makes it all right? Evicting the crofters? Burning down their crofts so they couldn't return?'

He shook his head. 'It's understandable, Kassia. The profit motive is a powerful one. It drives people to do things they might otherwise regret.'

She felt unease prick at her.

But there are some actions that shouldn't ever be undertaken. However profitable! However much money is at stake.

Her thoughts darkened. Her father would have no qualms about doing whatever was necessary to make a profit. Whatever it did to anyone else. Her expression softened again. But Damos was not like that at all. He'd just been stating blunt truths—not advocating them. Let alone practising them.

He was speaking again.

'And don't forget, as we learnt today, that crofting life was hard for the crofters. The idea was that they should move to towns, get other jobs—easier ones—or even emigrate, as so many did, and make a better life for themselves in the colonies. It wasn't completely black and white.' His voice changed. 'It seldom is,' he said.

She could hear something in his voice—a note of constraint—and looked across at him as he drove back towards their castle along the winding road. Some things *were* black and white, though, surely…?

As if he sensed her doubts over what he was saying, he turned towards her. A smile lightened his face.

'Let's not talk about such sad things,' he said. 'They are over and done with, thankfully. Let's talk about us, Kassia.'

His smile deepened, but then he had to flick his eyes back to the road again, as they climbed up towards a col. For all the warmth of his smile, Kassia felt a chill. Their fortnight was nearly up—what would come after?

Is this all there will ever be?

It was the question she did not want to ask…and yet the closer they came to the end of their holiday, the more intrusive it had become.

She knew the answer she wanted to give—longing filled her, and hope—but would it be the same for Damos? She had dared to hope…but hopes could be dashed. Discarded and dismissed.

Damos was about to speak again, still keeping his eyes on the road, his hands on the steering wheel. There seemed to be a lump forming in her throat…a stone… The dread of what he was going to say.

'I know I'm based in Athens, and you're not, but I think we'll be able to manage, won't we? For weekends together, at least?' he posed. 'And we can grab all the holiday time we can get together as well?'

The stony lump in her throat dissolved instantly as relief coursed through her—his words were music to her ears.

'Oh, I'm sure we can!' she exclaimed.

He reached towards her with one hand, flashing his warm smile at her, then looked back to the road again.

'Great—so that's sorted. Now, how do we make the most of our last day here tomorrow? What about a visit to the whisky distillery Duncan recommended?'

'Good idea,' she agreed.

Warmth was filling her, as if several wee drams had just

been consumed, making her glow from the inside. This time in the Highlands was *not* to be the end for her and Damos!

He still wants me—wants us to be together. How wonderful is that?

Again, she knew the answer. It was more wonderful than she dared believe…

To keep him in my life…and me in his…

'We can get a couple of bottles for the MacFadyens,' Damos was saying now. 'As a thank-you to them.'

'And maybe I can buy a scarf or a brooch for Mrs MacFadyen,' Kassia said.

Happiness at what Damos had said to her about them seeing each other in Greece was filling her.

They were descending now, towards the valley in which their own loch lay. Soon Damos swung into the driveway of their castle. As he did so, Kassia heard her phone beeping from her handbag. She reached down to fetch it out, but as she glanced to see who the message was from her happiness collapsed like a punctured balloon.

It was from her father.

Summoning her to Athens.

Damos stood by the edge of the loch, its dark water lapping near his feet. Kassia stood nearby, hands plunged into her jacket pocket, her face grave. He stooped to pick up a pebble, flat and thin, and stood up to skim it across the loch. The late sun, still high at this latitude at this season, despite the hour, had gone behind a cloud.

'You don't have to go,' he said.

He didn't look at Kassia. But he could tell from her tone of voice that she was troubled.

'I think I do, Damos. He isn't asking much—just that I show up for some dinner or other. You know that he does that from time to time. I turn up and be his docile daughter, and then he goes on being patron of the museum. It's… it's worked so far. And I suppose, in a way, I don't want to break with him entirely. I just wish, sometimes, that he—'

She broke off, then spoke again.

'That he wasn't always so dismissive of me. I know I disapprove of so much about him…how ruthless he is in business…but, well…' She swallowed. 'He's still my father, and it would be nice if sometimes…just sometimes…he might think something good of me.'

'Do you?'

He looked at her now. Her face was troubled. But then his thoughts were troubled too. He knew the reason for Andrakis's summons to his daughter. He was going to parade her in front of Cosmo, present her as a suitable bride, and set his scheme in motion.

But that was never going to happen.

Cosmo himself would to reject it out of hand.

The moment he knows what is between Kassia and myself.

On the short walk from the car down to the loch's edge thoughts had been marching through Damos's head. Now that the moment had come—now that Andrakis had shown his hand, made his move, set the timetable—Damos knew he had to react just as he'd always planned to do.

But do I have to do it in that way?

That was the question incising in his head now. What if he and Kassia simply flew back to Athens and went out and about together? Let word get out that they were an item? The trouble was, time was tight. Kassia had relayed, with reluctance in her voice—both at the summons itself and the high-handed short notice afforded her—that her father had demanded her presence the evening after tomorrow. The very day they were leaving the Highlands. And he had told her to present herself at, of all places, the Viscari Athena.

The irony was not lost on Damos.

The venue itself was a giveaway. It was newly opened, to great fanfare, and tables at the rooftop gourmet restaurant were like gold dust. Andrakis was clearly wanting to impress Cosmo.

Thoughts churned in his head. Unless Kassia refused the summons—and she seemed to be disinclined to do so, as she'd just said—there wouldn't be time for word to get out that he and Kassia were a couple. Which left only—

Only the way I originally envisaged.

And besides…

His question to her just now echoed in his head. Kassia's father had always sneered at his own daughter, castigating her cruelly for what he considered her lack of looks, condemning her to think so little of herself.

But now that is all changed!

No one—not even her cold-hearted father—could dismiss her now. Not any longer.

Kassia was speaking, answering his question. There was a sad, plaintive quality to her voice.

'But he never will, I know,' she was saying.

Damos's expression changed. Decisiveness fired in him.

He met Kassia's eyes full on. 'Oh, yes, he will,' he said, and there was something in his voice that only he himself could hear.

He stooped, picked up another flat pebble, straightened, and hurled it out across the loch. Then he took Kassia's hand.

'He will,' he said again.

CHAPTER TEN

KASSIA'S NERVES WERE stretched to breaking point. Oh, could she really go through with this? Inside she was trembling like a jelly. She had never enjoyed the times when her father summoned her, but she'd learnt to get through them with minimum stress. Simply by staying quiet and meek and docile, as she'd told Damos. By being as inconspicuous as possible.

But tonight…

Tonight was going to be totally different.

She felt her nerves jangle again as they made their way into the palatial lobby of the Viscari Athena. Given their early-evening arrival from the UK that day, Damos had booked them into a hotel that served the airport, to give Kassia the maximum time possible to get ready for the evening ahead. Even so, it had been a rush.

She'd had to shower, wash her hair, and then a hairstylist and beautician had arrived—Damos had seen to it—to style her hair, make up her face, do her nails, and then help her into the close-fitting bias-cut silvery dress she'd worn at the Viscari St James that unforgettable evening.

When she was finally ready, Damos's eyes had lit up.

'Sensational…' he breathed. 'Just sensational.' He came forward to take her hands, press them in his. 'Your father is going to be *stunned*!' He raised each hand to his lips in turn, then lowered them, holding them warmly still. 'Never,

never again will he be able to say the slightest derisive thing about your looks! Every head will turn when they see you!'

They were turning now, Kassia could tell as, nerves pinched yet again, they crossed the foyer heading to the elevators. If it hadn't been for Damos at her side, and her hand clutching the sleeve of his tuxedo, she would have cut and run. Not that running in these four-inch heels was possible...

But I won't run—I won't!

Resolve lifted her chin. All her adult life her father had disparaged her and belittled her for being plain and unlovely. Tonight she would show him.

It had been Damos's idea, out by the loch.

'It's the perfect opportunity to show him how fantastic you can look!'

And she did look fantastic—she knew she did. Her father would have to acknowledge it. It would be impossible for him to deny it. All the same, she knew that even with her new confidence about her looks she wouldn't have had the courage to look this incredibly glamorous for her father without Damos at her side.

As they stepped into the elevator she glanced at him, expecting to see a reassuring smile on his face for her. But he was looking ahead, not at her, and there seemed to be a tension across his shoulders. She wondered why...

Surely, she thought, he could not be apprehensive about turning up with her this evening? Whatever the reason her father wanted her to dine with him tonight, whoever he was entertaining, what did it matter if Damos was with her? They were a couple now—and it was something her father would have to accept.

Damos had said as much.

'If your father is happy with my joining the party, then fine—but if not... Well, there's no reason we need stay,'

he had told her. *'We'll have dinner together, by ourselves, and then why don't we hit a nightspot? I can't wait to start showing you off.'* His voice had been warm. *'I want all of Athens to see you with me!'*

The elevator was slowing, gliding to a halt. The doors were opening.

And now Damos did look at her. With her heels she was almost at his eye level, but not quite. Was it that slight angle that suddenly seemed to make his eyes look veiled...unreadable?

Then her nerves pinched again, and she tightened her grip on his sleeve.

He patted her hand briefly. 'You can do this,' he said, nodding at her.

She drew a breath, nodding wordlessly in reply and wondering, as they stepped out into the restaurant lobby, whether she had just imagined that she had heard him murmur, low and almost inaudibly, 'So can I...'

Damos led her forward. His shoulders were as tense as steel. Doubt knifed through him, but he thrust it aside. No time for that now. Whatever questions he'd put to himself about what he was doing had been set aside.

Out by the loch, with Kassia telling him of her father's summons, she had given him an opening he'd realised he could use. So she longed for her father not to deride her appearance as he habitually did? Well, tonight would be her chance. She would look as sensational at the Viscari Athena as she had at the Viscari St James.

And it's what I want too.

It would play perfectly to his own agenda. With Kassia looking such a knockout there could be no mistaking his interest in her—his involvement with her. And Yorgos Andrakis and Cosmo Palandrou would not mistake it either...

On his sleeve, he felt Kassia's fingers tighten. Well, there was no need. This would not take long. Oh, he'd told her that he'd be happy to join her father's party, if invited—but that was not going to happen. His presence would most definitely not be welcome, he thought grimly.

No, he would be whisking Kassia away the moment Cosmo and Yorgos got the message. He'd made a reservation for himself and her, requesting a table far away from Yorgos Andrakis. As far as anyone else would see, he and Kassia would simply be greeting her father and his guest, then dining *à deux* on their own. Reinforcing to all who saw them the fact that he and Kassia were together.

He paused by the desk, giving his name, and telling the clerk that they would be meeting with Kyrios Andrakis first. Then, with Kassia on his arm, he walked into the restaurant, raking his eyes over the tables, looking for her father.

He saw him immediately.

His mouth tightened. Yorgos had only one dinner guest with him.

Cosmo Palandrou.

Damos's eyes hardened. As they headed towards them he could see heads turning—Kassia, looking as sensational as she was, was drawing all eyes. But there were only two pairs of eyes he wanted to see her.

And see her they were...

He saw it happen. Saw her father, deep in conference with his dinner guest—his *only* dinner guest—glance up. Saw his eyes focus on who had just come into the restaurant. Saw, for a moment, complete blankness in them, as if he had no idea who the woman walking towards him was.

Then, as they approached, the blankness changed to incredulous recognition.

In one slow-motion movement, his incredulous gaze took in Damos, at Kassia's side. And his recognition changed to something else...a different expression taking hold of his face.

They reached his table, and Damos could feel Kassia's hand gripping his sleeve. But right now he had no spare attention for her. No attention for anything except what was happening.

Tension speared through him. So much was at stake.

And yet...

I want this done. Over and done with. So I can get the hell out of here with Kassia. I want Andrakis and Cosmo to get the message I am sending them, and for Andrakis to know his plan is now impossible. That I have made it so, and that now Cosmo will be looking elsewhere for a bride. And for a buyer...

It would not take him long to achieve all that—it was happening right now...

Cosmo Palandrou had looked up too.

Damos's eyes went from Yorgos to him. Then back to Yorgos. Then he smiled.

It was a smile, he knew, of victory.

Checkmate.

It was a sweet, sweet moment.

Kassia's grip on Damos's sleeve was rigid. Her father was staring at her as though he could not believe what he was seeing. Kassia could understand why.

Her eyes flickered for a moment, taking in the man dining with her father. Dim recognition plucked at her. It was Cosmo Palandrou. She'd met him before, at a larger dinner party a year or more ago, when her father had summoned her there. She took in the fact that the table was only set for three—which seemed odd. What was so special about Cosmo Palandrou that he was her father's only guest? And why would her father want her here as well?

She hadn't liked Cosmo Palandrou the first time she'd met him—he'd been as dismissive of her as her father always was, and he was physically repellent—overweight, with heavy jowls and small, pouchy eyes. His manner had been rude and abrupt, and she knew his company had often been in the press over a number of strikes and industrial disputes, as well as breaking environmental standards.

But she had no attention to give him now—all her focus was on her father. A tremor of trepidation went through her, and the sudden cowardly wish that she'd simply worn the unflattering green dress she'd bought in England and done nothing to her face and hair. Then she rallied. This was her golden chance to show her father that she was no longer the Plain Jane daughter he'd always castigated her for being. Maybe even finally to win his approval…

A stab of longing went through her, which she knew she should not allow. She had long ago given up on doing something right by his endlessly critical and dismissive standards…

But surely tonight there would be something different from the offhand way he usually noted her arrival? Surely this time he couldn't help but react differently, given her stunningly altered appearance?

But he was still staring at her—just staring—so she decided to make an attempt to break the moment, to give him some kind of greeting.

She never got the chance. Abruptly, her father was thrusting himself to his feet, his bulk considerable. Colour was riding up in his cheeks, his face working. Alarm speared in Kassia as he saw her father's beefy hands fist on the table.

Then words spat from him. Words that made her blench. Crude and explicit.

But they were not directed at her.

It was Damos who got them—full in his face.

Kassia's head shot round, She was appalled at what her father had hurled at Damos.

But Damos's mouth had merely tightened, his features steeled. There was a sudden hollowing in her stomach. He looked like a stranger to her. His face hard, his eyes harder.

Then Cosmo Palandrou was lurching to his feet as well, his expression ugly. He twisted his head, ignoring both Damos and herself. His focus was entirely on her father, and he was glaring at him with malevolence—a fury that contorted his ill-favoured features.

'What the hell are you playing at, Andrakis?' The question was a hiss, like a venomous snake.

She heard Damos's voice. Cutting across him like a knife. Answering him.

'Cool it—Andrakis is playing at nothing.' His voice was dismissive.

Cosmo's eyes flashed back across the table to Damos. He opened his mouth to speak, but Damos cut in again. His expression was still steeled, and there was a glint in his eyes too, a hardness in their depths.

His mouth twisted, and his voice changed as he spoke again. There was open mockery in it now. 'Relax. Andrakis's deal will still be on the table, Cosmo—if you still want to pick it up now, of course.' He paused, holding the other man's glaring gaze. '*Do* you?' he asked. It was a taunt—open and derisive.

Cosmo Palandrou surged forward across the table, rage in his face, mouthing expletives.

A cry broke from Kassia. What was happening? Dear God, what was happening? Nothing made sense—nothing at all.

Then her father was speaking. More than speaking. He was all but yelling, his features livid. And now it was not directed at Damos. It was coming at her. Right at her. Ugly and vile.

'Slut! You shameless, whoring slut!'

She gave another cry, horror and disbelief ravening across her face.

Her father's fisted hands slammed down on the table-cloth. *'Thee mou! Cristos!* How stupid can you be? Letting yourself be used by this…this…'

He used another word that made Kassia cry out again. But her father was storming on, his face filled with fury.

'He's used you—and you're too cretinously stupid to see it!'

'Enough!' Damos's voice was like a blade, slashing down. 'You will not speak to her like that!'

Her father's fury turned on him. 'I will speak to my *whore* of a daughter any way I want! The whore *you've* made of her!'

His lashing fury moved back to Kassia, his face enraged and twisting.

'You stupid, gullible, brainless idiot! You stand there, looking like the tart he's made of you… But do you really think that Damos Kallinikos would have looked twice at you if you hadn't been my daughter?' His scorn lashed at her. 'He wouldn't have given you the time of day, let alone warmed his bed with you! He's used you—made a whore of you—to get at me. Just to get at me! Attack me! Do you understand that? You imbecilic, whoring slut—'

She broke away from him, stumbling. A nightmare was enveloping her. She saw glass doors, staggered towards them blindly, hearing voices, harsh and ugly and raging, behind her. Her father's, Cosmo's—and Damos's too. Slicing through the air.

She had to silence them.

But they could not be silenced. How could they?

She reached the glass doors, pushed them open, plunged forward. She was out on some kind of paved terrace, set with tables. There were a few diners only, for the evening had turned chilly. The roof garden stretched beyond, framing the distant Parthenon, illuminated as it always was by night.

A path to the right opened up between high bushes and she stumbled along it, her ankles turning in her high heels. There was a voice behind her—urgent, calling her name. She reached a little clearing set with benches and lit with ornamental lanterns. Several more paths opened up. She paused, catching her broken breath, desperate still to get away…just get away…

'Kassia!'

Damos strode up to her. In the dim light his face looked stark. Like a stranger's.

But he *was* a stranger—a complete stranger—someone she had never known…

Till now. Till this nightmare.

He tried to reach for her arm, but she jerked away.

'Get away from me!'

His eyes flared. 'Kassia—I have to speak to you.'

'Get away from me!' she cried again.

She tried to plunge forward again, down a path—any path. Any path that would take her away from this nightmare. But she felt her arm taken in a grip she could not shake.

'Kassia, listen—*listen*!'

'To what? What else is there for me to hear? My father has said it all!'

Damos swore. Vehement and vicious.

'Your father is a brute! Don't take any notice of him—he isn't worth it!'

She rounded on him. 'And you? Are you worth anything more? *Are* you? Because what the hell was going on in there? What is all this *about*? Why is Cosmo Palandrou here? Why did you say my father's deal would still be on the table for him if he wanted it? What deal? And why... *why* did my father say those things about me? Those hideous, hideous things!'

The words, the questions, tumbled from her, anguished and uncomprehending. She was caught in this nightmare. She'd been catapulted into it. Her heart was pounding—she could feel it—and there was nausea inside her, rising up. She stared at Damos, still hearing her father's vile denunciation ringing in her ears.

Desperate denial filled her.

It's not true, it's not true!

'Damos, *why*?' she cried again.

Her eyes clung to his, but there was something wrong about them...something wrong in his face, in its starkness, in the tightness of his mouth, the set of his jaw.

A sudden fear went through her.

Damos was speaking, answering her. His voice was as tight as his expression.

'There is no good way to tell you this, Kassia—and I wish to God you'd never had to know! I never intended you to. But Cosmo Palandrou was there tonight because your father wants you to marry him,' Damos bit out, his face stark and grim. He gave a harsh, short laugh, bereft of humour, and his breath incised sharply. 'Make that *wanted* you to marry him.'

Kassia was staring at Damos. There was still something wrong with his face—but then there was something wrong with the universe right now. Something hideously wrong...

'Marry Cosmo?' she said. Her voice was hollow, her eyes uncomprehending.

'Yes,' Damos said grimly. 'Look, I have to explain...'

She heard him incise his breath again, as if forcing himself to speak, and when he did constraint tightened every word.

'Your father is after Cosmo's company. Cosmo's playing hardball and holding out for more. So...' His breath knifed again. 'Your father was going to throw you into play. Offer Cosmo the role of his son-in-law.' His voice changed. 'Kassia, I'm sorry. I'm so sorry that he said such things to you! I never—'

She raised her hand to stop him. What Damos had just told her about Cosmo Palandrou could not be true! It couldn't be! Her father couldn't possibly want what Damos said. And yet...

Why else would Cosmo Palandrou be here this evening?

The hollow inside her became suddenly a yawning chasm, And why else had her father been so angry to see her with Damos? So angry with Damos?

'He called me those vile things because you were with me,' she said blankly. 'But why?' Her words were suddenly as heavy as stones. 'Why was he saying...saying that you... you were only interested in me because I'm his daughter? And why was he so angry with *you*...?'

Damos's face was stark, his features like granite. She saw him take a breath—brief and harsh.

'Because,' he said tightly, his mouth set—as if, she

thought suddenly, he did not want to speak but was making himself do so, 'your father is not the only party interested in acquiring Cosmo Palandrou's company.'

Kassia heard his words. And as she did so a wheel started to turn very slowly somewhere in the recesses of her shattered mind.

'You,' she said. Her voice was empty.

He nodded. There was still that closed expression on his face, the same tightness in his voice and in the set of his mouth.

'Yes. I intend to acquire Cosmo's freight and logistics business,' he said. 'So I don't want him selling to your father—'

She cut across him. 'You knew Cosmo Palandrou would be here this evening, didn't you?' Her voice was still empty. 'You wanted to turn up with me—*didn't you*? So that he would see us together. So my father would see us…see us and know—' She broke off.

That same closed, stark look was in Damos's face.

'Yes,' he said. His hand tightened on her arm. 'Kassia, all I wanted was for your father and Cosmo to know about us. Then your father's scheme would collapse on the spot and we could just walk away. I never thought your father would react like that! Would say such things to his own daughter!'

The vile words her father had thrown at her were still slicing through her, each one drawing blood.

'My father does not take opposition well,' she heard herself say, her tone expressionless. 'And his temper,' she said, 'is very short.'

But that wheel in her head was still moving forward, slowly and agonisingly. Taking her to a place she did not want to go. A place she would have given all she possessed not to be taken to. But those words that her father had hurled at her, so vile and ugly, were taking her there.

She heard them again now, incising across her consciousness as if with sharpest knife.

'Do you really think Damos Kallinikos would have looked twice at you if you hadn't been my daughter? He's used you—'

Carefully, very carefully, she lifted Damos's hand off her arm and took a step back. The air felt thick, like the toxic air of a distant planet. The planet that she was now on. A million light years from all she had known. Had thought she knew...

'Tell me something,' she said, and she thought there was something wrong with her voice, as well as with the air she was breathing. It was starting to suffocate her. 'When did decide you wanted Cosmo's company? And when did you learn of my father's charming plans for me?' She stopped, trying to take another breath, but the toxic air was in her throat now, and it was suffocating her.

She forced herself on. Forced herself to ask the final question. The question she would have given everything not to ask, but must. *Must...*

'Was it before you showed up at the dig?'

He did not answer. His face had closed.

She let her eyes rest on him. On Damos. On the man who was not Damos. Not the man she'd just spent the three most wonderful weeks of her life with. Three weeks which had transformed her life. Transformed *her...*

Into a fool...a gullible, cretinous idiot.

Her father's vicious, excoriating, scathing castigation rang pitilessly in her ears. And more words too.

'Whore! Slut—shameless slut!'

She wanted to silence them, but it was impossible...impossible. Oh, dear God. To think she had wanted her father to see that she was no longer the crushed, dowdy daughter he'd always condemned her as being! To think that she'd thought her glamorous new look would achieve that...her fabulous transformation into a woman that any man might desire...

That Damos might desire.

A cry rose up in her from very deep, excoriating her.

Fool—oh, fool! It was never about you—never. Not for a single moment! It was only about—

'You knew,' she said, never taking her eyes from him though each word was like a scalpel on her skin. 'You knew that Cosmo Palandrou would not want to...to marry me if I had already—' She swallowed, and it was as if that scalpel was peeling the skin from inside her throat. 'If I had already, as my father so succinctly put it, *"warmed your bed..."'*

She fell silent. What else was there to say? What else could ever be said?

Except the word that fell from Damos's lips now.

'Yes,' he said.

She turned away.

She felt her arm seized, heard words breaking from Damos.

'Kassia—listen...listen to me! *Please!* It wasn't...isn't...'

She gave another cry, yanking her arm free, plunging down a path on feet that were stumbling, desperate.

Desperate to get away. Away from Damos.

For ever.

Damos watched her go. The universe seemed to have moved into another reality. One he didn't recognise. He had not given consent to it...given it permission to exist.

He turned. Headed back into the restaurant. He was conscious, with a fragment of his mind, that he was being looked at—the ugly scene at Andrakis's table had not gone unnoticed, unheard… The table was deserted now, and he could see the *maître d'* hurrying up to him, his expression anxious.

'Cancel my reservation,' Damos said, and walked past him, back out into the lobby beyond. Heading for the elevator.

He needed to find Kassia. Needed to find her, talk to her, explain to her.

It isn't the way she thinks it is! The way her thug of a father is making her think it is!

He felt his hands clench as he strode into the elevator. Hell, hell and hell! He should have realised that Andrakis would explode as he had. Take his fury at Damos out on his daughter.

He punched the button for the lobby and the lift hurtled down. Urgency filled him. Kassia might have come down in a service lift, but he could surely catch her as she left the hotel. He would wait by the entrance. If he missed her there, he'd find her at their hotel. But find her he must—he *must*.

How had he so misjudged the situation? Exposed Kassia like that? Self-castigation whipped through him.

The elevator doors sliced open, and he plunged out into the lobby.

He heard a snarl behind him. With a fraction of a second to spare, he whirled around.

Yorgos Andrakis was lurching up to him, coming out of the cocktail bar opening off the lobby.

'Looking for my *whore* of a daughter? She won't touch you—even though being your whore is all she's good for now!'

Yorgos Andrakis's face was ugly with fury and venom. Damos wanted to make it uglier still. His fisted hand moved faster than his thoughts. He smashed it into Yorgos Andrakis's face, his own face contorting, and then grabbed the man by his lapels, hauling him towards him.

'Don't *ever* call her that.'

His voice was a low, deadly blade, thrusting right into Yorgos's face. He drew back his fisted hand, ready to strike again. To pulverise. Smash to pieces.

He never made contact.

Kassia collapsed into the back of the taxi she'd flagged down when she'd emerged at the back of the hotel via the service staircase. Faintly, she gave the driver the name of the hotel near the airport and he set off. She closed her eyes, her face twisting painfully. She gave a smothered cry that was almost a sob, but she stifled it. She must not break down. Not now. Not yet.

At the hotel she made it to their room, terrified that she would find Damos there. But it was empty. She tore herself out of her gown, threw on some clothes to travel in, grabbed her handbag with her passport and credit cards.

Speed was essential—Damos could burst in at any point.

She made it downstairs, out of the hotel, and threw herself into the hotel shuttle bus. Minutes later she was in Departures, her eyes desperately scanning the board for a flight that had not yet closed. She didn't care where she went. Just away from this nightmare.

But she knew, with agony inside her, as she finally collapsed into her last-minute seat on a flight to Amsterdam, that she was taking the nightmare with her...

Damos emerged from the police station unshaven, his tuxedo crumpled, into the cold light of dawn. Both he and Yorgos Andrakis had been arrested after hotel security had rushed over, separating the two men, hustling them both out on to the pavement, then summoning the police. What had happened to Kassia's father he neither knew nor cared—he himself had been discharged with a caution.

The reason for his violent outburst at Yorgos Andrakis had been sympathetically regarded, hence his discharge. But for his night at the police station his phone had been removed from him. Now it had been restored to him he was phoning urgently, hailing a taxi to throw himself into, heading back to their hotel.

Heading back to Kassia.

Urgency drove him. Urgency and so much more.

But it drove him in vain.

His number had been blocked by her.

She had left the hotel.

There was no trace of her.

Over the following days there was no trace of her at her workplace either—and Dr Michaelis had been reserved in the extreme when Damos had finally badgered someone sufficiently to get him to speak to him directly. He had informed him, stiltedly, that Kassia had taken indefinite leave.

Damos's next attempt had been at her mother's house. The housekeeper there had been equally reserved. No, her employer's daughter was not there. She had no knowledge of her whereabouts, and she could not give out any information on where her mother was at the moment. She believed she was no longer in Spain, but would not take it upon herself to say when she might be returning to the UK.

Frustration bit through Damos.

More than frustration. Worse.

Desperation.

CHAPTER ELEVEN

KASSIA LAY ON the yacht's sun deck under an awning. Her eyes were shut, but she was not sleeping. Thoughts, bitter and toxic, were circling in her head.

I deserve what my father threw at me—I deserve it!

She had been as cretinously stupid as he'd said.

Thinking it was me Damos was interested in.

There had been only one thing he'd wanted—and it wasn't her.

Acid tears seeped beneath her eyelids. To think she had thought it mere chance, a coincidence, that she had bumped into Damos like that in Oxford...

Oh, fool to think that!

He planned it from the start—planned it all. Right from visiting the excavation. All that stuff about wanting to sponsor it...wanting me to tell him more over dinner on his yacht... Then 'accidentally' bumping into me at the Ashmolean, taking me for tea, visiting Blenheim together. And then that college dinner, where he 'just happened' to need a plus one—and needed another oh-so-convenient plus one at that Art Deco dinner-dance at the Viscari in London, dressing me up so that I was a fitting partner for him...someone a man like him would want to be seen with. And then—

Pain like a knife thrust into her.

Then taking me to bed...

For one reason only. The reason that had been slammed into her face that nightmare evening in Athens.

To get at my father...ruin his plans.

The pain of the knowledge forced upon her by her father was unbearable.

But I deserve it—I deserve it.

She deserved every last bit of the agony inside her.

'Darling?'

Her mother's voice came from the lower deck. It was full of concern. Concern that had been there since Kassia had thrown herself into her arms, swamping her petite frame, and burst into unstoppable tears. Despite her diminutive height, her mother had hugged her tightly. And now, days after she'd landed in Malaga from Amsterdam, following her desperate plea, her usually insouciant mother had gone into full maternal support role.

Kassia was abjectly grateful. She had never envisaged her butterfly mother being so full of feeling for her daughter's misery.

Kassia heard her footsteps coming up the stairs. 'Oh, darling...' she said again, pity in her voice.

Her mother, supple from all the Pilates classes Kassia knew she did to keep her figure trim, limbered down beside her onto a cushion. She helped herself to one of her daughter's hands, chafing it comfortingly.

'It will pass,' she said. 'I promise you, it will pass.' She drew back a little. 'Come and have some lunch,' she said. 'John's gone off in the launch—he and the first mate are after catching something big and inedible. It will probably take them all day. Goodness knows what the appeal of fishing is!'

Memory seared in Kassia... Damos learning how to fly-fish from Duncan MacFadyen, her sitting on the rug on the bank, watching him…

Loving him…

Her throat closed painfully, as if trying to stifle the word. How could she bear to hear it…think it…feel it? She wanted to silence it, deny it, thrust it from her. But she couldn't. That was the agony of it all…she couldn't…

Because that's what it was—I realise it now. I went and fell in love with him. I didn't know it, and didn't realise it, and now…

Now she was left with it—trapped with it. Imprisoned with it. And it was the worst thing possible.

To love a man who could use me like that. Oh, dear God, fool that I was! That I am. Fool, fool, fool!

A sob rose again, but she stifled it. Her mother had made such an effort for her, telling her to come straight to Spain, that she would be safe here, out on the yacht they'd hired, sailing off the coast.

Kassia knew from Dr Michaelis, who was so kindly allowing her indefinite leave, and from her mother's housekeeper in the Cotswolds, that Damos was trying to find her. Emotion twisted inside her, like painful cords tightening.

Heavily, she got to her feet, following her mother down to the main deck. The stewards had set the table for lunch, and memory knifed through her yet again. Of that very first evening with Damos. Aboard his yacht. When she had been tasked to do her best to persuade him to sponsor the excavation.

Her throat constricted.

All fake. All totally fake.

It hadn't been the excavation that he was interested in, that had brought him to the island.

It was me. He needed to get to meet me—it was a pretext, that was all.

A pretext that had gone on and on…

Until he had me where he wanted me.

In his bed. Ready to be paraded in front of her father.

Damos Kallinikos's latest squeeze. His latest bed warmer. Whom Cosmo Palandrou would never touch with a bargepole, so he'd walk away from doing any kind of business deal with her father. Leaving the coast clear for Damos to make his own move on Cosmo's company.

The only thing he was ever interested in…

Misery twisted again. And self-condemnation. And bitterness…

Dimly, she became aware that the captain had come down from the bridge and was addressing her mother.

'I do apologise,' he was saying, 'but I'm afraid we've been summoned back to port tomorrow. The owner requires the immediate use of a yacht—this particular one. You will be upgraded to a more expensive charter—gratis, of course—to continue your cruise.'

Her mother looked harassed, but could only comply.

And the next day, as the yacht nosed its way into the marina, its owner was waiting on the quay.

It was Damos.

Damos's expression was grim. Finally he had tracked down Kassia. Discovering that the yacht her mother and stepfather had chartered was one of his own had been the only piece of good fortune afforded him. He had recalled it immediately.

Kassia was on board—he knew that from the yacht's captain—and now she was clearly visible on deck as the yacht moored. He was seeing her again for the first time since she had fled from him that nightmare evening in Athens. He felt emotion kick in him—powerful emotion. Painful emotion…

As mooring was completed he walked up to the lowered gangplank. Kassia was as white as a sheet.

'I would like to talk to you, Kassia,' he said.

He kept his voice neutral, but the emotion that was as painful as it was powerful kicked in him again.

She didn't answer. Her mother did.

Barely touching her daughter's shoulder, Kassia's mother was indeed petite, with coiffed, tinted hair, a skilfully made-up face, and she was wearing exactly the kind of very expensive casual-chic yacht-wear that perfectly set off her trim, well-preserved figure.

Absently, he found himself realising just why Kassia— so tall, so racehorse-slender—had always compared herself so unfavourably to her mother, thereby excluding herself from any claim to beauty just because she was not like her mother in looks.

'My daughter has nothing to say to you, Mr Kallinikos,' Kassia's mother said crisply.

Damos's mouth tightened. 'But I have things that need to be said to her. Kassia?' He addressed her directly now. 'Please let me simply talk to you—that is all.' He paused. 'We can't leave it like this.'

He saw her whiten even more, but hesitate. Her mother murmured something to her and she seemed to tremble. Then, lifting her chin, she looked at him.

'Outside. At that café over there.'

She nodded towards one of the many cafés and restaurants lining the busy marina. It was the one closest to the yacht—her mother would be able to see them if they sat outside, Damos realised.

He gave a curt nod. Tension was racking through him.

He watched her walk down the gangplank, step past him. He caught a faint scent of her perfume and memory rushed back. Memory he had to thrust away. Not indulge…

She walked swiftly to the café across the cobbled stones of the quayside, and sat herself down at a table. Damos did likewise. A waiter came by and Damos ordered black coffee for himself and white for her. He knew her taste in coffee. Knew so much about her.

But not how she was going to respond to him now.

She wasn't looking at him—wasn't making eye contact. Her breathing was laboured, he could tell, and her expression tense.

The coffee arrived…the waiter disappeared. Damos began.

'We can't leave it the way it is, Kassia,' he said. His voice was low, intense. 'I have to try…try and make my peace with you.'

He sounded stilted, he knew. And he knew the words were inadequate. But they were all he had now…the only way he could express what he wanted to achieve. And so much depended on them—on what he was going to say now.

He felt emotion trying to rise up in him, but he crushed it back down. It would get in the way—complicate matters. And right now the matter was very simple. Brutally simple.

I want her back.

But even as he thought it he changed it. No, he did not *want* Kassia back.

I need her back—because without her my life is…

Unthinkable.

That was what these frantic days of trying to find her had shown him…shown him with all the tenderness of a fist slamming into his solar plexus. Over and over again.

'Peace?'

There was incredulity in her voice. She was staring at him. Now she was making eye contact—and he could almost wish she was not.

'Peace?' she said again. 'You did what you did to me and you think we can make *peace* over it?'

'I have to try, Kassia—' he began.

But she cut across him. 'Try what? Try to tell me that you *didn't* use me to get at my father? Try to tell me that everything that happened between us *wasn't* a lie from the very first? Are you going to try and deny that? You lined me up from start to finish! Knowing exactly what you were doing!'

He tried to interrupt but she would not let him. Vehemence was in her face, in her voice.

'You turned up at the excavation deliberately—are you doing to claim you didn't? And you got me to come to dinner on your yacht deliberately—are you going to deny that too? As for Oxford...' A choke broke from her. 'I thought it was a coincidence! Bumping into you like that. But it wasn't, was it? *Was it?*'

He drew a breath, his face as tight as if it were made of wire. 'No. But—'

She wouldn't let him speak.

'And after that it was easy, wasn't it? So damn easy. Spending time with me...coming up with one reason after another to do so. Reeling me in until you had me exactly where you needed me to be.' Her face contorted. 'In your bed.'

The bitterness in her voice was acid on his skin. Her eyes like knives plunging into his flesh.

'And then you could do what you'd intended to do right from the very start—make me a weapon to use against my father.' Her voice twisted. 'For money. For profit.'

Her eyes were on him still, but now there was a bleakness in them that struck him like a blow. And she struck him another blow with her next words, cutting him to the very quick.

'You once told me that there was a difference between using opportunities that presented themselves and using people to achieve them.' Her voice was hollow. 'But that wasn't a difference *you* took any notice of. I was an opportunity presenting itself to you and you took full advantage. You lied to me…made a fool of me…used me.'

She pushed her chair back, got to her feet. She looked down at him. Spoke again. But now her voice was hard. As hard as her expression. As hard as the look in her eyes.

'I thought you were different from my father, not cut from the same vile cloth.' She drew a breath, and he heard it rasp in her throat. 'How wrong I was.'

She turned away and walked back to the yacht, coffee untouched. There was something about the way she was walking, about the way her shoulders were hunching, her head dropping. He launched to his feet—then realised he had to pay for the undrunk coffee. He snatched out his wallet and dropped a note on the table, then strode after her rapidly.

He had to catch up with her.

Had to tell her what he had flown to Spain to tell her—what he would cross the world to tell her.

If she would let him…

She gained the gangplank and ran up it, head still bowed.

Someone stepped into his path. Not her mother, but her stepfather.

'Stay away from her, Mr Kallinikos. You've done quite enough damage. Leave our family alone.'

He spoke calmly, but with the authority of his years, of his place as Kassia's guardian right now. Keeping her safe from men who made use of her…

Damos looked past him. A taxi was pulling up on the quayside. Kassia and her mother were walking down the gangplank. Kassia's mother had her arm protectively around her daughter, despite the disparity in their heights. Kassia's head was turned away from him. A steward was following them with their suitcases.

Kassia's stepfather had gone to open the door of the taxi, ushering in his wife and stepdaughter. The steward put the suitcases in the boot, and Kassia's stepfather got into the front passenger seat.

The taxi moved off. Damos watched it go.

Then the taxi turned out of the marina into the traffic. Lost to sight.

Like Kassia—lost.

Damos went on staring. Though his eyes were blind.

CHAPTER TWELVE

KASSIA POSITIONED THE tip of her trowel over the protruding shard. She had to work carefully. And work she must. Without work she could not exist. Without work she would be a ghost. Without work she would be defenceless. Work could fill her days, her mind, her thoughts.

But it could not fill her nights.

That was the time she dreaded—feared. Nights brought thoughts, and thoughts brought memories, and memories brought dreams.

And dreams brought nightmares...

Her brow furrowed now, as she teased the earth from the shard. This was the last day of the dig and she wanted to get this shard out—and those that went with it. She was the last person in the trench, for the site was being shut down for overwintering. All the finds were packed away, all the notes and catalogues boxed up to be taken back to the museum. Her winter would be filled with completing the work done so far—typing up the paperwork, getting restoration work underway in the lab, choosing what should go on display, what should be sent to other museums, what archived.

Winter would keep her busy. And that was essential.

How long ago summer was. It was late autumn now, and the weather was breaking. Rain squalls were not uncommon, and a chill wind was sweeping down off the steppes. Time to hunker down...stay warm and dry.

Memory pierced… She and Damos, lolling by the roaring fire in the castle in the Highlands, rain spattering on the leaded windows, and she and he playing chess. Her mouth twisted and she dug the tip of her trowel in with more ferocity than she should. Damos had run circles around her playing chess. Just as he'd run circles around her in all the time he'd spent with her. Right from the very start.

She lifted her head. This trench, deserted but for herself, was an extension of where she'd been working all those months ago—the first time she had ever set eyes on Damos Kallinikos.

She felt her vision smear and dropped her head again. Her hand gripped the trowel so tightly her earth-stained hands went white. Dimly, she heard voices nearby, but her vision was still smeared.

Then someone tapped her hesitantly on the shoulder. She started, looking up. It was Dr Michaelis. But it was not only him she saw. It was the man behind him.

Damos.

Was he insane? The words were inside Damos's head, but it was as if he could hear them audibly. Insane to come here? Hadn't Spain taught him his lesson?

She wants nothing to do with me—nothing.

Yet he was here, all the same. Two months on. Months that had been like nothing he had ever endured in his life. Months that had made those brief weeks in the summer seem like a distant, impossible dream—a dream to torment him and torture him. For it was lost to him for ever.

As Kassia was lost to him.

Pain buckled through him at the knowledge of what he had done.

Everything she told me I had.

As he stood there now, looking down at Kassia hunkered in the trench, a terrible sense of *déjà vu* came over him. It was as if time were collapsing and he was seeing her as he had seen her for the very first time.

He felt a vice around his chest, tightening pitilessly.

But he deserved no pity...

Deserved only the pain that was now his constant companion.

Dr Michaelis was addressing her, and Damos could hear the awkwardness in his voice. He felt bad for him, but his need was too great. Too desperate.

'Ah, Kassia... Kyrios Kallinikos has...has asked the favour of a word with you.'

Kassia's expression did not change. Nor did she look at Damos. She got to her feet. She said nothing—only stepped out of the trench.

'Good, good...' said Dr Michaelis, sounding flustered. He hurried away.

Kassia's eyes went to Damos. There was something wrong with them, he could see. They looked...*smeared*.

She still didn't speak—just stood there. Memory poured through him. He could swear she was wearing the same earth-coloured baggy cotton trousers, the same mustard-coloured tee—though this time she wore a tan gilet over it against the chillier weather. Her hair was screwed up in a careless knot on her head, and she wore not a scrap of make-up—unless he counted the flecks of dirt on her cheeks.

The memory struck at him of how she'd walked back to the yacht at the marina in Spain, her shoulders hunched, head down. All the confidence that she'd glowed with once he'd got her to realise just how beautiful she was had gone. As if it had never been...

She was still not speaking, only looking at him with those smeared, blank eyes.

He made himself speak. Say what he had come here to say.

'I… I have something that I would like to tell you. That I… I would like you to know.'

His voice was hesitant—but how should it not be? Twice already she had not let him speak—in Athens and in Spain.

'I… I wanted you to know that I have been funding the museum. Your father…' his voice was strained '…withdrew his support after—'

He broke off, then made himself continue.

'I did not want the museum to suffer, so I stepped in. It was…something I could do. But I don't…don't say this in any expectation that you might…might think less ill of me—'

He broke off again. Those blank, smeared eyes conveyed nothing. Nor did she say anything.

He went on with what he had come here to say.

'My acquisition of Cosmo Palandrou's company has gone through—I used a proxy, whom I funded, who then sold it on to me. It had been badly mismanaged, and industrial disputes were endemic. Since my acquisition I have created an employee share scheme which allocates half the company to all the employees, at no cost to themselves. Profits will be shared fifty-fifty, and my share will be reinvested for the company's expansion. I,' he added, 'will not be benefitting financially.'

He stopped. What he had to say next was hardest of all. But he must say it. Even though Kassia still had not moved, her blank smeared gaze was still on him.

'I have done this because you told me in Spain that I had used you to make money for myself.'

His face contorted suddenly. Something broke inside him.

'Oh, God, Kassia, if only I could undo what I did to you! I regret it so, so much! But I can't undo it. All I can do is live with the consequences. Live with what I have lost.'

His voice dropped. There was a stone in his throat, making it impossible to breathe. To speak. But he must speak. Must say the most agonising words in the world.

'You,' he said. 'I have lost you.'

He turned to go. She was still motionless, still unspeaking, not reacting. There was no point in him staying here. No point at all...

But as he started to turn away he saw something happen to her face. Rivulets of tears were running down it...

The tears were spilling. She could not stop them. No power on earth could stop them.

'*Kassia—*'

Her name was on his lips. And then his arms were around her.

She should pull away—push him away, drive him away, force him away. For he was the man who had lied to her from the very first moment she had ever seen him, standing right here. Standing here, planning to lie to her, to make use of her, to make her the gullible, stupid fool her father had called her in his rage.

She should push him from her—but she did not. Could not.

His arms were holding her, cradling her. She heard his voice.

'Don't cry. Don't weep. I beg you! I can't bear that you should weep. I can't bear that I did to you what I did! It's an agony to me.'

She was clinging to him—but why she was, she didn't

know. How could she? How could she cling like this to a man who had used her as he had? Lied to her as he had?

'You lied to me Damos! You lied and you lied and you lied! Everything was a lie—all a lie! Every day we had together. Every hour. Every night in your arms.' Her voice choked, sobs racking her. 'It was all a *lie*!'

She felt his arms stiffen. Then they fell away, dropping to his sides. He let her go and looked away, out over the deserted trenches to the olive trees beyond. Then his eyes came back to hers. Held them fast.

'It started as a lie,' he said.

He paused, and the silence between them stretched like a chasm. Then he spoke again, his eyes still holding hers fast.

'But it became the truth,' he said.

He heard the words he had said. The words that were the most important words in the world.

'It became the truth,' he said again.

His eyes searched her face. He could read nothing there. Nothing to help him. But he did not deserve help.

After all that had been a lie between them she deserved the truth. The truth about the truth.

'The truth is brutal. Everything you threw at me in Spain—that I engineered meeting you, feigning an interest in sponsoring the dig, and invited you on board my yacht on that pretext…that I found out you were attending a conference in Oxford, so I turned up there myself, letting you think it was just by chance. I kept our acquaintance going, knowing exactly where I wanted it to lead. Knowing exactly why I was doing it. But then…then it changed.'

He knew his face was stark.

'It changed, Kassia. I realised I was enjoying your company…that I wanted more of it. That I wanted Kassia—

you. Not Kassia Andrakis, who was going to be the means by which I would outmanoeuvre your father, but you. Just you. For who you were yourself. I wanted you—I wanted to spend time with you—I wanted to be with you. And above all...' his voice changed now, and there was a husk in it that he could not hide '... I wanted you in my arms.'

He shut his eyes for a moment. Then flared them open.

'Oh, God, Kassia, how much I wanted that! And I wanted you to want it too! And the more I found out about you—how you lacked any confidence in your own beauty, which you could not see—the more I wanted to reveal it to you. And I did—I did just that! And when...when we came to-gether that night, I knew I had found someone.' His voice dropped, 'Someone I did not want to lose.'

He drew a breath. Words were still coming—the truth was still coming.

'Our time in the Highlands was the most precious time in my life. I felt a happiness I had never known before, being with you. We were good together—so very, very good. And I knew it was the same for you. I knew then that I did not want to be without you. I wanted our time together to go on, back here in Greece, just as I told you. But then—'

He broke off. Shut his eyes again for a moment, unable to bear seeing her looking at him. But he must bear it—must bear what he now had to say.

'I had to deal with what I had set up when I first came here. The plan to...to use you for my own ends. If...if there had been more time I'd have wanted us simply to be seen in Athens as a couple. The news would soon have reached Cosmo and your father. But there wasn't time for that. So I... I decided I just wanted it over and done with—the whole damn thing. I wanted to force the issue...have Cosmo and your father presented with us together and that would end it. I just didn't realise…'

He stopped again.

'It horrified me,' he said at last. 'Appalled me. What your father said to you.' His voice dropped. 'And it appalled me that I had exposed you to it—to that vile diatribe from your father…saying such things to you.'

He swallowed. There was a razor in his throat, but he swallowed anyway. He had no choice but to do so. He was telling her the truth about the truth.

'But I exposed myself as well. Exposed myself to your father's accusation of me. That I had used you.' He stopped again, then went on, making himself speak. His voice was low and drawn. 'I hadn't wanted you ever to know…to know that I had come here deliberately, wanting to use you. Oh, I'd told myself at the start, when I dreamt up the idea, that it would do you no harm, my taking an interest in you. That if you did not want to get involved with me then that would be that. And if you did, you would likely enjoy your time with me because—well, why not? I even told myself that since you couldn't possibly *want* Cosmo Palandrou foisted on you—what woman would?—you might appreciate the impact of our affair yourself. I told myself all that…'

He took another breath, ragged and razored.

'But when I realised that I wanted you for yourself, not for any other reason…then I didn't know what to do. I felt an impulse to come clean—to tell you why I had originally sought you out. But then I hesitated. It was too risky. It was safer not to tell you. I thought you need never know, because by then it did not matter. I wanted you for yourself, for real, and what we had together was so very precious to me, becoming more precious still with every day that passed. So why tell you anything about my original intentions?'

He stopped, his eyes veiled.

'But there was another reason I did not want to tell you—a reason I did not want to face. But in Spain you made me face it.'

He looked away, out over the serried trenches to the olive trees beyond. When his eyes came back to her they were bleak.

'In Spain, you told me I was exactly like your father—using other people for my own ends, as I had used you. And it shamed me—I deserved it to shame me.'

His eyes were bleaker still. Bleak as a polar waste where no warmth could ever come. His voice was just as bleak.

'But I am paying the price now, Kassia. Believe me, if you believe nothing else, I *am* paying the price. It's a price I deserve to pay for what I did. And it is a price I would not wish on anyone. I have lost you, and I cannot bear it. Except I know I must.'

I must bear this unbearable loss because I made it happen myself. And nothing can undo it—nothing.

Emotion speared him, right in his guts, twisting viciously. He had to bear that too…

He turned away. There was no point being here any longer. He had to go and live without her, all his days.

A hand touched his arm. Kassia's hand. And then there was Kassia's voice, speaking low and faint.

'Don't go,' she said. Her voice was almost inaudible. 'Don't go,' she said again. 'Don't leave me.'

His face stilled. His breath stilled. The world stilled.

He looked round at her. She wasn't looking at him. Her head was bowed, shoulders hunched.

'Don't leave me,' she said again. A husk…a whisper. 'I can't bear for you to leave me. I don't want to lose you. I lost you before, and I can't bear to lose you again. Not now…'

He heard her words but he did not believe them—dared not believe them. Dared not. And yet...

Slowly, he turned. The touch of her hand on his sleeve was so faint it was scarcely there at all. But he felt it tremble, as if it might fall from him at any moment.

She lifted her head now. What was in her eyes, he did not know. And yet he must speak. His heart seemed to be filling his chest.

'Don't say that,' he breathed, 'if you do not mean it.'

She shook her head. Slowly. As if she were moving it against the weight of the world. Against the weight of what he had done to her.

A rasp sounded in his throat, torn from his stricken lungs.

There was urgency in his words. 'Kassia, if you will have me after all I've done to you, what I would give all the world to undo, I would beg your forgiveness—but how can you forgive me?'

She lifted her other hand, and with a touch that was as light as the hand on his sleeve she brushed his cheek.

'But I do,' she whispered.

Her eyes were lifted to his, and he saw they were no longer smeared, but lit with a silver light.

'Kassia, dear God... *Kassia!*'

That emotion was sweeping up in him, powerful and strange and unknown—the emotion that had swept over him the night he had made Kassia his own. But now he knew what it was. Knew that the spear which had been thrust so deep inside him, twisting viciously as he'd faced walking away from her for ever, was suddenly gone.

With a jerking movement he folded his hand over hers on his sleeve. Pressed it down. Never to let it go. Never...

Then he slipped his fingers under hers. Lifted them. Lifted them to his mouth. Kissed them.

In homage and in plea—and in love.

Because that was what he knew was filling him—that was what had caused that unbearable sense of loss when she had fled from him that hideous night. That had been the desperation driving him to find her, to make his confession to her, to do whatever he could to make amends. To show her that what had started as a lie had become the truth…to beg her to believe him.

'I am yours,' he said, and his voice was low, filled with all he felt, all he had come to feel, would always feel. 'I am yours for however long you might want me. Yours for an hour, or a day, or a single night—or for a lifetime.'

She reached up a hand, enfolded his as it enfolded hers. She was looking at him now, and her eyes were filling again with tears. But her tears were diamonds…

'Or for eternity?' she said, and reached his lips with hers.

Was this love? Was this love pouring through her like a tide? Washing away all that had tarnished and poisoned and destroyed? Was it love she had tried to silence, to kill, after she'd realised what he'd done to her?

Oh, but it must be love! For what else could lift her like this? What else could turn agony and anguish into such joy? Such joy as streamed through her?

He was sweeping her to him, crushing her to him, saying her name, kissing her hair, her cheek, her mouth.

'I don't deserve you—I don't deserve a single hair on your head. I don't deserve a single moment with you! Oh, God, Kassia, if only I could undo—'

She pulled away—but only to place a finger across his mouth, to silence him.

'No more,' she whispered. 'It's gone…it's over—we will never let it come between us again. Simply to know how much you regret it means all the world to me. It…it heals us, Damos. Heals all the harm that was done.'

She kissed him again, to seal that healing. And then, as she drew back, she spoke again. There was something new in her voice now. A rueful note.

'And you know…maybe we should be grateful for your coming here for the reason you did. Because if you hadn't… would we ever have met? And if we had—in Athens, say— you would have had some gorgeous, glamorous female with you and you would not have looked twice at me.'

She was given no chance to say more. Words fell from him, urgent and vehement.

'Kassia, if you spend the rest of your life looking exactly as you do now, without a scrap of make-up and in clothes that should be buried deeper than those broken pots you keep digging up, I will love you and adore you and desire you all the rest of my days!'

He seized her hands, his eyes pouring into hers, and what she saw in them made her faint with love.

'It's *you* whom I love! And when I say I will always, *always* want you to look as stunning as I know you can, it is for *you*—not me!'

His mouth lowered to hers, and in the touch of his lips was all that she could ever desire. For a long time they kissed, and as at last they drew apart she saw he was gazing down at her, love light in his eyes…love light that was like a warming flame inside her, one that would warm her all her days, and all her nights, for ever and for good.

Her heart was singing. It would sing for ever now.

Damos's arms came around her and he held her close, against his heart, where now she would always be. Her arms wrapped him just as close, and closer still. Heart against heart—for all eternity indeed. And so much longer.

EPILOGUE

KASSIA COULDN'T STOP LAUGHING. Both she and Damos were making endless mistakes, but no one minded. All the other dancers were helpfully calling out to them which way they should be turning, whose hands they should be taking now. One thing was for sure, though, reeling was an energetic business. The foot-tapping music was driving them on, with fiddles, pipes, drums and accordions, and it was just impossible not to dance. They'd already Stripped the Willow, Dashed the White Sergeant, been to Mairi's Wedding, and were now completely confused in an eightsome reel.

When it ended she was more than ready to collapse down on one of the chairs around the edge of the village hall where the *ceilidh* was being held.

'Not bad, lassie…not bad at all.'

Duncan MacFadyen, looking not out of breath in the slightest, came up to her. He looked resplendent in his fi-libeg short kilt, simply worn with a white shirt and tie. His nephew was the piper in the band, and Mrs MacFadyen was presiding over the groaning supper table.

Damos came up too. He also looked not out of breath in the slightest.

Duncan clapped him on the shoulder. 'We'll make a Scotsman out of you yet, laddie,' he said approvingly.

Damos laughed. 'Kassia and I will practise in Greece in time for our visit in the summer,' he promised.

He'd procured a glass of beer for himself and Duncan, and presented Kassia with a glass of cider—which she knocked back thirstily.

'We'll be a respectable married couple by then, Duncan,' she said.

'So we're making the most of our last illicit romantic getaway here,' Damos said, with a glint in his eye.

'Och, well, winter's as good a time as any for keeping warm together,' Duncan chuckled with cheerful wickedness.

Kassia smiled, thinking of how very, very warm Damos kept her in the velvet-hung four-poster in the castle bedroom. She and Damos, after a Christmas spent with Kassia's mother and stepfather, hadn't been able to resist taking a Hogmanay break back here.

In the castle where we fell in love.

And where they'd be spending their honeymoon, too, next summer.

It was a long time to wait—but Kassia could not deprive her mother of the pleasure of organising a huge, full-works traditional wedding for them, with a reception at her stepfather's country house in the Cotswolds. There would be a marquee on the lawn, a lavish wedding breakfast, and dancing under the stars in the evening.

Her mother was in her element, and Kassia was giving her her head, knowing how much her social butterfly mother was enjoying it. As for herself—she'd have been just as happy taking her vows simply by hand-fasting, in the centuries-old Scottish union of those who loved each other, holding Damos's hand, quietly and on their own.

Perhaps that was what they would do. Walk down to the edge of the loch while they were here—warmly wrapped against the Scottish winter. Or perhaps at the summit of the Munro that Damos was determined to bag before they flew home. He'd already made the outdoor wear shopkeeper in Inverlochry an even happier man by taking Kassia there and kitting them out with winter walking gear.

'We'll bag our second Munro now,' he'd said. 'A nice easy one for winter walking. And then try a tougher one in the summer. And we'll keep going from there, doing another couple every annual visit, until we've bagged the lot!'

Kassia had laughed. 'There are close on three hundred!' she'd exclaimed.

Damos had dropped a kiss on her forehead. 'Well, maybe we'll settle for half. And that…' he'd taken her hand, his eyes warm upon her '…should see us into ripe old age. We might even still be tottering up them when we reach our centenaries!'

Kassia had squeezed his hand. That she and he should be granted so long a time together was all her heart's desire. She'd felt her heart swell then, and it was doing so again now, as she gazed up at Damos as he downed his beer, so tall, so gorgeous, and so infinitely dear to her.

How much I love him—how very, very much.

After their rapturous reconciliation everything had been so simple. Dr Michaelis had given her extra leave on the spot, and she and Damos had flown back to Athens, wrapped in each other's arms. They'd spent the weekend at his apartment in Piraeus, barely surfacing, and then he'd come with her to England. He had made his peace with her mother and shaken her stepfather's hand.

There was only one hand he could not, *would* not shake. Nor would Kassia ever expect it of him. Or of herself. Her break with her father was absolute—it could not be otherwise. And though it cast a shadow over her it was one she would not let blight her. It would be her stepfather who would give her away at her wedding.

Till then, she and Damos were doing what he had suggested to her when they'd left the castle in the summer. She could not let Dr Michaelis down, so would continue at the museum until her wedding, contenting herself with weekends with Damos. Then, once married, she would seek a post in Athens.

But it might not last that long. Already Damos was hinting.

'This apartment is all very well for the two of us, but it wouldn't suit a family,' he'd declared.

'But let's enjoy some time together first as a couple,' Kassia had said. 'Doing all the things you've promised me you'll do.'

Damos was stepping back from many of his business concerns. He had sold his yacht charter company, and was divesting himself of some of his merchant marine interests. And he had decided, once Cosmo Palandrou's freight and logistics business was in good order, to reduce his share even more.

'I want to enjoy life,' he'd said to Kassia. 'Learn scuba diving…go sailing with you…travel more. Our time together has taught me that.'

'I'm glad,' she'd said. 'You've worked so hard, Damos, to get where you are today—now relax, and enjoy the fruits of all your hard work. After all…' she'd given him a wry, quizzical look '…one day we'll be like all those souls who lived three thousand years ago in the Bronze Age, with the archaeologists of the future digging up the remnants of our lives, wondering what they were like. So…' she'd kissed him on the cheek '…let's make sure they are *good* lives.'

They were words that came to her again now, as the band struck up once more. Immediately her foot started tapping irresistibly.

Damos finished his beer and took her empty cider glass from her, placing both on the windowsill behind her chair.

'Away with you both now,' Duncan said jovially. 'Back to the *ceilidh*.'

He packed them off back to the dance floor. And as she and Damos took their places memory struck her.

'Do you realise,' she said, 'that this evening is the first time we've danced together since that night at the Viscari?'

She felt her heart swell again. The memory was sweet, so very sweet, and that night had started the affair that now would be their marriage, all their lives, for ever and beyond.

Her eyes went to Damos now, as they stood opposite each other, waiting their turn. He met her eyes full on, and in them was such a blaze of love that it made her reel.

And then the reeling was for real...

'It's you!' the woman next to her said.

Kassia started forward, and Damos did too, seizing her hand. Hand in hand, their eyes still locked together, they went down the line, hand-fasted, heart-fasted, united in their love for each other, dancing into the future that was theirs and theirs alone.

And always would be.

* * * * *

MILLS & BOON®

Coming next month

GREEK'S ENEMY BRIDE
Caitlin Crews

The priest cleared his throat.

Jolie took one last look at Apostolis, soaking in this last moment of blessed widowhood before he became her husband.

He looked back, that gleaming gold thing in his gaze, but his expression unusually serious.

For a moment, it was as if she could read his mind.

For a long, electric moment, it was almost as if they were united in this bizarre enterprise after all, and her heart leaped inside her chest—

'Stepmother?' he said, with a soft ferocity. 'If you would be so kind?'

No, she told herself harshly. *There is no unity here. There is only and ever war. You will do well to remember that.*

And then, with remarkable swiftness and no interruption, Jolie relinquished her role as Apostolis's hated stepmother, and became his much-loathed wife instead.

Continue reading

GREEK'S ENEMY BRIDE
Caitlin Crews

Available next month
millsandboon.co.uk

Copyright ©2024 by Caitlin Crews

COMING SOON!

We really hope you enjoyed reading this book.
If you're looking for more romance
be sure to head to the shops when
new books are available on

Thursday 19th December

To see which titles are coming soon, please visit
millsandboon.co.uk/nextmonth

MILLS & BOON

FOUR BRAND NEW BOOKS FROM
MILLS & BOON MODERN

The same great stories you love, a stylish new look!

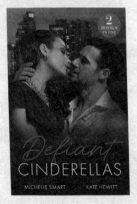

OUT NOW

Eight Modern stories published every month, find them all at:

millsandboon.co.uk

LET'S TALK

Romance

For exclusive extracts, competitions and special offers, find us online:

f MillsandBoon

X @MillsandBoon

◉ @MillsandBoonUK

♪ @MillsandBoonUK

Get in touch on 01413 063 232

For all the latest titles coming soon, visit
millsandboon.co.uk/nextmonth

afterglow BOOKS

Afterglow Books is a trend-led, trope-filled list of books with diverse, authentic and relatable characters, a wide array of voices and representations, plus real world trials and tribulations. Featuring all the tropes you could possibly want (think small-town settings, fake relationships, grumpy vs sunshine, enemies to lovers) and all with a generous dose of spice in every story.

♪ @millsandboonuk
⊙ @millsandboonuk
afterglowbooks.co.uk

#AfterglowBooks

For all the latest book news, exclusive content and giveaways scan the QR code below to sign up to the Afterglow newsletter:

SCAN ME

afterglow BOOKS

NAIMA SIMONE

Church Girl

She's always followed the rules.
Will she follow her heart?

KATY JAMES
THE GRUMP
WHISPERER

THERE'S NO REINING
IN THEIR CHEMISTRY

- 💻 Workplace romance
- 📡 Forced proximity
- 🌶 Spicy

- 💻 Workplace romance
- 🏠 Small-town romance
- ⛅ Grumpy/sunshine

OUT NOW

Two stories published every month. Discover more at:
Afterglowbooks.co.uk

OUT NOW!

3
BOOKS
IN ONE

Tawny WEBER

Tina BECKETT

Sharon KENDRICK

Workplace ROMANCE

A CHRISTMAS DATE

Available at
millsandboon.co.uk

MILLS & BOON

OUT NOW!

3
BOOKS
IN ONE

Fake
DATING

TEMPTED AT CHRISTMAS

CANDACE
HAVENS

MAISEY
YATES

JESSICA
LEMMON

Available at
millsandboon.co.uk

MILLS & BOON

OUT NOW!

3 BOOKS IN ONE

SECOND CHANCE FOR *Christmas*

A.C. ARTHUR MARION LENNOX SUSAN MEIER

Available at
millsandboon.co.uk

MILLS & BOON